"The Black
and
"The Salamanders"

TWO CLASSIC ADVENTURES OF

TM

by Walter B. Gibson
writing as Maxwell Grant

plus

Island of Ancient Death
by Gibson Scott Fox

with New Historical Essays by
Will Murray and Anthony Tollin

Published by Sanctum Productions for
NOSTALGIA VENTURES, INC.
P.O. Box 231183; Encinitas, CA 92023-1183

International Standard Book Numbers:
ISBN 1-932806-27-X   13 DIGIT 978-1-932806-27-4

Series editor: Anthony Tollin
P.O. Box 761474
San Antonio, TX 78245-1474
sanctumotr@earthlink.net

Consulting editor: Will Murray

Copy editor: Joseph Wrzos

First printing: February 2007

The editor gratefully acknowledges the contributions of Lou Nemeth.

Nostalgia Ventures, Inc.
P.O. Box 231183; Encinitas, CA 92023-1183

Visit The Shadow at www.nostalgiatown.com

Volume 5

CONTENTS

Two Complete Novels From The Shadow's Private Annals As told to Maxwell Grant

Thrilling Tales and Features

Cover art by George Rozen
Interior illustrations by Tom Lovell

FORESHADOWINGS by Will Murray

It was no accident that The Shadow struck a resonating chord in the minds of radio listeners when he first vented his sepulchral laugh in 1930. And no surprise that his sinister slouch-hatted silhouette soon became an iconic image, universally recognizable to all.

For The Shadow was nothing less than a Jungian archetype brought to life, an artifact of the collective unconscious that periodically bubbles to the surface of the cultural consciousness. For there were Shadows before Street & Smith coalesced the idea into a character so popular he refuses to die.

Going back to Plato, who once suggested that reality was like "shadows" on a cave wall, shadows have symbolized the dark destructive side of man, the unknown part of human nature.

Hans Christian Andersen once penned a tale of a man whose shadow detached itself and sought its own experiences. When it returned, the owner asked, "But now tell me everything that you saw."

"Everything," said the Shadow; "for I saw and know everything."

The origin of "The Shadow knows?" Perhaps.

Charles Dickens once ruminated on the idea of "...a certain Shadow who may go anyplace, by sunlight, moonlight, starlight, firelight, candlelight...and be supposed to be cognizant of everything," which eavesdrops, unsuspected, on malefactors, giving dire warnings before exposing their wicked schemes to the light of day.

Even F. Scott Fitzgerald toyed with a character he dubbed the Shadow.

Characters who strongly foreshadowed the Street & Smith hero had abounded in dime-novel literature long before Walter B. Gibson brought his version to life. Many were lurking felons tricked out in long black coats (or capes), slouch hats crushed down to disguise shaded features. This was the popular conception of the skulking spy or terrorist of a century ago.

Even Street & Smith had published an earlier version of the idea. In a 1929 issue of their *Fame and Fortune Magazine,* "The Shadow of Wall Street" haunted unscrupulous investors. In reality, this hooded figure, Compton Moore, looked very much like the earliest conceptions of The Shadow to come. But both Gibson and John Nanovic insisted they never saw this pulpy doppelganger.

The Shadow we know came about purely by accident. An advertising agency needed a device to present Street and Smith's *Detective Story Program* to radio listeners. Searching for an appropriate name, scriptwriter Harry Engman Charlot toyed with calling him The Inspector or The Sleuth. Then he hit upon something that transcended ordinary inspiration: The Shadow!

Charlot, who died under mysterious circumstances in 1937, was by all accounts a troubled man. Perhaps the idea for The Shadow arose from a very deep and dark well within his inner being. Or he might have simply gotten the name from police slang for "shadowing" a suspect.

"Who knows what evil lurks in the hearts of men? The Shadow knows" first reverberated out of radio cabinet speakers in the early 1930s. Unknown radio writers experimented with alternates to the seminal "weed of crime" line. "As you sow evil, so shall you reap evil" was one.

As brought to life by actor Frank Readick, the voice of The Shadow cut deep into the American psyche. Interest in the mocking mysteryman prompted Street & Smith to hire Walter B. Gibson to concentrate this nascent notion into a literary figure calculated to capture radio listeners.

Inspired in part by Bram Stoker's Count Dracula, Gibson also drew from a prior shadowy story. "[Edward] Bulwer-Lytton's stories fascinated me," he admitted. "There was one called 'The House and the Brain,' in which a man is in this house that was presumably haunted, where strange things happened. Every now and then you would see blackness gather and it looked like a shadow forming. I later used that kind of technique in The Shadow's approach. I would have crooks scared that something was lurking in the flap of a window shade. They would look and see nothing there. Somebody would just look long enough to think that they saw a shadowy form."

It was a radical innovation. Before, such sinister figures as The Shadow emblemized evil. Now the archetype of the Shadow was elevated into a force for justice.

As Gibson explained, "...in most mystery stories, somebody would look out and see a strange figure on the lawn. Then you knew there was going to be trouble, something sinister was afoot. Well, I reversed that process with The Shadow. I had trouble to begin with, and when they looked out and the sinister figure was coming in, he was somebody who was going to put an end to the menace. He was sort of like a benign Dracula, you might say."

The British have a saying: "No man can escape his shadow." Walter Gibson would agree. After The Shadow had completely infiltrated the popular imagination, he noted: "There are people of two classes. The ones who have read The Shadow and others who have heard it on the radio. They all recognize him."

The Black Falcon

A master fiend who knows The Shadow plots the black avenger's end. See how well his evil plans work out in this thrilling story

From the Private Annals of The Shadow, as told to

Maxwell Grant

CHAPTER I
THE BIG SHOT

A MAMMOTH limousine was parked in front of the Club Madrid. Curious bystanders, thronged beneath the lighted marquee of the glittering Manhattan night club, were buzzing among themselves. The chauffeur of the limousine, a grin on his tough face, was listening to the murmured comments of the handful who watched the car.

"That's Rowdy Kirshing's boat—"

"Say—it's a big bus—and you can bet those windows are bulletproof."

"Take it from me, that chauffeur's got a gun packed on his hip. Look at the face on him—"

"Here comes Rowdy Kirshing now!"

The final statement of a bystander caused all eyes to turn toward the entrance of the nightclub. A big man, his rough, scarred face looming uglily above a stiff tuxedo collar, was approaching from the door of the Club Madrid.

"The biggest of the big shots—"

The comment came from an onlooker as "Rowdy" Kirshing passed. It was whispered; and it brought a low answer from another bystander:

"Yeah—and that fellow with him is no softy. That's Pinkey Sardon, his bodyguard."

The man to whom attention had been directed was following close at Rowdy Kirshing's heels. Like his master, "Pinkey" was attired in a tuxedo. He, too, was the possessor of an evil face. A squat, broad-shouldered ruffian, Pinkey Sardon had risen from the ranks of ordinary gorillas to serve as bodyguard to the most notorious racketeer in New York.

Rowdy Kirshing paid no attention to the throng of persons who observed his exit from the Club Madrid. He left that to his trusted follower, Pinkey Sardon. The bodyguard, glaring from left to right, kept one hand menacingly in his side pocket, while his chief entered the limousine. With Rowdy Kirshing safely in the car, Pinkey sprang in behind him. The chauffeur slammed the door and clambered to the driver's seat. The wheeled leviathan pulled away from the curb, leaving the gaping spectators on the sidewalk.

"Plenty of gawks in New York," observed Pinkey, with a gruff laugh. "They stand around like a bunch of hicks. Everywhere you go there's a pile of mugs looking on."

"Lucky for you there is," growled Rowdy. "If those mugs weren't around, I wouldn't carry a bodyguard. It's just the chance that there might be some sharpshooter pretending that he was one of the goofs. That's why you've got your job, Pinkey."

"Don't I know it?" The bodyguard laughed. "Say, Rowdy, there's no guy tough enough to take a plug at you in the open. I know why I'm working for you. I keep my eye out for snipers. They know it wouldn't do them no good to take a pot-shot at you."

Rowdy Kirshing nodded in reply. He was reaching for the speaking phone that communicated with the front seat. He uttered words to the chauffeur:

"Tenth Avenue, Danny."

PINKEY SARDON grinned as he heard his chief's order. He knew the spot on Tenth Avenue where Rowdy Kirshing was going. The king of racketeers was headed for one of gangdom's strongholds—a place where bodyguards were not needed. This would mean a night off for Pinkey Sardon.

Rowdy Kirshing was evidently holding the same thought. From a side pocket the big shot brought out a massive roll of bills. He peeled off ten, each note of a hundred-dollar denomination.

"One grand, Pinkey," stated Rowdy, as he thrust the money into his bodyguard's hand. "That's for the week. And here"—the big shot was counting off five more bills as he spoke—"is some extra change for a present."

"Half a grand!" Pinkey whistled. "Thanks, Rowdy! Say—it's knocked me goofy, the way you've been slinging the dough the past week. You gave each of those chorines a century at the Club Madrid tonight—"

"There's plenty more where this came from," growled Rowdy, in a tone that stopped Pinkey short. "I don't have to look for the mazuma. It comes to me."

"I know that," agreed Pinkey. "But with the way some of the rackets have been taking it on the chin—"

"I've got others up my sleeve."

Pinkey nodded. As Rowdy Kirshing's body-guard, the ex-gorilla had a general idea of his employer's sources of revenue. He was frequent-ly present when Rowdy received collections from small-fry racketeers. Yet Pinkey realized that his knowledge was only partial. Racketeers had been low on contributions of late. Expenses of main-taining gang leaders and their mobs had been as large as ever. Despite these facts, Rowdy Kirshing had flashed and spent money with keen abandon.

The limousine swerved around the corner of a side street. It rolled along Tenth Avenue, slowed its pace and turned into the open doorway of an old garage. Danny guided the car across vacant floor space until he neared another door that opened on a side street.

The interior of the garage was dimly lighted. Peering from the window of the limousine, Pinkey Sardon saw that no one was in sight except a lounging attendant back at the door which the car had entered. Pinkey growled that the way was clear.

Rowdy Kirshing alighted. Pinkey watched him approach an obscure door at the back of the garage. He saw the big shot press a button. He could hear the click of a latch.

As Rowdy Kirshing entered the door, Pinkey spoke to Danny through the tube. The chauffeur nodded and started the limousine out through the door to the side street.

BEYOND the small door through which he had passed, Rowdy Kirshing had arrived at the foot of a stairway. The door closed behind him, the rack-eteer marched upward. Dim light showed a barri-er ahead; as Rowdy reached the top of the stairs, this proved to be a door of heavy steel.

A tiny peephole clicked open. An observing eye surveyed Rowdy's roughened countenance.

The peephole closed. The door slid to the right. Rowdy Kirshing entered a small anteroom where a brawny, red-faced fellow was waiting.

"Howdy, Steve," growled Rowdy.

"Hello, Rowdy," returned the guard, as he pressed a switch to close the outer door.

No further words were given. Steve gave a signaling rap against the inner door. It slid to the right. Rowdy walked through and Steve followed. Rowdy uttered a brief greeting to a beefy inner guard:

"Howdy, Mac."

The big shot was in the lounging room of a palatial club. In amazing contrast to the dingy garage beneath, this apartment was furnished, on an extravagant scale. The chairs and tables were of heavy mahogany. The ornate, tufted carpeting seemed inches thick. The paneled walls were decorated with gold-leaf ornamentation.

At the left were barred and shuttered windows, almost completely hidden by heavy velvet curtains. To the right was an open doorway, beyond it the cross-section of a mahogany bar with polished brass rail beneath.

The sight of a white-liveried bartender handling a shaker, the click of glasses and the tones of laughing conversation were evidence where most of the patrons of this club were lurking.

Rowdy Kirshing, however, did not turn in the direction of the barroom. He went straight ahead, crossing the deserted lounge room until he reached one of three doors that were set in a row. He opened the barrier and grinned as he poked his head into the room.

Four men, seated at a heavy card table, looked up as Rowdy arrived. With one accord, they beckoned to the big shot. Rowdy entered and closed the door behind him. One of the players, rising, invited the racketeer to join the game. Rowdy accepted.

These men were spenders. Hardened figures of the underworld, who gained their revenue through racketeering, they used this unnamed club as their meeting place. The size of their poker game was apparent when Rowdy Kirshing counted off five thousand dollars from the roll in his pocket and received fifty chips in return.

THE deal began. The game proceeded. Amid clouding cigar smoke, the five players kept up terse snatches of conversation as hundred-dollar chips changed hands as lightly as if they had been worthless disks of cardboard.

"Seen Velvet Laffrey lately?"

Rowdy Kirshing, squeezing five cards in his left hand, peered from the corner of his eye as he heard one player address the question to another.

"No," came the reply. "Maybe he's scrammed from town."

"They say the bulls are looking for him." The speaker paused; when no return comment came, he added: "Maybe they think he was the guy who hooked Hubert Apprison."

Silence followed, broken only by the clicking of chips. The speaker's reference had been to the disappearance of a prominent banker. Newspaper reports were to the effect that Hubert Apprison had been kidnapped.

The man who had brought up the subject said no more. Direct references to individual crime activities were taboo at this protected club. Rowdy Kirshing, his poker face inflexible, dropped four chips on the center of the table to raise a bet.

The game continued. Rowdy's stack of chips was dwindling. Some one commented on the fact. The big shot laughed.

"Guess I'll be buying some more," he asserted. "It always takes a few grand to get started."

"What's a few grand to you, Rowdy?" laughed one of the players.

"Not much," decided Rowdy. "I go in for big dough. And it's as big as ever."

With this retort, the big shot arose from the table. He reached in his right coat pocket and counted off the remainder of his roll, a matter of four thousand dollars. He pulled a revolver from his pocket and planked it carelessly upon the table, while he fished in his pocket for loose bills.

Grinning as he found none, Rowdy reached into his left pocket. He drew out a fat bundle of crisp notes. The stack was encircled with a broad strip of paper. The eyes of the players bulged as they saw the high denominations on the bills when Rowdy Kirshing riffled the ends.

Holding the stack in his left hand, the big shot tried to pull a group of bills free from the others. He wanted to do this without breaking the encircling paper band. The speculative players wondered why, but gave the matter little thought. Had they been able to view the side of the packet that was toward Rowdy's eyes, their passing curiosity would have become keen interest.

THE near side of the band was marked, not with a printed or written statement of amount, but with a most unusual emblem. Thrust through the band itself was a feather of jet-black hue.

It was this object that Rowdy Kirshing did not want the other men to see. That was why he did not tear the band. He glowered, as the tightly-packed bills failed to come free. The players leaned back in their chairs and waited.

Thus came momentary silence, that lacked

even the slight clicking of poker chips. It was the sudden lull that caused Rowdy Kirshing to look up quickly as his ears detected an unexpected sound from across the room.

Rowdy was facing the door; the other men stared as they caught the expression that appeared upon the big shot's face. Rowdy's hands stopped their motion. Gripping the ends of the packet of bills, the racketeer gazed in petrified horror.

The others turned their heads in alarm. Like Rowdy, they became as statues. Unseen, unheard, some stranger had entered the secluded gaming room. Like a specter from the night, a figure had appeared before these men of crime.

Looming just within the door was a tall form clad in black. A cloak of sable hue hid the arrival's body. The upturned collar concealed his features. The turned-down brim of a black slouch hat obscured the visitor's forehead. All that showed from that darkened visage was a pair of burning eyes that focused themselves upon the crisp bills gripped in Rowdy Kirshing's hands.

From a black-gloved fist extended a huge automatic, its mighty muzzle looming with a threat of instant death. It was the sight of that weapon that caused five watching men to quail.

Then, as no one moved, there came a token more terrifying than either the being himself or the mammoth gun which he displayed. A whisper crept from unseen lips. It rose to a quivering, shuddering laugh that echoed sibilantly through the room.

That was the laugh feared throughout the underworld. It was the cry that men of crime knew for a knell of doom.

The laugh of The Shadow!

CHAPTER II
THE SHADOW SPEAKS

THE SHADOW!

Every one of the five racketeers trembled at the sound of the visitant's laugh. Though four knew that the sinister sound was directed toward one— Rowdy Kirshing—there was no comfort for them.

These men were crooks. To them, crime had become a science. Payers for protection, they had found ways to offset the efforts of the police. But, like all denizens of gangland, they held a common fear.

They knew that all participants in crime were threatened by a common menace. They knew that a mysterious fighter was ever ready to battle with those who fought the law. They had heard tales of a being clad in black, a lone wolf whom none could balk; and they knew that he was called The Shadow.

Swift death came to those who sought to thwart The Shadow. Often had this phantom being arrived in spots where gangsters lurked, to deal vengeance upon fiends who plotted crime. But of all spots in Manhattan where security from The Shadow could have been expected, this guarded gaming room within the steel-domed club had promised greatest security.

The Shadow's presence was incredible. The trapped men stared as though viewing a ghost. There was an unreality about the black-clad shape; but it was brought to grim actuality by the tokens of The Shadow's power.

The blazing eyes; the looming automatic; the weirdly whispered laugh—these were signs of The Shadow's wrath. The men who saw and heard were quivering. Not a hand stirred as horrified minds hoped only that The Shadow would concentrate upon the man who first had seen him— Rowdy Kirshing.

A moment of chilling silence. Then came The Shadow's voice. A sneering whisper formed words that hissed with terrible threat.

"Rowdy Kirshing!" The Shadow's tones seemed to mock the name that they uttered. "I have found you with ill-gotten spoils. Before I depart, you will tell me of their source. You will betray the part that you have played in evil crime!"

The tall form was moving inward from the door. There was weirdness in The Shadow's approach. As his dreaded figure neared the table, the seated men crouched away; but all held their hands above their heads as token of surrender.

ROWDY KIRSHING'S face still wore its sullen fear. His hands, however, were trembling. The crisp bills crinkled between them. The big shot was cowed.

"Speak!" The Shadow's voice was commanding. "Tell me the name of the underling who has served you!"

Rowdy's lips were rigid. Then, like the big shot's hands, they began to tremble. The menace of The Shadow's automatic seemed imminent.

"Speak!" came The Shadow's harrowing tone.

"Terry," gasped Rowdy Kirshing. "Terry— Terry Rukes. He's the fellow—who's working for me. But I'm not in it—"

The Shadow's laugh came as a chilling interruption. Rowdy Kirshing's scarred face showed pallor.

"You are the go-between," sneered The Shadow. "The money in your hands is payment for your services. You have purchased men for crime."

Rowdy Kirshing's protest ended. There was

accusation in The Shadow's sinister utterance. The big shot could not meet it.

"Name the man," came The Shadow's order, "who has provided the funds for crime."

It was a moment before Rowdy Kirshing gained his voice. His words, when uttered, were hoarse, with a plaintive quaver that seemed incongruous from his roughened lips.

"I—I don't know"—Rowdy was gasping—"don't know—don't know who—"

The Shadow's blazing eyes were fierce. A soft, menacing taunt came from the lips that Rowdy could not see. A black finger pressed slowly against the trigger of the automatic.

"I'll tell"—blurted were Rowdy's words—"tell all I know! All I know! It was Velvet Laffrey! He—he started the game!"

A pause; Rowdy's voice became a pleading moan.

"I—I haven't seen Velvet." The big shot was insistent. "He—he told me I wouldn't see him. The dough comes in—I get it to pay Terry Rukes. I keep my cut—"

The racketeer was trembling from head to foot. He knew the menace of The Shadow; knew that in betraying others, he was confessing his own guilt. That was the explanation of his terror.

Rowdy Kirshing, here in gangland's most formidable stronghold, was a big shot no longer. He had become a pitiful crook, squealing on others and blabbing his own story while cowering racketeers crouched as listeners.

"I keep my cut!" Rowdy's voice rose to a tremolo. "It isn't my game, though. Honest—it was Velvet. It wasn't my game to start—"

The racketeer's eyes were bulging; his hands were faltering as they clutched the bills. His lips, however, had momentarily lost their quivering. The odd beginning of a smile had come instinctively upon Rowdy's face.

The big shot could keep an unflinching face in a poker game. In this situation, however, he was unable to keep from betraying the fact that luck had come his way. Rowdy's rising voice had been well timed. His eyes had sighted a motion of the door beyond The Shadow's form.

But the lips, with their unwarranted smile, explained the reason for Rowdy's louder words. The Shadow, although he could not hear the slight sound behind him, knew that danger lay in the direction toward which Rowdy stared.

THE black cloak swished. Its whirling folds revealed a crimson lining as The Shadow pirouetted toward the door. The barrier had opened. A hard-faced man, gun in hand, was peering into the room. There were others behind him. They had heard the sound of Rowdy Kirshing's voice.

The man with the gun caught his first view of the room just as The Shadow whirled. Responding quickly, the hard-faced fellow thrust his hand forward, with his finger against the revolver trigger.

Had The Shadow paused a split second, the rescuer would have gained the drop. But The Shadow, in his swift about-face, had taken it for granted that an enemy was at the door. The big automatic roared as The Shadow's rigid fist stayed with his line of vision.

The bullet found its mark. The man at the door sank back. His companions flung themselves away from the doorway.

The Shadow could have beaded one or more of them, but The Shadow had more important game. His swift whirl did not stop. It continued with a definite design; back to the spot which The Shadow had left.

The Shadow had foreseen Rowdy Kirshing's action. The instant that The Shadow had begun his whirl, Rowdy had shot his right hand to the table. There he had grabbed the gleaming revolver which he had taken from his pocket.

Rowdy was quick with the weapon. His finger found the trigger as his hand gained the gun. While The Shadow's automatic sounded its terrific roar, Rowdy, his eyes gleaming, came up to fire.

The big shot's eyes bulged as his finger drew against the trigger. A second roar came from the automatic. With listless finger quivering weakly, Rowdy slumped to the table. His dying gaze caught the glare of The Shadow's eyes.

The big shot had sealed his own doom. Acting rapidly, he had expected to shoot The Shadow in the back. Instead, the completion of The Shadow's whirl had ended in the second burst of flame from the deadly automatic.

Rowdy's hands, sprawling straight across the table, dropped two objects. One, the revolver, fell with a clatter. The other, the stack of bills, plopped softly. The side that the racketeer had sought to hide was downward. The Black feather did not show.

With one outward sweep of his free left hand, The Shadow sent the revolver flying from the table. It clanked against the wall beyond Rowdy Kirshing's crumpled body.

With the return sweep, The Shadow grasped the pile of bound bills. The packet went beneath the folds of the black cloak. With a quick, sidewise whirl, The Shadow glanced toward the door; then ended back against the wall, his automatic covering the four men who still cowered in their chairs.

TERRY RUKES

THE BLACK FALCON, master of crime, who pits his wits against The Shadow, master of crime detection. It is The Black Falcon who recognizes The Shadow beneath one of his disguises, and plans his capture in a bold stroke. TERRY RUKES, as henchman of The Black Falcon, leads the mob which carries out the orders of the hidden chief.

THE BLACK FALCON

A laugh resounded through the room. With the taunt, The Shadow pressed the light switch. His automatic barked two warning shots. In the gloom, the four racketeers dived for the shelter beneath the table.

The same swift shots stopped the men outside the gaming room. They dropped to the walls of the outer room. Drawing guns, they were preparing for an attack. Before they could acquire leadership, their opportunity was ended.

OUT from the gaming room swept The Shadow. His arrival was both swift and unexpected. With a long, springing leap, he shot from the blackness of the little room, and in three swift strides gained a spot well clear from the doorway.

The patrons of the club had chosen the corners near the gaming room. The Shadow, whirling as he came from cover, was beyond them.

Each gloved fist now held an automatic. Both weapons thundered as The Shadow, with the door to the gaming room as a center, began to spread his arms.

Screaming men flung themselves prone upon the floor to escape the spraying fire. The Shadow, as he increased the angle, was taking in every spot along the end walls; as his form moved swiftly backward toward the outer door, he covered the entire room.

Peering men ducked back into the barroom. At the steel door, The Shadow flung one hand against a switch. With this action, he extinguished the sidelights about the lounging room. Only the slight glow from the barroom remained; the shape of The Shadow dimmed against the steel barrier.

In his spraying fire, The Shadow had used remarkable strategy. Of a dozen men, three had tried to shoot in response. The Shadow's bullets, aimed a few feet above the wall, had clipped these ruffians while they aimed and had dropped them wounded.

The others had flung themselves upon the floor.

They were unscathed; but they had lost the opportunity to deliver a quick response. After the lights went out, they rose to fire at the steel door.

Bullets zimmed against the barrier. The four racketeers in the cardroom joined in the shooting. Men surged forward through the gloom. A cry came to end the fire. A man pressed the switch by the steel door.

Where every eye expected to see the crumpled form of a black-cloaked figure, there was no one in view! The Shadow had pressed the switch that opened the steel door. He had left as the volley of shots had begun. All had been foiled, for there had been no light from the anteroom to show that the door had opened.

The answer was discovered when someone slid away the barrier. The lights in the anteroom were out. Steve and Mac, the guards, were lying gagged upon the floor. They were released; Steve pointed to the outer door of steel.

"I heard the ring," he explained. "I looked through the peephole. There wasn't no one there. I opened the sliding door; then he got me."

"Same here," grunted Mac. "I heard a rap. I thought it was Steve. Then I was yanked out as soon as I opened the door. The lights were out."

"It was The Shadow," gasped Steve, in an awed tone. "I seen him, but Mac didn't. He grabbed both of us. But he put the lights out here before he knocked for Mac."

Foiled crooks stood disgruntled. Pursuit was too late. To seek The Shadow was the last deed that anyone intended. None cared to risk a new encounter with that fierce fighter of the night who had invaded this stronghold alone to deliver deserved death to Rowdy Kirshing.

WHILE the baffled men of crime lingered in their stronghold, a trim coupé rolled to a stop on a side street near Times Square. Black-gloved hands came from darkness. They showed in the dim glow from the sidewalk.

ROWLAND RANSDALE, millionaire, and HAZZLETT, his servant, who are the first ones to successfully withhold the attack of The Black Falcon. The fire of these two men, aided by the unseen help of The Shadow, brings the first respite from the depredations of this master crook.

HAZZLETT

RANSDALE

Keen eyes surveyed a packet that rested between those hands. It was the stack of crinkly bills that The Shadow had taken from Rowdy Kirshing. The eyes now saw the strange marking that adorned the paper strip about the packet.

A black feather! This was the only symbol of the person who had paid Rowdy Kirshing, big shot racketeer, a price for service. That marking, as yet, was the single clew to the man behind some insidious game of crime.

A soft, echoing laugh came from hidden lips as the eyes of The Shadow identified the species of the plume. That bit of evidence denoted a bird of prey.

It was the feather of a falcon—dyed black!

CHAPTER III
CRIME FOREWARNED

A BLACK feather!

Such was the trophy that The Shadow had brought from the secret stronghold on Tenth Avenue. Unaided, the master fighter had raided the palatial club where big shots met. Departing unscathed, he had left death lying in his wake.

Rowdy Kirshing had died in an attempt to slay The Shadow. Before his death, the big shot had blurted his connection with "Velvet" Laffrey. There lay another link. The police—so rumor had it—were looking for Laffrey in connection with the disappearance of Hubert Apprison, prominent New York banker.

Gangland rumors are usually backed by truth. Such was the case with this one. Less than half an hour after the echoes of The Shadow's shots had ended within the confines of the Tenth Avenue club, a swarthy, stocky man stepped from a subway entrance near the corner of Thirty-third Street.

This individual walked along at a steady pace until he arrived at the entrance of an apartment house. He rode upstairs in an automatic elevator

and knocked at the door of an apartment. The door opened to show a small anteroom. A short man, of military bearing, stepped back to admit the arrival.

"Good evening, Detective Cardona," he said, "The commissioner is waiting to see you. Step in."

The servant conducted the detective into a living room. He led him through to a hallway beyond and paused to knock on a closed door. A brusque voice responded from the other side of the barrier.

"What is it, Kempton?"

"Detective Cardona is here, sir," replied the servant.

"All right," came the voice. "Have him enter."

The servant opened the door and ushered the detective into a small, lighted office. A desk occupied the middle of the room; beyond it was seated a firm-faced man who was going over a stack of papers.

Cardona seated himself in a chair on the nearer side of the desk. He waited for several minutes until the police commissioner laid the papers aside, rested back in the chair and eyed his visitor.

There was a marked contrast between these two men who represented the law. Police Commissioner Ralph Weston was of a powerful, executive type. His strong face, his steady lips with pointed mustache above them, showed him to be a man who believed in action and demanded it.

Detective Joe Cardona, with keen, dark eyes and solemn visage, was one who could follow instructions that were given. His impassiveness was the sign of his ability to observe. Long experience in hunting down perpetrators of crime had gained him recognition as an ace among sleuths.

IT was Cardona's practice, when he visited Weston, to let the commissioner begin the conversation. Cardona had learned that his superior was both impulsive and impatient. When Weston had questions, he asked them. Cardona had become wise enough to govern his replies along lines that were close to the commissioner's train of thought.

Thus Cardona waited for a full minute while Weston stared in his direction. The detective knew that a question was coming. He wanted to hear it. At length the commissioner snapped his inquiry.

"Anything new on Apprison?"

"Nothing since my last report," replied Cardona.

Weston fingered a sheaf of papers on his desk. He nodded slowly as he considered Cardona's noncommittal answer. Then, with his characteristic brusqueness, he gave an order.

"Let me have the details to date," he said.

Joe Cardona repressed a smile. This was an old trick of the commissioner's. Weston had a habit of digesting every detail of a written report; then demanding a verbal resumé. He was quick to catch any variance that might occur. Cardona's way of meeting this was to make verbal reports concise.

"At eight o'clock last Wednesday night," declared the detective, "Hubert Apprison was in the study of his home on Seventy-fifth Street. With him was his secretary, Jonathan Blossom. Mrs. Apprison was entertaining guests downstairs.

"Shots were heard. The guests hurried upstairs. They found Jonathan Blossom lying dead, on the floor of the study. In his grasp was the top portion of a letter addressed to Hubert Apprison. It bore a date—Tuesday—and Apprison's name and address with the words 'Dear Sir.'

"Hubert Apprison was gone. Evidently intruders had entered by the backstairs, had seized Apprison and carried him away. The letter which Apprison had received was probably important, for most of it had been torn from Blossom's grasp.

"The important evidence was the presence of thumb and fingerprints upon the portion of the letter that Blossom held. These have been examined"—Cardona paused to bring photostatic copies from his pocket—"and have proved to be the impressions of a former confidence man named Peter Laffrey—known as Velvet Laffrey."

Again the police commissioner nodded. He waited quietly. Cardona's eyes narrowed momentarily; then the detective added a short statement.

"Two theories," he said. "One, that Apprison killed Blossom and made a getaway. The other, that Velvet Laffrey headed a crew that carried off Apprison. I am working on the last named."

Cardona eyed the commissioner upon the completion of this statement. He expected a criticism. He was ready for it when it arrived.

"Why," questioned Weston, "do you reject the possibility that Apprison may have slain his secretary?"

"I do not reject it," returned the detective, with a steady smile. "My job is to find Hubert Apprison. Once he is quizzed, we will have a lead on whether he or someone else was responsible for Blossom's death."

"So you are trying to locate Velvet Laffrey—"

"As a step to finding Apprison. We have evidence that Laffrey was present when Apprison disappeared."

COMMISSIONER WESTON arose from his desk. He paced across the room while Joe Cardona watched him. At last the commissioner turned and faced the detective.

"Cardona," he declared, "you are using commendable tactics. I want to compliment you upon your keenness. You have learned to combine theory and practice. It is an ability which you did not fully possess when I first knew you."

The compliment was something of a backhanded one. Commissioner Weston seemed to take upon himself some of the approval that he was extending to the detective. That, however, did not curb Joe Cardona's secret elation. The detective was used to Commissioner Weston's brusque, egotistical manner. He knew that Weston was pleased. Cardona retained his flickering smile as he gazed at his superior officer.

Weston paced a while longer. His face clouded. He stopped short and snapped a question at his subordinate.

"Why have you not traced Velvet Laffrey?"

"We're using the dragnet," returned Cardona calmly. "If Laffrey is in New York, we'll get him."

"Hm-m-m," mused the commissioner. "I see your point. Velvet Laffrey may have left town. Quite likely. Meanwhile, of course, a search is being made for Hubert Apprison."

"Yes. Under Inspector Klein's supervision."

"Exactly. Therefore, the only excuse for the inability of the police force to locate either the kidnapped man or the supposed kidnapper is the fact that both may be absent from the city."

"That would be a good reason for not finding either of them."

"Cardona,"—Weston became serious as he spoke—"there is a clever crook behind the disappearance of Hubert Apprison. That crook may be Velvet Laffrey. I think he is Velvet Laffrey, but I am not willing to express a final opinion until more evidence is obtained in the matter.

"We must find the master crook. Naturally, if he has been outside of New York, we can say that the task is one that might be excusable if it failed. But if the crook should be in New York—if he should positively return to the city—"

"We ought to get him, Commissioner."

Weston nodded at Cardona's words. The detective became a bit uneasy. He had a hunch that Weston was holding something back.

"If," remarked the commissioner thoughtfully, "our man were to enter New York on a stipulated date and there attempt a crime similar to the kidnapping of Hubert Apprison—a crime with murder again involved—we, as representatives of the law in New York, should certainly be expected to apprehend the miscreant. Am I right?"

"Yes," agreed Cardona with a short laugh. "If we knew what the crook is going to do, we ought to get him."

"And if," added Weston, "we should be somewhat in the dark regarding his actual plan of action, it would be our part to illuminate the subject in time to forestall crime?"

"Absolutely."

"Good. I am glad to hear you talk that way, Cardona. Very glad, especially"—Weston was smiling—"because I am able to give you an opportunity to prove your statement."

There was a biting challenge to Weston's tone. Joe Cardona shifted uneasily. He watched the commissioner pick up a folded sheet of paper from the desk.

"The crook," remarked Weston quietly, "will be in New York. Do you understand that, Cardona? The man behind the disappearance of Hubert Apprison is coming to New York. There is information that I want you to put to good use. If there is anything more that you want to know about the man in question, ask me."

"All right," returned Cardona. "Why is he coming here?"

"To repeat his crime," answered Weston promptly. "To perform murder as well as abduction."

"When?"

"Tonight."

THE quickness of the commissioner's response took Cardona aback. The detective stared in stupefaction; then, recalling Weston's statement that he would answer required questions, Cardona put another query.

"How do you know all this, Commissioner?"

"Because," declared Weston, "I have received a letter from the crook himself."

With that response, the police commissioner unfolded the sheet of paper. He planked it on the desk in front of Cardona's amazed eyes. A sheet of white paper—a beautifully engraved letterhead in the upper left corner—a series of typewritten lines as the body of the message itself—these lay in plain view.

But to Joe Cardona, these meant nothing at first sight. The detective's gaze was glued to the bottom of the page, upon the spot where one might have expected a signature to the communication.

The object which Cardona saw there was one that commanded his complete attention. Thrust through two small slits in the sheet of paper was a symbol identical with the one that The Shadow had tonight gained from the dead grasp of the big shot, Rowdy Kirshing.

Detective Joe Cardona was staring at a feather which formed a glistening black-dyed blade against the white paper to which it had been affixed!

CHAPTER IV
THE COMMISSIONER'S PLAN

COMMISSIONER RALPH WESTON stood smiling grimly while his ace detective stared at the queer signature beneath the letter. Then, as Cardona made no immediate effort to read the message itself, Weston offered explanatory suggestions.

"Up here," remarked the commissioner, pointing to the top corner at the left, "you will find the name by which our correspondent chooses to call himself."

Cardona looked at the corner indicated. Printed in jet-black was the artistic drawing of a bird. The detective took it to represent an eagle or a hawk. Then, noting three neatly lettered words below the depicted bird, he read them aloud:

"The Black Falcon!"

"The Black Falcon," repeated the commissioner. "An appropriate name, Cardona, for one who swoops down to gain his prey by night. The falcon, Cardona, is a bird trained in methods of effective capture.

"The author of this letter calls himself The Black Falcon. If you will read the message, Cardona, you will see why; and I, by watching, may gain an inkling of the effect which The Black Falcon's statements have upon their reader. When I perused the message myself, I must confess that I was too tense to consider my own reactions."

Cardona nodded silently. He held the letter before him and scanned the typewritten lines which appeared as follows:

Ralph Weston,
Police Commissioner,
New York City
Dear Sir:
　　You, as chief representative of the law in New York City, have chosen to concern yourself with the disappearance of one Hubert Apprison.
　　In order to save you time and annoyance in a futile search for this missing person, I take the liberty of announcing that Hubert Apprison is at present in my charge.

Inasmuch as Hubert Apprison is a man of great wealth, it is my intention to hold him prisoner until I have arranged suitable means of delivering him into the hands of friends. This service is one for which I shall receive a ransom commensurate with my prisoner's wealth.

Since, however, I am willing to relieve you from trouble in connection with Hubert Apprison, I expect the same courtesy in return. Undue interference on the part of the police will merely disturb my plans—not balk them.

May I suggest that you announce to the public that Hubert Apprison vanished of his own accord? Such a course will relieve you of troublesome responsibility. It will also enable me to conduct quiet negotiations with Apprison's associates. I can assure you that if you act as I suggest, all will be handled to satisfaction.

I shall look forward to seeing your definite statement in the evening newspapers on the day that you receive this letter. Should you, however, fail to act in accord with my plans, I shall act again, as I did with Apprison, before midnight.

In return for your failure to cooperate, I shall kidnap another person of wealth from within the limits of New York City. My second crime, like the first, will be committed in an area under your jurisdiction.

It will stand as proof of my ability to kidnap and return people at will. My only regret will be that you will have committed the folly of putting my unique skill to the test.

Joe Cardona, when he had finished the reading of this singular epistle, remained in deep thought. Commissioner Weston, watching the detective, was ready for a comment. None came. The commissioner put a question.

"What do you think of it?" he asked.

"When did you receive it?" parried Cardona.

"This afternoon," was the commissioner's reply. "Here, at my apartment."

"I've seen a lot of crank notes," decided Cardona, "but this doesn't look like one."

"It is too specific," agreed the commissioner. "Furthermore, if it were intended as a hoax, it would defeat its own purpose—"

"Because it names tonight as the time limit," interposed Cardona, as Weston paused.

"Precisely," declared the commissioner. "You caught that point excellently, Cardona. More promptly than I did. If the purpose of this letter was to cause mere annoyance, the writer would have given me a week to make my statement. However, with midnight as the time set—"

"We'll know quick enough if this bird is a faker."

"He is a bird," announced Weston, solemnly repeating Cardona's slang expression. "He calls himself The Black Falcon. That feather, if my ornithology is correct, is the plume of a falcon, dyed black. This man is a schemer, Cardona. His challenge is open defiance."

THE detective's fingers were beating a soft tattoo against the arms of the chair. Cardona was staring speculatively at the letter. He chanced a new remark.

"I've had a look at the afternoon papers," he declared. "I read them coming up on the subway. I didn't see the statement The Black Falcon asked for."

"I know you didn't," returned Weston, with a firm smile. "I could have inserted one—just as a blind—but I refrained. I would rather meet this schemer openly for the time. Let us learn whether or not his boasts can be made good."

"You're right, Commissioner," agreed Cardona. "We've struck a stone wall on the Apprison case. If The Black Falcon pulls another job tonight, we'll have a chance to trail him, maybe. At the same time—"

"The chance of murder is not to be overlooked," admitted Weston, in interruption. "I know that, Cardona; and I considered long before I made my decision. Killing as well as abduction is possible. However, I have reasons for my decision. Before I give them, let me hear what your impression is regarding the possible identity of The Black Falcon. Give me theory if you wish—I shall not criticize it under these circumstances."

"All right, Commissioner," responded Cardona. "Take a look at that letter while I show you something."

He handed the letter to Weston and picked up the photostats from which he had selected a specimen of Velvet Laffrey's fingerprints. Cardona chose one of these which showed the entire portion of the torn sheet which had been clutched by Hubert Apprison's secretary. He passed it to Weston and pointed to the typing on the photostat. Weston read it:

Hubert Apprison, Esq.
New York City.
Dear Sir:

The letter had been torn below that point; hence no more typing showed on the photostatic copy. Cardona, however, seemed to think that the wording was sufficient.

"Typed on a Mangus Portable," remarked the detective. "Model Eight. I had an expert look at it. He spotted it quick, by the type style. Said the machine was off the market; never sold well, and that funny type was a giveaway. Now look at your letter from The Black Falcon. I'm no expert on typewriters, but I can see that it was the same kind of a machine. Expert examination may prove it to be the identical typewriter."

Weston pulled a magnifying glass from the desk drawer and compared the letter with the photostatic sample of typing. He uttered a cry of elation as he nodded.

"I think you're right, Cardona!" exclaimed the commissioner. "We can have an expert examine it later. But for the present—"

"Right now," interposed Cardona, "it's close enough to support my theory. I figured right from the start that a smart crook was in the game—and Velvet Laffrey was smooth enough to be the guy.

"Here's the way I dope it. Laffrey sent some kind of a letter to Apprison. Probably it veiled a threat. Not getting a reply, Laffrey blew into Apprison's house. He had a gun; he made Apprison dig up the letter. He took Apprison with him and Blossom tried to grab the letter from Laffrey. So Velvet gave the secretary the works."

"Logical," admitted Weston. "Particularly because Blossom may have known too much."

"Right. Velvet Laffrey didn't get all of the letter though, and he left his fingerprints on the part that Blossom kept. Velvet was wise enough to cast Apprison out of town with him. He wants dough—all kidnappers do—and naturally he's bothered because the police are on the job."

"Which would account for The Black Falcon letter," mused Weston. "So far, Cardona, it may fit."

"It does fit," asserted the detective. "Velvet Laffrey used to do some smooth confidence work. He's the kind of bird who would go in for abduction. He was seen around New York only a week before Apprison was grabbed."

"But the abduction was accomplished swiftly—"

"Which means that Velvet has mobsters working for him."

Cardona made this statement with finality. Without realizing it, the detective was following the same course of reasoning as The Shadow. But there the detective's findings ceased.

THE SHADOW, like Cardona, had decided that gangsters must have aided in the swift capture of Hubert Apprison. Thinking further, he had placed a racketeer above them. Rowdy Kirshing, a big shot whose income had recently been curtailed, had been spending money freely since Apprison's abduction. Thus had The Shadow taken up the trail of Rowdy Kirshing.

A faint glimmer of the money angle reached Commissioner Weston as the dynamic police official considered Joe Cardona's statement.

"Mobsters," mused the commissioner. "That means cash paid out. Was this confidence man—Velvet Laffrey—well supplied with money?"

"He could be, easily enough," returned Cardona. "It doesn't take much to buy a few gorillas. Chances are, his crew was small—and you can bet they're hiding out."

"Why?"

"Because of that letter in your hand. Velvet Laffrey is holding them for another job—tonight."

"Jove, Cardona!" The commissioner's voice denoted new elation. "You're striking it right! Let me mention, however"—Weston's face began purposely to mask its enthusiasm—"that I must have more evidence before I can agree with you that Velvet Laffrey is the supercrook behind this game."

"If it isn't Velvet Laffrey," protested Joe Cardona, "who is it?"

"The Black Falcon," declared the commissioner, tapping the letter that he held in his hand.

A wry smile appeared upon Cardona's swarthy face. The stocky detective had long been waiting for a moment such as this. His next remark, though mild in tone, was a triumphant one.

"Commissioner," said Joe reflectively, "I once included on my reports the mention of a person called The Shadow. I took it for granted that there was such a person—that he threw his lot in to help out against crooks when the going got too hot.

"You put sort of a curb on my reports. You said that until we could identify The Shadow as a definite person, he wasn't to be mentioned."

"Of course not," snorted Weston. "The Shadow is a myth—a name—"

"And so is The Black Falcon," interrupted Cardona.

Weston's face puffed. The commissioner showed momentary anger. He set a heavy fist upon the desk; then his rigor lightened. A smile appeared upon the lips beneath the mustache. Weston chuckled.

"You're right, Cardona," he admitted. "You've given me my own medicine. I like your frankness. This letter is an anonymous communication—that's all we can take it for. The Black Falcon is a name—like The Shadow—"

"Unless," interposed Cardona, "we speak of Velvet Laffrey, alias The Black Falcon."

Weston leaned back in his chair. He smiled broadly. He had no answer. Cardona was showing him a way out—to take it, the commissioner would have to agree with the detective's belief that Velvet Laffrey was the abductor of Hubert Apprison.

"We'll let it rest your way," decided Weston, in a slow tone. "We'll assume that Velvet Laffrey is The Black Falcon. Only for the time being, though, Cardona. Only for the time being. Until"—Weston paused again to tap the feathered letter—"until midnight."

"You mean—"

"That we may, by that time, have captured this man who signs himself The Black Falcon."

It was Cardona's turn to be perplexed. Weston seemed triumphant as he referred to the letter. He pointed to certain sentences; then spoke slowly.

"This message," he declared, "is carefully worded. Here, for instance, the writer states that he expects to act before midnight. Next, he states that he will kidnap another person of wealth. Finally, he specifies within the limits of New York City.

"Why does he say midnight? Because, evidently, he knows where a certain person will be up to that hour. Why does he say person instead of man? Because that person may be a woman. Why does he say within the limits of New York City? Because the criminal may have been thinking of some portion of the metropolis other than Manhattan.

"My theory, Cardona, is that the criminal expects to raid some residence where a number of wealthy guests may be assembled. That will give him the opportunity to seize the victim that may be most available. Such a spot would very probably be somewhere on Long Island."

"Maybe," agreed Cardona. "But you're taking a long shot there, Commissioner—"

"One moment," interposed Weston, quietly. "My original thoughts were vague, yet good in theory. While I was awaiting your arrival, Cardona, I looked through the newspapers to learn of society events scheduled for tonight. I learned that Elias Carthers, the tobacco magnate, is giving an exclusive reception for his niece, at his Long Island home."

"You called Carthers?"

"I did. I learned that the guests will not arrive until after ten o'clock. While talking to Carthers, I had what you would term a hunch. I asked him if he knew Hubert Apprison. I learned that Apprison had been expected as a guest at the Carthers' home tonight.

"We are dealing with a smart crook, Cardona. The Black Falcon—Velvet Laffrey for the present—must have learned facts regarding the exclusive social set which contains both Hubert Apprison and Elias Carthers. Viewing the situation from the criminal's angle, I should say that his most logical action would be to abduct some one who is present at the Carthers' reception tonight."

Impulsively, Joe Cardona pulled a watch from his pocket. The time showed twenty minutes before ten. Commissioner Weston was smiling as the detective looked up with an anxious gaze.

"That is the reason," remarked Weston, "why you and I are leaving at once in my car. It has been waiting below since half past nine. We shall require less than half an hour for our journey."

RISING, the commissioner pressed a button on the desk. The front door of the office opened. Kempton appeared and stood in military attitude.

"We are leaving, Kempton," remarked Weston. "Detective Cardona and I are going to the home of Elias Carthers, on Long Island."

"Yes, sir."

"Also, Kempton," added Weston, as an afterthought, "I do not want anyone to know where we have gone. No one, Kempton. Do you understand?"

"Yes, sir."

His final admonition given, Weston beckoned to Cardona. Together, the commissioner and the detective left the apartment. As they entered Weston's limousine, which was waiting on the street, Joe Cardona smiled a grin of secret elation.

The ace sleuth was a man who followed hunches. He liked them, even when others supplied them. Joe Cardona was convinced that tonight, he and Commissioner Ralph Weston would have their opportunity to forestall the crook whom Joe believed to be Velvet Laffrey.

Two keen men of the law were setting forth to outwit The Black Falcon!

CHAPTER V
THE SHADOW'S MOVE

A CLICK sounded in a pitch-black room. A glimmering light of blue cast its eerie sheen upon the polished surface of a table. White hands appeared beneath the strange illumination. Upon one appeared a sparkling jewel of ever-changing hues.

The hands moved away. Something crinkled beyond the range of light. The hands reappeared, bringing with them the paper-encircled band of banknotes that The Shadow had wrested from Rowdy Kirshing.

The pile of pelf meant nothing to The Shadow. The token on the hand, however, was significant. Well did The Shadow divine the meaning of that blackened falcon feather. It was the sign of a perpetrator of crime, a crook de luxe who had paid for aid obtained through Rowdy Kirshing.

A white hand stretched across the table. It produced a pair of earphones. A tiny light glimmered on the wall. A voice came over the wire:

"Burbank speaking."

"Instructions," replied the voice of The Shadow, as it shuddered through the gloom. "Tell Marsland to obtain information concerning Terry Rukes, gang leader."

"Instructions received," returned the quiet tones of Burbank.

"Reports." The Shadow's voice hissed from the dark.

"None received," came Burbank's answer.

The earphones clicked back into place. The hands of The Shadow returned to the table. In this brief conversation, the master who ferreted out crime had spoken to Burbank, his contact man.

Through Burbank, The Shadow's instructions would go to Cliff Marsland, a stalwart agent who served The Shadow in the underworld. It would be Cliff's task to seek facts concerning the whereabouts of Terry Rukes, the man whose name Rowdy Kirshing had gasped in confession.

The feather on the stack of bills! A tantalizing clue, it baffled further traces. The Shadow had been forced to slay Rowdy Kirshing in order to save his own life. The one man who might have furnished information thus was dead. Yet The Shadow had gained a step tonight.

Upon a piece of white paper, the right hand inscribed three names, as follows:

Velvet Laffrey
Rowdy Kirshing
Terry Rukes.

Solemnly, The Shadow crossed out the central name. Rowdy Kirshing had been obliterated. The racketeer had served purely as a go-between.

Then, from the stack of bills, The Shadow's hand removed the falcon feather. The black plume dropped from the long white fingers. It fell directly upon the name of Velvet Laffrey.

THERE was significance in the action. Some master crook—he who used a falcon feather as his signature—was the abductor of Hubert Apprison. Was that man Velvet Laffrey?

The Shadow's action denoted present doubt. Until further evidence was gained, The Shadow would let that telltale feather cover the name that lay beneath it.

Fate had been freakish tonight. The Shadow, following Rowdy Kirshing's trail of easy money, had found the odd emblem of the one who had supplied the racketeer with cash. Meanwhile, Police Commissioner Weston had held an actual letter from the same supercrook.

The man who had defied the police had ignored The Shadow. Well for him that he had. With the letter as further evidence, The Shadow might have gained a prompt and effective trail. As it was, The

Shadow, through active efforts, had gained less than had the police through purely passive behavior!

Commissioner Ralph Weston and Detective Joe Cardona had gone to a spot where they believed that crime would strike. They had followed evidence that a supercrook had deliberately provided. Meanwhile, The Shadow, whose keenness had outstripped that of the law enforcers, had gained a clue that could lead to no definite action on this night.

The little light gleamed from the wall. The Shadow reached for the earphones. The voice of Burbank came quietly over the wire.

"Report from Marsland," announced the contact man. "No facts whatever concerning Velvet Laffrey. The man has disappeared. Instructions given to Marsland. He will look up Rukes."

The earphones went back to the wall. The Shadow's gleaming eyes still lingered on the markings which lay before him. A falcon feather; the crossed-out name of Rowdy Kirshing; the uncrossed name of Terry Rukes—these formed a trio in The Shadow's plans to reach the plotter who had seized Hubert Apprison.

Long minutes went by. The Shadow's hands made cryptic notations; then obliterated them with quickly penned lines. Intuitively, The Shadow could sense that crime was brewing. He was not content to wait until the kidnapper of Hubert Apprison chose to move.

Once again, the light showed on the wall. This time the voice of Burbank brought a new announcement, as The Shadow gave the word: "Report."

"Report from Burke," was Burbank's statement. "Cardona called to conference with Weston."

A soft laugh sounded in the gloom as the earphones clicked back to the wall. This was news. Clyde Burke, agent of The Shadow, was a newspaper reporter on the staff of the New York *Classic.* Burke was a frequent visitor to detective headquarters.

The Shadow knew that Joe Cardona was working on the Apprison case. The fact that the detective had gone to see the police commissioner indicated that some evidence might have reached the law.

The hands moved from the table. The light clicked out. A whispering laugh rose weirdly through the room. It reached a strange crescendo; then ended abruptly. Ghoulish echoes responded from the blackness. Silence followed. The sanctum was empty.

NOT long afterward, a tall man in evening clothes strolled into the lobby of the exclusive

Cobalt Club. The doorman bowed as the visitor passed. He had recognized the solemn face of Lamont Cranston, millionaire globe-trotter.

An important member of the Cobalt Club, Lamont Cranston was regarded as a cryptic individual. It was known that he traveled to many foreign lands and never announced his plans to anyone.

The only proof that Cranston was residing in his New Jersey home was found when he made his occasional visits to the Cobalt Club. Yet even then, the persons who saw him were not always correct in their belief that Lamont Cranston was back at home.

Little did they suspect that a strange, sinister being of mystery had adopted the guise of Lamont Cranston as a convenient personality to use on certain occasions. This tall, immaculate person-age whose face was almost masklike, was a masquerader who had chosen a part that would not be questioned. The arrival at the Cobalt Club was none other than The Shadow.

Strolling through the lounge, The Shadow passed through a doorway and approached a group of telephone booths. There, with the leisurely manner of the man whose part he was playing, he entered a booth and gave a number. A few moments later, a voice came over the wire.

"Commissioner Weston's apartment."

"Hello," The Shadow's voice was a quiet, deliberate one. "Is that Kempton?... Ah, yes... This is Mr. Cranston... Yes, the friend of Commissioner Weston. Is the commissioner there?"

A pause; then the quiet voice resumed. "He is out? Where could I reach him?... I see... I see... You have instructions that he is not to be called... Of course; of course... I understand. You are to inform no one."

A smile appeared upon the calm features of Lamont Cranston as the tall figure appeared from the phone booth. Still playing the part of the millionaire, The Shadow strolled through the lounge and took a chair. A thin smile appeared upon his lips as he pressed a cigarette between them.

Completing his smoke, this personage who played the role of Cranston, arose and returned to the phone booth. He dialed the same number that he had called before. Kempton's voice came over the wire.

THIS time, The Shadow, although he still appeared as Cranston, did not use the voice of the millionaire. Instead, his tone was brusque. It was a perfect representation of the voice of Commissioner Weston.

"Is that you, Kempton?" queried The Shadow.

"Were there any calls for me?... I see... Cranston. You told him where to reach me, of course..."

A pause; then, still in the tone of Weston, The Shadow delivered an angry outburst.

"Sometimes you lack sense, Kempton!... Of course... Yes, of course I told you not to inform anyone where I had gone... Once in a while, though, you can use good judgment... Yes, Lamont Cranston is an exceptional case."

Kempton was apologizing in a profuse tone. The Shadow listened; then responded in mollified fashion, exactly as the police commissioner would have spoken.

"All right, Kempton... Yes, perhaps Cranston would call again. Tell him where I am, if he does. By the way"—The Shadow was adopting the sarcastic touch of which Weston was capable—"you haven't forgotten where I am, have you?... Yes, that's right... Visiting Elias Carthers, on Long Island..."

The Shadow hung up the receiver as Kempton completed an apology. Rising, he strolled in Cranston fashion from the club. Reaching the street, he signaled to the doorman, who, in turn, hailed a limousine parked down the street. The pretended Lamont Cranston entered the car when it arrived.

"Long Island, Stanley," he said to the uniformed chauffeur. "Out to the home of Mr. Carthers."

A soft laugh came from Lamont Cranston's thin lips as the limousine rolled eastward. It was the whispered laugh of The Shadow; the laugh that denoted the mysterious and subtle nature of its utterer.

In feigning the voice of Police Commissioner Ralph Weston, The Shadow had paved the way for another call by Lamont Cranston. At the same time, he had made the extra call unnecessary; by feigning the commissioner's sarcastic tone, he had drawn from Kempton the information that he wanted.

Yet there was another reason for the soft laugh. The Shadow was thinking of the destination to which he had ordered Stanley.

Lamont Cranston was a friend of Elias Carthers. He would be welcome at the tobacco magnate's home. In fact an unanswered invitation to this very reception lay on a table in Lamont Cranston's New Jersey residence.

The Shadow had cause for mirth. He sensed why Commissioner Weston had gone to visit Elias Carthers. It was probable that Weston had Cardona with him; the fact that Weston had given orders to Kempton not to name his destination added to that conjecture.

The Shadow knew that the dual presence of Weston and Cardona could mean but one thing. Danger or crime—an aftermath of Hubert

Apprison's abduction—must be threatening the Long Island mansion.

The Shadow, in addition to watching men of crime, kept in touch with the activities of the police. The policy had served him well tonight.

The Shadow had made his move. He, like Weston and Cardona, had the thwarting of The Black Falcon as his objective!

CHAPTER VI
THE BLACK FALCON

IT was quarter after ten. Police Commissioner Ralph Weston was seated in a mahogany-furnished room that served as the study of Elias Carthers. On the other side of the table was the tobacco magnate. The third occupant of the room was a tall, pale-faced man whose tortoise-shell glasses gave him an owlish expression.

This room formed a quiet, detached portion of the Carthers mansion. Weston had chosen it as the best place to confer with Elias Carthers, particularly as the tobacco king had arranged for the police commissioner to meet him here.

"You believe then," Carthers was questioning, "that it would be unwise to inform my guests of the danger which may be lurking here?"

"Yes, exceedingly unwise," expressed Weston firmly. "This kidnapper has made no specific statement in reference to his plans. I have picked this reception as the likely spot at which he will act—before midnight."

"And if the guests knew of this fact—"

"They would talk among themselves. The criminal would be warned. He would avoid trouble here."

"A very good reason," decided Carthers, "why the guests should know. Let me have that list, Wistar"—he turned to the man with tortoise-shell glasses—"and I can tell the police commissioner exactly who will be here tonight."

The bespectacled individual, whom Weston took to be a social secretary, produced a typewritten sheet and handed it to Elias Carthers.

Weston studied the tobacco king. Carthers was a pudgy, droop-faced man of sixty. His flabbiness showed a life of ease; yet there was a squareness to his jaw and a flash in his eyes as he looked toward the commissioner and passed the list across the table.

"Prominent people," asserted Carthers. "This is an important social event. I don't like such affairs—I'll have to stroll in and out, however. But that isn't the point, commissioner. I think that the guests should be informed. You want to forestall crime, don't you?"

"I do," returned Weston. "That is exactly why I do not intend to speak to your guests. You have seen the criminal's letter." Weston tapped the projecting end of The Black Falcon's note, where it showed from the commissioner's side pocket. "You can readily appreciate that we are dealing with a supercrook."

"All the more reason—"

"Why we should say nothing. Let me repeat, Mr. Carthers, that the man has been specific upon but one point only. He intends to act before midnight. I have picked this affair as the logical one where he would make an attempt. These people" —Weston was tapping the typewritten list—"are representative of wealth. One of them would be a logical victim.

"The criminal calls himself The Black Falcon. He is unquestionably a supercrook. He believes that he can defy the law. There is one weakness in his armor; he undoubtedly has no inkling of the action that I have taken tonight. Should he come here, we shall be able to forestall him.

"If, however, he becomes cognizant of the fact that your home is being guarded, he will certainly avoid this place. That would not mean that The Black Falcon would fail to fulfill his threat. He has sworn that he will act before midnight. In all probability, he has alternate plans.

"Finding the police here, he could strike somewhere else. There are many wealthy residents of Long Island. Between now and midnight, The Black Falcon would have an opportunity to swoop down upon some other house and abduct a person of reputed wealth."

"I understand now," nodded Carthers. "You are right, commissioner. Say nothing to my guests. You understand that, Wistar?" Carthers turned to put the question to his secretary. "The only fault, however"— Carthers paused as he swung back to face the police commissioner —"is one of your own making, commissioner. You have come here, so you tell me, with subordinates at your command. If The Black Falcon is the smart crook that you reckon him to be, he will probably observe the presence of your men."

"I do not think so," smiled Weston. "No one except yourself and Wistar know that I am here. I have brought only one man with me and he is the cleverest detective on my force. I am speaking of Joe Cardona, the man who is working on the Apprison case.

"Cardona is strolling about on your front veranda. No one could recognize him in the semi-darkness. The lighted windows of the reception room, however, enable him to see what is happening inside. I intend to rejoin Cardona; together, we will observe all who come in and go out between now and midnight."

With an angry gesture at Elias Carthers, he forced the magnate back against the open window.

"We'll keep the guests in the reception room," affirmed Carthers. "That will not be difficult. The Black Falcon will have no opportunity to strike before midnight."

"Also," added Weston, "there are two men in my darkened limousine, which is parked among the cars in your driveway. They can be summoned instantly in case of trouble. They are watching for signals from the veranda."

Elias Carthers arose from his chair. His face was serious. He extended his hand to the police commissioner.

"I appreciate your efforts, sir," stated the tobacco king. "I shall have Wistar move back and forth from the veranda, so that we may be in direct communication."

"Have him check this list to begin with," suggested Weston, also rising.

"Certainly," agreed Carthers. "All the guests will be here by now. That will be Wistar's first action. After he has made his check, I shall send him to the veranda. Following that, I shall join the guests myself."

POLICE COMMISSIONER WESTON stepped toward the massive door of the study. Wistar leaped ahead of him and turned the large brass knob. The muffled babble of distant conversation came to the study as the secretary opened the door.

"Through the passage to the right, sir," explained Wistar to Weston. "You can reach the veranda without encountering any of the guests."

The secretary closed the door when Weston had departed. He turned to see Elias Carthers facing the rear of the study. The tobacco magnate was looking into a full-length mirror that was set in a large closet door. He was adjusting the necktie above his tuxedo collar.

"Shall I check on the guests now, sir?" questioned Wistar, in a mild tone.

"Yes," ordered Carthers. He wheeled to pick up the paper from the table. "There is only one person whom I do not expect. That"— Carthers rested his finger upon a name —"is Lamont Cranston. There is a chance that he may still be out of town. We received no reply after sending him the invitation. Of course, Cranston is always likely to arrive. You may, however, consider his name as doubtful."

"Very well, sir." Wistar picked up the list and carried it toward the door as Carthers turned back to view the closet mirror. "I shall check every one. I shall return as promptly as possible. Are there any other instructions, Mr. Carthers?"

Still reading the list, the secretary paused with his hand upon the brass doorknob. He waited for a reply from Carthers. None came.

"Are there any further instructions, sir?"

As Wistar repeated the query, he looked up from the list. He saw Elias Carthers standing before the mirror. The secretary blinked his eyes in wonderment as he observed what he first thought was the reflection of his employer. Then a gasp of terror came from Wistar's lips.

DURING the interim in which Carthers had faced the table, the door of the closet had silently opened. Framed in the space where the mirror had been was the form of a stockily-built man. The fact that this man also wore a tuxedo accounted for Wistar's momentary belief that he had seen the reflection of Carthers. The features of the stranger, however, soon dispelled that thought.

All that Wistar could see of the man's face was a square-set chin with gloating lips above it. The eyes and nose were covered with a black mask. His gaze dropping, Wistar observed a glittering revolver that covered Elias Carthers.

Eyes from the mask caught Wistar's gaze. The secretary quailed. The revolver took a forward thrust; Elias Carthers, his hands rising, backed away from the man who stood in the closet doorway.

The revolver, moving easily back and forth, held both Carthers and Wistar under its control. A contemptuous chuckle came from the gloating lips below the mask.

"Excellent plans." The masked man spoke in a dry tone. "I was pleased, Mr. Carthers, to hear you voice your approval of the police commissioner's methods. I assure you that your guests will be safe tonight."

Elias Carthers was glowering. Wistar was clutching the doorknob with a trembling grasp.

"However," resumed the masked man, "I am still able to make good my threat. A person of prominence — abducted before midnight — with Commissioner Weston standing by. An odd loophole in your plans, Mr. Carthers.

"Unselfishly, you have taken care to insure the protection of your guests. Somehow, both you and the commissioner overlooked the fact that you, yourself, would be eligible for seizure. You, Mr. Carthers, are the person of wealth who will accompany me from this house tonight."

"Who—who are you?" blurted Carthers. "Are you—are you—"

"I am The Black Falcon," interposed the man with the mask. "The past abductor of Hubert Apprison; the present abductor of Elias Carthers."

The gloating lips formed a cunning leer as The Black Falcon announced his identity.

CHAPTER VII
THE ABDUCTION

THE BLACK FALCON had plotted well. Whether or not he had anticipated the arrival of the police commissioner was a matter of secondary consequence. The chief point was that he had chosen the best lurking spot that existed within the Carthers mansion.

The tobacco magnate's study was isolated. It was easily accessible without passing through the principal rooms of the big house. Located on the ground floor, with its windows opening toward the side and rear lawn, it afforded easy opportunity for quick escape.

Elias Carthers realized this. He knew that The Black Falcon must have entered the study some time before. He was also sure that the criminal had overheard the entire conversation which had passed between Carthers and the police commissioner.

This was proven by the deliberation with which The Black Falcon acted. The masked crook seemed to know that this room would be free from intrusion. Carthers, fuming helplessly, glanced toward Wistar. One look at the secretary's pale, scared face was sufficient to tell Carthers that this weakling could not offer aid.

The Black Falcon apparently held the same opinion of Wistar. His gloating lips hardened; they formed a vicious snarl as the armed man turned his entire attention to Elias Carthers. Thrusting his revolver forward, The Black Falcon forced Carthers backward, step by step.

Carthers did not understand his enemy's purpose. He endeavored simply to retreat from the menacing gun before him. Thus, amid gloomy silence, the tobacco magnate slowly neared the window that opened toward the rear of the house. He came to a standstill with his back against the wall.

With a snarling laugh, The Black Falcon reached out with his left hand and raised the window sash. He raised his free hand to his lips and produced a soft, hissing whistle. With an angry gesture at Elias Carthers, he forced the magnate back against the open window.

As Carthers shrank from the menacing gun which The Black Falcon suddenly shoved in his face, four hands came through the window and caught the tobacco magnate from behind. A gasp came from the prisoner's lips. The hands yanked him backward; a forming cry died as these outside captors overpowered him.

Scuffling sounds were muffled in the outside darkness. The Black Falcon, gazing from the window, smiled in gloating fashion. The dim glow from the window showed his squad of husky henchmen lugging Elias Carthers helpless across the side lawn.

There was a certain lack of caution in the masked man's attitude. The evil grin upon his lips betrayed that fact.

Apparently The Black Falcon had forgotten all about Wistar, the secretary. The pale-faced fellow at the door was too frightened to realize that the evil abductor was toying with him.

IT dawned on Wistar that escape was possible. That was the very thought that The Black Falcon sought to create. While the abductor's attention remained upon the window, Wistar, with a frantic effort, fumbled with the doorknob and managed to open the door.

The instant that the secretary started to spring for safety, The Black Falcon acted. He swung his revolver and fired. Wistar, leaping into the outer passage, let out a shrill shriek as he staggered forward. The Black Falcon leaped across the room in pursuit. He saw Wistar floundering ahead, gasping as he clutched the wainscoting of the passage. Deliberately, The Black Falcon fired a second shot that stretched the secretary upon the floor.

There were cries from beyond. Faces appeared at the end of the passage. Men leaped back to cover as they saw the masked man within the study.

Snarling, The Black Falcon fired two warning shots above Wistar's body. He slammed the door of the study and pressed a brass bolt that was set above the big doorknob.

THE sounds of The Black Falcon's shots had been plainly heard in the front of the house. On the veranda, Commissioner Weston had swung to Joe Cardona in alarm. Through the windows, the detective saw people rushing toward the rear of the house.

"Where were those shots?" asked Cardona quickly.

"From the study!" exclaimed the police commissioner. "Through to the back. Quick, Cardona! While I call the men!"

Joe Cardona plunged against a French door and smashed it open. With drawn revolver, the ace detective broke through astonished guests, heading in the direction that Weston had indicated. The police commissioner, as he neared the edge of the veranda, shouted to the men stationed in the official car. The pair came scrambling out at his call.

"Through the window!" ordered Weston. "Hurry. Work with Cardona."

For an instant, Weston made move to follow. Then, with an afterthought, he hurried to the end of the veranda. He reached the side of the house on which the study windows opened. Drawing a revolver, the police commissioner skirted the driveway, then hastened toward the rear of the building.

Weston could hear the hubbub from within. A shattering blow indicated that Cardona must have opened an attack upon the study door. Weston heard a second crash as he arrived beside the open window of the study.

Raising his head above the sill, the commissioner stared into the study. He gaped in amazement as he observed the stocky figure of a man crouched against the door. The intruder seemed to have his hand upon the knob, waiting as though he expected to attack the moment that the barrier broke.

That time would not be long forthcoming. A resounding smash made the big door tremble. As the police commissioner raised his revolver, the man at the door suddenly turned toward the window. Weston stared at the mask above the snarling lips. He knew that he was facing The Black Falcon!

Opportunity lay in Weston's grasp; in his surprise, the commissioner faltered. The Black

Falcon stopped short at sight of the face in the window. With a quick movement, the masked man shifted as he jerked his revolver from his pocket.

Commissioner Weston fired hastily. His shot whizzed past the masked man's shoulder. The Black Falcon sprang forward. Weston, seeing the revolver coming at him, ducked away from the window, firing a second wild shot as he took to cover. He was ready to get the intruder when the man came from the window; but Weston's scheme was interrupted by the sound of shots from across the lawn. Henchmen of The Black Falcon were firing from beyond a hedge by the side road.

Bullets flattened against the stone wall of the house. Weston headed for the shelter of an alcove. His only protection until he reached that spot was the distance of the range. For a few moments, Weston was out of sight of the study windows; then, as he neared the drive, the commissioner looked back to see The Black Falcon dashing across the side lawn.

The kidnapper was taking a semi-circuitous course to avoid any fire from the study windows, should Cardona and the others break through. This gave Weston a chance to intercept him. Trusting to darkness, the police commissioner sprang across the lawn, believing that he would not be noticed from the hedge.

SHOTS from the study window aided Weston. Cardona had broken through the door. The detective was firing, but his shots were wide. The Black Falcon neared the darkness of the hedge; he paused to fire a shot back at the house. Then, as Commissioner Weston stopped to take aim at the spot where the revolver had spoken, an unexpected light broke over the scene.

A car had swung into the Carthers drive. The man at the wheel had heard the shots. He had brought his car to a quick stop; now the long beam of a searchlight spread across the lawn.

As plain as in the light of day, The Black Falcon was shown by the hedge. Beside him stood a rangy henchman. The two were holding revolvers; both were uncovered by the sudden illumination.

Instantly with the arrival of the light, The Black Falcon sprang through the hedge. His henchman remained, staring along the line of the searchlight's beam. Spying Commissioner Weston, caught in the same glare, the big mobster fired. Weston, dropping away, stumbled upon the lawn and fell to one knee before he could catch himself.

The commissioner was a perfect target for The Black Falcon's henchman. As the mobster aimed to kill, Weston was unable to bring his own hand up in time to beat the shot.

A gun boomed from the driveway. The arrival in the car with the headlight had leaped to the ground. His shot, at hopelessly long range, was both perfect and timely. Commissioner Weston saw the threatening mobster crumple on the turf.

Cardona and others had piled from the study window. They were hastening across the lawn, firing wildly toward the hedge. Then came the roar of a motor. A car on the side lane shot off into the darkness. The Black Falcon and his band were escaping from the scene with Elias Carthers as their prisoner.

Not even the perfect marksman from the driveway could stop that flight. He had arrived in time to drop the mobster who had gained the bead on Commissioner Weston, but the car to which The Black Falcon had dashed was protected by trees beyond the hedge.

Commissioner Weston regained his feet. He saw Joe Cardona reach the hedge and stop short staring toward the lane. Then the detective turned back to examine the body of the dead mobster. Still in the glare of the headlight, Commissioner Weston turned toward the car in which the sharpshooter had arrived. Coming across the lawn was the marksman who had saved Weston's life.

"Cranston!" exclaimed the commissioner, as he recognized the faultlessly garbed figure of his millionaire friend. "You! Great work, old man! You saved my life."

"A bit different from big game hunting," returned Cranston, with a quiet smile. "Fortunately, Commissioner, I have used the permit which you gave me. I always have a gun in my car. It came in useful upon this occasion."

Joe Cardona was striding across the lawn. The detective's face was glum. Joe became active, however, as he reached the commissioner.

"They've made a getaway," he announced reluctantly. "Looks like they took Elias Carthers with them. I'm going to the house to call headquarters. Maybe the patrols can grab them. That was The Black Falcon—"

"I know it!" snapped the commissioner. "Get into the house, Cardona! Get the call through—and clear the study! Where is Wistar, the secretary?"

"Dead," returned Cardona, as he turned and began a quick jog toward the mansion.

"Come, Cranston," urged Weston, turning toward the one who had saved his life. "This is serious business. Murder and abduction. We must study the evidence."

Side by side with his millionaire friend, Commissioner Weston started for the gray stone mansion. Weston was alert. Though he had failed to stop The Black Falcon, he was hopeful that he and Cardona might uncover clues that would lead to the trail of the daring crook.

Little did Weston, relying upon his own capability, realize that beside him was a person whose skill as a sleuth far exceeded that of Weston and Cardona combined.

The commissioner had no inkling whatsoever that he was conducting The Shadow to the scene where crime had befallen!

CHAPTER VIII
THE PROVING CLUE

COMMISSIONER WESTON had formed a new headquarters. The dominating police official was seated behind the table in the study from which Elias Carthers had been abducted. With him were two others: Detective Joe Cardona and Lamont Cranston.

Guests had been cleared from this part of the house. The two men who had been in Weston's car were in charge. Word had been sent out to cover all roads leading from the vicinity of the Carthers mansion.

Details of police had arrived; they had been sent to trail The Black Falcon and his band of miscreants. Here, on the scene where crime had fallen, Commissioner Weston was planning his next campaign against the supercrook.

Lamont Cranston, his privilege as a friend of the commissioner increased because of his timely aid in saving Weston's life, was seated quietly at one side of the table. Joe Cardona, his brow grimly furrowed, was pacing back and forth across the room.

"I'd like to have talked with Elias Carthers, Commissioner," announced the detective bluntly. "Maybe if I'd come in here with you, I'd have spotted something brewing."

"That is speculative, Cardona," returned Weston. "I had a long conversation with Carthers."

"We found part of a note at Apprison's place," asserted Cardona. "You've got the photostats there with you. Maybe, if you had quizzed Carthers, you might have learned something from him."

"I had no idea that Carthers was threatened," responded the commissioner. "Nevertheless, I am sure that he received no communication from The Black Falcon. When I began my interview with Carthers, I told him the details of the Apprison case. Had Carthers received any kind of a note, he would have mentioned it."

"Did you tell him that we were looking for a crook named Velvet Laffrey?"

"No," admitted Weston. "I showed him the letter from The Black Falcon. I told him that the man was a supercrook. If Carthers had ever heard of Velvet Laffrey, he would probably have mentioned it."

"Not necessarily," insisted Cardona. "Laffrey was always a smooth egg. This is a new game for him. I guess he hoaxed Apprison with a note, but when it caused trouble, he decided not to try that system again."

THE police commissioner was nodding as he went over the stack of photostats. Noticing a curious look on Cranston's firm face, Weston pushed the photographs over to his friend. He then drew The Black Falcon's letter from his pocket and passed it to Cranston.

"See what you make of these," suggested Weston.

"You know what I make of them," remarked Cardona to the commissioner. "I've got the right trail. Velvet Laffrey is the crook. He's working with a mob behind him. Velvet was the fellow in this room. His crew grabbed Carthers. Velvet had to kill Wistar."

"Let us speak of the criminal as The Black Falcon," decided Weston. "That is the name which he has used. We have seen him. We can only assume that The Black Falcon is Velvet Laffrey. For the present, Cardona, I intend to reconstruct the scene. Let me give my version as I have grasped it. Tell me if you check anything that is incorrect."

"All right, Commissioner."

"I visited this study," resumed Weston, "and talked with Elias Carthers at approximately quarter past ten. I went out to join you on the veranda. Almost immediately after that, The Black Falcon entered."

"By the window?"

"I suppose so. We have examined the footprints on the lawn. They are barely distinguishable because of the dry grass. However, it is probable that The Black Falcon entered by the window."

"Hardly, Commissioner."

The interposition came from Lamont Cranston. Weston turned to raise his eyebrows as he faced his friend.

"What makes you reject the window, Cranston?" asked Weston.

"You say that there were two men here," observed the millionaire, in a calm, even tone. "An entry through the window would have attracted too much attention. Especially"— Cranston's keen eyes were fixed toward the open sash—"since the window sash was probably locked."

Weston's gaze followed that of his friend. The commissioner saw the logic of Cranston's remark.

There were three windows altogether. The two that were closed were locked. It was probable that the third had been also.

"The Black Falcon," decided Weston, "could not have come through the door. His arrival came too closely upon my departure. I suppose that he opened the window himself, in order to summon his waiting men. But where did he come from?"

"The closet, perhaps," remarked Cranston.

Joe Cardona stepped over to the mirrored door. He opened it. The space was more than ample for a man to have been in hiding. Cardona turned to Weston with a definite nod.

"He must have been lying in here, Commissioner," said the sleuth. "That would have let him hear everything that was said. It would account for why he acted so soon after you were gone. He came out of here"—Cardona was acting the part as he visualized it—"and covered Carthers with his gun. He backed Carthers to the window, this way. That left Wistar at the door of the room. Wistar made a break for it. Then Velvet—The Black Falcon—got Wistar. He banged the door of the room and bolted it. He was standing by when we were smashing through."

"Sound reasoning, Cardona," approved Weston, with a nod. "Your only mistake was a partial reference to The Black Falcon as Velvet Laffrey. Those fingerprints from Apprison's are not sufficient! Do you understand?"

"All right," returned Cardona. "I figure The Black Falcon had figured the door as the best way for a run-out after he bumped Wistar. That's why he stayed there so long. It must have been three minutes at least. Then, just as you came around to cover him, he changed his mind and took to the window."

Cardona stared toward the door of the study as he spoke. The barrier had been smashed. One hinge was broken. The bolt was out of place; the door was hanging crazily inward.

LAMONT CRANSTON was watching Joe Cardona closely. It seemed as though the detective was thinking of something apart from The Black Falcon's actions. Cranston's knowing look apparently divined the mental process through which Cardona was passing. A thin smile appeared on the millionaire's lips as Cardona turned suddenly toward the closet door.

Commissioner Weston stared curiously as the detective began to examine the small brass doorknob on the outside. Then, stepping half into the closet, Cardona made a second ineffective inspection. Stepping out into the study, Cardona strode across the room and took a look at the knobs on the door to the passage.

It was here that Cardona's face assumed a look of triumph. The detective turned toward Weston and his eye lighted as he spied an object that was lying on the table. This was a magnifying glass—evidently one that had belonged to Elias Carthers.

Without a word, Cardona picked up the magnifying glass. He smiled as he tested its power. Quickly, he plucked up one of the photostats from those that were lying in front of Lamont Cranston. He stepped back to the outer door.

With the photostat beside the doorknob, Cardona made a magnified comparison. Staring through the glass, he beckoned to Commissioner Weston. The official arose from the table and joined the detective. Lamont Cranston also approached to learn what Cardona had discovered.

"Here you are!" exclaimed Cardona. "Velvet Laffrey's fingerprints on the doorknob—the same as they were on the paper in Apprison's. I told you Laffrey was The Black Falcon!"

Weston took the magnifying glass. The comparison was an excellent one. Plainly impressed upon the doorknob were the marks of a thumb and two fingers. There were lesser smudges, roundabout; these, however, were predominant.

Detailed through the glass, the prints on the doorknob appeared identical with those that were registered on the photostat. The commissioner handed the glass to Lamont Cranston. Stepping back, Weston turned to Cardona.

"You are right," commended the commissioner. "Keep up the search for Velvet Laffrey. He made his mistake tonight, when he closed the door and kept his hand upon the knob, preparing for a getaway. Let me have the glass, Cranston. I want to examine the bolt."

No traces showed when the commissioner made this inspection. With Cardona at his side, Weston looked at the knob on the passage side of the door. This was smudgy. Cardona gave the reason.

"We were all trying to turn that knob," explained the detective. "Laffrey didn't handle that knob anyway—at least not after the others were at it.

"Say—we're lucky, Commissioner! Look at this inside knob. Its been polished since the outer one. That's why it took the impression so perfectly. The closet doorknobs are too grimy. This one"—Cardona paused to look again at the telltale knob—"has a nice smooth lacquer on it. Say—when Laffrey grabbed it, he was leaving his mark just like a kid stepping on a soft cement pavement! We've got the goods, Commissioner. Velvet Laffrey is the crook we'll have to grab!"

Cardona studied the knob again; then, with a grin, he pulled a penknife from his pocket. He opened the blade and used it as a screwdriver on the single screw which held the doorknob in place. The screw was loose; a few quick twists made the knob wobble. Catching it at the neck, where there were no impressions, Cardona removed the knob and held it up as an exhibit.

"We'll take it down to headquarters," he said to Weston. "Photostats of this will clinch things. We've got the goods on Laffrey twice."

COMMISSIONER WESTON went back behind the table. He took his chair and thrummed with his fingers. At last he rendered his verdict.

"Cardona," he said, "we know whom we are after. Velvet Laffrey is the crook we want. For the present, however, we shall preserve secrecy.

"The public must be warned against this dangerous kidnapper. He is likely to commit a new crime, if we persist to seek his trail. Therefore, to aid us in the job ahead, we must blind him.

"We shall speak of the criminal as The Black Falcon. Let him be known by the name that he has chosen. Continue the quest for Velvet Laffrey, but conduct it with discretion. Use the dragnet; through it we may haul the crook that we want."

"I get you, commissioner," assured Cardona. "Maybe it's leaked out that we're after Velvet Laffrey, but I don't think so. Sooner or later, I'll get my mitts on him, wherever he's hiding. Leave that to me, Commissioner. We can beat this fellow at his own game by throwing The Black Falcon alias right back at him."

"Exactly," declared Weston, rising. "Now, Cardona, we can complete arrangements to leave here. Perhaps Laffrey has been rounded up. Let us hope so. In any event, what you say is true. Once we have captured the man, we shall be sure that we have taken The Black Falcon."

Placing the magnifying glass upon the table, Weston looked toward Lamont Cranston. The commissioner's face was beaming. He was pleased because of Cardona's finding. Weston took great pride in the successes of his ace. He was glad that Cardona had shown prompt work in the presence of so critical an observer as Lamont Cranston.

"Cardona and I shall return in a few minutes," informed Weston. "If you prefer to ride back to Manhattan with me, I can detail one of my men to bring in your coupé."

"Excellent, Commissioner," returned Cranston.

Weston and Cardona walked out of the study. The keen eyes that peered from the masklike countenance of Lamont Cranston watched them go. Then those same eyes looked at the brass doorknob which Joe Cardona had carefully placed, bulky end balanced, upward, upon the table. The same gaze turned to the axis that projected

from the door itself; the stump from which Cardona had unscrewed the telltale knob. A soft, whispered laugh came from the thin, straight lips of Lamont Cranston.

The laugh of The Shadow! It was significant. Although neither Cardona nor Weston had realized it, The Shadow had turned their attention to the closet; from that point, Cardona had caught the possibility of impressions on the doorknob.

To The Shadow belonged the credit for the discovery of the proving clue. That was the reason for The Shadow's laugh. The Shadow, like the police, was seeking the trail of The Black Falcon!

CHAPTER IX
FROM THE UNDERWORLD

SEVEN days had passed since the episode at the home of Elias Carthers. During that week, the name of The Black Falcon had swept the headlines. All New York, from the highest social circles to the scum of the badlands, talked of the nefarious abductor who had dared the police to trail him.

The Black Falcon had eluded the surrounding cordon that the police had summoned to Long Island. An abandoned automobile—a stolen sedan—had been found eight miles from the Carthers mansion. It was believed to be the car in which the marauders had escaped.

Theories galore circled about the escapade of The Black Falcon. One rumor claimed that he had changed to another car and had slipped through the police cordon. Another theory attributed his elusiveness to a hideout on Long Island. A third idea involved a swift speed boat, fleeing across the Sound. A fourth claim persisted that he had taken to the air by means of a plane quartered in a vacant field.

The Black Falcon! The name, itself, suggested a master criminal descending from the blackness of the sky to snatch up an unsuspecting victim. Commissioner Weston had released the news of The Black Falcon's letter. This, in itself, made every one understand the menace of this man who dealt in crime.

From highest to lowest—all talked of The Black Falcon. Logically enough, the circles in which he was most discussed were those that represented the extremes of society. The upper crust talked of The Black Falcon because they feared him. The vilest of evildoers talked of him because they envied his ability.

No word of either Hubert Apprison or Elias Carthers! This fact marked The Black Falcon as a crafty fiend. Unlike the usual kidnapper, he was in no hurry to demand ransom money. His silence did not take him from the headlines. Instead it kept the newspapers throbbing with every vague report, making copy out of trivial news; giving space to crank theories and wild guesses that bore no semblance of truth.

The dragnet was at work. Detectives were scouring the underworld. Every suspicious character was quizzed. This made gangdom seethe; and it also produced the very result that Commissioner Weston had anticipated. Velvet Laffrey, although his name was mentioned, was not heralded in gangland as The Black Falcon. Rumors of the underworld named various identities as possible claimants to the title.

On this evening, exactly seven days after the abduction of Elias Carthers, a stoop-shouldered, rat-faced little fellow was slouching along an alleyway on the East Side. Satisfied that he was not being followed, he ducked into a passage between two dilapidated houses and scurried down a flight of cellar stairs. In the darkness of what appeared to be an empty basement, he rapped twice upon a closed door; then repeated with two slower knocks.

A MINUTE passed. The door opened. The little man edged into the space. A low voice challenged amid the dark:

"Who is it?"

"Cull," replied the little man. "That you, Terry?"

"Yeah."

The door closed. A light clicked on. The pasty-faced rat eyed a husky, fierce-visaged rowdy who motioned him to enter another door on the left. The two reached a crumply, stone-walled room. The big man pointed to a broken chair. The little fellow sat down.

The big mobster was Terry Rukes, a tough gang leader who had been missing from the badlands. The little man was "Cull" Buzbee, one of the minor characters in the underworld. So insignificant was Cull that even the police had passed him up. They had rejected him as a stool pigeon.

"Well?" questioned Terry, as he studied the little man. "Wotcha got to tell me?"

"Nothin', Terry," returned Cull, "Nothin' new. I got took in by the dragnet onct again. That didn't mean nothin'. They let me go."

"Got a paper?"

Cull pulled a crumpled journal from a pocket of his grimy jacket. Terry Rukes studied the sheet by the single light that hung from the ceiling of the room.

"Still after The Black Falcon," growled the gang leader. "Well—they'll never get the guy. Any new ideas on who he is?"

"No," responded Cull. "I been listenin' to find

out if they thought he was Velvet Laffrey. They ain't been much talk about Velvet, no more, but they's still some guys that figure Velvet is The Falcon."

The little man looked at Terry Rukes with beady eyes. The gang leader saw his quizzical expression and delivered a grunt.

"Don't look at me," he snorted. "I ain't sayin' that The Black Falcon is Velvet Laffrey—"

"Velvet knowed Rowdy Kirshing was—"

"Sure he did. An' there was lots of other guys knew Rowdy, too. I got my instructions from Rowdy—an' my dough, too. But Rowdy never told me who was handin' him the gravy."

"You seen The Falcon—"

"Sure I seen him. Mostly in the dark an' with blinkers over his eyes. I've heard him talk, too. Givin' me orders over the telephone—I get 'em right upstairs here in this empty joint. But that don't mean that I know who he is." Terry's voice was cautious. "I ain't sayin' he's Velvet. Don't forget that, Cull."

"You know me, Terry."

"I know you all right. You can play dumb. That's why I'm keepin' you on the payroll. But I ain't seen nothin' worthwhile, Cull. Up at Apprison's I was there with the mob. The Black Falcon gives the whistle; out comes Apprison an' we cart him away while The Black Falcon was shootin' that guy Blossom.

"Same thing when we got this guy Carthers. The whistle; the old gent plops out the window. We drag him away. Then The Black Falcon bops off that mug Wistar.

"Both times we drive him away in a buggy that we'd copped. Tie up the guy he grabbed and let him out of the car when he tells us. Then we ditch the bus we swiped an' slide back here. That's all. That's why we're waitin'—an' it's why I'm worried."

Cull Buzbee nodded. He seemed to understand the cause of uncertainty which gripped Terry Rukes.

"THE BLACK FALCON is a sweet bimbo when it comes to a getaway," resumed Terry. "But that ain't helpin' us. I've got four gorillas here with me an' they're as worried as I am. I had to tell 'em that Rowdy Kirshing took the bump. That means no more dough unless we hear from The Black Falcon. An' we know he ain't callin' until he needs us. But we're stickin', because it's the game.

"Goofy Hornell was a sap out there when we grabbed Carthers. The Black Falcon ducked through the hedge an' rode away with us. Goofy stuck around to do some shootin' an' he got his. Luck was with me there, though. Nobody knew that Goofy was workin' for me. He was an odd gorilla that I tacked on. If it had been one of my regular gorillas, Joe Cardona might have got a line on who was workin' with The Black Falcon."

"Why're you worryin', then, Terry?"

"Why'm I worryin'?" Terry snorted. "On account of Rowdy Kirshing getting his. You know who got him—"

"I know who some guys say got him. But the guys that was over there on Tenth Avenue ain't talkin' about it. I ain't heard direct from nobody that The Shadow handed the one-way ticket to Rowdy—"

"No, you ain't heard 'em say it," broke in Terry, in a sardonic tone. "You don't hear many people say The Shadow got a guy—not if they was anywhere near when it happened. Say, bozo, when they think The Shadow got anybody, you can bet it was The Shadow that got him."

Cull had no reply to this sally. Terry Rukes stalked across the room and gave an impatient kick to a rickety chair. The gang leader, despite his fierce appearance, was plainly bundled with nerves.

"I'll tell you what," announced Terry suddenly. "I'm goin' to talk turkey to The Black Falcon when he calls. I ain't goin' to be the fall guy. I ain't no squealer, but it's drivin' me sappy here in this hideout. Maybe The Black Falcon thinks he can buck The Shadow, but—"

There was a rap on the door. Terry Rukes started nervously, then strode over and opened the barrier. One of his gorillas was standing there.

"Phone's buzzin' upstairs," the man announced anxiously. "Figgered you'd want to answer it, Terry."

"Sure thing. Scram, Cull. I ain't needin' you no more tonight. Come back tomorrow."

HURRYING through a short corridor, Terry Rukes ascended a flight of rickety steps and came to a door. He opened it and turned on a light in a closed closet. A telephone showed on a shelf. A buzzer, formed from a discarded bell, was giving its insistent signal. Terry grabbed the instrument.

"Hello..." The gang leader's gruff voice eased. "Yeah. Yeah..."

Gleaming, eager eyes. Terry Rukes knew the voice at the other end. The Black Falcon!

"Yeah... Yeah..." It came the gang leader's turn to speak. "Sure, I knew that you'd count on me stayin' here after Rowdy got the works. He musta been plugged just before the time we was startin' out to get Carthers.

"What's that?... Yeah... You figured out just what I been told. There was only one guy who could have got Rowdy Kirshing... Yeah, you guessed it... The Shadow.

"That's why I'm leery... No—I ain't told the mob... Sure, they'd turn yellow if they knew The Shadow might be in it... Say—this hideout may be a good one, but I'm tellin' you that when we move out of it, we're takin' chances..."

A harsh look appeared upon Terry's roughened face. For a moment, the gang leader appeared enraged as he heard the smooth voice over the wire. Then he laughed sheepishly.

"You guessed it. That's why I've been layin' low here. On account of The Shadow... I'm tellin' you, I'm ready to give the gang the word to bust up... No, it ain't the dough..."

A sudden gleam appeared upon Terry's features. Eagerness again dominated the gang leader.

"You mean tonight?" he ejaculated. "An' after that we can scram? Two grand apiece to the gorillas an' five grand to me?... I getcha! Sure... I knowed Rowdy musta been gettin' the real gravy. Nobody gets a cut this trip an' we're through... Sure thing... Say—will we risk it? Give me the lay...

"Yeah... Yeah... O.K. The fire tower... I got that... No move, just lay easy, until we get the whistle... Say—this'll be the berries. O.K., boss."

Terry Rukes hung up the receiver. He opened the door and went down the stairs. In the dim light of the passage below—illumination that came from the room opposite the one where Terry Rukes had conferred with Cull Buzbee—four hardfisted men were waiting. The gorillas had sensed that Terry had been talking with The Black Falcon. They wanted the news.

"Wot's de woid, Terry?" came a question.

"It's all set, boys," returned the mob leader. "Listen—one more job for The Black Falcon an' we quit. I'll tell you what you're gettin'—two grand each from The Black Falcon himself. Then we scram."

"Yeah, bo!" came from one of the gorillas. "When we startin', Terry?"

"Right away. An' it's goin' to be a snap. A swell apartment way uptown—the Garman Apartments—only two apartments on a floor. We hit the fourth floor, to grab another silk hat bimbo named Rowland Ransdale."

"The Falcon?"

"He'll be there—an' he's goin' to give us the same signal. This bloke Ransdale will be easy. He's got a valet workin' for him—the other apartment on the floor is empty. Down the fire tower—"

"An' the dough?"

"In the car. We'll pick up a buggy on the way."

Murmurs of approval. Terry Rukes ordered lights out.

WITH his mob at his heels, The Black Falcon's aide opened the door toward the alley. Cull

Buzbee had gone before. That was why Terry was venturing forth so promptly.

For the gang leader had used the insignificant creature of mobland with definite design. Cull Buzbee kept out of crime himself, but he was an observant individual. Coming and going, he watched the approaches of this hideout.

Had Cull suspected any watchers lurking in the night, he would have returned. Terry Rukes grinned at the thought. Cull was scary; that was why he would have returned. A bolder rat might flee; Cull would pile back for safety.

The mob moved along the alleyway. Terry Rukes paused to listen. He thought that he had detected a sound; but he heard it no longer. He did not know that eyes were watching vainly in the dark; that ears could hear the footsteps of himself and his tribe.

Slouched, bound and gagged in the pit that led to a cellar window of a house across the street was Cull Buzbee. Swift action had swept over the little rat the moment that he had left Terry's hideout. Phantom hands from the dark had plucked him from the very doorway. Whirled into dizzy senselessness, Cull had regained his wits to find himself helpless.

Terry Rukes and his gorillas sneaked on toward the alleyway, totally unaware of Cull's vain efforts to notify them of danger. Emerging from darkness, Terry looked about; then gave the word to start. The gang leader grinned as he glanced back from the end of the alleyway and convinced himself that all was clear.

Terry Rukes was thinking of The Shadow. But his thoughts were not of shadows. He saw nothing suspicious in the long black streaks of darkness that shrouded the sides of the dim alleyway.

Not until after the mobsters had moved further on their way did one long mass of blackness detach itself from the wall of a decadent building and transform itself into the shape of a tall and spectral being. The laugh that came from the phantom form was no more than a sinister whisper.

The Shadow, supersleuth, had spent this week within the underworld. He had traced Cull Buzbee to the hideout of Terry Rukes. Unseen, he was trailing the gang leader who served The Black Falcon!

Gasped words from Rowdy Kirshing; long search throughout the underworld for some insignificant character who might be connected with Terry Rukes, whom Rowdy had mentioned— thus had The Shadow gained the trail.

Through tracing The Black Falcon's henchmen, The Shadow was taking a course to thwart the supercrook!

CHAPTER X
WESTON STRIKES LUCK

WHERE The Shadow, a lone wolf of the darkness, trailed through the underworld to place his finger on the spots where crime was fostered, Police Commissioner Ralph Weston was content to sit back and trust to the strength of the forces under his command.

Yet all the commissioner's men, with their dragnets and their stool pigeons, had been unable to gain a single thread that would lead to The Black Falcon's doings. Even Joe Cardona, the ace detective, had been helpless; and Commissioner Weston, seated in the office of his apartment near Lexington Avenue, was fuming at the futility which had possessed the law.

A rap sounded at the commissioner's door. Weston looked in that direction and snapped a query:

"What is it, Kempton?"

"Detective Cardona is here, sir," came the voice of Weston's military servant.

"All right," ordered the commissioner. "Have him enter."

Joe Cardona came into the office. The ace detective shifted uneasily as he took his chair. He saw a glower on the commissioner's face.

"Sorry, commissioner," said Joe. "I was checking up on some joints where I thought I might find Velvet Laffrey. The man isn't in New York—"

"He will be," interposed Weston.

"Will be?" questioned Cardona.

"Yes," assured Weston. "Tonight. This arrived at three o'clock."

Weston tossed a sheet of paper across the desk. Cardona stared, and a firm challenge showed upon his chin. This paper was a letter. In the upper left corner was the neat engraving of a hawklike bird. Thrust through the bottom of the sheet was the symbol that served as a signature—a black feather.

Another message from The Black Falcon!

"Read it!" ordered Weston.

CARDONA studied the letter. It was addressed to the commissioner and it was couched in the same ironical terms as the previous epistle of warning:

Ralph Weston,
Police Commissioner,
New York City.
Dear Sir:
    Despite my advice to forget the disappearance of Hubert Apprison, you chose to put me to the test. The result of your folly was the abduction of Elias Carthers, not only from a spot under your jurisdiction, but almost from beneath your very nose.

Elias Carthers, like Hubert Apprison, is a man of great wealth. I am holding both as prisoners in order to obtain the ransoms that I desire. I am offering you the opportunity to cease your annoying interference, which consists only in stirring up ridiculous rumors.

I suggest that you announce that both Hubert Apprison and Elias Carthers will soon be returned and that there will be no effort on the part of the police to trouble the abductor.

Unless such a statement appears in the evening newspapers upon the day that you receive this letter, I shall be forced to teach you another lesson by abducting another gentleman of prominence.

This third proof of my ability—if you unwisely choose to force it—will be demonstrated within the limits of Manhattan. This time, I shall experience no regrets.

Joe Cardona had no comment. He stared blankly at the letter as he placed it on the table; then looked vaguely toward the police commissioner.

"This is serious, Cardona," stated Weston. "When I received The Black Falcon's last note, I was fortunate enough to strike upon a theory that gave me a trace of his intended crime. Tonight, I have no theory.

"There are many men of wealth in Manhattan. We can limit the location of The Black Falcon's activity only to a place where a suitable victim may be available. Our only hope is that the vigilance of the police may be rewarded with a stroke of good fortune.

"The public is aroused, of course, because of the newspapers. All sorts of calls have come into headquarters. Other crime is somewhat passive. Yet to apprehend The Black Falcon, we should be forewarned. We lost our opportunity when we failed to save Elias Carthers. I greatly fear that we shall not gain a second stroke of such good fortune."

The commissioner settled glumly back in his chair. His usual criticism was absent now. Weston realized that Joe Cardona had been doing his utmost. The helplessness of the present situation was beyond control.

Yet Cardona knew that Weston had summoned him here in the hope of some useful suggestion. The detective racked his brain. His hunches were missing. Like Weston, he felt that he was beaten. The Black Falcon, crook extraordinary, had found the weak spots in the armor of the law.

WHILE the two men sat in silence, each ticking minute increased the gloom. Somewhere— tonight—The Black Falcon was due to strike. The time of his crime was approaching with ominous

regularity. Cardona, like Weston, sensed that the next news would be a call from detective headquarters stating that word of another kidnapping had been received.

The jingle of the telephone bell on Weston's desk snapped the commissioner into life. Cardona saw the tenseness in his superior's face. Weston lifted receiver to ear and spoke in a listless tone.

"Hello... Yes, this is Commissioner Weston... Who? Ransdale... Rowland Ransdale... The mine owner... Yes... Yes..."

For a moment, Cardona thought that the expected call had come. He recalled the name of Rowland Ransdale, a wealthy mine owner who had returned from the West. Here was a victim for The Black Falcon!

But as Cardona saw an eager expression creep over Weston's face, he sensed that the commissioner was not receiving news of a kidnapping. This was a message of another sort.

"You are sure of it, Mr. Ransdale?"

As he heard these words, Cardona realized that Weston was talking to Ransdale himself. Listening intently, the detective tried to catch the voice over the wire, but succeeded only in judging the conversation by Weston's own replies.

"Yes... Yourself and your servant... I understand... You have investigated, you say... You are sure... What's that? Two revolvers?

"Good... Yes... I shall have men there at once... Yes... Wait as long as possible. Give us time to form a cordon... The Black Falcon... Yes... We shall enter as soon as the apartment building is surrounded... A shot—in case of emergency—as a signal... Yes... Protect yourself as you see fit."

Down went the receiver. Commissioner Weston leaped to his feet. He paused for a tense moment; then grabbed up the telephone again and put in a call to headquarters. Joe Cardona was on his feet also.

He heard the commissioner's eager voice, giving orders in quick, disjointed phrases that brought an inkling of the story to Cardona's excited mind.

"Garman Apartments—fourth floor—Rowland Ransdale—fire tower entrance on Ninety—fourth Street—cordon—The Black Falcon—enter when completely surrounded—radio patrols—"

ALL was hectic until the call was ended. Cardona realized that Weston had been talking tensely; that his own anxiousness had brought about much of the broken impression. Weston, standing in back of the desk, faced Cardona and spoke, with a steadying tone in his voice.

"Rowland Ransdale," declared the commissioner, in explanation, "lives in the Garman

Apartments. The window of his servant's room opens by the fire tower. The servant—Ransdale's valet—heard men talking there. Ransdale has been listening. He heard the words 'The Falcon.'

"Ransdale has a gun. So has his valet. They are waiting in darkness, with a light in Ransdale's den as a lure. I have given orders for a cordon to surround the apartment house.

"Ransdale will hold out; in emergency, he will fire. The shot will bring in all our men. The fire tower is being covered."

Regaining his dynamic bearing, Commissioner Weston strode from behind the desk. He gripped Joe Cardona by the arm and drew him through the front door of the office.

"Let us hope," announced Weston, "that the cordon will be waiting when we arrive; that Ransdale will still be watching for The Black Falcon. My car is downstairs, Cardona. Luck is with us. If it continues"—the commissioner laughed sternly—"you and I shall rectify the mistake which we made at Long Island.

"We, Cardona, shall be the first to reach the fourth floor. Tonight, we may meet The Black Falcon at the moment when he strikes!"

CHAPTER XI
AT THE APARTMENT

SILENCE rested over the Garman Apartments. A large building, away from heavy traffic, it formed a huge mass in the darkness, with lighted windows far apart.

Crouched in the gloom of the fire tower was Terry Rukes. The mob leader's henchmen formed a group close by him. Tensely, they were awaiting the signal that would bring them through the corridor to the apartment on the left.

Terry, peering through the door to the corridor, returned to offer growled advice which his gorillas accepted. The gang leader's nervousness was no longer apparent.

"Leave it to The Falcon," he said. "He'll get in there and cover the guy. The door will be open for us when he gives the signal. This is a pipe."

Grunted assent came from the listeners. One mobster stared down the dark stairway up which the group had come. He saw nothing in the gloom, nor did he hear a sound.

The gorilla's alertness was justified. His gaze, however, was directed to the wrong spot. Watching eyes were close at hand; listening ears were near. But the being who could overhear the mumbled conversation of the mobsters was not within the confines of the fire tower.

A batlike shape was clinging to a wall which projected at an angle from the set-in fire tower.

Invisible in the darkness, this hidden creature seemed other than a human form. Above a shrouded head was a darkened, open window of Rowland Ransdale's apartment.

Something squdged upon the wall. The mobster who had turned back to his fellows paused to listen. The sound was so elusive that he gave it no second thought. He did not hear another similar noise that followed.

The batlike shape was moving away from the fire tower. Past the angle, it crept with sidewise, crablike motion along the extended wall. The glow of city lights revealed the figure dimly. Like a huge vampire, The Shadow was sidling across a vertical surface!

Hands and feet were pressing against the wall. Each was equipped with a large concave disk of rubber. Each pressure of a suction cup gave its wearer purchase upon the wall. Each twist released one of the supports.

THE SHADOW had become a human fly. So familiar was he with this method of progress that his motions were timed to perfect precision. Terry Rukes and his followers might choose the corridor as the way to gain access to Ransdale's apartment; The Shadow preferred the outer wall.

One light glowed as a beacon. The Shadow knew that the room which it indicated was probably the one in which Ransdale would be found. It was The Shadow's goal. With remarkable ease, the creeping master reached his objective. His eyes peered through the space between a lowered shade and the windowsill.

The room within was empty. Furnished with comfortable chairs, a long lounge and ornate tables, it constituted Rowland Ransdale's den. Every window of the apartment opened on this wall; there were no other lights in view. Hence The Shadow knew that Ransdale must, for some reason, be waiting in darkness.

Had The Black Falcon already arrived? If so, action was essential at once. A gloved hand released itself from a suction cup. A long, thin strip of metal was thrust between the portions of the window sash. The lock turned noiselessly.

Up came the sash. Like a ghost from the beyond, The Shadow gained the windowsill. His tall form cast a long black silhouette upon the floor. The door of the den was ajar. Wisely, The Shadow kept away from the opening. He made a circuitous tour of the lighted room and reached an alcove near the opening of the door. There, The Shadow listened.

Soft voices sounded suddenly. The Shadow caught the words that were uttered. A man was speaking in well-chosen accents. The Shadow, his keen eyes watching toward the door, sensed that Rowland Ransdale must be the speaker.

"Are they still waiting, Hazzlett?"

"Yes, sir," came a voice that was less refined. "I just heard them talking. They seem to be a bit impatient, sir."

"It's time to be ready for them, then." Ransdale's voice broke with a slight chuckle, that showed a note of nervousness. "The police commissioner promised that a cordon would surround the place before the officers entered."

"He was sure about The Black Falcon when you called him?"

"Absolutely. That means prompt action. I told him I would leave the den lighted, as a lure. Wait here, Hazzlett. I'm going through to listen a moment by the window toward the fire tower."

Then silence followed. The Shadow waited. Long, tense moments; then, from somewhere came the soft note of a hissed whistle. Black gloves emerged from The Shadow's cloak. Each fist held an automatic.

More moments of silence. A cautious whisper told that Ransdale was back with his servant, Hazzlett. Ransdale's words concerned the sound that had reached The Shadow's ears.

"You heard it, Hazzlett?"

"The whistle? Yes, sir."

"Steady. Be ready for an attack. I'll be at the door opposite."

Footsteps creaked. Ransdale was crossing his living room. Even though he could not see beyond the door of the den, The Shadow knew how the arrangements stood. Ransdale and Hazzlett were waiting, armed, each on a different side of the living room. They expected an invasion; they knew that the den would be the objective of the invaders.

The whistle was the signal of The Black Falcon!

THE supercrook must be lurking somewhere, perhaps in the outer corridor. In this attack, it seemed, he was sending in his henchmen, under the command of Terry Rukes. Even yet, The Black Falcon might precede them. Perhaps, because of the broad layout of the apartment, he felt it best to invade with a squad in order to gain quick coverage.

So far as Ransdale and Hazzlett were concerned, the mine owner and his valet held the advantage, even against a squad of ruffians, provided only that their nerve did not fail them in the test. The Black Falcon, however, held the key to the situation. The Shadow knew the ability of this adversary.

If Ransdale and Hazzlett should let the invaders reach the lighted den, The Shadow would bear the brunt of this attack. If, however, the beleaguered men should fire too soon, it would be The Shadow's part to stand in readiness. Peering from the opening of the den door, The Shadow kept his keen eyes fixed upon the dim spot which he knew must be the door from the corridor.

As The Shadow watched, the door moved slowly inward. A bulky form appeared against the light of the corridor.

It was Terry Rukes, at the head of his small mob.

The Shadow glided back into the den. Either The Black Falcon had sent the men ahead, or he was waiting elsewhere. The apartment was a large one; the supercrook could have hidden in some well chosen spot.

Terry's form was near the den. The big mob leader was coming cautiously, as though expecting another signal. His men were behind him, all within the living room. Suddenly, Terry made a forward plunge. The den door shot inward as he pushed it.

Two revolvers barked. Ransdale and Hazzlett had opened fire. A bullet whistled past Terry's shoulder and flattened itself against the doorway. Momentarily paused upon the threshold, the gang leader uttered a wild cry.

It was the sight of the being before him that gave Terry Rukes such consternation. The gang leader was staring squarely at the dreaded form of The Shadow. Blazing eyes—a looming automatic —these were the silent sights that brought his frenzied utterance.

"The Shadow!"

As Terry screamed the warning, shots came in quick rapidity from the sides of the living room. A second bullet dropped the gang leader in his tracks. The other mobsters were in confusion. They were turning in the gloom, to aim at flashes of flame that came from partly opened doorways.

Ransdale and Hazzlett were in the dark. The men whom they were shooting were midway between the streak of light that came from the den and the outer shaft of illumination from the corridor.

Terry Rukes had collapsed. Down went a second mobster. A third, cursing, staggered and gripped a wounded arm. Of the two who remained, one leaped for the den, forgetful of Terry's warning scream. With outstretched revolver, he was ready to fire. The Shadow's finger rested on the trigger of an automatic.

Then came a spurt from Hazzlett's gun. The mobster, as he spied The Shadow, sprawled headlong at the feet of the dread being whom all evildoers feared. The Shadow had not been forced to fire his shot.

Momentarily paused upon the threshold, the gangster uttered a wild cry.

The last mobsman was hurtling toward the outer door. It was Ransdale, this time, who applied good marksmanship. The mine owner's revolver barked twice. The second shot picked off his quarry. The last of Terry's gorillas rolled in agony.

Whistles were sounding from without. Shouts came from the fire tower. The police were arriving. Still, The Shadow waited. One menace still remained: The Black Falcon.

A click sounded as Rowland Ransdale turned on the light in the living room. The Shadow, peering from his alcove, saw the mine owner, in a smoking jacket, heading toward the corridor with a revolver in his grasp. Hazzlett, plainly attired, was hurrying to join his master.

A shrill whistle burst through the corridor. The police had entered. Ransdale and Hazzlett had met them. Where was The Black Falcon? Swiftly, The Shadow cut into the living room. He could hear the sound of feet and excited voices in the hallway. With a swift motion, the black-garbed visitor swept into the darkness of an adjoining room.

Loud talk sounded in the living room as The Shadow reached the little window that opened near the fire tower. He could hear the voice of Commissioner Weston. The official had arrived with Joe Cardona. He was ordering a prompt search of the place.

The Shadow could not remain. The window by the fire tower was open. Swiftly, the black-clad protector swung over the sill. Remaining there, he adjusted the rubber suction cups that had served him so well. Then, with faultless action, he began his descent along this blackened section of the wall.

The police cordon had closed in. Men were pounding up the steps of the fire tower as The Shadow descended alongside. The Shadow, at the second floor, swung inward to the rail. He removed the suction cups and descended the steps to the ground. But as his tall form appeared within a patch of light that glistened on the paving, a shrill whistle sounded.

Swiftly, The Shadow merged with the darkness of an opposite wall. He found an opening which his keen eyes had spotted from above. He chose this way between two walls to find a quick exit from the scene. Again that whistle. As The Shadow neared the end of the narrow area, a policeman came pounding straight against him.

The officer did not see the crouching shape that dropped instantly to the paving. The first inkling that he gained of a living presence was when powerful arms blocked his path and a heaving form of hidden muscle lifted him towering in the air. Dizzily, the policeman plunged headlong. He seemed to dive at an angle from a pair of shoulders. For a moment, the gripping clutch restrained him. As he fell, the officer had time to thrust out his arms and break the force of the drop. His revolver clattered on the cement.

By the time the policeman had gripped his gun and risen dazedly to his feet, no living presence remained. The Shadow, fleeting through the last short space of darkness, had gained the street beyond. He had passed the encircling cordon.

THE Garman Apartments were in full possession of Weston's forces. Policemen and detectives were everywhere. The commissioner and Detective Joe Cardona were with Rowland Ransdale and his servant, Hazzlett.

Ransdale, a keen-faced man of medium height, was giving the details of the raid. Hazzlett, taller and more powerful than his employer, was standing by with a grim expression on his firm, hard-visaged face.

"This is Terry Rukes," announced Cardona, pointing out the dead gang leader. "Now we know who was working for The Black Falcon."

Commissioner Weston surveyed the other mobsters. He turned to Rowland Ransdale.

"These men were the only ones who entered?" he questioned.

"Yes," assured the mine owner. "Fortunately, Hazzlett and I are good shots. We handle revolvers well out West. But there was another— someone who gave a whistle signal—"

"Where from?" queried Weston eagerly.

"I don't know," admitted Ransdale. "It came just before the attack. I heard it while I was listening at the window to the fire tower. I couldn't trace it from—"

"I think it was from the corridor," broke in Hazzlett. "I heard it, too—and I was waiting here in the living room."

"That explains it!" asserted Weston, in a disappointed tone. "The Black Falcon reversed his game tonight. He must have sent his mobsters in first. He was wise enough to hurry away when he heard the firing."

"He may have had time to get through the cordon," added Joe Cardona. "Our men were all ready, though, when the shots were fired—"

A gray-haired man appeared at that moment. Cardona stopped speaking as he recognized Inspector Timothy Klein entering from the corridor. With the inspector was a uniformed policeman.

"Officer Dellin," announced Klein. "He has a report to make on someone who escaped."

"Bumped into me down below," declared the policeman, sheepishly. "I was comin' through a little alley—just wide enough for one man. Answerin' a whistle, Commissioner. This fellow tackles me in the dark an' throws me head foremost. Out at the far end of the alley—he got to the street before I could follow him."

"Another officer caught a glimpse of the man," added Klein. "He had come from the fire tower. They are searching for him now, but apparently he has made a getaway."

"The Black Falcon," declared Joe Cardona.

Commissioner Weston nodded.

"He has eluded us again," declared the official.

"This time, however, we have thwarted him. His mobsmen are dead. He cannot afford to defy the law again. My congratulations, Mr. Ransdale, to you and your man Hazzlett, for the work that you have done tonight."

Joe Cardona was grim. Though he did not voice his thoughts, the detective could not agree with the commissioner. To Cardona, the escape of The Black Falcon was new proof of the master crook's amazing ability.

The elusiveness with which The Black Falcon had passed through the police cordon; the quick ability which he had shown in dealing with Officer Dellin—these were things of which Cardona believed only The Shadow could be capable.

Greater would have been Cardona's wonder had the detective known that it was actually The Shadow who had broken through the narrow alleyway! The Black Falcon, in his own evanishment, had gone The Shadow one better.

For The Black Falcon had disappeared without a trace, while The Shadow, master of the darkness, had been forced to physical encounter in order to leave this scene where crime had failed!

CHAPTER XII
MILLIONAIRES CONFER

ON the second evening following the episode at the Garman Apartments, Rowland Ransdale was seated in his comfortable den. Wearing his slippers and smoking jacket, the millionaire mine owner was puffing at a large-bowled pipe as he studied the headlines of the evening newspapers.

Ransdale's face showed a pleased smile. The journals were still filled with talk of The Black Falcon; and they teemed with credit for Ransdale's part in submerging the kidnapper's gangster minions.

The Garman Apartments were still under police observation. Patrolmen were on the lookout for suspicious characters. Detectives were in the vicinity.

The cordon had disbanded after the disappearance of The Black Falcon, but there were still men available in case of emergency.

Rowland Ransdale and his servant Hazzlett were armed. They had been within their rights in defending themselves against Terry Rukes and his mobsters; moreover, Ransdale had acted with the telephoned sanction of the police commissioner.

According to the newspapers, The Black Falcon had met his match when he had tried to abduct the wealthy mine owner; and editorial comment upheld Ransdale as the type of man upon whom the law could depend. Ransdale, in interviews with reporters, had expressed the hope

that The Black Falcon would return. The mine owner had shown self-confidence rather than boastfulness when he had made this statement.

Ransdale looked up quietly as he heard Hazzlett enter. The husky valet had come with an announcement.

"Call from the lobby, sir," he said. "A gentleman named Lamont Cranston has come to see you. A friend of the commissioner's, sir."

"Lamont Cranston." Ransdale was speculative. "Yes—I recall the name. I've heard of him before—have met him in fact. He's the chap who travels everywhere. Tell him to come up, Hazzlett."

The servant went to the living room. Ransdale, rising, stacked newspapers in orderly piles. While he was relighting his pipe, he heard the outer door of the apartment open. Facing the door, Ransdale stepped forward to greet a tall, quiet-faced individual whom Hazzlett had ushered across the living room.

"Good evening, Mr. Cranston," greeted Ransdale. "I recall that we have met before."

"At the Cobalt Club, perhaps?" questioned Cranston.

"That must have been the place," nodded Ransdale. He motioned Cranston to a comfortable chair.

Although he did not express it, Ransdale was curious as to the purpose of Cranston's visit. As a preliminary gesture, he beckoned to Hazzlett, and the valet brought a box of expensive cigars from which Cranston selected one.

WHILE his visitor was lighting the perfecto, Ransdale noted him closely. The light of a match revealed Cranston's unusual features. The visage which Ransdale saw was a hawklike countenance, with a calmness that reminded the observer of a living mask.

A pair of sparkling eyes turned toward Ransdale as Cranston shook out the lighted match.

Those eyes, in turn, saw an unusual face. They took in the firmness of Ransdale's countenance. The mine owner had a pleasant, well-formed visage; it was one, however, that showed hidden determination. Ransdale's eyes were keen; he was obviously a man who could rise to action, as he had proven in his battle with Terry Rukes.

"I come to congratulate you, Mr. Ransdale." The words issued in even tones from the thin lips of Lamont Cranston. "You have done society a great service through your prompt action here. In delivering death to that gang of ruffians, you performed a duty I should have been pleased to aid."

"It was really nothing much," protested Ransdale, with a modest laugh. "Hazzlett—my servant—and I were in ambush. We are both good shots. We practice marksmanship a great deal out at the mines in Colorado."

"I held no doubts as to the capability of your marksmanship," came Cranston's smiling reply. "My only regret was that you did not have an opportunity to spot the hidden leader of the game—The Black Falcon."

"I hold the same regret," returned Ransdale. "The villain never appeared within the apartment. Neither Hazzlett nor I caught a glimpse of him. Police Commissioner Weston told me that he had seen The Black Falcon, out at the home of Elias Carthers."

"I saw him there also," remarked Cranston. "I was just too late to aim for him. I did, however, bag one of his henchmen, at long range."

"The one who was killed on the lawn?" queried Ransdale.

"Yes," answered Cranston.

"I recall the incident," nodded Ransdale. "Commissioner Weston mentioned it. He said that a friend had saved his life on that occasion. You were the friend?"

"I was."

"Then," decided Ransdale, "you are a member of our select trio. Like Hazzlett and myself, you bagged a minion of The Black Falcon. I realize, Mr. Cranston, that you, like myself, would be pleased to take a shot at the master criminal himself. If you have any scheme for falcon hunting, the suggestion would interest me."

"That work belongs to the police," declared Cranston. "Nevertheless, Mr. Ransdale, I feel that I should take a personal interest in the case. In fact, I am willing to spend a great deal of time and money in this matter. I knew Hubert Apprison. Elias Carthers was also a friend of mine. They are prisoners of The Black Falcon; and they should be delivered."

"Precisely," agreed Ransdale. "I knew both of those men by acquaintance. My social contacts in New York are wide, but spasmodic, due to my frequent absence from the city. You are right, Cranston. Any clue to The Black Falcon is important. Commissioner Weston tells me, however, that his men are on the trail of the crook himself. They know his identity."

"They are after a man named Velvet Laffrey," said Cranston with a nod. "That has not been made public—"

"Wisely so," returned Ransdale. "Weston spoke to me regarding the matter, in hopes that I might be able to provide some information. I have encountered confidence men at rare intervals—but I could not recall anyone who answered to the description of this man Laffrey.

"After all, Mr. Cranston, The Black Falcon needed only a passing acquaintance with the affairs of his victims. Apprison—Carthers—myself—all of us were open to attack. We were men of wealth who never gave a thought to our security.

"It was merely good fortune that Hazzlett happened to be in the room at the far end of the apartment. The window was open. He went to close it. He heard voices on the fire tower. He suspected danger, as this is the only occupied apartment on the fourth floor. That was how I came to call the police commissioner; and at his advice, Hazzlett and I prepared the trap."

"You may still be in danger," interposed Cranston's meditative tone. "Have you considered that fact, Mr. Ransdale?"

THE mine owner smiled, and his lips showed his confidence. Reaching in the pocket of his smoking jacket, he produced a .38-caliber revolver and broke it so that Cranston's eyes could view the loaded chambers.

"Hazzlett is similarly armed," informed Ransdale. "Let The Black Falcon launch a new attack. We shall be ready for him. Moreover, the police are guarding this vicinity. No, Mr. Cranston, I am convinced that The Black Falcon will leave me alone hereafter. I doubt that The Black Falcon would be foolish enough to let a grudge interfere with his plan of action.

"If such were his policy, he might have it in for you—presuming that he has learned that you were responsible for the death of one of his henchmen on the night that he kidnapped Elias Carthers. Have you considered that fact?"

"Yes," returned Cranston, "and I, like yourself, have ignored it. I happened to be armed on the night when I arrived at the Carthers house. That was simply because I was traveling alone in my coupé and I usually carry an automatic on such occasions."

"A .38?"

"No. A .45."

Ransdale's eyes opened widely. He snapped his revolver shut and laughed as he dropped the weapon back into his pocket.

"You go in for heavy artillery!" he exclaimed.

"Anything up to an elephant gun," declared Cranston, with a smile. "I handle weapons in accordance with their size. A .45 obtains results."

"Yes," agreed Ransdale, "but as a pocket weapon"—he shrugged his shoulders—"even my own revolver is too large. I would prefer a short-barreled gun for ordinary occasions."

"I need no weapons," explained Cranston, "except when I am alone. I have servants at my New Jersey home; ordinarily, when I ride back and forth from New York, I travel in my limousine, with my chauffeur, Stanley, at the wheel.

"I have never encountered trouble either at home or on the road with Stanley. It is only when I ride by myself that I require precautions."

"Like the rest of us," observed Ransdale, "you are ordinarily careless. Hazzlett and I had our guns packed away two nights ago. It was merely fortune that aided us. Had we not heard the men on the fire tower, we would have been easy prey for The Black Falcon."

"I choose to be careless," declared Cranston. "I shall never make my home into an armed camp. Like yourself, I am a man of wealth. But I feel convinced that such rascals as The Black Falcon prefer to attack those who are apparent weaklings, like Apprison and Carthers. Particularly"—the thin lips were smiling in approbation—"after the reception that he and his mobsmen received when they tried to seize a man who could fight."

RANSDALE'S responding smile was a pleased one. The mine owner liked Cranston's commendation. He puffed his pipe; then became serious.

"You are right, Mr. Cranston," asserted Ransdale. "We both have done our part in thwarting The Black Falcon. However, as men of wealth, we represent a distinct class of society. So long as this hawk of crime remains uncaptured, it is our part to be ready to cooperate with the police.

"I appreciate your visit. Should you require my aid, financially, in any measure that you plan to undertake, you may count upon it. I feel, however, that I should make my present situation plain to you. Frankly, I am nervous, since my combat with those mobsters. I am going to take a trip from New York."

"To the West?"

"No. To a secluded residence in the Catskills. The weather is pleasant and I have an excellent house far off in the confines of the forestland. Hazzlett is going with me; I have caretakers at the place upon whom I can rely. I am the one upon whom The Black Falcon has real reason for revenge. I need a vacation. Like yourself, I prefer to be careless—or let us say carefree. A gun in readiness—police on the watch—such things annoy me."

"We are of the same mind," came Cranston's statement, as the tall visitor arose from his chair. "I am glad to have met you again, Mr. Ransdale. Let us hope that the renewal of the acquaintance will lead to a future meeting."

"It will," assured Ransdale, walking to the door with his guest. "I assure you, Mr. Cranston, that immediately upon my return to New York, I shall communicate with you."

"Either at my home in New Jersey," invited Cranston, "or at the Cobalt Club. You are welcome at either place at anytime. And let us hope that when we meet again, we shall be able to discuss the matter of The Black Falcon as a more tangible subject."

"Agreed," responded Ransdale, as he shook hands with his guest at the door to the corridor.

The mine owner waited at the door until the tall form of Lamont Cranston had entered an elevator. Then Ransdale turned back into his apartment. He strolled across the living room and entered his den. He puffed his pipe; then chuckled and called to his servant. The husky valet entered.

"Hazzlett," then remarked Ransdale, "what is your opinion of our recent visitor?"

"A quiet sort of bloke," returned the servant.

"Who do you think he is?" A knowing smile was creeping over Ransdale's lips.

"He said," replied Hazzlett, wondering, "that his name was Lamont Cranston—"

"I know that," interposed Ransdale. "But you know well enough, Hazzlett, that one individual can sometimes play two parts—"

"You—you don't mean"—Hazzlett was stammering—"that—that Lamont Cranston is—"

"You are guessing it, Hazzlett," prompted Ransdale, his smile becoming an evil twist. "Lamont Cranston is The Shadow!"

CHAPTER XIII
THE FALCON SCHEMES

ROWLAND RANSDALE laughed harshly as he stared at his servant, Hazzlett. The valet's countenance had whitened. Hazzlett slumped into a chair and stared at his employer. Even the contemptuous look of complete assurance that Ransdale wore was not sufficient to overcome the valet's consternation.

"Take a drink, Hazzlett," snarled Ransdale suddenly. "Brace up. I told you this would be coming."

The servant nodded weakly. He arose and went to a small cabinet. He brought out a bottle, poured himself a long drink and downed the liquor. His face had lost some of its whiteness when Hazzlett again turned toward Ransdale.

"You don't think"—Hazzlett was trying to be steady—"and he knows—that he knows about you—"

"That I am The Black Falcon?" Ransdale laughed scornfully. "Not a chance of it, Hazzlett. He's fallen for the game, just like the rest of them. I knew that he would be here, two nights ago.

That, Hazzlett, was why I made you play your part. I went through with everything, just as though we were being watched. You heard Terry Rukes scream when I dropped him."

Hazzlett nodded.

"Terry saw The Shadow," declared Ransdale. "In this room. I suspected that The Shadow might be here. The Shadow is clever, Hazzlett, but a nighttime prowler who trails crooks is no match for The Black Falcon."

"But you always said"—Hazzlett was protesting as he sat down in a chair and unsteadily placed his glass upon a table beside him—"that if The Shadow would—"

"I always considered The Shadow to be a menace," interposed Ransdale brusquely. "I said that we would have to watch out for him. I have done so all along. I never planned to bait him as I have the police commissioner. I wanted The Shadow to reveal himself—unwittingly—and he has."

"But he may know—"

"He is ignorant, like the police. My game has been too well planned. Until now, Hazzlett, it has scarcely been interesting. The real game is just beginning. I want you to understand it perfectly, Hazzlett, because your aid will be important. Hence I shall trace the whole scheme from its inception."

Hazzlett nodded. The valet was gaining confidence from his chief. His eyes were steady as they viewed Rowland Ransdale's scoffing face. The expression on the mine owner's lips was that contemptuous one that Elias Carthers had seen beneath the mask of The Black Falcon.

"Velvet Laffrey was a clever swindler," began Ransdale, in a reminiscent tone. "He made his mistake, however, when he tried to fool me with a confidence game. You remember how I cornered him, Hazzlett. I knew him for a crook."

The valet grinned at the recollection.

RANSDALE puffed his pipe and resumed his discourse.

"When Laffrey broke down and told me all about his past, I began to see how his connections with the underworld would serve me well. I can remember how pleased Velvet was when I began to unfold promises of great reward through super-crime.

"His part looked easy. He arranged the connection with Rowdy Kirshing and told the big shot of the funds that would come through The Black Falcon. Rowdy, in turn, lined up Terry Rukes and an undercover mob. That made the going easy.

"Then came our little episode with Velvet Laffrey," Ransdale chuckled. "He was to be the goat, yet all the while the police would be looking for him, he would be out of the country. I offered him a hundred thousand dollars and told him that I would not start the kidnapping game until he was safely in South America.

"No wonder he gave me his fingerprints! Those that we have on sheets of paper are valuable enough, for they can be used in letters and documents.

"But the doorknob impressions were the best. I dropped out to see Elias Carthers one night just to look that doorknob over. Carthers never suspected what I was doing, while I talked to him about my mining interests."

"Velvet Laffrey didn't suspect much either," observed Hazzlett, grinning as he spoke. "He didn't know where he was going after he put his prints on that doorknob. They showed up great in that lacquer stuff."

"Velvet," mused Ransdale, "was trusting enough to believe that he was actually going to South America. He planned to spend a last night with me in the Catskills. He never realized the danger in that lonely spot. He did not see me take the revolver from my desk drawer, when he was strolling toward the door. One shot in the back—that was all."

"He looked funny when he dropped."

"Yes, as you saw him, Hazzlett. You were standing by the door. I recall that you told me of the annoyed expression that seemed to come over his face."

"He looked like a kid that had just found out Santa Claus wasn't real!"

"So much for Velvet Laffrey," resumed Ransdale. "The torn paper that I placed in the hand of Apprison's secretary, Blossom, had Velvet's finger impressions on it. That was an easy matter. The doorknob, when I captured Carthers, was ticklish, however. I had to shoot that fool Wistar. I had to stay around long enough to take our doorknob from its velvet bag and affix it to the door instead of the one that belonged there."

"You worked cool enough."

"It was ticklish, Hazzlett, but not difficult. It allowed time, though, for Commissioner Weston to circle the house. I was wise in wearing my mask.

"My getaway, too, was somewhat fortunate. I was careful enough to smudge the knob a bit without touching Velvet's well-planted impressions. Then that smart detective, Joe Cardona, proved as wise as I had hoped. He found the impressions on the knob. That, with the paper from Apprison's, clinched the deal. Velvet Laffrey is established as The Black Falcon."

"And Velvet Laffrey is dead!"

RANSDALE chuckled as he nodded in response to Hazzlett's exclamation. Then the millionaire mine owner became solemn. His lips twisted and the snarl of The Black Falcon issued from between them as he spoke.

"The Shadow!" exclaimed Ransdale. "There was the uncertain quantity, Hazzlett! The police have been mere dupes; but The Shadow has been a possible menace all along. I suspected that The Shadow was the one who killed Rowdy Kirshing after word came out in the newspapers that the big shot had been put on the spot.

"Rowdy's death was lost in the shuffle with the disappearance of Elias Carthers. But I tell you, Hazzlett, that I was glad Rowdy was dead. He may have known too much about what Velvet Laffrey had been doing."

"Maybe," agreed Hazzlett, "but Terry Rukes didn't know much, did he? He may have thought you were Velvet Laffrey—"

"He probably did," interposed Ransdale. "But Terry constituted a danger. He and his mob met me twice and aided me with the abductions. Each time, I left their car taking my prisoner with me and marched my victim to the spot where you were waiting in the plane. All that Terry could say—if quizzed—was that he had helped me; and he could have given the approximate locality of each place where he and his mob had taken me.

"With Rowdy Kirshing dead, however, Terry Rukes became the next link. I foresaw that; I began to doubt the value of keeping Terry. I realized that The Shadow, if in the game, would possibly be on Terry's trail. So when I called Terry, two nights ago, I was prepared.

"Best of all, Terry told me over the wire that he had heard who killed Rowdy Kirshing. Terry named The Shadow. That meant that Terry must be put away. Whom could I entrust to do it satisfactorily? No one but myself. How could I reach Terry Rukes? By bringing him here. That was perfect, Hazzlett. It gave me opportunity to cover my own traces. What an alibi for The Black Falcon— to be his own prospective victim!"

"You did it great, chief," agreed Hazzlett.

"I did," admitted Ransdale. "But I saw further ahead, Hazzlett. I saw that where Terry Rukes went, I might expect The Shadow also. Terry Rukes walked into my trap. I called the police commissioner. Our explanation of overhearing the mobsters talking was a perfect one. I wanted the police here—and I had an idea that The Shadow would be here also."

"It was neat the way you gave the signal. In there by the window. It sounded like it might have come from anywhere. Terry and his crew heard it right enough."

"But they didn't talk about it afterward. We had them in our power as soon as they entered. I aimed to kill Terry first of all. The others were not so important. But we bagged them all, Hazzlett. Meanwhile, the police were coming in to aid us."

"Great stuff, chief, the way you brought in the police."

"Not only the police. The Shadow also. He was there to stop them. There in the den, Hazzlett, waiting to protect me from The Black Falcon. That is why I drew you out into the corridor after we had dispatched Terry Rukes and his crowd."

"So The Shadow could get away?" Hazzlett's tone was puzzled. "That was something I didn't quite figure out. It would have been better if the police had thought The Shadow was The Black Falcon."

"Not a bit of it, Hazzlett," remonstrated Ransdale. "The Black Falcon is a masked criminal. The Shadow is known as a being who battles crime. Had The Shadow been trapped, the consequences would have been unfortunate.

"If The Shadow had fought his way out; if he had been captured or killed and thus identified as someone other than Velvet Laffrey, for whom the police were searching, the issue would have been clouded. This was to appear as a regular raid by The Black Falcon; to keep him as the criminal personality, with the issue unclouded. It was my chance to establish a perfect alibi; to make myself a public hero.

"The game succeeded. The Shadow, it proved, was actually here; and the chance he had to get away turned to our advantage. The police did catch sight of The Shadow escaping. That proved to them that The Black Falcon had been here. They mistook The Shadow for The Black Falcon."

"But what about The Shadow? What did he think about it?"

"He figured that The Black Falcon fled when the first shots were fired. After that, he was too busy with his own escape. He is worried now, Hazzlett. He is worried because he has learned of a clever personage who is quite as elusive as himself!"

HAZZLETT pondered. He saw the logic of Ransdale's remarks. The valet stared in awed fashion at his master. Here was one who had duped The Shadow as well as the law!

"Since night before last," observed Ransdale, slowly puffing smoke rings from his pipe, "I have been studying The Shadow's plight. His trails are ended. Hubert Apprison and Elias Carthers are prisoners. Rowdy Kirshing is dead; so is Terry Rukes and all his mob. I saw clearly that The Shadow would have to search for new clues."

"Where?"

"Here. This is the scene of The Black Falcon's last attempt. I am one man of wealth who managed to save myself from being kidnapped. The Shadow, to gain further leads, would have to come to me. I have been expecting him.

"I have supposed, all along, that The Shadow might be a man of wealth. He has terrorized the underworld for years; yet he has never profited by his work. He is not an agent of the law. Therefore, being a person of wealth, it would be natural for The Shadow to visit me—another man of means—in his undisguised personality.

"He came tonight. Lamont Cranston is The Shadow. He talked with me about his friends, Hubert Apprison and Elias Carthers. He gave himself away without knowing it, for he had no idea that I might be The Black Falcon.

"A friend of the police commissioner! Certainly, The Shadow should be such, to keep his finger on the pulse of crime. A man who prefers automatics of large caliber. Those are the guns for which The Shadow is famous.

"Tonight, Hazzlett, I have chatted with The Shadow. Lamont Cranston and Rowland Ransdale are friends. The Shadow and The Black Falcon are enemies. Through the friendship of Ransdale and Cranston, The Black Falcon will move to thwart The Shadow."

Rowland Ransdale's face was glowing. The master crook paused to stare at Hazzlett with a knowing gaze. The servant realized that some daring scheme was brewing.

"Rowland Ransdale," declared the mine owner, pronouncing his own name with emphasis, "is regarded as a potential victim of The Black Falcon. Since, however, The Black Falcon failed in his attempt to capture Ransdale, it is logical that he would choose a new victim for his next attempt. Am I clear, Hazzlett?"

"Yes," responded the valet.

"Another man of wealth," continued Ransdale. "One whose abduction would create a great sensation; one whose abduction would strike close to Commissioner Ralph Weston. Does that sound logical?"

"It does."

"More desirable still, one whose abduction would remove the real obstacle in The Black Falcon's path: namely, The Shadow. The way, Hazzlett, must be cleared for The Black Falcon to continue with his plans of wholesale kidnapping, to be followed by vast ransoms when the victims are released."

"It sounds good, chief," stated Hazzlett, "but you've got two jobs ahead of you. One is to get rid of The Shadow; the other is to snag another victim—"

"Both will be performed at once," broke in Ransdale, with an evil leer. "Before this week is ended, Hazzlett, The Black Falcon will swoop down again. His next victim will be—"

"Who?" questioned Hazzlett, as Ransdale paused.

"Lamont Cranston," announced the supercrook.

With that decision, Rowland Ransdale chuckled. His lips, as they formed the dry, insidious sound, were the twisted lips of The Black Falcon!

CHAPTER XIV
THE SHADOW'S AGENT

ON the following afternoon, a complacent chubby-faced man was staring from the window of an office high in the Badger Building. This gentleman was an investment broker, Rutledge Mann by name, and he spent much of his leisure time in gazing at the pinnacled skyline of Manhattan.

A knock at the door. Mann swerved in his swivel chair and called for the visitor to enter. The door opened and an alert young man stepped in from the outer office. He closed the door behind him. Rutledge Mann smiled as the visitor took a chair beside the desk.

This arrival was Harry Vincent, a friend who called occasionally for business conferences with Mann. To all appearances, Rutledge Mann was an investment broker who made a comfortable living, while Harry Vincent, a man of considerable leisure, constituted one of Mann's clients.

This surface indication was entirely incorrect. Actually, Rutledge Mann was a contact agent of The Shadow and Harry Vincent was one of the active operatives who served the invisible master. When Harry Vincent called to see Rutledge Mann, it meant that The Shadow's orders were to be discussed.

"Vincent," remarked Mann, in a complacent tone, "there is work ahead for you. The duties will be specific ones and they will require vigilance."

Harry nodded. He knew that Rutledge Mann was speaking for The Shadow. The investment broker had evidently received a communication from the mysterious chief.

"Three nights ago," Mann went on, "an attempt was made to abduct Rowland Ransdale, a wealthy Western mine owner, from his uptown apartment. This attempt was made by the notorious kidnapper known as The Black Falcon."

"I have read the details," Harry stated.

"Ransdale," asserted Mann, "is leaving New York. He wants more security, because he apparently feels that The Black Falcon may make another attempt to abduct him. He is going to a house in the Catskills—a place which he has long owned.

"Naturally, Ransdale has said very little about this prospective trip and he believes he will be safe where he is going. Nevertheless, it is quite possible that The Black Falcon may have agents on hand at Ransdale's mountain residence.

"I have investigated through real-estate agents and I have learned the location of Ransdale's place. It is fifteen miles from the town of Cuthbury and it is located in a region which is almost entirely forest. Ransdale has certainly chosen a safe spot—if seclusion can be called safety.

"You are to go to the town of Cuthbury. Take your coupé with its complete wireless sending equipment and make a complete investigation of the entire terrain. Learn all that you can concerning the protective measures which Rowland Ransdale has instituted.

"Make your reports to me, by mail, so far as ordinary data is concerned. In case that you encounter unusual circumstances, communicate with Burbank by wireless. Remember: your task is to learn all that you can regarding Rowland Ransdale's location and the trustworthiness of the men who live with him. At the same time, however, do not give any inkling that you are watching Ransdale himself."

"I understand," said Harry, with a nod. "Ransdale might think that I was there for The Black Falcon."

"Exactly," affirmed Mann. "Your duty requires the utmost discretion. Your reports must be exact in every detail. Be particularly observant whenever Ransdale leaves his place. Those are the times when danger from The Black Falcon may be threatening."

"How soon do I leave?" questioned Harry, rising.

"At once," stated Mann. "You can reach Cuthbury this evening. There is a small hotel in the town; you can stay there. Take along the real-estate credentials which you have used on other occasions. They will serve you in this case as the town of Cuthbury is on the border of a vacation district and interest in land development is budding."

HARRY VINCENT left the investment broker's office. He rode down in an elevator, strolled to Broadway and hailed a cab. Harry rode to the Metrolite Hotel, his New York residence, and packed a large bag, in which he placed the credentials which Rutledge Mann had mentioned.

Calling a garage, Harry ordered his car to the hotel. Half an hour later, he was crossing the huge George Washington Bridge, in order to reach the west bank of the Hudson River.

Harry Vincent scented adventure. He had found it often in The Shadow's service. Time and again, Harry had been dispatched upon special duties for The Shadow. As a tried investigator who could play the part of working on his own, Harry had proven his worth.

Yet in his remarkable career as an agent of The Shadow, Harry had never gained facts concerning the identity of his mysterious chief. That was the intriguing feature. Instructions came through Rutledge Mann; Harry sent reports to the investment broker. Burbank, a second contact man, could always be reached by telephone or by special wireless communication.

The Shadow's mysterious ability to keep his astounding personality shrouded in complete darkness was one that made Harry constantly aware of the power of his chief. There had been other manifestations of The Shadow's might, however; these had imbued Harry with even greater confidence.

Often, Harry had encountered hopeless situations. He had fallen into the hands of superfiends. Certain death had threatened him and others who sought to obey The Shadow's bidding. On every occasion, The Shadow had brought aid, even though the attendant difficulties had demanded superhuman prowess.

Thus Harry Vincent had no fear. He was ready to embark on any enterprise which The Shadow commanded. His belief in his own ability was limited; but Harry knew that The Shadow possessed incredible strength and he relied fully upon his master's strength.

The Black Falcon!

Harry had been sure that The Shadow was on the trail of the supercrook who had stirred Manhattan. Until now, however, no duty in this case had fallen upon Harry. The expected time had arrived. Harry's part seemed small; yet Harry had played other roles which at the outset had promised little action. This trip to the Catskills, to gain data regarding Rowland Ransdale, was one which might prove of tremendous consequence.

The Shadow, Harry knew, seldom sent his agents on idle quests. Rowland Ransdale, Harry felt sure, must be an important factor in The Black Falcon's schemes. Harry, as he rode along, was filled with determination to learn every available detail regarding Ransdale's position.

Then, should The Black Falcon choose to strike, The Shadow, through Harry, would he able to counteract the supercrook. This was Harry's positive opinion.

The Shadow's agent held a high sense of the responsibility which involved upon him in assuring the protection of Rowland Ransdale. The Black Falcon was a menace who must be offset at any cost.

Had Harry Vincent known the true situation that lay ahead, his determination would have been tempered with amazement. As yet, however, Harry had gained no inkling of the truth. The instructions from The Shadow, though they had mentioned the threat of The Black Falcon, had shown no knowledge of the insidious facts that lay beneath the unruffled surface of Rowland Ransdale's affairs.

Harry Vincent was completely ignorant of the fact that Rowland Ransdale was The Black Falcon himself!

CHAPTER XV
THE FALCON SWOOPS

A LULL had followed The Black Falcon's attack at Rowland Ransdale's. In the days since the time when the mine owner and his valet had shot down the invading mobsters under Terry Rukes, there had been no new demonstration of The Black Falcon's power.

Speculation, however, was still rife on the fate of Hubert Apprison and Elias Carthers. It was obvious that The Black Falcon must be holding both millionaires as prisoners; yet there had been no effort on the part of the abductor to demand ransoms.

The newspapers had taken the repulsion of The Black Falcon as a sign that the supercrook had lost his nerve. News columns had been awaiting more activity before their space would be devoted to new blasts concerning The Black Falcon. During this period of relief, the police were busy. Public fear of The Black Falcon had waned.

Of the two classes that had felt most interest in The Black Falcon's doings, one had subsided. That was the underworld. The dragnet and other efforts of the police had been accepted as mere routine. The fact that The Black Falcon had lost his mob—represented by Terry Rukes and gangsters—had produced the feeling that The Black Falcon was crippled.

Among the upper crust, however, tension still persisted. Whatever The Black Falcon's situation, the man of crime still held two victims; and, from the fact that he had invaded Rowland Ransdale's apartment, it was still possible that he fostered his plans of wholesale abduction.

Every place where the elite gathered, the topic of The Black Falcon was a pressing one; and such proved to be the case among a group of persons assembled in the sumptuous home of Lamont Cranston.

Seated in a luxurious living room, half a dozen men in evening clothes were discussing the activities of the uncaptured kidnapper.

"It's good to be outside of New York City," admitted one gentleman, in a rueful tone. "I have great confidence in the police; but I must honestly state that I expect The Black Falcon to bob up everywhere I go."

"We're not far from New York now," interposed another speaker. "This part of Jersey is a portion of greater New York—just as much as Long Island."

"Why mention that?" quizzed a third man. "Are you trying to make us all feel uneasy? How do you feel, Cranston, living out here?"

LAMONT CRANSTON, seated in an armchair, indulged in a quiet smile. There was something lackadaisical about the globetrotting millionaire. Perhaps it was the comfortable atmosphere of his home.

"I'm keeping away from Manhattan," observed Cranston, in a quiet tone. "Not entirely through fear of encountering The Black Falcon, although I must admit that has something to do with it, but chiefly through desire for a rest."

"From your last trip?"

"Yes. I stopped off in Florida after my return from the jungles of the Amazon. Then I received telegrams referring to matters that meant business pressure. That is why I came home. Everything seemed to clear up automatically upon my return, so I have kept away from New York during the past week."

"I should think," remarked a guest, "that you would relish an encounter with someone like The Black Falcon. You are a big-game hunter, Cranston."

"Jungle hunting and man hunting are different occupations," returned the millionaire. "There are great risks attendant upon elephant hunts, for instance; but those come under the head of sports. I am a sportsman, not a representative of the law. I do not care to embroil myself with criminals."

"Maybe this Black Falcon business has subsided," declared a guest. "The criminal depended upon a crowd of ruffians. They were killed when they tried to capture Rowland Ransdale. Since then, The Black Falcon has been a nonentity."

"The police," observed another man, in a wise tone, "are on the trail of The Black Falcon—at least, so I am informed. They know his identity, but have not made it public. He will run tremendous risks coming into New York."

"They have clues?" inquired a guest.

"So I understand," asserted the informant. "Commissioner Weston is a competent official. What is more, he has this case under his own supervision. He, himself, is one of the Four

Hundred. It is good to have a man of his caliber in charge. Most meritorious, in my opinion—"

The conversation stopped as a servant entered the living room and approached Lamont Cranston.

"What is it, Richards?" questioned the millionaire.

"A telephone call, sir," answered the servant. "Police Commissioner Weston is on the wire—"

A gasp came from the listeners. This was a most unexpected announcement. Buzzing words began; then stopped as Cranston arose and faced his guests with an easy smile.

"I am acquainted with the commissioner," he remarked. "This is probably a mere coincidence. However, since our talk has turned to The Black Falcon, I shall ask Commissioner Weston if any new developments have occurred."

With that, Cranston strolled from the living room. The guests watched him cross the hall to a room that was opposite at a distant angle. It was Cranston's private smoking room, where the downstairs telephone was located.

CRANSTON passed by a side door that led from the house and entered the smoking room. He closed the door behind him. The desk telephone was off its cradle. Cranston picked up the instrument and spoke across the wire.

"Commissioner Weston?" he inquired in his calm tone. "Yes, this is Lamont Cranston... What's that?... In answer to my call?... You must be mistaken, Commissioner... Let me get this exactly. You say that you received a call five minutes ago... A call from here... My home... A servant saying I wished to speak with you... Then the connection was cut off.

"I don't understand it, Commissioner... I can question my servant... What's that? The Black Falcon?... I don't quite understand... You say that you thought I might have some theory regarding him? I don't quite follow you, inspector.

"Because of the matter on Long Island?... You mean the abduction of Elias Carthers... You have kept quiet regarding my action, you say... That sounds a bit puzzling, Commissioner. I don't see why you should be worried on my account... Yes... I feel quite competent of caring for my own safety..."

Cranston ceased speaking of a sudden. The long fingers of his right hand had been toying with a sheet of paper that was lying beneath the telephone standard. Drawing the paper forth as he spoke, Cranston found himself staring at a black object thrust through the center of the white sheet. It was a long feather, dyed black.

"One moment, Commissioner." Cranston's voice became tense but steady. "I have just found

something that will interest you... Here, on my desk. A sheet of paper... Blank, but with a mysterious symbol... A black feather... Yes, it appears to be the feather of a falcon..."

A chuckle came from across the table. Lamont Cranston looked up. He was staring squarely into a pair of eyes that peered through a black mask. A gleaming revolver bulged directly in front of the millionaire's nose. An opened door to a passage beyond the study was indication of where the intruder had been stationed.

Lamont Cranston had no opportunity to move. One hand was holding the double-ended telephone. The other was on the desk. The Black Falcon held his victim helpless.

Reaching out with his left hand, The Black Falcon plucked the telephone from Cranston's unresisting grasp. Coldly—in a voice that veiled the accustomed tones of Rowland Ransdale—The Black Falcon spoke to the police commissioner; but all the while his evil gaze and his covering revolver were fixed on Cranston across the table from him.

"Good evening, Mr. Commissioner," snarled the supercrook. "This is The Black Falcon... In person... It was I who called your home... From this room.

"I must apologize"—The Black Falcon was chuckling gleefully—"for sending you no letter. My reason was twofold. First, because I failed with my last threat and am making amends for it now. Second, because I am outside of your jurisdiction.

"The fault is not mine. You can blame it on Mr. Cranston. I have been waiting for him to come to the Cobalt Club. Since he has not done so, I have visited his home instead."

The Black Falcon's evil lips held a twisted smile while sputtered protests came over the wire. Then the snarling voice recurred with a tone of finality.

"Cranston is going with me," declared The Black Falcon. "The token which I left him—the feather through the sheet of paper—will remain here as proof of his veracity—"

With that, The Black Falcon clamped the telephone on the hook. As he had done with Elias Carthers, so did he do with Lamont Cranston. He poked the revolver forward and ordered the millionaire to rise.

Cranston's face was calm. Half smiling, the millionaire obeyed the injunction. Cranston seemed to regard this episode as a pleasant adventure; but he made no effort to balk his enemy. Opportunity for resistance was impossible.

"Arms up—turn around—"

Cranston followed the order. The Black Falcon,

Lamont Cranston looked up. He was staring squarely into a pair of eyes that peered through a black mask.

shoving his revolver into the small of Cranston's back, forced his prisoner toward the door. With a deft maneuver, The Black Falcon opened the barrier without losing his hold over the millionaire.

As Cranston walked helplessly into the hallway, The Black Falcon guided him to the right, toward the door that led outside. The door opened as the two arrived. A man was standing on the outer steps.

"Face around!" ordered The Black Falcon, in a snarling tone. "Arms behind you!"

Cranston obeyed mechanically. Handcuffs clicked as the waiting man snapped them to the millionaire's wrists. The Black Falcon's aide thrust his own gun into the small of Cranston's back. With his free hand, he gripped Cranston's shoulder and yanked the prisoner out into the night.

THE BLACK FALCON wheeled. The sound of his voice had reached the living room. Men were stepping forth into the hall. They stopped in consternation as they saw the masked enemy who faced them. The Black Falcon snarled a warning as he raised his revolver. Like frightened hares, the guests scurried for the cover of the living room.

Scoffing, The Black Falcon fired shots across the hallway. Three roaring reports echoed through Cranston's mansion. Then, his unaimed threat delivered, The Black Falcon sprang through the open door and pulled it shut with a resounding slam.

It was Richards who came to action. The servant had gone upstairs after notifying Cranston that Weston was on the wire. The sound of the shots brought him scurrying down. The cries of the guests told him what had happened.

Leaping to a hall closet, Richards found a revolver and hurried to the door through which Cranston had been taken. As the servant opened the door, he heard the sound of a car pulling away from the drive beyond.

Richards fired futile shots. Answering spurts of flame sent bullets spattering close to the spot where the faithful servant stood. Then, with roaring motor, the car took a curve in the driveway and was gone.

Again, The Black Falcon had scored a new triumph. From a house where guests were present, he had swept away another victim. Lamont Cranston, multimillionaire friend of Police Commissioner Weston, had been abducted from his home.

With daring, the supercrook had talked over the wire to the police commissioner, during the actual moments when his crime had begun. Another challenge from The Black Falcon to the law!

More than that, however, The Black Falcon's action was a stroke that showed a superhuman boldness. His abduction of Lamont Cranston was not only a step in his plans for wholesale kidnapping; it was an expression of his contempt for the awesome being whom all the underworld dreaded.

Rowland Ransdale—in his own character—had identified Lamont Cranston as the enemy whom he sought. Rowland Ransdale, as The Black Falcon, had kidnapped Lamont Cranston.

In catching Cranston unaware, the master crook had gained his double triumph. Riding free with Hazzlett at the wheel of the car in which they had departed, The Black Falcon was snarling his elation.

Tonight, when he bestowed Cranston among his other prisoners, The Black Falcon would not only have a captive worth a mammoth ransom; in his toils would be the only foeman who might have thwarted his evil schemes.

Rowland Ransdale—The Black Falcon—was gloating with the surety that The Shadow was in his power!

CHAPTER XVI
THE LAST REPORT

FAR out in the wilds of the Catskills, a young man was seated in a coupé parked beneath the branches of trees that overhung a rough dirt road. It was Harry Vincent. By the dome light of the car, The Shadow's agent was studying sheets of penciled notations.

Harry had kept these memos at his hotel. He had sent copies of them to Rutledge Mann. He had brought them along with him tonight, in case there would be need for reference if he communicated with Burbank.

Harry went over the brief pages one by one. They were filled with terse information that Harry checked. First was the location of Rowland Ransdale's house, a large, stone-walled building that was stationed in a clearing fifteen miles from the town of Cuthbury.

Harry had specified the size of the clearing. It measured less than fifty yards in greatest depth. About half of that distance—some sixty feet—formed a space in back of Ransdale's house.

The place was surrounded with heavy barbed wire. Harry had made his way past that obstacle and had viewed the clearing, close at hand. He had given a completely defined description of the open space that was surrounded by huge, overshadowing trees.

Also, in his observations, Harry had estimated that there were seven men in Ransdale's employ. He had seen these fellows on the premises. All were hard individuals. Rowland Ransdale was well protected.

In all the surrounding terrain, Harry had found no other clearings of importance, although he had driven his coupé over miles and miles of stony dirt roads. He had found a few old houses in the woods.

It was not until he had reached a spot some fourteen miles from Ransdale's—in the direction opposite the town of Cuthbury—that Harry had found a sizeable open space. This appeared to be a pasture land, of several acres in extent, well surrounded by barbed wire. Harry had not investigated it except by peering from the road.

Each afternoon, Harry had kept late vigil from a hidden spot beyond the road that ran in front of Rowland Ransdale's secluded estate. Having learned essential facts, it was Harry's duty to make sure that Ransdale remained within the shelter of his protected abode; and also to watch for prowlers.

Such had been a thankless task until this evening. Then, just after nightfall, Harry had seen the lights of a sedan as they swept from the unclosed gate that was in front of the obscure house.

HARRY had spotted the direction in which the sedan had gone. He had followed far behind. At every crossroad, he had stopped to examine traces. Fortunately, the roads were muddy in spots. After a slow trailing, in which the sedan had gained miles, Harry had found himself approaching the vicinity of the pasture fourteen miles from Ransdale's.

Harry had stopped once at the distant sound of a motor. He had recognized it as an airplane; then had dropped the matter. Planes were uncommon in this portion of the Catskills; the one that Harry had heard seemed several miles away.

Now, however, Harry had reached the end of his journey and he was wondering what next to do. He had spotted the final tracks of the sedan when he had reached the pasture that was surrounded by barbed wire. The car had turned into a narrow road that led through a heavy gate into the pasture!

How long ago? Harry estimated that it must have been considerably more than an hour—closer to two perhaps—since Ransdale's car had reached this spot. The trailing had been a slow task on which Harry had followed wrong roads more than once.

Had Ransdale been in the car? Harry did not know. He was preparing a specific statement to add to his other notes. At present, Harry was in a spot of security, for he had parked the coupé in a road that led away from the pasture.

The only course was to investigate. Before he did so, however, Harry planned to be ready for emergency. He could not understand this visit of the sedan to the isolated pasture—the only stretch of open ground within miles of Ransdale's home.

Clambering from the coupé, Harry opened the rear. Instead of a rumble seat, he produced a heavy box from which he drew out wireless equipment. This constituted a sending apparatus of The Shadow's own invention. With prompt efficiency, Harry rigged up the sending station through which he could communicate with Burbank.

The Shadow's agent worked rapidly in the silence of the night. His task completed, he tested with the key. At last he gained a response. In special code, Harry clicked through a brief report:

Ransdale car at pasture clearing. Forty minutes minimum from house. Investigating.

With this assurance, Harry left the coupé. He had turned out the dome light. The car was lost in blackness. Following the untraveled road, Harry finally turned off and cut through bushes until he encountered the barbed wire.

This barrier was not so formidable as the one about Ransdale's house. Harry passed it and crept along the fringe of the woods. He could see the clearing in the starlight. Harry decided to circuit the entire area.

At one end of the clearing, Harry stopped short as he saw a broad path cut beneath high, overhanging branches. Creeping to the edge, Harry saw what appeared to be a low building in the darkness. The front end looked like a solid wall of black. Harry moved closer. Then came realization.

The front wall was an opening. This low-built structure was a hangar for an airplane!

Stopping, Harry fancied that he could hear whispered voices from the hangar. Then came the thought of the airplane motor that he had heard. Harry knew the truth.

Rowland Ransdale must have come here tonight with a squad of his men. They had pulled the airplane from its hidden hangar and Ransdale—with one or more companions—had taken off for parts unknown! Other men had been left in charge, awaiting the return of their employer.

WHAT was Ransdale's purpose? Evidently the mine owner had utilized this hangar before. Until now, Harry had regarded Ransdale as a man who sought seclusion. This placed a new light on affairs in the Catskills. Ransdale—for some unknown reasons—had cause to leave his abode in secret fashion, with a rapid mode of travel at his ready command.

Was Ransdale's return expected soon? Probably, because the men were waiting in the hangar. This made a report important. Harry crawled back through the woods, passed through the barbed wire and hurried to the coupé.

Establishing communication with Burbank, Harry sent his new message. He gave Burbank every detail he had discovered, including the approximate time of the airplane's departure. Then, with the final statement that there would be more information when Ransdale returned, Harry went back to the vicinity of the hangar.

The Shadow's agent placed himself at the edge of the clearing. Then, with caution, he moved down the cut-out alleyway below the trees until he neared the hangar. Here, in darkness, he might be able to overhear some conversation. Any details would be important.

Mumbled voices reached Harry's ears as the young man edged toward the blackened front of the hangar. Just away from protecting trees, he tried to make out the jargon that he heard, but the words were indistinguishable. Then came a distant sound that made Harry turn.

Ransdale's airplane was returning! Far up beyond the clearing, Harry caught the twinkle of tiny lights. Fascinated, The Shadow's agent watched. It was that action that made him unready for what suddenly occurred.

A click came from the interior of the hangar. A light blazed from the front of the building. Other lights came on about the field. This hidden landing spot was illuminated; and Harry Vincent, out from the trees a few yards from the hangar, was caught in the glare.

Leaping to his feet, Harry turned to dash for cover. He was too late. Two men, pouncing from the hangar, fell upon him before he could gain the shelter of the trees. A stunning blow dazed Harry. While one man gave instructions, the other strapped a belt about the arms of The Shadow's agent.

The roar of the descending airplane sounded like tremendous waves in Harry's ears. Prostrate, on his back, his head swimming and his eyes blinking at the lights, Harry saw the ship come to earth and zoom closer and closer as it crossed the field. The brakes applied, the plane came to a stop less than a hundred feet away.

One of Harry's captors dragged him to his feet. Stumbling, Harry moved forward toward the plane. As he stared ahead, he saw three men alighting. One, he recognized as Rowland Ransdale. The second—whom Harry did not know—was Hazzlett.

Between them, standing wearily, was Lamont Cranston. Harry saw the captured millionaire as a calm-faced individual whose features showed dejection. He realized that this man was a prisoner.

SHOVED face to face with Rowland Ransdale, Harry Vincent caught the gleam of evil eyes. He heard words of explanation from his captors. Then, apart from Lamont Cranston, Harry Vincent was marched across the field, to the spot where the sedan was parked among the trees.

Rough hands shoved Harry Vincent into the car. Lamont Cranston tumbled in from the other side. Ransdale's pair of waiting ruffians piled into the back to growl commands for silence, which they backed with threatening revolvers.

The glow of the lights about the field disappeared. A few minutes later, Rowland Ransdale arrived; then Hazzlett. The latter took the wheel.

The sedan pulled out through the gate; it stopped long enough for Hazzlett to alight and close the barrier.

The sedan started on; and as it jounced along the bumpy dirt road, Harry Vincent, silent, began to grasp the truth. He knew—too late—the true motives that guided Rowland Ransdale. He realized that the dignified man who was a prisoner beside him must be another abducted man of wealth.

Too late to inform Burbank, Harry Vincent had learned that Rowland Ransdale was The Black Falcon! Amazing discovery though this had been, its stupefying effect was small compared to the one which would have gripped Harry had he known the identity of the prisoner beside him.

For Harry did not know Lamont Cranston. Nor had he—even as The Shadow's agent—ever connected the personality of a New Jersey millionaire with the mysterious master known as The Shadow.

The Black Falcon had gained another prisoner in Harry Vincent. The coupé, with its wireless equipment, was resting hidden among the trees. Burbank had received enough information to know that something must be wrong when no new word came from Harry.

Moreover, Burbank had gained sufficient to lay suspicion upon Rowland Ransdale. Coupled with Harry's previous information, notes of specific value had been obtained.

But of what avail could all this information be? Who was to take up The Shadow's work now that Lamont Cranston, like Harry Vincent, was helpless in The Black Falcon's clutching talons?

CHAPTER XVII
THE FINAL SCHEME

NEARLY twenty-four hours had elapsed since Lamont Cranston and Harry Vincent had been carried prisoners in Rowland Ransdale's sedan. The plotting criminal who called himself The Black Falcon was seated in a lighted room on the second floor of his stone-walled abode in the Catskills.

Behind Ransdale were half-opened French windows that showed a projecting roof toward the darkness at the rear of the clearing. Ransdale, leaning back in a chair behind a desk, was puffing at his pipe. His face showed its evil gloat. The Black Falcon, unmasked, had no cause to hide his identity here.

The door opened and Hazzlett entered. The pretended valet who served as The Black Falcon's chief henchman was grinning as he crossed the room. He slapped a New York newspaper on the desk. Ransdale picked up the sheet and scanned the headlines.

"Good!" he snarled. "That's the ticket. Weston has come out with it. Announcing that the police have uncovered the identity of The Black Falcon."

"Name and all," returned Hazzlett. "Velvet Laffrey is the guy they're after."

"I knew that sheet of paper I left on Cranston's desk would clinch it," asserted Ransdale. "I used the one on which Velvet's impressions were barely noticeable. A subtle touch like that, Hazzlett, is just what a criminal needs to use."

Leaning back in his chair, Ransdale emitted a harsh chuckle. He puffed speculatively at his pipe, blew a few smoke rings, and indulged in comment for Hazzlett's benefit.

"The way is clear," decided the supercrook. "Lamont Cranston is good for as big a ransom as Hubert Apprison and Elias Carthers. He is The Shadow—and that makes it all the sweeter. I can deliver him for cash along with the others."

"But you're taking chances, with him being The Shadow."

"Why? You know the game, Hazzlett. I can't cover up who I am, after I turn these prisoners back. The truth will come out then. But you can be sure that I shall be so far away they can never hope to find me.

"Cash and plenty of it. No delivery of the prisoners. Let them cool as long as their friends hold out. Years if necessary. My terms will be accepted. This wholesale work is something so big that people are bound to give up in despair.

"We aren't through yet, though, Hazzlett. Weston is still after The Black Falcon. Until the police give up, I'll keep on, while they follow their hopeless, blind trail. Rowland Ransdale is safe. Velvet Laffrey is the man they're after."

Ransdale pounded the desk as he spoke; then, with an evil leer, he arose. He strolled across the room toward the door and motioned to Hazzlett to follow him.

"We're going down to talk with the new prisoner," declared Ransdale. "I want you to be there. It will be interesting."

THE man who called himself The Black Falcon proceeded downstairs with Hazzlett at his heels. He passed through an archway on the ground floor and descended into a large basement. On all sides were heavy, barred doors. The place constituted a cellroom. One of Ransdale's henchmen, a husky, dark-faced fellow, was standing on guard.

"Vincent?" questioned Ransdale.

"In there," indicated the guard.

Ransdale drew a revolver from his pocket. With sweeping action, he unbarred the door, opened it and stepped into a square, windowless room that was illuminated by a single light.

The place was stone-walled. Harry Vincent was seated on a chair beside a cot. Ransdale motioned to Hazzlett to close the door.

"Comfortable?" questioned Ransdale.

"All right," returned Harry, in response to the note of sarcasm.

"I trust," stated Ransdale, in an easy tone, "that you appreciate the courtesy that I am showing you. It is not my policy to take unprofitable prisoners. However, you may prove useful later on, because of your connections."

With that, Ransdale produced a sheaf of papers from his pocket. Harry recognized them as the memos that he had not had an opportunity to destroy.

"Evidently," declared Ransdale, "you were keeping a close checkup on my actions. From these notes, however, I can see that you were probably apprehensive for my safety. I learned your name, Vincent, through papers in your pocket; and I also divined your purpose.

"You are working—so I take it—for a mysterious employer known as The Shadow. He is a weird personage who battles crime. Because I was once attacked, presumably by The Black Falcon, you were sent here to watch what might occur."

Ransdale eyed Harry as though he expected a comment. The Shadow's agent made none. Ransdale's smile was not unpleasant. The criminal seemed to be enjoying himself.

"You did your duty well," he commended. "In fact, you handled it up to a point where you finally began to expose the truth about The Black Falcon. Here is a blank piece of paper. Will you kindly jot down the remainder of your experience up to the present moment?"

Harry was puzzled. He could not, however, see any reason to refuse Ransdale's request. He took the sheet of paper and briefly listed remarks concerning his capture. Ransdale bowed as he received the paper.

"Thank you," he said. "I shall see to it that your complete notes reach The Shadow himself. You have served him well. I may have occasion to use you later. Perhaps, in return for my kindness in delivering your memoranda, The Shadow may place you at my disposal when I require your services."

The insidious tone of Ransdale's remark left Harry Vincent stupefied. As his captor left the cell, followed by Hazzlett, Harry began to grasp the meaning.

Ransdale had promised to deliver these notes to The Shadow. How? Dimly, Harry realized the only possible answer. The Shadow—like Harry—must be a prisoner in the hands of the villain whom Harry now knew to be The Black Falcon!

ROWLAND RANSDALE, when he had closed the door through which he had left Harry's room, turned immediately toward Hazzlett. He flourished the sheaf of papers and made a significant gesture.

"This chap may prove useful," he announced. "Later on, when we are ready to deliver the prisoners for ransom, a go-between may be necessary. Vincent has evidently been a capable agent for The Shadow. He can serve us as well."

"He might try to give the game away."

"With his master as our prisoner? Not a chance of it, Hazzlett. I'll tell you something, though"—Ransdale's expression was a wise one—"regarding this man Vincent. He does not know The Shadow's true identity."

"You mean that he doesn't know that Cranston is The Shadow?"

"He is ignorant of that fact. Did you see how blank he was when I told him that I intended to deliver his messages to The Shadow? That was the test, Hazzlett."

"But Vincent has been working for The Shadow—"

"Certainly; and that is a proof of The Shadow's cleverness. Even his agents have been in the dark about his true personality. The Shadow has been too wise to trust his complete secrets to anyone."

"Then how will Vincent know after you have forced The Shadow to comply with your plans?"

"There must be some form of recognition between them. That will come later, Hazzlett. For the present, I shall play a very subtle game. Come. We shall interview our prize prisoner."

Ransdale's gun was in his hand when he unbarred the door to another cell. Hazzlett, at his master's bidding, also produced a revolver. The guard rose in readiness. Rowland Ransdale was about to enter the room in which Lamont Cranston was a prisoner. The Black Falcon was taking no chances with The Shadow.

Ransdale opened the door and entered the room. Lamont Cranston, seated in a chair, looked up to view the visitor in quiet fashion. Ransdale's smile held but a trace of its gloating. The Black Falcon advanced and extended the papers which he held.

"These may interest you, Cranston," he announced.

Lamont Cranston appeared curious as he took the notations which Ransdale had obtained from Harry Vincent. The calm-faced millionaire read them one by one and then passed them back to Ransdale.

"Outside of the fact," he declared quietly, "that I now know where I am and the conditions which surround me, I can see no value or meaning to these notations."

"You do not recognize their source?" queried Ransdale.

"No." Cranston's tone was emphatic. "I am amazed, Ransdale, to learn that a man of your standing should deal in crime. To think that you, whom I first met at the Cobalt Club, could play the part of The Black Falcon!"

Ransdale's eyes narrowed. His smile, though evil, showed a cunning that was not to be outdone. A question stopped upon his lips.

"I have chosen the role of crime," he admitted sternly. "It pleases me, Cranston; moreover, it offers me tremendous return for the investment which I have made. You are one of my prisoners. The terms of your ransom will be fixed—like those of the others.

"In the meantime, you will remain guarded. I warn you that escape is impossible. New victims will be brought here; after that, I shall arrange for the delivery of all. Do not be impatient. The time will soon arrive when the police will find that it is hopeless to antagonize me."

Cranston settled back in his chair. He seemed to take his imprisonment in philosophical fashion. His gaze showed no animosity. It was more a sign of reproval. Ransdale eyed his prisoner; then laughed scoffingly. He turned and went to the door; there he signaled Hazzlett, and the pair left the room, bolting the door behind them.

RANSDALE was silent as he led the way up to the second floor. There he took the chair behind his desk and tossed Harry Vincent's notes into a drawer. He lighted his pipe and leaned back to enjoy the cool breeze that came from the half-opened French doors. After a short period of speculation, Ransdale noted a disappointed look on Hazzlett's face.

"What is it, Hazzlett?" he inquired.

"The way you talked to Cranston," replied the servant. "I thought you were going to lift the lid—to tell him that you knew he was The Shadow."

"That, Hazzlett," remarked Ransdale, "would have been poor policy. I tried him out, Hazzlett, when I asked him if he recognized the source of the memoranda which I gave him. You heard his emphatic denial. He followed it with an indignant protest against my ways of crime."

"You've got the goods on him—"

"Certainly. I picked Lamont Cranston as The Shadow the night that he came to my apartment. I did not betray my discovery then. Why should I do so now? Cranston wants to cover up the fact that he is The Shadow. You saw the way that he pretended ignorance. Let him continue to think that I do not know his true identity.

"The Shadow, Hazzlett, is dangerous, even when a prisoner. At present, a waiting game is his best policy. So long as he thinks that he is known only as Lamont Cranston, he will make no trouble. The time is close at hand, Hazzlett, when I shall be ready to demand ransoms for my prisoners."

"With the police still fighting you?"

"Their persistent efforts are to cease, Hazzlett." Ransdale's face wore a shrewd but ugly smile. "My last coup was a great one—the capture of Lamont Cranston and the elimination of The Shadow accomplished with a single swoop. My next move will be equally as cunning. I have gained a new inspiration."

"You are going to abduct another man?"

"Yes. A warning will precede the act. The deed itself will force the law to listen to my mandates. Bring me the typewriter, Hazzlett. I shall make use of it."

The servant produced a portable machine from the corner. He opened the case and placed the typewriter upon the desk. Rowland Ransdale opened a drawer and brought out a sheet of paper that bore the singular letterhead of The Black Falcon. He placed it in the machine. Slowly and with deliberate care, he typed a letter.

As he drew the sheet free and placed it on the desk, Ransdale opened another drawer. From this he produced a similar piece of stationery. He examined this sheet carefully by the light and his lips formed their gloating smile. Inserting the second piece of paper in the machine, Ransdale began a new typing process slower than the first.

At last, he laid the second letter beside the first and beckoned to Hazzlett. The servant approached to read the letters. He saw that both were identical—new messages to Police Commissioner Weston.

ROWLAND RANSDALE produced two falcon feathers. He examined them carefully, then thrust one through the first letter and the other through the second.

"Why two letters?" questioned Hazzlett.

"One would be enough," admitted Ransdale, "but I do not wish to risk this one." He indicated the second sheet which he had typed. "It is better that I should hold it myself. Then I can be sure of an effective conclusion to the plan which I am contemplating."

Hazzlett looked puzzled. Ransdale enjoyed a smile at his servant's bewilderment. He folded each letter. He addressed an envelope and inserted the first letter. Sealing the envelope, he passed it to

Hazzlett. Then, from a desk drawer, he produced a stack of bundled bills. Taking a falcon feather from the little drawer where he kept these symbols, he thrust it through the paper wrapping that encircled the banknotes.

"Rowdy Kirshing," remarked Ransdale, "had a bodyguard named Pinkey Sardon. A capable fellow—ready for any crime—and admirably free from the toils of the law."

Hazzlett nodded.

"Pinkey Sardon," resumed Ransdale, "knew nothing about The Black Falcon, but it is probable that he wondered about Rowdy Kirshing's source of mysterious wealth. With his salary of a thousand a week cut off, Pinkey must be anxious for new revenue."

"Velvet Laffrey told us all about Pinkey—"

"Yes. I am recalling Velvet's information. Also his description of Pinkey Sardon. The ex-bodyguard has aspirations to become a big shot. More than that, he has a penchant for taking part in crime himself always—something that Rowdy Kirshing was anxious to avoid.

"You are going to New York, Hazzlett. Take this money with you. Call Pinkey Sardon. Make it plain that you used to deal with Rowdy Kirshing. Say that you represent The Black Falcon and tell Pinkey that you have work for him to do. He must be in readiness, with a picked squad of mobsters at his call."

"Pinkey's hangout is the Club Madrid?"

"Exactly. You can phone him there. The facts that you discuss with him will lead him to believe what everyone else now suspects: that The Black Falcon is Velvet Laffrey. Pinkey will listen to your plans. Arrange to get this money to him—and tell him that another ten thousand will be his pay when he has served The Black Falcon's bidding."

"Ten grand in this bundle," nodded Hazzlett, tapping the pile of cash. "Ten grand again when he has done the job."

"Precisely. He must be ready at the Club Madrid. The Black Falcon will call him there and give him final orders. After you have made sure of Pinkey Sardon, post the letter to the police commissioner and return here at once. You may start for New York now, in the sedan."

His orders given, Rowland Ransdale arose and walked with Hazzlett through the door. The two men descended to the ground floor. Hazzlett left. Ransdale returned upstairs.

SEATED at his desk, Ransdale relighted his pipe. He picked up the folded second letter, opened it, and reread its lines. With a chuckle he creased the message and placed it in his inside pocket.

Rowland Ransdale's lips formed an insidious leer. This expression was a token of final triumph. To Ransdale, the game was safe from now on.

Confident that he had eliminated his greatest enemy, The Shadow, The Black Falcon had prepared the final stroke in his chain of supercrimes.

With Pinkey Sardon at his beck, the way would be clear for the most audacious abduction in the history of New York; one that would far eclipse the kidnapping of Lamont Cranston, so far as the public was concerned.

Yet The Black Falcon expected no interference. The very boldness of its scheme constituted its surety. Only The Shadow could have fathomed the crime that threatened; and The Black Falcon no longer feared The Shadow!

CHAPTER XVIII
THE FALCON'S THREAT

Two nights later, Police Commissioner Ralph Weston was seated at the desk in the office of his apartment. The official's face showed anger. Detective Joe Cardona, grim-mouthed, was seated opposite. The detective was perusing a letter which Weston had handed him.

Another message from The Black Falcon! The birdlike letterhead; the feathered signature—both were tokens of the mysterious criminal who had bewildered the police. The lines that Cardona studied were a new and final threat:

Ralph Weston,
Police Commissioner,
New York City.
Dear Sir:
Despite my repeated warnings you have persisted in your pitiful efforts to thwart my schemes. Three men of millions now are in my power, to wit: Hubert Apprison, Elias Carthers and Lamont Cranston.

It is your duty to protect the public. You have failed in that duty. Cranston, it is true, was abducted from a territory beyond your jurisdiction; but he was taken by The Black Falcon—the kidnapper whom you are seeking.

You have announced that you know the identity of The Black Falcon. You have given the name of Velvet Laffrey to the public. You have created the impression that since this identity has been revealed, The Black Falcon has deliberately avoided New York.

You have even made the claim that no further abductions can take place within the limits of New York City. You have narrowed your task to that of tracing The Black Falcon to his place of hiding.

Absurdities! I, The Black Falcon, shall challenge them. I give you warning; but this time there is no alternative. Tonight, before midnight,

I shall come to Manhattan. There, with you standing helpless, I shall abduct a man of wealth, to hold him for ransom with my other prisoners.

This will stand as so notable an achievement that the public will cry out against the puny interference of the police. I predict that my success will lead to the appointment of a new commissioner in your place.

"What do you think of it, Cardona?" quizzed Weston anxiously.

"It looks bad," admitted the detective. "You haven't any idea where The Black Falcon will hit—like you had with Elias Carthers?"

"Cardona," returned Weston, in a serious tone, "the previous crimes have been daring. This one will probably exceed them all. The Black Falcon is determined to beat down our resistance. He is stubborn—as stubborn as he is crafty.

"He had the temerity to call me from Cranston's own home, the night of that abduction. I do not doubt but that he will act with similar boldness tonight—but from a spot closer at hand. I have placed police on guard at the homes of many wealthy persons. Nevertheless, The Black Falcon is a supercriminal; we shall find it difficult to frustrate him."

"He makes his threats good," admitted Cardona. "I don't like this talk of his—his wisecrack that there will be a new commissioner."

"Forget that part," laughed Weston. "It is mere braggadocio. No action of The Black Falcon could cause me to resign from my post."

"Tonight's our chance, Commissioner," decided Cardona, in a grim tone. "The whole force is on the lookout for Velvet Laffrey. If there's a chance to bag him, he'll get bagged. But if he once starts on a getaway he—"

"His escape will be probable," interposed the commissioner, in a glum tone. "Cardona, there is no doubt but that The Black Falcon uses a plane. The New Jersey State police found an abandoned car a few miles from Lamont Cranston's home. We found abandoned cars after the previous abductions."

"He can't land a plane in Manhattan."

"Granted. But he can choose a spot on Long Island. That means a dash after he has seized his victim. The air patrol is ready; but it is difficult to trace an escaping airplane."

Cardona had no comment. The detective was as glum as the commissioner. Cardona had felt that some new trouble was in the offing when he had been summoned here from headquarters.

"We'll sit tight, Cardona," decided Weston.

"We had a stroke of luck that night when The Black Falcon tried to kidnap Rowland Ransdale. Perhaps, tonight—"

"What has become of Ransdale?" queried Cardona. "He went out of town, you told me—"

"Yes," interposed Weston, "I thought the move was a wise one. Ransdale wanted seclusion. He promised, however, to notify me immediately upon his return to New York. The Black Falcon has failed but once. Ransdale caused his failure. There is reason why the criminal should again seek to capture Ransdale."

There was a knock at the door, just as Joe Cardona tossed The Black Falcon's letter on the desk. The police commissioner called an inquiry.

"What is it, Kempton?"

"A gentleman here to see you, sir," came the servant's response. "He is in the anteroom. Mr. Rowland Ransdale."

"Ransdale!" exclaimed the commissioner.

"Yes, sir," came Kempton's reply. "He says that he has just arrived in New York; that he must speak to you at once."

"Usher him in, Kempton! Immediately!"

THE police commissioner was on his feet. He pounded the desk emphatically and The Black Falcon's letter trembled. Weston was staring hard at Joe Cardona.

"The Black Falcon may be after Ransdale again!" exclaimed the commissioner. "Perhaps there is a new threat at the apartment. I have my men in the limousine out front. Let us hope, Cardona, that Rowland Ransdale has some clue."

The detective nodded. He was keyed like Weston, although he did not show it. A tense moment passed. Then came a knock at the door. Weston gave a summons to enter.

Cardona was looking at the police commissioner. Weston was staring at the door. Cardona was about to glance in the same direction; he stopped suddenly as he saw a fixed look come over Weston's face. The commissioner's eyes were bulging in disbelief; his lips had tightened to a state of rigidity.

In alarm, Joe Cardona swung toward the door. The detective, like the commissioner became tense. The sight of the man who stood there brought home the reason for Weston's strange alarm.

Both men had expected to see Rowland Ransdale. Instead, they were facing a visitor who had not been announced. Framed in the doorway was a man whose eyes were glaring through the openings of a mask; whose lips were framing an evil gloat.

In his right hand the intruder held a shining revolver as a threat to the men whom he had surprised. There was no mistaking the identity of the insidious stranger.

Commissioner Ralph Weston and Detective Joe Cardona were at the mercy of The Black Falcon!

CHAPTER XIX
THE SIGNAL OF DEATH

FOR a short interval, The Black Falcon remained gloating in the doorway. Then, assured that the men before him could offer no resistance, he entered the room with quick, short steps.

Keeping his revolver in constant readiness, the masked abductor reached a point at the end of the desk. His back was toward the side door that formed the second exit from Weston's office.

His new vantage point enabled The Black Falcon to keep watch on both Weston and Cardona; at the same time it brought him facing the window and cleared the doorway through which he had entered. That entrance was at The Black Falcon's right.

With twisting lips, The Black Falcon spoke. His tone was a snarl, yet it contained no disguising effort. Weston and Cardona blinked as they caught the familiar voice. Both had heard it before; the fact that they had been waiting for Rowland Ransdale told them the truth that The Black Falcon disdained to cover.

"Ransdale!" gasped Weston.

"Yes, Ransdale," snarled the masked man. "Fools! You have been seeking the wrong man. Velvet Laffrey is dead. I killed him. I have been The Black Falcon, the criminal that you sought."

Weston could volunteer no reply. The statement was too bewildering for the commissioner.

"Velvet Laffrey was my dupe," laughed The Black Falcon. "He was to take the blame for the crimes I planned. He was to be far away, and with that thought he kindly provided me with fingerprint impressions.

"I killed Velvet Laffrey so he would make no further trouble. I planted a torn paper with his finger prints at Apprison's. I changed the doorknob in the room from which I abducted Carthers. The single feather that I left on Lamont Cranston's desk was attached to a sheet of paper that bore very faint impressions of Velvet Laffrey's fingerprints."

With his left hand, The Black Falcon pointed to the letter which lay on Commissioner Weston's desk.

"That message," he stated, "came from me. It bears no identifying marks. This one, however, does. I brought it with me, in hope that I could substitute it."

Reaching in his pocket as he spoke, The Black

Falcon brought out the second letter. He dropped it on the desk and pocketed the first one. Commissioner Weston, staring, could see the blur of fingerprints on the edge of the white sheet, below the feathered signature.

"I promised a startling crime," announced The Back Falcon. "You shall have it. I intend to kidnap a man of wealth. I also promised that New York would have a new police commissioner after tonight's episode. That promise, too, will be kept.

"Tonight, Commissioner Weston, your term of service ends. I shall make the appointment of a new commissioner a matter of necessity. You are the man of wealth whom I intend to take to join my colony of captives at my isolated house deep in the forest!"

POLICE COMMISSIONER WESTON gasped. Joe Cardona was grim. It was evident that The Black Falcon meant to go through with his threat.

"I travel swiftly," announced the masked criminal, with his ugly snarl. "My measures are effective; and I strike where least expected. Yet had either of you been anything but dullards, you might have sensed the meaning of my message.

"Less than two hours have elapsed since I left my stronghold. It required more than half an hour to reach the spot where my airplane was in readiness. The Black Falcon has wings—as you surmised. One hour of flight brought me to Long Island. Less than half an hour by car; and I am here.

"My trusted servant waits me. He and I will conduct you, Commissioner, to the plane. You remember my valet, Hazzlett? He is my chief aide. It was wonderful how he and I slaughtered off Terry Rukes and his gang of mobsters. It was easy, for I, The Black Falcon, summoned them into the trap which I, Rowland Ransdale, had prepared for them."

THE BLACK FALCON paused as though the reminiscence pleased him. Weston and Cardona were silent as they heard the villain's explanation of the affray at the Garman Apartments.

"I came here," resumed The Black Falcon, with a scoffing chuckle, "because I knew that the police commissioner would never dream that any one would attack him in his own abode. I entered as Rowland Ransdale. Your men outside, Commissioner, had no suspicion of who I am.

"Do not, however, cherish the thought that I came alone. Others have entered through the side way. They followed when they heard a signal, given by my henchman Hazzlett, who is waiting. Men of crime, they are pleased by the thought of aiding The Black Falcon in his abduction of the police commissioner."

The eyes that looked through the black mask were evil. Weston and Cardona realized the insidious character of this supercriminal who dealt in murder as well as kidnapping. Both knew that The Black Falcon would readily shoot them dead; that he was sparing Weston's life only because the police commissioner would be a valuable prisoner.

"I announced myself to your servant," chuckled The Black Falcon. "When he returned to the anteroom, I was masked. The door was open to the corridor. Mobsmen had come at my soft whistle. They overpowered your man; they did not kill him. He will be a victim later on. He is lying, helpless, in a corner of your living room.

"My new minions think, like you, that I am Velvet Laffrey. So will all others, after your abduction, Commissioner. The final evidence is that letter"—The Black Falcon was pointing to the sheet that he had laid on the desk—"with another faint touch of Laffrey's fingers. Your servant must die; and so"—The Black Falcon was staring hard at Joe Cardona—"must this other man who knows my true identity."

Joe Cardona did not quail. Yet he saw the merciless glint in The Black Falcon's eye. The fiend's purpose was apparent. Cardona and Kempton were to be found dead in the wake of The Black Falcon's deed of abduction.

"It is more than you deserve," said The Black Falcon to Cardona. "In life, you have been a bungler. In death, you will be a hero. That letter with Velvet Laffrey's imprints will be discovered in your dead clutch. It will appear that you fought to restrain The Black Falcon."

A pause; then The Black Falcon's voice became an impatient growl.

"This is enough!" declared the supercrook. "Come, Weston. You are going with me. Hesitation will not avail you. My henchmen will rush in from the corridor when they hear my signal. That signal, tonight, will be a single shot. It will be a shot that delivers death!"

With his pronouncement, The Black Falcon aimed his gun at Joe Cardona. Commissioner Weston sat aghast. The fiend's finger rested on the trigger; his lips formed his vicious snarl.

Then came sudden rigidity.

THE BLACK FALCON did not budge a muscle as his eyes, staring beyond Joe Cardona, affixed themselves upon the doorway at the right.

Standing there was a figure clad in black. Blazing eyes peered from beneath the brim of a broad slouch hat. An automatic projected from a fist that seemed part of an inky-hued cloak.

Like a grim avenger from nowhere, this master of darkness had arrived to stay The Black Falcon's cruel attempt to murder Joe Cardona. There was no mistaking the identity of the unexpected visitant.

The Black Falcon's lips were fuming. His eyes were blinking behind the mask. The supercrook was staring at the weird avenger whom he had thought was in his power.

Rowland Ransdale, The Black Falcon, was facing the burning gaze of The Shadow! The death signal—the shot that the fiend was about to fire—remained withheld as The Black Falcon shrank from The Shadow's glare!

CHAPTER XX
THE FALCON'S FLIGHT

CONSTERNATION was evident in Rowland Ransdale's face. The visage of the millionaire mine owner was apparent now, in contrast to the scowl of The Black Falcon. Bewilderment had seized the supercrook.

Two hours before, Ransdale had left his house in the Catskills. His last act had been to make sure that Lamont Cranston was a hopeless prisoner. As The Black Falcon, the fiend had traveled hither in his fast plane.

It was impossible, The Black Falcon knew, that Lamont Cranston could have reached this spot in pursuit, even if he had escaped. The presence of The Shadow, therefore, seemed miraculous.

The Black Falcon was trapped. He dared not fire at Joe Cardona. Such a shot would mean his instant doom. The Shadow's mighty automatic was covering the crook.

Luck had served The Black Falcon before. It was to avail him now. Joe Cardona, facing The Black Falcon's revolver, was waiting unflinchingly for the shot of death. Cardona could not see The Shadow.

Nor did Commissioner Weston observe the eerie personage who had brought this strange denouement to the strained situation. Weston, staring toward The Black Falcon, saw only that for some reason the fierce crook had faltered. He could note the palsied tremor of Rowland Ransdale's hand. He saw the trigger finger waver in the trigger guard.

With a tigerlike spring, Ralph Weston leaped from the chair behind the desk and hurled his bulky form upon The Black Falcon. A man of courage, Weston had launched this attack to save Cardona's life, not caring what had caused The Black Falcon's momentary failure.

Up went The Black Falcon's arm. The crook staggered backward and fell beneath Commissioner Weston's powerful frame. It was

then that his luck availed him. As he collapsed hopelessly, the criminal was saved from The Shadow's aim, for his body was automatically shielded by the bulk of the police commissioner.

As a second stroke of fortune, the revolver remained in Rowland Ransdale's clutch. Though his arm was flung sidewise, the cornered crook managed to press the trigger. The bullet struck the wall; but the frantic purpose of the shot was gained. The Black Falcon had sent his signal!

JOE CARDONA was on his feet, yanking his revolver. Instinctively, the detective turned toward the door. He gasped as he saw The Shadow.

Joe Cardona understood, as he observed The Shadow's free hand pointing toward the floor. Nodding, Cardona leaped forward to aid Commissioner Weston in the capture of The Black Falcon.

The Shadow's pointing left hand moved inward. The black cloak swished as the left hand snatched forth a second automatic to match the one in the right. With the same motion, The Shadow whirled and faced out into the passage that led to Weston's living room.

The maneuver was well timed. Just as The Shadow aimed his automatics toward the dimly lighted living room, Pinkey Sardon appeared, armed at the head of his squad. The toughest gorilla in Manhattan was coming in response to The Black Falcon's signal.

Pinkey stopped short as he saw The Shadow. The gorilla's revolver was pointed. Reputed to be the swiftest shooter that the badlands had produced, Pinkey had his opportunity. Before him was The Shadow! The enemy of all crooks; the avenger who had dealt death to Rowdy Kirshing!

Pinkey and The Shadow were gun to gun. The gorilla, as he pressed finger to trigger, steadied his aim with almost instantaneous action. The movement, however, required the tiniest fraction of a second. It was the slightest sort of gesture, yet one which The Shadow did without.

A roar sounded through the passage. By a hairbreadth of time, The Shadow had beaten Pinkey Sardon to the shot. The terrific report came from the automatic that loomed from the avenger's right hand.

So close was the timing that The Shadow could not prevent Pinkey's shot. The mob leader's faltering finger twitched convulsively as Pinkey crumpled to the floor. The gorilla's drooping wrist, however, had not retained the aim. The bullet which Pinkey delivered in the throes of death, whistled past The Shadow's form.

Instantly, the black-garbed master sprang forward. His automatics boomed in quick succession as his keen eyes caught the glare of leveling revolvers, held by the mobsters who had stopped short to watch their leader collapse.

Roaring shots echoed in quick tattoo. Zimming bullets scorched through flesh and bone as The Shadow's metal found its mark in human targets. Screaming gangsters dived for shelter; others, dropping grimly, tried to fire at the weaving mass of blackness which surged upon them.

The Shadow's long arms were sweeping wide. The barks of his dread guns were timely. His keen eyes guided the aim to those mobsters who had sought to fight. Cursing men withered and useless revolvers dropped from loosening hands.

One mobster, alone, fired a shot that clipped a gap in the side brim of The Shadow's slouch hat. He was the last to meet The Shadow. A burst of flame almost in his face settled the venomous gunman. He sprawled headlong.

The others—they had fled for cover in the anteroom—had stopped in hopes of delivering a counterattack. But before they could plan an onslaught, The Shadow was upon them. Bursting flashes from the automatics sent the rogues scurrying through the corridor. As they fled in wild confusion, a terrifying burst of mockery overtook them.

The Shadow had reached the outer door. In tune with new bursts of the automatics, The Shadow delivered a weird, sinister laugh of triumph. The sardonic taunt rose to a crescendo; then broke. Shuddering echoes followed the din of gunfire. Gangsters, staggering down the stairway, kept on in their mad flight.

BACK in Weston's office, Joe Cardona was ready with his revolver. The police commissioner had yanked the gun from The Black Falcon's grasp. He had thrown it across the room. The crook seemed helpless in his clutch; and Cardona risked no fire.

Then came a swift turn. With a sidewise lunge, The Black Falcon hurled Weston backward. As the commissioner clutched for his enemy's throat, a swift fist swung in answer. The blow reached Weston's chin. The commissioner sank to the floor. The Black Falcon, rising, leaned against the wall.

His eyes, blurred by the twisted mask, spotted Joe Cardona. The tables were turned. The detective, grimly aiming his revolver, held the crook beneath control. Firing had died from without. Cardona was holding The Black Falcon alive.

The crook, weakly raising his arms as Cardona growled an order, seemed pitifully fagged. Joe yanked a pair of handcuffs from his pocket. He moved forward to thrust his revolver into the stomach of the man before him.

It was then that The Black Falcon made his break. With a frenzied leap to the right, he swung his left hand backward, in an attempt to block Cardona's aiming hand. The move was a lucky one. The Black Falcon's fist encountered the barrel of the revolver and knocked Cardona's aim astray.

As the detective swung to fire, The Black Falcon's right fist swung to action. The punch met Cardona's face. The detective flopped back against the desk and rolled to the floor.

While Cardona was groggily coming to his knees, The Black Falcon, weaponless, leaped for the side door of the room. He yanked the portal open and plunged into a hallway beyond.

Cardona fired. His quick shots shattered plaster from the walls of the passage through which The Black Falcon had fled. The bullets, hastily aimed, went wide. Cardona, stumbling to his feet, caught himself against the desk.

As the detective faltered, unable to take up the chase, a tall figure appeared at the front door of the office. The Shadow had returned. His keen eyes saw the chaos.

Commissioner Weston was slouched on the floor, his hand pressed to his chin. Joe Cardona was leaning back against the desk, trying to regain his sense of balance.

The opened door at the side of the room told its story. The Black Falcon had fled. Vital seconds had given him an opportunity to put good space between himself and any pursuers.

With a quick sweep, The Shadow crossed the room and headed through the passage. He reached a rear door of the apartment: one that opened on a fire tower. From the side street below came the roar of a departing motor. Shots followed. Policemen had arrived and had tried to prevent The Black Falcon's escape.

Swiftly, The Shadow descended to the street. Two uniformed men were at the curb. It was plain that The Black Falcon had eluded them. Joe Cardona had failed in the duty that The Shadow had entrusted to him. These men of the law had been too late to rectify the ace detective's error.

Swiftly, The Shadow merged with darkness. When he again came to light, he was more than a block away. A fleeting, evanescent form, he entered a trim coupé that was parked beside the curb.

The car headed downtown. Its objective, as it sped through traffic, was the Holland Tunnel. Beyond that tube lay the Newark airport.

The Black Falcon, fleeing to an unknown spot on Long Island, had taken to the air. The Shadow, with his knowledge of The Black Falcon's hidden lair, was off to intercept the supercrook before he reached his final goal!

CHAPTER XXI
WINGS OF THE NIGHT

A SWIFT plane was speeding northward. Lightless, its black wings were unseen against the clouded sky. A grim pilot was at the controls; beside him, a stalwart henchman. Rowland Ransdale, alias The Black Falcon, was fleeing with his minion, Hazzlett.

The ship was one which coupled speed with manageability. This combination was essential to The Black Falcon's needs, for the winged abductor had a habit of choosing rough and unkempt landing fields when he swooped to the earth.

Both The Black Falcon and his scowling aide realized that a swifter plane could overtake them, but they were relying on their start. Coming from Long Island, they had successfully dodged any police planes that were about; now, above the wooded mountain land, they were nearing their goal, an hour from New York.

Lights flickered from the plane. The Black Falcon eased the speed. Far below, a patch showed in the woods. It was The Black Falcon's abode, fourteen miles from the landing field by road; not more than half that distance by air.

A few minutes later, the plane was circling over the pastured clearing, which showed dull white among the trees. Floodlights glowed suddenly. A grim smile on his unmasked face, Rowland Ransdale, The Black Falcon, prepared for his final landing.

The plane reached its objective. It bumped along the rough ground straight toward the hangar, and came to a stop some fifty yards from that hidden building. As The Black Falcon clambered from his ship, two henchmen came rushing up.

Rowland Ransdale's face was steady as the supercrook gave his order. He paused as he spoke to gaze up toward the sky; then told his henchmen of his plans.

"Hazzlett and I are going to the house," he declared. "We shall return for you in about an hour. In the meantime, wait here. There is a chance that someone is on our trail. Be ready with the machine gun. Give them the works."

The henchmen growled in pleased fashion. Ransdale smiled. He motioned to Hazzlett. With the others aiding them, they warped the airplane to the hangar. Then Ransdale and his chief minion strode away to the spot where the sedan was parked.

AS they rode along the jouncy road, Ransdale, in his own voice, talked with Hazzlett. The Black Falcon's air was one of calm speculation.

"I don't know how Cranston could have gotten away," he declared. "He was here when we left; it seems impossible that he could have followed so quickly even if he did escape."

"Maybe we're running into trouble," observed Hazzlett uneasily. "If he broke loose, he could have raised hob at the place."

"No time for that," returned Ransdale, in a tone of surety. "We can take it for granted that he escaped by stealth. His quick trip to New York proves the fact. I am sure that he left without releasing the others."

"Why?"

"Because that would have meant an alarm—a fight—the danger of missing his chance to stop my abduction of the police commissioner. I can't understand it, Hazzlett! Something is wrong somewhere!"

"You mean—"

"How could Cranston have done so much in so short a time? Why didn't he call the police commissioner? How did he learn that I was going there? We have held Cranston prisoner—and Cranston is The Shadow!"

"Maybe," observed Hazzlett in a doubting tone, "you have been mistaken all along about Cranston—"

"That may be it," snarled Ransdale, in the style of The Black Falcon. "We'll know soon enough. When we get to the house."

A pause as the two rode on in silence. The sedan was traveling slowly along the turns in the rough road. Progress here was slow.

"We are not going back for our men," observed Ransdale, in a tone of decision. "Let them shift for themselves, Hazzlett. We have our own skins to look after."

Hazzlett seemed pleased by this decision.

"The game is over," resumed Ransdale, in a bitter tone. "We must say nothing to the men at the house. I, myself, shall kill our prisoners and leave their bodies in the cells. Then we can tell the crew that we are going back to the landing field. Our men at the house can hold the bag."

"We'll travel in the sedan?"

"Yes. Up to that secret hangar near Binghamton. We'll head for Canada in the monoplane. That will be the last seen of us, Hazzlett."

"It will be an easy getaway. Even if the police planes do find our landing field—"

"They won't find it tonight, Hazzlett. I didn't tell the commissioner where my place was located. It wasn't the police from whom I was hurrying."

"The Shadow?"

"Yes. He may be on our trail. Let him come. The only place that he can land his plane—if he has one—is on our field. They'll have the machine gun on him the minute that he lights—"

As the detective swung to fire, The Black Falcon's left fist swung to action.

"But what if he manages to get by with—"

"With the machine gun there? The best break he can get will be to clear off the ground before he steps out of his ship. He may be wise enough to do that, if they start to use the machine gun too soon. That will mean another landing place. More delay.

"Even if he should get clear"—Ransdale's tone was tense—"he will have to follow this course that we have taken. He has no car—even if he did have one, we have gained too good a start.

"Ten minutes will be all that we require at the house. Five to clear out my papers and money. Five to kill the prisoners while you are talking to our men upstairs. Then for our final getaway."

The gleaming headlights of the sedan cut a swath through the darkness of a turn. The entrance to Ransdale's secluded residence showed within the range of the glare. The Black Falcon swerved the car through the open gate. As the sedan pulled to a stop, a man appeared on the front steps of the gray stone house.

"It's Sharpless!" whispered Hazzlett, as he recognized one of Ransdale's henchmen. "You are right—nothing has happened here."

"Good," returned Ransdale, as he alighted from the car. Then, as he approached the steps, he called: "All well, Sharpless?"

"Yes, sir," responded the man on the steps.

"No trouble with the prisoners?" questioned Ransdale.

"All doors safely barred," came the reply.

"Say nothing about Cranston," whispered Ransdale. "Go down to the cellar, but don't touch the door of the room where we had him imprisoned. Bring all the men together—up to my room. I'll be there, packing the papers and the cash."

Hazzlett was still nodding when the pair reached the spot where Sharpless stood. They walked through the door; the waiting henchman followed. All was quiet in the clearing about Rowland Ransdale's hidden abode.

WHAT Ransdale had said to Hazzlett was true. The start that they had gained was valuable. A following plane, if it were headed hither, would have to choose the landing field fourteen miles away.

But had Rowland Ransdale remained outside his house; had he stared upward toward the darkened sky, he might have seen a phenomenon that would have brought him consternation. No sound came as a token from high above; only an amazing sight that marked the coming of a phantom being from the night.

Descending straight toward the clearing was an autogyro. The ship was coming from a high altitude. Its motor had been slowed until the sound was inaudible below. Sharp eyes from that strange machine of the sky had spotted the house of Rowland Ransdale. The same eyes had viewed the arrival of the sedan, betokened by the glare of the car's headlights.

Rowland Ransdale had never dreamed that his small clearing could serve as a landing field. The space in back of the stone house was less than sixty feet across. It was no more than a sloping patch of greensward.

Yet that was the spot that The Shadow had chosen. He had not taken his autogyro from the Newark airport without clear forethought. Traveling at maximum speed, he had followed on an average of nearly two miles a minute—almost the same pace set by Rowland Ransdale's plane.

But The Shadow, with his later start, had been forced to take the road travel into consequence. He had also perhaps considered the possibility of a fray at the landing field. He had chosen the one way by which he could either anticipate or duplicate the time of The Black Falcon's arrival at the house in the forest.

That was by a landing at the house itself. The autogyro, its four blades whirling above it like a horizontal windmill, was making a beautiful landing. Like a bird coming to earth, it descended into a crater-like space between the trees.

Settling with silent ease, The Shadow's ship came to rest upon the sloping green. Its shock absorbers took the brunt of the landing. The autogyro rolled forward a few short yards and stopped.

From the darkness of the strange machine stepped forth the shrouded figure of The Shadow. Blazing eyes turned upward. A soft laugh hissed from hidden lips as a light came on beyond the French doors of Rowland Ransdale's room.

The Shadow, mysterious avenger from the darkened sky of night, had arrived to settle scores with The Black Falcon!

CHAPTER XXII

THE REVELATION

ROWLAND RANSDALE was standing by his desk. Smoking his inevitable pipe, the fleeing crook was rapidly opening drawers and removing documents along with bundles of cash. Stationery that bore The Black Falcon's letterhead; special sheets of paper, a little box of blackened feathers—these were items what he was taking as mementos of his reign of crime.

On the desk beside him lay the black mask that he had drawn from his pocket. Ransdale's revolver was there also. The evil villain's eyes were gleaming; a fierce smile flickered on his lips. The Black Falcon, frustrated, had lost the patience that had characterized his criminal activities.

Thoughts of death were burning through Ransdale's thwarted brain. The fiend was contemplating what he considered now to be a pleasant prospect: the slaughter of those victims whom, until now, he had held for ransom.

As Ransdale paused in his activity, a curious stare came into the man's glaring eyes. Ransdale seemed to sense a presence in this room. He placed his right hand on the desk close beside his revolver, then turned to gaze behind him at the half-opened French doors.

The instant that Ransdale turned, those doors shot wide apart. The crook's hand was frozen. The sight that greeted his astonished gaze was one that petrified him. Standing in the opening was the same figure that had appeared at Weston's.

The Shadow!

A looming automatic was directed squarely between Rowland Ransdale's eyes. The crook's trembling fingers dared not approach the revolver that lay so close to them. A gesture of The Shadow's weapon was sufficient. Ransdale slowly raised his hands and stared fiercely at the weird intruder who had so silently entered.

It was then that Ransdale heard The Shadow's laugh. A sardonic taunt, it did not rise above a whisper; but its weird tones carried a note that chilled the evil man who caught its sound. The Black Falcon, at the end of his career of daring, had learned how fear felt!

THE SHADOW'S turn had come. Coldly, his whispered voice began to speak. The Shadow was using The Black Falcon's own tactics. Time and again, The Black Falcon had scoffed at his prospective victims. The Shadow's sneer was a just one.

"Rowland Ransdale!" The Shadow hissed the second name. "Your career of crime has ended. You are to pay the penalty for the murders that you have committed. Flight will not be yours.

"Your schemes were well planned, but they did not deceive me. From the outset, I knew that some such brain as yours was in back of this insidious game."

Ransdale, though trembling, was defiant. His evil face indicated that he doubted The Shadow's words. A laugh came from the lips that were hidden by the upturned collar of The Shadow's cloak.

"Fingerprints at Apprison's," sneered The Shadow. "Weston suspected them as fakes. It was the doorknob that convinced him. But to me, that knob was spurious. Its newness; its lacquer that kept the impressions safe—those were proof to me that you, The Black Falcon, had substituted it for the one that belonged there."

The Shadow approached the man before him.

Ransdale quaked as he tried to pierce the blackness that hid the master avenger's countenance. Sparkling eyes were all that he could see.

"I searched for Velvet Laffrey in the underworld," asserted The Shadow. "I searched for others also, and I found them. Terry Rukes—your henchman—slain at your own apartment. Others thought that The Black Falcon had failed. I suspected the truth!

"It was as Lamont Cranston that I visited the home of Elias Carthers. It was as Cranston that I visited you. At that time, I suspected evil strategy; your manner and your talk convinced me that you might be the criminal I sought. So I subtly offered facts that would make you know who I was—that I was The Shadow."

Again the sneering laugh. Ransdale's face was blank. The wretch was pitiful as he cowered and quailed before The Shadow.

"I talked to you as if I were Lamont Cranston. I paved the way for you to plan an abduction. I am not Lamont Cranston; but his features are ones that I have often adopted. The real Cranston had returned to his home; summoned by supposed business telegrams that I arranged. For when I play his part, even his friends and servants are deceived!

"Cranston is still your prisoner, in the cell below. So is my agent, Harry Vincent. I, however, received his report. The final notes, up to the time of his capture, came by wireless. That report brought me here"—The Shadow's whispered tones became slow and emphatic—"on the very night when you made your final plans.

"Through these opened windows I watched you. While you were gone, I entered and read your duplicate letter. I trailed Hazzlett in New York. I kept watch on Pinkey Sardon and his minions.

"That is how I reached Commissioner Weston's at the time you did. I had divined your purpose by that time. I entered ahead of you and was stationed in readiness. Had you sought to kill Kempton, Weston's servant, I would have slain you then. But you let him live—to be killed at a later time—which never came!"

With his left hand, The Shadow pointed to a telephone which lay on Ransdale's desk. As though in answer to a spoken command, Ransdale reached for the instrument. He lifted the receiver mechanically to his ear, awaiting The Shadow's orders.

"Call New York!" The Shadow's command was powerful. "Get Commissioner Weston on the wire. He is to receive another message from The Black Falcon!"

Rowland Ransdale, trembling, obeyed. Minutes

ticked by. The connection was completed.

"Speak!" ordained The Shadow. "Tell him where you are. Challenge him to come here and find you!"

"This is The Black Falcon," declared Ransdale, in a voice which seemed controlled by The Shadow's bidding. "I am at my stronghold. Fifteen miles from Cuthbury. In the Catskills. Come and capture me—"

"If you can!" prompted The Shadow in a sinister whisper.

"If you can!" gasped Ransdale into the telephone.

The receiver clicked on the hook. Rowland Ransdale faced The Shadow. For a moment, The Black Falcon's role had returned. Although at bay, Ransdale snarled a question.

"If you are not Cranston," he demanded, "who are you?"

"You shall learn!" The Shadow's tone was ominous. "You, Rowland Ransdale, shall see the face of The Shadow. It will be your deserved warning— you who call yourself The Black Falcon. For those who have seen the true face of The Shadow have never lived to recite their discovery!"

THE collar of the black cloak wavered as The Shadow's gloved left hand unfolded it. A frightened gasp came hollow from Rowland Ransdale's lips. The crook slumped as his bulging eyes viewed the countenance beneath the brim of the black slouch hat. As The Shadow's hand refastened the collar of the cloak, Rowland Ransdale slumped pitifully to the floor.

The man's face was ashen. A whispered laugh came from The Shadow's lips. Only The Shadow knew why the sight of his dread face had brought terror to this evil fiend who never before tonight had known fear.

The face of The Shadow! The face that was never seen except when disguised to represent some other countenance. Roland Ransdale had met The Shadow face to face. The Black Falcon, he who had terrorized the law, had lost all nerve when he had viewed the true visage of The Shadow!

Only brilliant eyes remained in view. They were burning eyes that surveyed the gasping shape of a man who had once thought himself invincible. Then, with sudden keenness, The Shadow's eyes were raised. Staring toward the door, they saw the barrier move.

The Shadow's automatic rose to aim as Hazzlett, a revolver in hand, appeared upon the threshold. The henchman, wondering what had kept his chief had come to investigate. Instead of Rowland Ransdale, Hazzlett had found The Shadow!

CHAPTER XXIII
THE HOODED FALCON

HAZZLETT had arrived expecting trouble. He had been awaiting Ransdale's call to bring the men upstairs. Hence, when he had flung the door open, Hazzlett was ready armed; behind him, on the stairs, were the others.

Keyed to excitement, Hazzlett acted on the instant. With a snarl as vicious as any that The Black Falcon had ever uttered, Ransdale's minion pressed finger to trigger of his upswinging gun.

As Hazzlett performed this deed, The Shadow made a double action. With a quick shift to the left, The Shadow executed the fadeaway maneuver which had made him an impossible target for hosts of gunmen. At the same instant, he pressed the trigger of his automatic.

The huge .45 declared itself with a terrific roar. The Shadow, in his shift, had not lost his aim. The speaking muzzle of the automatic was still on its desired objective—Hazzlett.

Directly following the spurt of flame from The Shadow's gun, Hazzlett pitched forward into Ransdale's room. The minion's arms sprawled crazily. With a convulsive effort, Hazzlett managed to gain his knees. He snapped the trigger of his revolver. The shot, unaimed, was futile. The effort was Hazzlett's last. Coughing blood, the evil servant of a vicious master, rolled dead upon the floor.

The men behind had glimpsed The Shadow. Like fiends, they sprang in through the wide doorway, to battle with this marksman who had edged away from view. Ransdale's henchmen had not yet learned their master's perfidy. They were out to slay the enemy who had dropped Hazzlett.

Revolvers spurted as wild shots echoed through the room. All were fired toward the spot where The Shadow had last been. Not one found its mark, for The Shadow, reaching the end wall of the room, had crouched in waiting. A second automatic had joined the first; now, as one of the four henchmen shouted his discovery of the foe, both hands performed their deadly work.

Thundering automatics belched hot lead into the ranks of the would-be rescuers. While return shots spattered wildly, The Shadow's guns completed their work. Rowland Ransdale's henchmen collapsed in pairs. They had come to slay The Shadow; they, in turn, had met their fate.

THE SHADOW'S tall form rose beside the wall. A weird laugh echoed from sinister lips. It was not a tone of mockery; rather was it a knell for these foolhardy minions who had served an evil and unrewarding master.

The Shadow's gaze turned toward the desk. Rowland Ransdale, aroused from his terror by the sound of gunfire, had regained his feet. With a wild gleam in his eyes, the supercrook pounced upon his revolver and aimed the weapon toward The Shadow.

The vicious leer of The Black Falcon was upon Ransdale's lips. Snarling, the criminal had gained the aim. His steadying hand was ready; but before his finger could press the trigger, the glint of The Shadow's eyes was full upon him.

Ransdale quavered. The venom of The Black Falcon remained traced upon his features, but his countenance was ashen. His hand began to shake as it pointed the revolver which it held. The steady grip that had enabled Ransdale to slay Terry Rukes as well as helpless victims, was failing in this dire emergency.

Rowland Ransdale had seen the face of The Shadow! That sight, he knew, had been his sentence of doom! The words of The Shadow, the power of the master fighter—all these came surging through Ransdale's brain as the fierce crook caught the burn of The Shadow's eyes.

Ransdale fired. The echo from his revolver seemed deafening in his ears. Then, from across the room, came a strident burst of mockery. Ransdale caught himself as he was sinking to the desk.

The face of The Shadow! Rowland Ransdale had seen it. His nerve had passed with that revelation. He, The Black Falcon, marksman extraordinary, had beaten The Shadow to a shot—and had missed.

With a wild cry, Ransdale aimed again. The fury of The Black Falcon was upon him. Hate blazed in his own eyes; hate that matched the mastery of The Shadow's gaze. This time Ransdale knew that he would not miss in his aim!

This shot would kill The Shadow—so Ransdale thought; and such might have been the outcome, had Ransdale fired. But The Shadow had allowed one lone opportunity. Ransdale's first shot was to be the last. The burst of flame that came from a trigger-pressed gun was a flash from The Shadow's left-hand automatic.

The Black Falcon had had his turn. This was The Shadow's. The gloved hand did not fail. Rowland Ransdale, the snarl still issuing from his lips, collapsed upon the desk. The revolver dropped from his nerveless fingers and clattered on the woodwork. It slid off and fell upon the floor. Rowland Ransdale followed a few seconds later. His clutching hands had weakened. His body sagged. It sprawled face-first upon the useless gun; then, with a last writhe, turned back upward on the floor.

Slowly, The Shadow advanced. His automatics went beneath his cloak. From beneath that garment he drew a cloth of black. As he held it in his right hand, he reached forward with his left and drew an object from the desk.

Stooping above the body of The Black Falcon, The Shadow hovered like a monster of the night. When he arose, the black cloak swished as The Shadow turned and swept across this room of carnage.

Past the body of Hazzlett just within the door; down the stairs and through the archway to the cellar. Such was The Shadow's course. The black-clad avenger reached the cellroom.

There, like a mammoth specter, his shadowed outline silhouetted on the floor, The Shadow unbarred the doors of the cells. His keen eyes, peering through an opening, spied Harry Vincent. In whispered tone, The Shadow hissed a summons to his agent.

HARRY leaped to his feet. Pounding to the cellroom, he saw The Shadow on the stairs. His chief was beckoning. Harry followed. Out into the night, Harry followed the course that was marked by The Shadow's hissing summons. Around the house, there Harry stopped short as he saw, with astounded eyes, the hulking, fan-topped shape of The Shadow's autogyro!

In response to an order from the ship, Harry clambered aboard and entered the rear seat. The blades above began their revolution. The rhythm of the motor increased. The autogyro started forward.

To Harry it seemed that the impetus would carry them into the wall of Ransdale's house. The gyro, however, performed a sudden revolution as The Shadow maneuvered it with remarkable skill. With gaining speed, the craft headed for the trees at the rear of the clearing. It took off with a perfect upward lift.

Climbing almost vertically, taking a spiral course as The Shadow, master pilot, handled the controls, the autogyro rose from among the trees. Harry, staring from the side, saw the gray walls and light-colored roof of the house as the building dropped away beneath.

Higher, with motor throbbing for the climb, the autogyro ascended into the night. This ship had dropped like a phantom craft from the sky when danger had beckoned. Now that The Shadow had accomplished his appointed mission, the roar of the motor needed no further muffling.

RANSDALE'S house was far below. Within the walls of The Black Falcon's lair, three men were making a startling discovery. Hubert Apprison, Elias Carthers, and Lamont Cranston formed a bewildered trio of freed investigators.

The prisoners had come forth to the cell room.

Finding the way clear, they had ascended to the ground floor and had taken the stairs to the second story. There, in the room where The Shadow had met The Black Falcon and his minions, they viewed the bodies that were lying on the floor.

"Look there!"

The others followed Hubert Apprison's pointing finger. By the desk lay the figure of a man. At a distance, the dead form appeared headless. As the three released prisoners approached, they saw that a black bag had been placed upon the head of the reclining corpse.

"The hood!" exclaimed Elias Carthers, with sudden understanding. "The hood! It means—The Black Falcon!"

"The hood?" questioned Hubert Apprison.

"Yes," explained Carthers. "The falcon, when captured, is kept hooded. Someone—to whom we owe our safety—has trapped The Black Falcon and has left this as his token!"

Stooping, Carthers seized the hood and drew it from the victim's head. The trio stared at the evil face that showed uncovered. Contorted lips formed a vicious leer, even in death. Above that lay the final evidence of The Black Falcon's identity. Covering the eyes was the black mask that had been upon the desk. The Shadow had placed it upon The Black Falcon's visage.

Lamont Cranston pulled away the mask. He named the man whose face he saw beneath. The rescued men remained staring at the death-stilled features of their abductor.

THOUSANDS of feet above, the autogyro poised as it turned to take a direct course. Harry Vincent, still staring downward, saw Rowland Ransdale's stone house as a toylike structure in a tiny patch among the trees.

As the thrumming of the motor paused, a weird sound came to Harry's ears. A chilling taunt of mocking triumph rose to an eerie pitch, then ended as the motor roared and the autogyro sped forward on its course.

The laugh of The Shadow! Victorious, it had pealed forth amid the heights from which The Black Falcon had so often swooped; through which the criminal of the skies had carried home his prey.

The echoes of that laugh persisted in Harry's ears, amid the thrumming of the motor. The laugh of The Shadow lingered as a parting jest from the master who had ended a fiend's career.

The Black Falcon's reign of crime was ended, doomed through The Shadow's might!

THE END

Coming in THE SHADOW Volume 6:

THE SHADOW'S JUSTICE

A wealthy man leaves a legacy to his son—a legacy that must be won through skill, perseverance and courage. It's an excellent test of the willingness of the young, adventurous son. But the father did not know of the evil being plotted in his own home, or that his bequest would put his son's life in danger! However, The Shadow knows! And, knowing, The Shadow acts, meting out his own brand of deadly justice!

Then, the superfiend called The Vulture acts as the cashier in a bizarre game of evil! Follow the trail of

THE BROKEN NAPOLEONS

as The Shadow battles an amazing master crook, and against circumstances that would spell doom to anyone else. Don't miss these two book-length novels in the next thrilling volume of

Only $12.95. Ask your bookseller to reserve your copy now!

SPOTLIGHT on THE SHADOW
by Will Murray

The mysteries of The Shadow were many. Who was he? Where did he come from? What motivated him to combat evil?

Walter Gibson only hinted at such secrets during the formative years of The Shadow's campaign against crime. The Dark Avenger played many roles and wore multiple faces. But his deepest secret was not his true identity, which was finally revealed, but what lay concealed beneath the crimson collar of that flowing black cloak.

In the initial novel *The Living Shadow,* "Maxwell Grant" dropped a fascinating hint. An underworld crook known only as Spotter recounts the story:

> "Then, out of nothin', comes this big black shadow. It was a man, all right—but it didn't look human. It wraps around Birdie and shoots him with his own rod. He flops in the street, and The Shadow moves right across without a noise, and that was the last we seen of it."
>
> "That's The Shadow, all right," declared English Johnny. "I was never quite sure he was real."
>
> "I seen The Shadow again,"said Spotter eagerly. "Down by the Pink Rat. This time I looked for his face. I saw nothing but a piece of white that looked like a bandage. Maybe The Shadow ain't got no face to speak of. Looked like the bandage hid somethin' in back. There was a young guy once who the crooks was afraid of—he was a famous spy in the War, and they say he was wounded over in France—wounded in the face. I think The Shadow is this guy come back—maybe he—"

Seven novels later, this mystery is addressed again when the Master of Darkness confronts the bloody terrorist known as The Black Master. The Shadow is trapped:

> The curtains began to close, forming a smaller space in the center of the room. The blue lights flickered and The Shadow's form wavered.
>
> His mind could resist all that the enemy had to offer, but his physical being could not withstand the currents that swept through his frame. He stood numbed and powerless. The curtains were close about him.

The blurred white face had vanished. Only a black shape remained, outlined against the front of the curtain. An arm came from the curtain. It reached forward and plucked the black hat from The Shadow's head.

> A low sound of amazement came from the curtain when the face of The Shadow was revealed.
>
> "The secret of The Shadow," came the monotonous voice. "At last it is understood! The man of many faces—with no face of his own!"

Not long after, in the classic 1933 adventure known as *The Shadow's Shadow,* the face of the Black Eagle—as the Knight of Darkness had been called during his wartime spy career—is once more revealed to a mortal foe:

> Zubian's snarl became a cry of triumph as he saw The Shadow roll upon the floor. The slouch hat was carried away by the bullet. The head of The Shadow lay obscure beneath the folds of the cloak.
>
> In that wild moment, Zubian thought that he had slain his enemy. He did not realize that The Shadow's plunge had enabled him to escape the shot; that the black hat had alone received the bullet.
>
> Zubian was aiming to fire further shots, to make sure of The Shadow's death; but he never accomplished that final purpose.
>
> An arm swept upward from the floor. Behind it came those glowing eyes; but it was not the eyes that stopped Felix Zubian. He was staring into the face of The Shadow—not the disguised features of Lamont Cranston or Henry Arnaud, but the visage of The Shadow himself!
>
> What Zubian saw there; what expression on The Shadow's countenance made even that fiendish villain gasp in horror; no one could ever know. For Felix Zubian knew his last moment of life in that fateful instant.
>
> His trembling finger faltered on the trigger of his gun. The Shadow's unfailing hand did not yield. The last shot that was fired on that night came from The Shadow's automatic.

A similar scene graces this volume's lead novel *The Black Falcon.* Wisely, Walter Gibson did not describe what these men beheld. He was trying to keep his readers guessing. But after *The Black Falcon,* all references to this grisly aspect of The Shadow's murky past were dropped.

Was The Shadow disfigured? Did this motivate his actions? Was his threatening laugh a sign of a man tormented in mind and body?

Walter Gibson never fully explained these mysterious events. At least, not in the pages of *The Shadow Magazine.* In 1975, he revealed his thinking. "It wasn't too long after the War that The Shadow started," Gibson recalled. "It was ten years after. There had been war aces, and things of that sort, and so the idea [was] giving him a past with the things he had done over in Germany. That he could have been injured. And there's almost a nebulous history about him."

Many veterans of the First World War returned with horrific facial injuries. Gibson did not deny the possibility that The Shadow had at some point had his face surgically repaired.

"That was more or less hinted at," he revealed. "That he had plastic surgery, or something. And if he just took the [collar] away, it would look weird, almost skeletonish. But I never went into it because I didn't like to get too much on the gruesome side. It was one of those things that we didn't find any reason to go ahead with."

Instead of delving further, Gibson preferred to leave the answer to the imagination. "The idea was to stir the reader up," he confessed. "I mean, get the reader wondering. It accomplished this very aim. I had sort of a metaphysical answer for it; which could have been that he had them see something strangely gruesome or weird, that almost hypnotized them. But I never had reason to go into a lot of details about it. I just let it hang a bit."

The Shadow stories selected for this Nostalgia Ventures volume represent a stark contrast.

In Walter Gibson's approach to his Shadow novels, the wizard of pulp illusions prided himself on not falling into formula writing. Every Shadow story was crafted in response to the specific demands of the plot. If he were writing an underworld thriller like *Gangdom's Doom,* Gibson wrote blazing action. If the tone was gothic suspense, as in *The Ghost of the Manor,* he focused on mood and mystery. When the villain chosen to challenge the Master of Darkness was a superfoe like The Cobra, "Maxwell Grant" bore down on the melodrama. With a traditional tale of crime and detection like *Murder Every Hour,* Gibson adhered to the rules of the formal mystery.

The Shadow Magazine was launched during a period of transition in what Frank Gruber called the "Pulp Jungle." The Stock Market Crash of 1929 and the resulting Depression were already flattening magazine sales. Gangster heroes had been all the rage during those roaring Prohibition times. Now they were on their way out. The American public had become sickened by the wave of hoodlum violence that had overtaken its greatest cities. Corruption infiltrated the police and the political establishment. "Crime Must Go!" became a national catchphrase. Calls to repeal the Volstead Act—which banned all sales and consumption of alcohol and so opened the door for organized crime's bootleg beer and liquor "speakeasies"—were growing stronger.

These were the circumstances that forced the Department of Justice to organize the F.B.I. to combat lawless forces local police departments were unable or unwilling to confront. In Chicago, a city virtually in the octopus grip of organized crime, Eliot Ness and his "Untouchables" were closing in on mob boss Al "Scarface" Capone, who had been declared Public Enemy Number One by that city's Crime Commission.

The day before the first issue of *The Shadow* landed on newsstands, George E. Worthington of the Mayor's Commission on Crime Prevention warned that "Conditions are ideal in New York for the rise of a super-criminal who will organize the city's underworld after the manner of Al Capone in Chicago." He cited Manhattan's ubiquitous speakeasies and "hideaway nightclubs" as the breeding grounds for organized crime.

Into these dark dens of iniquity, a new power was about to plunge. At least in the pages of *The Shadow Magazine*. Mythical dives like the Black Ship, the Pink Rat, and the Club Cadiz were soon to quake to his shuddering laugh, their rafters splintered by mortal lead, the shadowy hoods who inhabited them driven back into the shadows that spawned them by a greater and more terrifying Shadow.

Audiences were also becoming bored with the cliched amateur criminologists who had dominated the Roaring 20s mystery genre as well. At home investigating murder in the genteel mansions of the wealthy and powerful, they were not up to the brutal challenge of the underworld. The rising tide of lawlessness required a hero who, when faced with bursts of tommy-gun lead, would shoot back—and shoot to kill.

The "hard-boiled" approach exemplified by Dashiell Hammett and Carroll John Daly in the pages of *Black Mask* magazine kept gaining ground. Tough times needed heroes as tough as their vicious opponents. Pulp magazine editors started searching for new approaches. They began asking writers for stories of movie-style "super-action" or "ultra-mystery," which one pulp agent described as "bordering on the weird." The so-called "weird menace" pulp sub-genre was slowly emerging.

Walter Gibson's cloaked avenger combined all these new styles. The Shadow was as drawn to investigating a rumored haunted house as he was cleaning out an underworld den with his unerring .45 automatics. Colorful supervillains were as much his prey as terrorists and secret spy rings. Serial murderers were especially the Dark Avenger's meat. He slew them by the score.

As Gibson himself once wrote, "Almost any situation involving crime could be adapted to The Shadow's purposes; hence the novels ran the gamut from forthright 'whodunit' plots to forays into the field of science fiction."

The Black Falcon is a classic example of the formative Shadow story wherein mystery, suspense and a formidable mastermind were woven together to create a satisfying tale. Here Gibson depicts the early "mysterioso" Master of Darkness who is a gun-punishing terror to the Underworld and whose face cannot be looked upon except upon penalty of death. And another strong assertion that somewhere the true Lamont Cranston is roaming the world while a shadowy impersonator

occupies his New Jersey mansion reminds readers not to become too comfortable with The Shadow's frequent appearances as the millionaire world traveler. One day he may unmask for real.

By contrast, *The Salamanders* is a radical departure from Walter Gibson's usual approaches to storytelling. From the beginning, Street & Smith was surprised by the sales success of *The Shadow Magazine*. In 1932—the worst year of the Depression—it was selling 360,000 per month. When they stepped up the frequency to twice-a-month, sales leveled off at an amazing 300,000 per issue. Yet the company projected that such sales success would be good for only five years.

At the end of 1935, after Gibson had produced over 100 Shadow novels, sales started sagging and the competition, which included *The Phantom Detective* and *The Spider,* began to bite into the loyal *Shadow* audience.

After a typical story called *The Yellow Door*— in which The Shadow virtually decimated New York's ratty underworld—editor John L. Nanovic and S&S Business Manager Henry W. Ralston sat "Maxwell Grant" down to plot new directions. It was time to retool. Gibson explained the situation this way:

> Increasing competition had led to new trends in the character magazine field. Instead of building up to some great menace, then unravelling it and defeating it, writers were plunging into a full-blown horror that called for immediate demolition. Injecting stories of this type into The Shadow series seemed advisable if only as a matter of expediency.

This was exactly the approach used on *The Spider,* a particularly crazed Shadow clone. Now it was Gibson's turn to take back some of his own borrowed thunder. The first of these new experimental stories was *The Salamanders*. It's remarkable because Maxwell Grant completely dispensed with his trademark atmospheric opening and other time-tested devices. Here, a new brand of criminal arsonist is torching Manhattan, the police are helpless, and The Shadow rises up to wage withering war against this vicious gang.

Operating virtually alone, the Knight of Darkness faces an unremitting succession of fiery perils and death traps in this astounding episode—and once more Walter Gibson proved himself to be a true pulp virtuoso.

The Salamanders was followed by two other format-busting efforts, *The Man from Shanghai* and *City of Doom,* which brought back the soundly-defeated Voodoo Master. This electrifying rematch is scheduled for an upcoming Nostalgia Ventures *Shadow*

The
Shadow

All the world knows of The Shadow and his astounding deeds against the menace of crookdom. Wherever crime is known; wherever justice seeks to rule, there the deeds of this master of the night, this weird creature of blackness, are common knowledge.

His source unknown to the public, nevertheless, his prowess is feared by the underworld. He works as a lone hand, yet he has able aides in Harry Vincent, a presentable young man who can make himself at home anywhere; Burbank, who serves as communications contact for all the agents; Clyde Burke, reporter on the *Classic;* Cliff Marsland, who served a term in prison for a crime he did not commit and whose innocence was known only to The Shadow. Marsland, rather than show that innocence, was willing to work for The Shadow as a branded crook, for The Shadow had rescued him from death in the past. Mann, the calm-looking broker, is another link in The Shadow's small but compact army of crime-battlers.

The Shadow himself assumes the guise of Lamont Cranston, Henry Arnaud, or "Fritz," the janitor at police headquarters, whenever necessary. As Cranston he hobnobs with the police commissioner; as Fritz, he learns what Joe Cardona is doing. And he uses this knowledge to coordinate all efforts so that crime might be punished.

Other agents are at The Shadow's call, and various means which only this dark master of the night can wield, are used by him. He battles crime with thrills and chills, and smoking automatics. Let him thrill you in these tales, gathered from his private annals. Join with The Shadow to end crime.

Twice a Month      *10 Cents a Copy*

At Your News Stand!

ON THE AIR!   **ON THE SCREEN!**

—Adapted from the original 1930s Street & Smith house advertisement

The Salamanders

In dead of night a flaming monster rears its drooling head and bellows forth its challenge with searing breath! It was a terrible menace The Shadow sought to overcome as he went forth to combat the dragon of Fire!

A Complete Book-length Novel from the Private Annals of The Shadow, as told to

Maxwell Grant

CHAPTER I
FIRE OF DOOM

"FIRE! Fire!"

The shouts rose hoarsely on the midnight air. The glare of rising flames showed wild-eyed men as they dashed to spread the alarm.

Madness had gripped the town of Riverport; excitement of a sort that the little Southern city had never before known. The crackling blaze that had come into sudden life was a threat that promised great disaster.

The fire had started in the Capitol Hotel—the principal structure that adorned the main street of Riverport. The blaze had arisen like a living monster coming out of hiding.

A burst of flame; smoke pouring bodily through ground-floor windows; then demonish tongues of fire, lapping upward, crackling on to fury.

The Capitol Hotel was a firetrap.

"Fire!"

Faces were answering the shouts. White faces peered from upstairs windows. Staring eyes saw the flickering reflections of the flames. Faces disappeared from sight. Occupants of the hotel were hastily preparing for escape.

The wail of a fire siren split the night air. The alarm had been given. The clanging of bells told that Riverport's fire engines were emerging to fight the flames. Those engines were coming to a hopeless task. Nothing could stop that fire. The flimsy, wooden walls of the old frame hotel were perfect fuel for the devouring flames.

Within the burning building, commotion reigned. Men were dashing about, pounding upon doors, shouting through corridors. Their one hope was to arouse their fellow guests, then make a dash for safety. There was no time to linger.

Nevertheless, in all that bedlam, there was one man who acted with calmness. He was the occupant of Room 408. His name was Harry Vincent. Aroused by a hammering upon his door, Harry had shouted his response. Out of bed, he was donning his clothes by the light of the fire that other buildings reflected through his window.

There was a reason for this man's precision, his ability to avoid the panic that had overtaken others. Harry Vincent was an agent of The Shadow. He was a man trained to remain calm in the face of danger.

Though he knew that speed was necessary, Harry had other thoughts than those of escape. He was remembering the mission that had brought him to the city of Riverport, to register at the Capitol Hotel.

Chester Woldorf.

THE name drummed through Harry's brain, more vividly than the clanging of bells, or the wailing of the shrieking siren. Woldorf was the cause of Harry's presence here. Like Harry, Woldorf was a guest at the Capitol Hotel.

Harry had seen Woldorf in the lobby last night. He knew the man's room number: 411, almost across the hall from Harry's own room. Woldorf had retired at eleven o'clock. He had left a call for seven in the morning. Harry had left a call for the same hour.

Harry had guessed that Woldorf would take the eight o'clock train to New York. It had been Harry's plan to do the same. Woldorf, for some reason not yet determined, was a man who feared a threat.

That fact had been learned by The Shadow.

Threats indicated crime; The Shadow, always at war with men of evil, had delegated Harry to take up Woldorf's trail.

Bells were clanging from the street below. Water from fire hoses was fizzing uselessly, drowned by the increasing crackle of the flames. The light of the fire had become a ghoulish, crimson glow. The glare outlined Harry Vincent as he yanked open the door of his room.

Dressed, Harry was ready for departure. An overwhelming cloud of blackish smoke greeted him in the corridor. Harry was prepared for it. Burying his face in the bend of his elbow, he groped his way across the hall. His free hand found the knob of Woldorf's door.

Smoke had cleared partially, thanks to the draft created when Harry had opened his own door. The flames had not reached this floor. There was time to make sure that Woldorf had heard the alarm. Harry pounded furiously upon the door of Room 411.

There was no response. Smoke thickened as it floated along the corridor. Holding his breath, Harry backed away, then launched himself like a battering ram against the door of Woldorf's room. Shoulder first, he splintered the rickety barrier. Stumbling, Harry caught himself before he sprawled upon the floor.

Smoke had followed Harry's charge. Clutching like a shroud of doom, it was filling Woldorf's room. The opened window sucked smoke outward. Flickering flame light became dim, but the glow remained enough for Harry to view the room. Steadied by the broken door, The Shadow's agent gazed in horror.

On the floor, beside the bed, lay an upturned figure clad in pajamas. Harry saw a pale face, with lips half opened, fishlike beneath a droopy mustache. Below was a mass of crimson, splotched and streaked across the front of Woldorf's pajama jacket.

That blotted mass of crimson was Chester Woldorf's lifeblood. The man had been stabbed in the heart!

A CRACKLING drilled Harry's numbed brain. Yellowish flicker weaved across the inner walls of the room. From somewhere came the muffled crash of falling beams. Harry turned about toward the corridor.

The fire had reached this floor. Brief minutes would make the room a trap. There was no aid for Woldorf—no time to search for clues. Harry had gained enough. He had learned what some assassin had sought to cover: namely, that Chester Woldorf had been murdered before the fire had begun in the Capitol Hotel.

Springing from the room, Harry chose a direction away from the flames. Smoke had lessened. Though he was choking, Harry knew that he would be safe if he could reach a stairway or a fire escape.

Smoke destroyed the lighting effect of the flames. It was only by pressing his hand along the wall that Harry found the stairway he wanted.

Harry stumbled as he struck the first steps. He caught himself against a rail beside the heated wall. A fist clamped his arm; he heard a gasped voice beside him:

"Steady, friend. Take it easy. We'll get out this way."

Harry coughed his thanks. He turned his head as they descended. The flickering flame light from a stairway window showed the features of the man whom he had encountered. Harry took the fellow for another guest who had blundered toward this path to safety.

The man on the stairway was sallow of countenance. His hair was dark; his eyes, bulging, carried a blackish glitter. Seeing the man's profile, Harry noted a solid, outthrust jaw.

As the man's face turned and grinned toward him, Harry observed a hardness of the lips that was matched even by the wrinkles of the furrowed forehead.

"We'll make it."

The hard-faced man spoke raspily, as they reached a landing and continued downward.

"Easily," returned Harry. "The smoke has thinned. We are almost to the second floor."

"We're there. Keep your head down. it's going to be smoky the rest of the way."

The hard-faced man was right. He and Harry continued their descent blindly, clutching to the rail. Harry took a false step as he reached the bottom. His heel clanked stone. He knew that he had struck a side exit on the ground floor of the hotel.

Blinking in the smoke, he saw his companion. Ruddy light from the interior of the burning hotel showed the hard-faced man stumbling toward another flight of steps.

"Hold it!" coughed Harry. He sprang across to block off his companion. "Don't go any farther! Those steps lead down into the basement!"

The hard-faced man no longer wavered. He straightened. His grin was livid as he saw Harry, arms outstretched, at the very top of the stone steps. A hoarse gasp came from Harry's lips. At that instant, Harry knew who this man must be.

The hard-faced man was the murderer of Chester Woldorf!

Harry's cry told what he knew. It was all that the hard-faced man wanted. Before Harry could bring his arms up, his leering companion swung a tough, swift fist. The punch clipped Harry's jaw.

WITHOUT an outcry, The Shadow's agent tumbled backward. Slugged clear of the top step, he went tumbling, rolling to the bottom of the stone stairs.

Leering, the hard-faced man saw the final crash. Rolling over twice, Harry Vincent lay still and helpless, deep in the basement of the doomed hotel.

Smoke enveloped the prone body. The hard-faced man turned about. As he stumbled toward the exit, it was wrenched open. Rescuers from outside grabbed the murderer and helped him to the outside air. Coughing, two firemen clattered inward and stared through thickening smoke.

"See if there's any others," ordered one. "Maybe down those steps—"

"There's nobody there. That's the basement."

Smoke had totally obscured Harry Vincent's unconscious form. The opening of the outside door had brought the smoke upward. Peering through the dense smoke, the firemen saw nothing. They stood, shouting at the exit. They heard no answering calls. While they waited, the finish came.

Fire crackled wildly from above. Walls trembled. Beams burst with a roar. Downward, a flaming mass, came the whole interior of the old hotel. As the firemen leaped to outside safety, the walls crumbled.

From a blazing framework, the hotel was transformed into a pitlike furnace, where flames rose rampant and sparks soared high into the night.

The bed of that furnace was the basement where Harry Vincent had sprawled. No human being could have lain there and survived.

Crushing timbers, ablaze from end to end; masses of flaming woodwork; an entire ruin that crackled anew like a mammoth bonfire—such was the remains of the old hotel.

Survivors had scattered. Other buildings were ablaze. The fire had reached an office building; it had swept to a garage in back of the hotel. Automobiles were being removed by frenzied owners. Puffs of flame formed twenty-foot torches as gasoline tanks ignited.

Firemen were everywhere, working like madmen to save other buildings. Riverport's small police force was on hand. Tumult reigned as the holocaust continued. Volunteers were joining in the fight against the flames.

The ruins of the Capitol Hotel were forgotten by all men except one. He was the hard-faced murderer, the last to grope his own way out from the interior of the hotel fire, alive. A block away, he was standing beside an automobile. His face showed an evil gloat, his dark eyes surveyed the spreading flames.

The hard-faced man was pleased. He had slain Chester Woldorf. He had removed Harry Vincent—the only man who had learned that Woldorf was murdered. All evidence of crime lay buried in that fire-seethed pit that had once been topped by the old Capitol Hotel.

The murderer's leer showed that he expected no reckoning. In that, the gloating killer was to find himself mistaken.

Crime would soon receive its challenge from The Shadow.

CHAPTER II
THE LONE TRAIL

SMOLDERING ruins marked the business section of Riverport. The spreading hotel fire had not been curbed until dawn. Twelve hours more had passed; at last the fiery pit had cooled sufficiently for searchers to approach it.

Just outside the fire-devastated area was an undertaker's establishment that had been called into service as a morgue. There, searchers were bringing whatever objects appeared to be human remains.

They had made few finds. The principal exhibit at the morgue was a typewritten list of guests who had been at the hotel.

This list had been prepared by a hotel clerk who had a good memory. The hotel register had been lost in the fire. One clerk, who had gone off duty earlier, had perished in the blaze. As near as could be guessed, there had been about a dozen victims. The names of the survivors had been checked with a red pencil. The other names stood barren on the list.

Among the persons who studied the list of names that afternoon was a tall, calm-faced stranger who had arrived at Riverport on the later afternoon train. Though distinctive in appearance, he had attracted but little attention, for his quiet manner rendered him inconspicuous.

This arrival was The Shadow.

In New York, The Shadow had read of the holocaust at Riverport. There had been no word from Harry Vincent. Though the newspapers had classed the fire as accidental, The Shadow was sure that it had been designed.

Two names—unchecked in red—showed on the list to prove The Shadow's belief.

One was the name of Chester Woldorf. Though the public did not know the fact, Woldorf had been a man of considerable wealth—a shrewd speculator who had kept his affairs strictly to himself.

Woldorf had moved out of sight some months ago, to bob up at intervals in unexpected places. He had shown by his actions that he feared some menace. That was why The Shadow had decided to learn more about him.

The other name was that of Harry Vincent.

Fire had struck the hotel where Woldorf was located. That, in itself, was significant; yet The Shadow could concede that Woldorf might have perished through an accident. But with Harry also named on the death list, the aspect changed.

Harry, alert and on duty, ready for any emergency that might arise, would have learned of the fire soon enough to leave the doomed hotel.

THERE was only one answer. Something had happened to Woldorf. Harry had investigated. He had met with trouble before he left the hotel.

Walking from the morgue, The Shadow approached the ruins of the hotel. A small group of men were clustered at one corner. Their discussion told that they were officials who had taken charge of the search. The Shadow paused close by the cluster. Unnoticed in the settling dusk, he listened to the conversation.

"Some of the victims may have blundered into the basement," one man was saying. "A couple of firemen told me they found one fellow who nearly stumbled down there."

"That sounds likely," came the comment, "except that there haven't been many human remains picked up."

"There won't be. That fire lasted long enough to burn them to a frazzle. It was hot enough inside that fire to melt that old safe that was in the hotel!"

"Who says that? A safe won't melt!"

"This one must have. There's no sign of it. Nobody could have lugged it away."

"What was in it? Anything important?"

"No. Old Millick, who owns the hotel, says the safe didn't count for much. It wasn't often that folks put things there while stopping at the hotel."

The speakers moved away. The Shadow gained an immediate deduction. One hotel clerk had survived the fire, to give from memory, the names of registered guests. The inclusion of Woldorf's name was proof of that clerk's honesty.

But there had been a second clerk—off duty— who had presumably died in the blaze. It was possible that Woldorf had given the dead clerk valuables for deposit in the hotel safe. To The Shadow, the absence of a safe amid the ruins was a matter of high importance.

Could that safe have been removed during the fire?

The Shadow's answer was yes. His decision, however, was modified to suit the circumstances. The safe could not have been carried away openly. It must have been removed in some secret fashion.

STARING across the ruins of the hotel, The Shadow saw the grayish-white outline of other crumbled walls. They represented the garage that had adjoined the Capitol Hotel. Skirting the smoldering pit, The Shadow reached the site of the garage.

Between the hotel and garage was an elongated pit, half filled with debris. A man in overalls was poking about with a long stick, dislodging chunks of charred wood and stone.

The Shadow approached the man and spoke an affable greeting. When the man looked up, The Shadow made a casual inquiry.

"Was this the storage tank," he questioned, "where they kept the gasoline for the garage?"

The searcher shook his head.

"The storage tank was up there, sir," he replied, pointing to the remains of the garage. "This was the cellar of an old annex that used to run back from the hotel. They tore it down a couple of years ago."

"And left the cellar covered over?"

"Yes, sir. 'Twouldn't have done for gasoline storage. Too close to the hotel. Maybe it wouldn't have mattered much, though. The hotel burnt like a tinderbox as it was."

In the dusk, the man noted that The Shadow was well dressed. He looked like a stranger who might have been a guest at the burned hotel. The man questioned:

"You had a car, sir? In the garage?"

The Shadow nodded.

"Maybe it was saved, sir," informed the man in a hopeful tone. "You'd better inquire down at the Southern Garage, just past the depot. That's where they took what cars they could."

The Shadow headed for the Southern Garage. Strolling toward that destination, he checked his new information. The old cellar in back of the Capitol Hotel had existed as an unseen route from the hotel to its garage. Through that underground passage, men could have easily carried the missing safe.

To do so, they would have been forced to dare the flames. A dangerous task; one so formidable that it seemed almost impossible. The hotel had burned with amazing rapidity; and the interval of action had, therefore, been brief. These facts pointed definitely to a scheduled fire. They were bringing The Shadow along a trail that showed crime.

ARRIVING at the Southern Garage, The Shadow entered to find a crowded floor. Cars were jammed into every foot of space. No attendants were about. The Shadow pressed his way between crammed automobiles and found an office.

There, a grimy-faced man was seated at a bat-tered desk, going over account books. He looked up as The Shadow entered.

"Good afternoon," greeted The Shadow, quietly. "You are the manager here?"

"Yes, sir."

"I came for my coupé," remarked The Shadow. "It was brought here from the garage at the Capitol Hotel."

"You were in the fire, sir?"

The Shadow made no response to the manager's question. Instead, he merely continued his statement.

"Unfortunately," he said, "I no longer have the owner's card. Of course, I can identify the car. It was a green coupé, with a New York license—"

"I know the car, sir. It's right inside the front door. You can drive it out without any trouble—"

The car in question was Harry Vincent's. It actually belonged to The Shadow; hence his statements were correct. The garage manager took them at their face value. Riverport was a town where most men were accepted at their word.

The manager accompanied The Shadow from the office. As they pressed their way between stored cars, The Shadow made a quiet comment.

"Odd that you have no trucks stored here."

The garage manager turned quickly. He had reached the side of Harry's coupé; an overhead electric bulb showed a troubled look on the man's face.

"Why did you say that, sir?"

"For no special reason," replied The Shadow. "I suppose that few trucks choose the route through Riverport?"

"There was a truck here," declared the manager, biting at his lip. "It came from the burned hotel garage last night. The men who brought it wanted storage here; I told them that there was no space. They kept the truck outdoors until early this morning."

"And then?"

The Shadow's query was impressive. Almost in spite of himself, the garage manager answered. His tone was cautious.

"I overheard one of the truckmen making a telephone call," he stated. "He was in my office, without permission. He was telling someone that he would bring the truck on to Westhampton, about fifty miles from here.

"He was arranging storage at Westhampton, sir. To keep the truck there all day, in a garage. He said something about driving on to New York tonight. It sounded like they didn't want that truck to be seen by day. Right after that, the truck left here. It wasn't daylight; they had time to reach Westhampton before dawn. Maybe I'm suspicious, sir, but—"

A massive monkey wrench in his clutch, the hoodlum had delivered a vicious swing for the garage manager's head.

With an amazing spring, The Shadow leaped into action. Coming from the front of the coupé, he interrupted the garage man with a wide, swinging left arm, that sent the astonished fellow sprawling to the running board of Harry's car.

His right hand jabbing upward, The Shadow

stopped a swinging arm that was coming downward. A huge, sweatered thug had sprung from behind a parked car.

A MASSIVE monkey wrench in his clutch, the hoodlum had delivered a vicious swing for the garage manager's head. Only The Shadow's swift intervention had prevented the crushing blow. With one stroke, The Shadow had hurled the garage manager from the path of the deadly bludgeon, had caught the thug's arm in the middle of its drive.

The attacker writhed. With a harsh oath, he wrested his sweatered arm free and took a sweeping sidewise swing at The Shadow's head. The wrench whisked space. Dropping, The Shadow ducked the sweep by a clear inch.

Bobbing up, he drove a hard fist straight across the thug's arm before the attacker could recover and ward off the punch.

Knuckles landed just beneath the thug's chin. An ugly gargle told how deep The Shadow's fist had driven into the attacker's windpipe. The thug thudded floorward, his head cracking against the coupé's bumper.

The garage manager came to his feet and blinked. The Shadow was stepping aboard the coupé; the thug was lying senseless on the stone floor.

"Inform your local authorities," ordered The Shadow, quietly. "You will have ample time. That fellow will not recover within the next fifteen minutes."

"Yes, sir."

"Say nothing about the truck that went to Westhampton." The Shadow pressed the coupé's starter as he spoke. "I shall investigate the matter."

"I understand."

The garage manager was impressed by the hawk-visaged stranger who had saved him from a murderer. He thought that The Shadow must be a Federal agent, who had trailed the missing truck to Riverport. He saw no connection between the hotel fire and the truck.

The coupé rolled from the garage. It swung toward the road that led to Westhampton. The garage manager scurried forth and dashed toward the local police station, which was less than two blocks away.

AN approaching pedestrian had stopped short when he saw the coupé pull from the garage. Lost in the dusk, this arrival watched the taillight twinkle as The Shadow turned the corner toward the Westhampton road. Still watching, the pedestrian spied the garage manager's hasty exit.

With a growl, the man from the dusk hurried into the garage. Electric lights showed his features. He was the hard-faced man who had steered Harry Vincent into the flaming basement of the Capitol Hotel.

Dark eyes showed an ugly glint as they saw the thug flattened on the floor. Hard lips uttered a savage curse. Striding to the fallen thug, the hard-faced man raised the fellow's shoulders and growled:

"Broddy! What happened here?"

Questioning Broddy was useless. The thug was senseless. The hard-faced man moved rapidly between the packed cars. He reached the office, seized the telephone and quickly gave a number. He was holding a watch when the response came. In choppy tones, the hard-faced man snapped orders:

"Car due at seven ten. Coupé with New York license. Handle it, then wait."

Smashing the receiver back on its hook, the hard-faced man hurried out into the garage. He shoved an arm under Broddy's shoulders and hoisted the thug into the back seat of a parked touring car. Springing to the wheel, he drove from the garage.

As he took the turn at the corner, the hard-faced man saw figures emerging from the police station. The garage manager was bringing two of Riverport's policemen. They were coming on a vacant quest. They would not find the stunned thug whom The Shadow had left upon the garage floor.

Like Harry Vincent, The Shadow had crossed the path of a dangerous murderer. Driving full speed for Westhampton, hard on the trail of the missing truck, The Shadow was heading into unexpected disaster. The chance arrival of the hard-faced man boded ill for The Shadow.

The lone trail had suited The Shadow for the present. It had promised him a chance to encounter enemies who dealt in crime. But the encounter which The Shadow sought would be gained much sooner than he believed.

Peril lay along The Shadow's lone trail.

CHAPTER III
THE BROKEN TRAIL

THE road from Riverport to Westhampton was a lonely highway. For miles, it followed the river gorge between the two towns. Sharp curves impeded continual speed but the lack of traffic on the highway partly offset that disadvantage.

The Shadow had left Riverport at ten minutes of seven. He was managing an average of fifty miles an hour. Fifteen minutes out of Riverport had carried him slightly more than a dozen miles along his way.

Hands firmly clutching the wheel, his eyes fixed on the road ahead, The Shadow observed the contour of the highway. Every curve was different; yet all bore one point of similarity. To the right were rugged, towering slopes; to the left a guard rail that fringed the riverbank.

The rail was one that had been built to stand a severe test. Taut wires ran between stout wooden posts, fixed deep beside the left shoulder of the highway. In all that monotony of posts, the ordinary observer would have seen no change. To The Shadow, however, differences were apparent.

Certain posts had weakened. Though they remained upright, there were tell-tale depressions at the base, sure signs that freshets had washed away supporting soil. Those posts needed strengthening supports. The Shadow made a mental note of that fact. Curiously, his observation was to serve him well before his trip was ended.

Except for those infrequent weaknesses, the guardrail was strong enough to resist the onslaught of a ten-ton truck. It needed to be strong. The river that lay below was deep and blackly sinister.

This gorge was narrow; its waters were slow, for the river was dammed some miles ahead. Fully thirty feet of depth lay below the dark surface of the river.

Mile after mile, The Shadow saw no other cars. He was traveling at the highest speed that any car could maintain along this winding road. At a fifty-mile-an-hour average, there was a chance that he might reach Westhampton soon after the departure of the mysterious truck. Inquiries; new clues; then The Shadow would resume pursuit. He was confident that a trail could be picked up at Westhampton.

The clock on the coupé's dashboard showed seven ten. It was the exact minute mentioned in the hard-faced man's telephone call. Timed almost to the second, The Shadow whizzed past an obscure side road that led upward to the right, through the ravine of a little stream.

THOUGH his headlights were pointing ahead, The Shadow was conscious of a small house nestled at the outlet of the dirt road. His momentary glimpse gave him the impression that the house was deserted.

The impression was justified. Supposedly, that house had been vacated a month before. Tonight, however, it was occupied. Peering eyes were stationed at a blackened upstairs window, to note The Shadow's coupé as it whirled past. Observers saw the New York license plate.

The hard-faced man at Riverport had made a perfect estimate of the time interval. He had done better than produce a haphazard guess. He had been familiar with the river road; he knew the maximum speed that its curves allowed. He had assumed that whoever had departed in the coupé would be riding at the fastest possible clip.

Gripping the wheel of the coupé, The Shadow swung hard as he finished a leftward curve. The road swung to the right; then left again, to a jutting point that hung above the river. The turn was one that required brakes. Safety signs showed twisted lines to indicate the sharpness of the turn. The right side of the road was a mass of mixed rocks.

The Shadow's foot moved to the brake pedal. There it halted, momentarily. His ears had caught a muffled boom, dimly heard despite the closed window of the coupé.

It was a blast from the jutting hillside straight above.

Almost coincident with that muffled blast, The Shadow's keen eyes saw a quivering of the rocks to the right side of the road. Stones rocketed to the highway.

Some drivers would have applied their brakes, to stop short of the falling stones. Others might have preferred to run the gauntlet, hoping to get past before the hail of stones increased. To The Shadow, both courses were hopeless.

He knew the meaning of that blast. Those stones were the forerunners of a man-made avalanche. A wall of rock had loosened. Already, high above, a stretch of massive stone was dropping to overwhelm the coupé.

There was no escape for any car upon this stretch of road. Neither a halt nor a burst of speed could carry The Shadow free in the brief moments that remained.

Instinctively, The Shadow chose a course entirely his own; one that was based upon previous observation.

A quick foot left the brake pedal. It drove the accelerator to the floorboard. Swinging the wheel hard to the left, The Shadow launched the coupé straight for the nearest guard rail, at the river side of the road.

No time to learn if that rail was held by loosened posts. Chances were that the supports had weakened; for here, the gorge was steepest. Conditions favored The Shadow. Speed, plus luck, should serve him. His hope was that the rail would meet a test that would prove too severe.

CABLES twanged as the coupé struck. They bellied outward like the string of a bow, threatening to resist the strain. One post gave way. Its yield was sufficient.

The rear of the coupé lurched upward; as the wires sagged, carrying over a dangling post, The Shadow's car catapulted into a huge somersault toward the river, thirty feet below.

As the car dived toward the gleaming water, a terrific roar sounded from above. Tons of rock crashed upon the highway, shattering the concrete paving as if it had been flimsy pasteboard.

A mammoth cliff had been blasted loose, along a stretch of fully sixty yards. Dynamite, drilled deep into the rock, had accomplished its devastating work in the space of three brief seconds.

As The Shadow's car hit the water, a landslide followed. Rocks buried the ripped guardrail. Scattering stones poured into the river, adding to the splash of the coupé. The downpour lasted for a dozen seconds; then came a sifting trickle of powdered stone and loosened dirt.

A feeble gleam showed dimly from the bottom of the river. The glow came from the lights of the coupé, sunk at a depth of more than twenty feet. The gleam ended. In its overturn, the coupé had nosed in toward the riverbank. Stones and mud blanketed the headlights.

The Shadow was still in the coupé.

Water had filled the interior of the car. Gripping the wheel, The Shadow could feel the pressure about him. One deep breath, gained before the plunge, still served him as he waited. Half a minute of this ordeal would mean that the landslide had lessened.

Stones thumped the coupé, but their landings were puny. Slowed by the water, the chunks of rock had no effect. The coupé was intact. It afforded complete protection while The Shadow remained within it. The danger that faced The Shadow was the possibility that the entire car would be buried by debris from the road.

That, however, was unlikely. The Shadow preferred to chance it. Too early a departure from the car might bring him up into a delayed downpour of stone. The Shadow waited a few more seconds, then gripped the handle of the door to his right. The coupe had tilted on its left side. It was imbedded among rocks; but the right door was clear.

BRACING his feet upon the lower door, The Shadow pressed his shoulder upward. The door forced open, against the pressure of the water. The car itself was filled with water; that rendered The Shadow's task possible.

Crawling through the half-opened door, The Shadow gave an upward push. His body shot toward the surface; those final seconds seemed interminable. Suddenly, The Shadow's head bobbed clear.

Propelling himself with hard strokes, he made sure of his self-rescue by swimming away from the bank where overhanging rocks still threatened to plunge upon him.

The Shadow found no current. He swam northward, along toward the portion of the bank which he had followed in the coupé. Clear of the rock-shattered area, he took strong strokes to the shore. Clutching clusters of tough shrubs, The Shadow climbed the bank and reached the guardrail.

As he gripped the lowest cable, The Shadow heard the purr of a motor. He saw a red light turning on the road. A touring car was swinging about; it had come from the direction of Riverport and had stopped when it had reached the fallen mass of rock. The Shadow edged down the embankment completely out of view from the road.

A moment later, a powerful searchlight glared above The Shadow's head. It formed a glaring path toward the river. The Shadow watched the beam sweep across the waters.

The searchlight's rays scoured the surface of the river, pausing near the very spot where The Shadow's coupé had performed its plunge.

The searchlight clicked off. The Shadow heard voices at the guardrail. He distinguished words that came in a rasped tone. A voice said:

"That was the fellow we were after, all right. He'll give us no more trouble. Come along back to the house. We'll clear out by the dirt road."

Men boarded their car. Weaponless, The Shadow had no way to deal with these murderers who had sought his life. Beyond the guardrail, he was unable to gain the road in time to board the rear of the departing car.

Rising to the guardrail, The Shadow watched the headlamps of the touring car as they weaved their way back along the road. The lights diminished, then blinked from view.

ON foot, The Shadow followed. He had an objective; that house which had been mentioned. There, even should he find no clues, The Shadow could remain for the night. Crooks would be gone before he arrived.

The Shadow had been balked in his pursuit; nevertheless, he had thwarted criminals in their attempt to eliminate him. He had heard the voice of one man who must certainly be a leader of the crooked band. The Shadow would recognize those rasped tones when he heard them again.

Beneath the towering slopes beside the lonely road, a grim laugh quivered in quiet night air. Fierce, strident, that mirth was heard only by the one who uttered it.

That laugh was The Shadow's new challenge. It boded ill to men of crime.

CHAPTER IV
CROOKS AGREE

WITH his hearing of the voice beside the guardrail, The Shadow had formed a mental picture of the man who had spoken. He had visualized a hardened face with stony lips and sharp, glinting eyes. The image that The Shadow composed was accurate.

The man who had sneered his evil glee was the hard-faced rogue who had steered Harry Vincent into trouble—the same man who had visited the Southern Garage in Riverport. He had followed The Shadow's car after his telephone call ahead to warn the others.

That man of crime had left no trail. When morning came, he was far from the deserted house near Riverport. In faultless attire, a cane beneath his arm, he was riding in an elevator to the fiftieth story of a Manhattan skyscraper. With a cigarette pursed between his sallow lips, he looked like a New York business man en route to his office.

When he stepped from the elevator, the hard-faced man went directly to an office that bore the legend:

GREAT AMERICAN POWER COMPANY

The door was the entrance to a suite. The hard-faced man entered a large reception room and spoke to a girl who was seated at a desk. His lips were eased into a confident smile; his tone held but a slight touch of its harshness as he announced:

"I have come to see Mr. Huxley Drune."

"Your name, please?"

Politely, the hard-faced man tendered an engraved card. The girl read it; then picked up a telephone. She pressed a button and received a response.

"Good morning, Mr. Drune," said the girl. "Mr. Gordon Colgarth is here to see you."

Words came across the wire. The girl hung up and nodded to Colgarth.

"Go right in, sir," she said. "Mr. Drune's office is straight ahead."

HALF a minute later, Colgarth was closing a door behind him. He turned to face a gray-haired man who was seated behind a large, flat-topped desk. Windows beyond showed a panorama of New York's skyline. Withered of face, the gray-haired man studied his visitor solemnly. Colgarth delivered a hard smile.

"Hello, Drune," he greeted. "Here's the bacon."

Approaching the desk, the hard-faced man produced a slender stack of papers and planked them in front of Drune. The gray-haired man thumbed the papers slowly. His withered face displayed a satisfied smile. Drune laid the papers aside.

"Good," he asserted, in a cold crackle. "Woldorf was worthwhile. You had trouble, though."

"Not much," returned Colgarth. "There was a chap who looked like he was covering Woldorf. I ran into him while I was leaving the hotel—right in the middle of all the smoke and fire."

"You left him there?"

Drune's crackled query was significant; his face showed an expectant gloat. Colgarth returned a hard grin.

"Better than that," he declared. "I gave him to the Salamanders."

Drune leaned back and chuckled.

"The truck left yesterday morning," continued Colgarth. "I met it at Westhampton and kept it there until night. I went back to Riverport to see how matters were."

"And found them satisfactory?"

"Not quite. Some meddlesome stranger found out about the truck. He slugged Broddy and headed for Westhampton in a car. I was lucky enough to head him off. I telephoned ahead and they gave him the blast. That was your idea, Drune, having that charge set in the hill. It proved useful."

"I read about it," chortled Drune, tapping a newspaper on his desk. "Down in Riverport, they think it was a new disaster. A landslide. No lives lost."

"There was one lost," put in Colgarth. "They'll never guess it, though. That car was bowled down into the river underneath twenty tons of rock!"

Drune had swung about in his swivel chair. He was staring through a side window; his face appeared reflective. Colgarth expected a question. Instead Drune turned around. He picked up Woldorf's papers.

"We needed these," clucked Drune. "They are worth the trouble that we took to get them. Woldorf had ambitions. He could never have realized them. This stock gave him full control of one holding company; but that was all."

"Worth a full million," inserted Colgarth. "That's pretty good money."

"Only a trifle. With other securities, with options, this should be worth ten millions. But Woldorf could never have secured the other stocks that he needed."

"While we can."

Drune nodded as he replaced the papers on the desk.

"WE had three objectives," he asserted.

"Woldorf's holdings were the first. They have been gained. Next will come our acquisition of the securities held by Lincoln Breel."

"Which will be easy," stated Colgarth. "The Salamanders worked perfectly at Riverport. They can do as well here in New York."

"After that," continued Drune, "we must obtain the securities that belong to the Cruikshank estate, in Sheffield. That means a bank robbery, Colgarth."

"We can handle the Sheffield National Bank. Everything is arranged, Drune. The torches will be ready. The dynamite will be on the railroad siding. We know that we can count on the Salamanders. There can be no trouble interrupting—"

Drune raised his hand in interruption. Solemnly, he shook his head.

"Remember, Colgarth," he asserted, "one job is not enough. We must hold all the securities that we need. We must control every company involved. That accomplished, we shall have a fifty-million-dollar proposition. I can make Great American Power dominant. You say there can be no trouble. There was trouble."

"Only from some dub who found out about the truck. He knows nothing else."

"Why did he suspect the truck at all?"

Drune's query was a sharp one. It made Colgarth wince. The hard-faced man had no answer. His eyes showed alarm.

"I shall tell you why," asserted Drune, his crackly tone harsh. He leaned across the desk and glared at Colgarth. "Because he traced everything, step by step. He knew that Woldorf was in danger. He learned that the safe could have been removed from the hotel. He went to find out about the truck."

Drune leaned back. Colgarth protested.

"That can't be!" he exclaimed. "No one could be wise enough to—"

"No one?" queried Drune, with a quick interruption. He chortled an ugly laugh. "Do you call The Shadow no one?"

"The Shadow?"

Colgarth blurted the name. His hard lips quivered, then gained their stony front. Drune watched the man's fists tighten.

"You're right, Drune!" rasped Colgarth. "It was The Shadow! I should have known it, the way he handled Broddy! But I finished him. The Shadow is through!"

"So others have thought," reminded Drune. "They have invariably found themselves mistaken."

RISING, the gray-haired man exhibited hunched shoulders. Tightening a clawlike fist, he pounded hard upon the desk. The words that came from his dry lips were emphatic.

HUXLEY DRUNE—mastermind who controls the Salamanders.

"Be sure of nothing, Colgarth!" pronounced Drune. "Nothing where The Shadow is concerned! Unless you see him dead, an absolute corpse, you cannot be sure that he is gone. Even then, he should be cremated; his ashes scattered to the winds.

"You say The Shadow is buried in that riverbed? Bah! He is as much alive as you or I! Earth, water, even fire—those are mere elements. The Shadow can conquer them. Those tons of rocks—that—river—"

Drune paused. His eyes showed shrewdness.

"Earth—water—" he repeated the words slowly. "They would not suffice. But fire might. Very well, The Shadow shall have fire. We shall see, if he is still alive, whether or not he can withstand the same ordeal as our Salamanders."

"You're taking too much for granted, Drune," scoffed Colgarth. "I admit that the meddler could have been The Shadow. It was also possible that he escaped death. Nevertheless, we can forget him.

"The truck has reached New York. Every trail has been covered. The Shadow—if he lives—cannot even guess the secret of the Salamanders. They are ready for their next duty, here in New York. Then to Sheffield, where my estate will be our final headquarters. The spoils are ours, Drune. Fifty millions will belong to us."

GORDON COLGARTH—lieutenant of the mastermind

Drune was smiling sourly; his elbow was on the desk, his chin in his hand.

"We must cash those millions, Colgarth," he reminded. "Do you think we can accomplish it?"

"You yourself have arranged the method, Drune. It will be a simple matter."

"While The Shadow lives?"

New alarm registered on Colgarth's hard face. Drune raised his head. Wagging a forefinger, he drove home his message:

"Sooner or later, Colgarth, The Shadow will divine our game. We accomplished crime in Riverport. We shall succeed here in New York and at your home city of Sheffield. With the Salamanders to aid us, our work is purely mechanical.

"But The Shadow will remain a menace, if we permit him to stay at large. Even if we proceeded too rapidly for him to overtake us, our venture will be threatened later. We have only one logical course, Colgarth."

"And what is that?"

Drune chuckled as he heard Colgarth's question. Tilting back in his chair, the power magnate spoke sagely.

"The Shadow will seek a trail," he predicted. "Very well. He shall gain one—a trail that shall lead him straight to the scene of our next crime."

"To Breel's house?"

"Yes. Where disaster will overwhelm The Shadow. You tried earth and water, Colgarth. I shall use fire."

Colgarth's eyes shone in admiration of his evil partner's scheme. Then a question rasped from his lips:

"How can we bait The Shadow?"

IN answer, Drune opened a drawer of the desk. He produced a letter. Holding it between his hands, he eyed Colgarth and asked:

"Chester Woldorf had an office here in New York?"

"Yes," returned Colgarth. "In the Greystone Building. His name, however, was not listed."

"The Shadow, nevertheless, should find that office."

"Yes, if he is as good as he is supposed to be. But The Shadow will find no clues there. You removed them, Drune."

"I shall replace one clue."

Chuckling, Drune held up the letter. "Chester Woldorf wrote to Lincoln Breel," he reminded. "That is how we learned that Woldorf intended to be at Riverport."

Colgarth nodded.

"Breel replied to Woldorf's letter," continued Drune. "This letter came from Breel. Woldorf never received it. I found the letter, unopened in Woldorf's office at the Greystone Building."

Another nod from Colgarth.

"Very well," concluded Drune, in a precise tone. "I shall replace the letter where I found it. The Shadow, when he discovers the office, will read the letter."

A pause; then Drune added:

"The Shadow will come to Breel's."

Colgarth stroked his hard chin; anxiously, he inquired:

"Will that be before or after we make our stroke at Breel's?"

"Neither," returned Drune, with a savage chortle. "We shall hold crime until a definite moment. We shall await a signal; then we can make our thrust."

"And that signal?"

"Will be The Shadow's own arrival. All will be prepared for that occurrence. Our torches will be ready; our watchers posted—"

"And the Salamanders?"

"They will be at their station. Everything will move as scheduled, Colgarth. We shall gain our spoils; and with that gain, The Shadow will be destroyed."

Leering, Colgarth thrust his hand across the desk. Drune received it with an iron grip. The pact was made. Partners in crime had agreed upon their plan.

Colgarth departed. Soon afterward, Drune strolled from his office. Clad in hat and coat, the power magnate paused in the reception room. In a dry tone, he told the girl there that he would return within an hour.

In his pocket, Huxley Drune was carrying the letter that he had shown to Gordon Colgarth. Drune was on his way to plant the missive that would seal the Shadow's doom.

CHAPTER V
THE TRAIL REGAINED

LATE that same afternoon, a pedestrian stepped aboard a taxicab near Times Square. In level tones, he ordered the driver to take him to the Greystone Building. Glancing over his shoulder, the taxi driver caught a glimpse of an impassive, hawk-faced passenger.

The Shadow had returned to New York. Hours of investigation had produced the result that Huxley Drune had expected. The Shadow had learned of Chester Woldorf's office at the Greystone Building.

As he rode along, The Shadow studied report sheets. Aided by competent agents, he had gained some facts concerning Chester Woldorf. The man who had died in the Riverport hotel fire was something of a mystery figure in financial circles.

Wall Street men had known Woldorf. They had guessed that he had money, but had finally classed him as a speculator. Only The Shadow had divined Woldorf's real purpose. The Shadow knew that Woldorf had been acquiring securities that would give him control of important holding companies.

The dead man had posed as a speculator merely to cover his real activities. He had succeeded, in that game, so far as the public was concerned. The Shadow knew, however, that crooks had learned of Woldorf's true capacity.

Men of crime had slain Woldorf to gain his holdings. But of what sort were those holdings? Oil—mines—shipping—manufactures—power?

Any one might be the answer. So might a host of others. The Shadow knew only that Woldorf had sought mastery of some specialized field, that the dead man, though shrewd, had been honest in his efforts.

There was a chance that the riddle of Woldorf's purpose could be answered through a visit to the office that had been Woldorf's mailing address in New York.

ARRIVING at the Greystone Building, The Shadow entered the lobby in a leisurely fashion.

Apparently, he was unconcerned with persons about him. Actually, he was eyeing every face.

The Shadow noted the man behind the cigar stand. As he made a purchase and paused to light a cigar, he observed the elevator starter; also the operators of all the cars that were waiting with opened doors. Well did The Shadow know that Woldorf's office might prove to be a trap.

Satisfied that no agents of crime were watching, The Shadow entered an elevator and rode to the eighth floor. When he stepped from the car, he waited a few moments, then chose a stairway that led up to the ninth.

Reaching the corridor above, he studied various closed doors. Sure that no lookouts were posted, he approached a door that bore the number 906.

The Shadow produced a ring of skeleton keys. His first choice was the right one. Probing the lock of 906, The Shadow was rewarded by a slight click. He turned the key and entered the office. Closing the door behind him, The Shadow pocketed the keys and produced a heavy automatic pistol. He laid the weapon upon a nearby desk, in case of trouble.

The Shadow doubted that there would be a surprise attack in this well-tenanted office building. Nevertheless, he was prepared for any emergency.

Daylight was fading. The windows, however, still produced sufficient light for The Shadow to make a search without betraying his presence by turning on the electric lights. There were two places that called for inspection. One was the desk; the other, a small filing cabinet.

Five minutes was all that The Shadow required to complete his preliminary search. In that time, he found nothing of consequence. The desk drawers contained pencils, blank stationery and paper clips. The filing cabinet held nothing but steamship circulars and railroad timetables.

Either Woldorf or some other person had cleared this office of all telltale contents.

The Shadow removed the drawers from the desk. Peering into the hollow, he saw something white. It proved to be an envelope, stamped and postmarked, torn open at the top. The envelope was addressed to Chester Woldorf, at this office.

The Shadow removed the letter from the envelope. He unfolded it and read a brief, scrawled note:

Dear Woldorf:

Sorry, but your plan does not appeal. Do not expect to hearfrom me when you reach Riverport. Am leaving tonight for the Adirondacks. Will be home in about ten days, perhaps sooner.

Sincerely, Lincoln Breel.

Studying the letter, The Shadow promptly gained its full meaning. He had been right. Chester Woldorf must have held control of important companies. To strengthen his position, Woldorf had sought some arrangement with Breel.

A logical procedure. Everyone knew of Lincoln Breel, wizard of finance, whose contacts were many and whose methods were devious. Breel had lost millions in a stock market crash.

He had gone into retirement, apparently soured with the world. But those who knew Breel held their doubts. They claimed that despite his losses, he still held wealth.

SOMEDAY, it had been predicted, Lincoln Breel would come out from retirement and begin a new campaign of finance. It was believed that Breel had acquired key stocks that would give him dominance in certain fields of industry.

No one, however, had hazarded a guess as to Breel's particular specialty. When it became known, it would arrive as a bombshell.

From one riddle, The Shadow had arrived at another. He still had no clue regarding Woldorf's plans. He knew only that they must be identical with those that Breel had undertaken. That, however, shifted the mystery from Woldorf to Breel.

What Woldorf, dead, could not answer, Breel, alive, could. At present, however, Breel was still absent from New York. The postmark on the envelope—the date on the letter—both showed the correspondence to be eight days old. Breel had stated that he would be home in about ten.

A soft laugh issued from The Shadow's disguised lips. A super-sleuth, The Shadow had seen another meaning to this letter.

Chester Woldorf had never received it!

The deduction was plain. Had Woldorf received the letter, he would certainly not have misplaced it. Nor would he have gone to Riverport, for the letter stated that he would not hear from Breel when he reached that city.

Woldorf had written Breel. Convinced that the financial genius would be interested in his terms, Woldorf had not waited for a reply by mail.

Who, then, had opened the letter?

The Shadow knew the answer. Some man behind the game of crime. There could be only one reason why the rogue had not kept it. He had planted it in this very office as bait for just such an investigator as The Shadow.

Though The Shadow did not know the identity of Huxley Drune, he clearly traced the super-crook's game. He knew exactly what Drune wanted. That was a visit, by The Shadow, to the home of Lincoln Breel.

Pocketing the letter, The Shadow stowed his automatic beneath his coat. He left the office and took an elevator on the same floor. He had no further need to look for spies. He knew that the master crook would have posted none. Watchers might have spoiled the bait.

In the lobby of the Greystone Building, The Shadow entered a telephone booth and put in a call. He gave instructions over the wire. Facts were to be assembled promptly; all available data concerning Lincoln Breel must be gained by agents and sent through to their chief. With such at hand, The Shadow would prepare his next move.

EARLY evening found The Shadow in his sanctum—the hidden abode that served him as headquarters in New York. Beneath a bluish lamp, long-fingered hands opened a six-by-nine mailing envelope. From this, The Shadow produced papers.

Agents had done well. From Mann, an investment broker, The Shadow had gained accurate facts concerning Lincoln Breel. The financial wizard's home was a secluded brownstone mansion in a block on the West Side. Breel, it appeared, had chosen that locality because the houses close to his were untenanted. Breel had no love for neighbors.

It was known generally that Breel had gone to the Adirondacks, but no one could give the location of his obscure hunting lodge. Breel had not returned from his trip to the mountain region; but his arrival was expected. Breel was accustomed to go and come as he chose, with no set announcement of his plans.

There were three servants at Breel's home; all were old retainers who had been in his service for many years. Except for these employees, Breel lived alone.

From Burke, a newspaper reporter, The Shadow had a report that tabbed closely with Mann's. In addition, he found a photograph of Lincoln Breel. It showed a heavy-browed face distinguished by a Vandyke beard. The Shadow studied the flowing hair above the forehead; he noted every detail of the countenance.

The Shadow had seen Breel in the past; he remembered the financier's precise manner of speech in addition to these facial characteristics. The photograph enabled The Shadow to improve his recollection of Breel's appearance. A soft laugh whispered in the darkness above the shaded lamp. The Shadow picked up the photograph, then clicked off the light.

Soon, a light glowed elsewhere in the sanctum. The illumination showed The Shadow's hawkish features reflected in a mirror. Set against the looking glass was Breel's photograph. The Shadow opened a makeup kit.

Then began a remarkable process.

Dab by dab, feature by feature, The Shadow changed his countenance. Long fingers pressed waxlike substance against the hawklike face. Molding his face, The Shadow built up the contour of his forehead. He added constructive touches to his cheeks, filling them, tapering their shape to resemble the outline of Breel's countenance. The Shadow's nose lost its hawkish aspect.

With spirit gum, The Shadow added a goatee that was a perfect replica of Breel's. His final touch was a wavy wig that resembled the financier's flowing hair.

This required rearrangement; artfully, The Shadow perfected the final feature of his disguise. He lifted the photograph and compared it with his own reflection.

DETAIL for detail, The Shadow's physiognomy matched the distinguished face of Lincoln Breel. Had The Shadow chosen to visit Wall Street in this disguise, Breel's own friends would have passed the word that the financier had emerged from retirement.

Wall Street, however, was not The Shadow's goal. His destination was to be Breel's own home, where servants, instead of friends, would believe that their master had returned. As Breel, The Shadow saw opportunity for an investigation that might lead him to men of crime.

Schemers would be watching for The Shadow. Unquestionably they were covering Breel's home. Battle with a cordon of crooks would produce no material gain for The Shadow. His desire was to enter the trap while watchers maintained their vigil; to keep them lulled and waiting while he had time to learn all that was possible concerning Breel's affairs.

Through this clever process of deception, The Shadow could arrive at Breel's home openly. By fooling Breel's own servants he would be able to go through the house as he chose. The Shadow was planning craft instead of stealth.

The light clicked off beside the mirror. A final laugh quivered through the sanctum. The Shadow was departing amid total darkness; within the next hour he would be at his goal. The Shadow had prepared a game to outmatch the scheme of his unknown foeman, Huxley Drune.

Well had The Shadow planned; but he had not yet learned the full extent of Drune's machinations. Clever though his method was, The Shadow had chosen an unfortunate method.

Due to circumstances unknown to him, The Shadow was adding to the danger that awaited. In using craft instead of stealth, The Shadow was playing straight into the hands of Huxley Drune.

CHAPTER VI
THE VOICE OF DEATH

IT was exactly nine o'clock when a taxicab stopped in front of Breel's old mansion. All was silent on this obscure Manhattan street. One spot alone was free from darkness. That was the top step of the brownstone flight that stood in front of Lincoln Breel's home.

There, servants had turned on a brilliant light. The glare testified that they expected their master hourly. The light was to The Shadow's liking. It offered him an opportunity to display his guise to watchers from the darkness.

As the taxi rolled away, The Shadow ascended the steps. He was carrying a suitcase; he placed it beside the door. Turning half toward the street, he removed a pair of gloves and began to reach in his pockets as if searching for a key.

The glow from above the doorway shone directly upon The Shadow's face. It showed the detailed features of Lincoln Breel. The Vandyke beard was conspicuous in the light.

The Shadow showed annoyance at being unable to find his key. He thrust his gloves into his pocket. He shrugged his shoulders and turned toward the door. With short jabs, he pressed the doorbell, in impatient fashion.

Eyes were watching.

The Shadow had almost felt their presence. With sidelong gaze, he had spotted a vacant house across the street, where shuttered windows tilted outward at a trifling angle. Behind those shutters were men of crime, noting the arrival of the pretended Lincoln Breel.

The Shadow gave no inkling of his knowledge. He had chosen to play the part of an unsuspecting man returning to his home.

The front door opened. A servant eyed The Shadow, then bowed in welcome. Entering, The Shadow handed the suitcase to the servant, then turned to another menial who had also arrived at the door. The second servant helped The Shadow take off his coat.

"Carry that suitcase upstairs, Yocum," ordered The Shadow, in a precise, but short-clipped tone. "Place it in my study."

"Certainly, Mr. Breel."

"And you may go, Tobias," added The Shadow, to the second servant. "I shall be in the strongroom, where I do not wish to be disturbed."

The second servant bowed and departed.

THE SHADOW walked to the rear of the hall.

Reaching an alcove, he paused before a heavy door. This time, when he reached into his pocket, he produced a set of special picks.

In the report concerning Breel, The Shadow had not only learned the names and descriptions of the financier's servants; he had also gained facts regarding the house.

Breel had a strongroom on the ground floor. It housed a large safe that probably held Breel's private fortune. The second-floor study was a room wherein Breel received occasional callers.

The Shadow expected a task with the strong-room door. The fact that Breel was willing to leave the house in charge of his servants was proof that both the strongroom and its safe would be formidable.

The Shadow had deceived the servants completely with his disguise; but he had dismissed them abruptly because he did not want them to watch his efforts at the door of the strongroom. He knew that they would wonder why he did not unlock the door immediately.

Picks clicked softly within the lock; but the door did not yield. The Shadow had encountered a formidable obstacle. This barrier required patience. Once in the strongroom, The Shadow would have time to dally with the safe. For the present, however, he had to remember the servants. Their possible suspicions could not be disregarded.

Close against the door, The Shadow continued his probe. One pick was working. Deft fingers pressed. The pick failed to hold. Carefully, The Shadow started to repeat his maneuver. He stopped abruptly as he heard a faint sound from upstairs. It was the ringing of a telephone bell.

Stepping from the alcove, The Shadow listened at the foot of the stairs. He heard the voice of the two servants. Yocum had met Tobias in the upstairs hall.

"A call for Mr. Breel—"

"He is in the strong-room, Yocum."

"I shall inform him."

"The master does not wish to be disturbed."

"But the call may be important, Tobias."

"I am repeating the order that was given me—"

The Shadow thrust his face past the post at the bottom of the stairs. He called up to the servants.

"Come! What is the trouble?"

It was Tobias who answered: "A telephone call, Mr. Breel."

"Very well." The Shadow spoke testily as he pocketed his picks. "I shall answer it."

THE SHADOW showed no haste as he ascended the stairway. At the top, he saw the open door of a lighted room and knew that it must be the study.

In dignified fashion, he walked past the servants. At the doorway, he turned and delivered an impatient gesture. The servants went downstairs.

The study door was open, inward. Its base was blocked tightly by a rug.

Apparently, Breel seldom closed the door; but The Shadow decided to do so. Chances were that this call would be for him.

Burbank, The Shadow's chief contact man, knew that his chief had gone to Breel's. To talk with Burbank, The Shadow needed privacy.

Despite The Shadow's caution as he turned the knob, the latch clicked sharply. The sound did not trouble The Shadow. The two servants had gone downstairs; they could not have heard the sound.

A telephone was resting on a desk beside a curtained window. The receiver was off the hook. The Shadow raised it and spoke in Breel's precise tone.

"Hello."

There was no response. The Shadow spoke again, in testy fashion.

"Hello... This is Mr. Breel..."

A harsh chuckle sounded from the receiver. It carried a gloating tone. That chortle was issued by Huxley Drune.

Though The Shadow did not know the identity of the master foe, he recognized at once that he was in direct contact with the criminal whom he had sought to thwart.

Was this a message for Lincoln Breel?

The Shadow had a way to learn. That was to continue his role of Breel. Impatiently, he demanded:

"Come! Who is on the wire?"

Drune's answer was raucous in its glee. Avoiding all mention of his own name, Drune expressed a fiendish challenge that marked him only as the foe that The Shadow sought.

"You found my bait," came Drune's triumphant crackle. "You are The Shadow. You were crafty, to play the part of Lincoln Breel. But therein lay your own folly. You, The Shadow, gave away your game. It was impossible for Lincoln Breel to return to his home.

"Breel is dead. His life was ended three days ago, by my own hand. His body lies buried deep beneath his hunting lodge. When you entered Breel's house tonight, I knew you for The Shadow."

A pause; then with evil emphasis, Drune added: "You have served my purpose well. You came as Lincoln Breel; you shall die as Lincoln Breel. Servants will bear testimony to the fact that Breel returned to New York. You are trapped. I heard the click of the door that locked your prison. Earth and water did not doom you. Fire will!"

A CLICK followed Drune's prophecy. The Shadow was standing with a dead receiver in his hand. He clattered it upon the hook. He swung toward the window and hauled back the curtains. Massive iron shutters showed beyond the glass. The Shadow knew that the master fiend had seen to it that they were clamped on the outside.

The Shadow reached the door. The knob spun uselessly in his hand. Another of Drune's devices. Arranged for Breel but never used. Murder in the Adirondacks had made it unnecessary in Breel's case. The self-locking door had served to snare The Shadow.

The door was massive, heavy-paneled, as formidable as the barrier that blocked Breel's strongroom on the floor below. It was an obstacle that no one man could conquer bare-handed. It stood between The Shadow and the path to safety.

For, already, shouts were proving Drune's prediction that fire would be The Shadow's foe. From below came the frenzied shrieks of Breel's servants. They were giving the loud-lunged alarm in one wailed word:

"Fire!"

The Shadow heard the cry within his prison. Grimly, he faced the door that blocked escape.

CHAPTER VII
FOEMEN OF THE FLAMES

FRANTIC footsteps pounded on the stairs. The Shadow heard beating fists against the heavy door. Voices of frightened servants shouted in confusion:

"Mr. Breel! The house is ablaze!"

The Shadow waited until the hubbub subsided. Then, in loud, testy tones, he answered:

"The door will not open. Smash it down."

"No time, sir!" It was Yocum who gasped the cry. "The fire is everywhere, Mr. Breel—"

There were scudding footsteps. The other two servants were fleeing downstairs. Yocum blurted something about getting aid. The Shadow heard him dash away. With their last chance for escape, the servants had been forced to abandon their supposed master.

A hissing crackle told The Shadow that the servants had not exaggerated the menace. The odor of smoke was heavy through the crack beneath the door. The Shadow realized that incendiaries had been posted in the empty houses that adjoined this one. Paid "torches," they had fed the flames with oil.

Breel's house was doomed. Despite its stone walls, it was a firetrap, with wooden beams, laths that would flame like kindling. Its fate would soon match the destruction that had overwhelmed the hotel in Riverport.

The Shadow had waited in hope that the servants might effect a rescue. He had entered this house as Breel. He had intended to depart in the same guise, to prove his contempt of Drune's prophecy. That chance was ended.

With quick hands, The Shadow plucked away his false beard. He tugged the puttylike mold from his face. He whisked away the wig that topped his head.

THIS room contained no object that could be used as a battering ram to smash the door. Drune knew it: that was why he had fully depended upon the trap. But The Shadow, himself, had dispatched a useful item to the room.

He turned to the suitcase that the servant had carried upstairs. Deliberately, The Shadow placed the flat bag upon Breel's desk.

From the bag, he produced a black cloak that he immediately slid over his shoulders. He lifted a slouch hat and clamped it to his head. A brace of automatics went beneath his cloak.

The Shadow then picked up thin, black gloves and laid them to one side. From a little pocket at the side of the bag, he removed three small bottles, which were separately packed.

One bottle contained a black powder that resembled graphite. Stepping to the door, The Shadow poured a line of powder along the opening at the bottom of the barrier. From the second bottle, he added a thin stream of grayish powder that formed a weaving line through the black.

The last bottle held a colorless liquid. Uncorking it, The Shadow blobbed the entire contents along the line of mixed powder. Wheeling, he crossed the room. Crouched behind the desk, The Shadow muffled his head in the folds of his cloak and waited. The intermission was brief.

A sudden blast shook the room. The air shivered as it compressed and coughed a puffing echo to the explosion. When The Shadow arose, he sniffed a pungent odor that was stronger than the oily smell of the fire.

The heavy door was loose upon its hinges, half-tilted into the room. It was a barrier no longer. Springing to the door, The Shadow wrenched an opening. He pressed outward into the upstairs hall.

The Shadow had come prepared to blast his way into Breel's strongroom, if all other devices failed and entrance would have proved necessary. Trapped in the study, he had made use of the chemical powders that he had brought for another purpose. The Shadow had offset the snare devised by Drune.

Had he escaped too late?

Volumes of smoke were pouring upward from the floor below. His head muffled deep in folds of

Framed against the glow of the passage were enemies, perhaps the strangest that The Shadow had ever encountered. Grotesque foemen stood to block The Shadow's path.

his black cloak, The Shadow groped his way downward. He was taking the outlet that Breel's servants had utilized; but they had gained a start before the fire had reached its present intensity.

Even through the black cloth of his cloak, The Shadow could see licking tongues of flame, devouring the woodwork on the ground floor, gnawing at the rails of the banister.

Outside, alarms were clanging; sirens had joined with a wail. Manhattan fire engines were arriving; but even efficient firemen would be balked.

The flames were fed by oil.

THE ground floor was an inferno when The Shadow reached it. The whole front of the house was ablaze with fire. Crackling from the other direction told that the rear of the building was a furnace. One spot alone offered temporary security. That was the alcove in the very center of the house, where the door of the strongroom loomed.

The Shadow retreated to that refuge. He placed his hand upon the knob of the strong-room door. He wrenched. The door swung inward. Firelight, vivid everywhere, gave The Shadow a complete view of the strongroom before blackish smoke poured inward.

The strongroom was completely empty.

The Shadow's laugh came strident amid the crackling of devouring flames. His sinister mirth was significant. The Shadow had expected this discovery.

As at Riverport, a safe had been removed under the cover of a terrific fire. The strongroom had been opened while The Shadow was still trapped in the study. Drune's henchmen had come, carrying Breel's own keys. They had opened the strongroom; they had removed the safe bodily.

Outside, clangor told that no criminals would have dared to leave by any door. The Shadow knew their only route. They had come through the cellars, from one house to another, until they had reached Breel's. Their only outlet was the path by which they had arrived.

Beneath the stairway was a door, also protected in this alcove. The Shadow ripped the door open; he saw a stairway to the cellar: He, too, had a route to safety. Through keen deduction, The Shadow had gained his chance for escape. Stumbling through the smoke, he descended, yanking the door shut behind him.

Fierce flames hissed; a burst of fire swept the alcove. A wall tumbled; blazing beams covered the very spot where The Shadow had been, but moments before. Sizzling, crackling, the fire roared like an angry monster deprived of a helpless victim.

Free from the fire's wrath, The Shadow had reached the bottom of the steps. There was smoke in the cellar; from the cloudy mass, flames were rising to consume wooden bins and boxes. The blaze, however, had not reached a high intensity.

The stone floors offered pathways. The Shadow groped through sweeping smoke. He knew that the cold air from some pathway was blowing the smoke in his direction.

His head enveloped in his cloak, The Shadow continued through the smoke. Despite his upraised arm, with its folds of cloth, he could sense the thickness of the oily cloud about him. Suddenly, the atmosphere cleared. The Shadow had passed through the smoke. He was near the outlet that he knew existed. The Shadow dropped his arm; he stopped his progress instantly.

Off to the side of the cellar was an opening in the wall. It was a passage leading to the house next door. Flames, shooting sparks, showed that the adjoining cellar was ablaze. The outlet offered hazard. But it was not that fact that caused The Shadow's halt.

FRAMED against the glow of the passage were enemies, perhaps the strangest that The Shadow had ever encountered. Grotesque foemen stood to block The Shadow's path.

They were men, attired in bulky garments that looked like diving suits. Above their chunky shoulders were round helmets with glass fronts, through which peered glaring faces. In this distorted scene, they had the appearance of demons.

There were eight men in the group. Each was provided with a hose line that came through from the adjoining cellar. Just as divers are equipped to fare to the ocean's bottom, so were these interlopers protected against flames.

Massive gloves formed a portion of each uniform. With clumsy hands, these brawny invaders were setting down a heavy iron box. It was Breel's safe, that they had lugged from the strongroom on the floor above. The fireproof men had heard The Shadow's approach. They had stopped their departure in order to meet the lone pursuer.

They were human Salamanders, these foemen of the flames. Like mythical creatures who could live in fire, they had no fear of the blaze about them. Drune, the master crook, had chosen fire as the cover by which he could accomplish robbery. He had also devised equipment that enabled his henchmen to do their work with safety and precision.

The Salamanders had removed the safe from the Riverport hotel. They were carrying off Breel's strongbox in the same bodily fashion. They were capable, however, of a different duty.

They were ready to fight anyone who tried to block their work.

Odds were with the Salamanders. They could defy the flames. The Shadow, unprotected against the roaring fire, was confronted by a double menace. The blaze was behind him; the Salamanders stood in front. Moreover, they had weapons, a sort more deadly than guns.

With clumsy hands, the human monsters were drawing pipelike torches from belts at their waists. Thick-gloved thumbs were fumbling with catches that topped the strange weapons. The Shadow could guess that those pipes were designed to issue withering blasts of flame.

FROM above, a crackle told that minutes of safety were few. The ceiling of the cellar was yielding to the fire. Soon beams would topple, blazing. The Shadow would be entombed in a fiery pit.

Already, the stairs from the ground floor were on fire. The Shadow could see bright tongues amid the smoke as he turned for a quick glance over his shoulder.

Venomously, two Salamanders were advancing; another pair were ready for the march. Creatures of doom, they intended to drive back The Shadow at close range; to force him to a corner where either flame or blowtorches would wither him to death.

In coming from the upstairs trap, The Shadow had found another mesh, more desperate than the one that he had left.

CHAPTER VIII
THE ODDS FAIL

EVEN in this moment of complete desperation, The Shadow chose a course. He took the choice that no other would have accepted, a return to the flames. Close-range battle with the Salamanders would have been suicidal. It was better to dare the fire.

Whirling about, The Shadow plunged into the smoke at the front of the cellar. Beams fell, blazing. Flames licked from the stacks of burning boxes. The smoke, itself, was blinding. Yet The Shadow leaped forward, almost to the toppling stairway.

Escape was impossible up the steps. They were a mass of flames. The Shadow, however, had not intended flight. As he reached the front wall of the cellar, he turned. From his cloak, he whipped a pair of automatics.

Smoke obscured the Salamanders; but they gave signs of their deliberate advance. Long jets of flame roared from their blowtorches, jabbing through the smoke, blindly seeking The Shadow as a target. Those singeing blasts did not reach the wall beside the stairs.

The Shadow had understood the reason for the prompt advance that the Salamanders had made. Their blowtorches could work only at close range, within a radius of about twelve feet. The Shadow, through his quick dart, had placed a full twenty feet between himself and the foemen. Through that strategy, he had gained short seconds in which to use weapons of his own.

The Shadow jabbed shots with his automatics, firing toward the fiery jets that sought him as a target. Somehow, his bullets seemed futile. The smoke—the weaving firelight—all distorted The Shadow's vision. Dropping beams made him shift as he fired.

Moreover, only two of The Salamanders had led the advance. Despite their fireproof suits, they did not care to come beneath a mass of falling timbers. Two thrusts of withering fire jets were advancing in the face of The Shadow's shots. A few seconds more, those blasts would sweep The Shadow's wall.

Suddenly, one fire jet stopped. The Shadow had scored a hit. One Salamander clipped, he aimed grimly for the other, pumping bullets through the smoke. The jet ceased; then began again. The second Salamander was retreating.

THE SHADOW ceased his fire. He waited amid terrific heat, close against the wall, one cloaked arm raised to protect his stinging eyes. He realized why his shots had not been accurate. Blinding smoke had handicapped his vision.

Nevertheless, The Shadow had gained hope.

One Salamander down, the other had wavered. When The Shadow had ceased firing, the surviving Salamander had been ready to believe that his torch had found the victim or that The Shadow had succumbed to the flames. That Salamander was returning to the others, to tell them that there was no need to stay.

Huddled in the smoke, The Shadow lingered, undetermined how soon he should proceed in the direction of the Salamanders. His decision was forced by the blaze about him. A roar sounded in the cellar; the entire stairway gave. A huge sheet of fire, the entire mass tumbled sidelong toward The Shadow. With it, beams thundered downward. The whole front ceiling was in collapse.

The Shadow took the only possible course. He hurried through the smoke, toward the rear of the cellar, seeking the Salamanders in preference to the hot flames. Spark-shooting woodwork crashed about him.

One burning beam glanced from his shoulder.

Half staggering, The Shadow stumbled clear of the smoke and sprawled upon the stone floor. Rolling over, he looked for the Salamanders.

They were through the opening to the next cellar. Five were lugging Breel's safe; two were hauling away the prone Salamander whom The Shadow had dropped with a bullet.

This pair saw The Shadow as he sprawled. They reached for their blowtorches. They were too late. The Shadow had an automatic in his fist.

Dropping their comrade, the two Salamanders leaped beyond the five who carried the safe, showing speed despite their clumsy garb. The Shadow fired twice; again, his smarting eyes handicapped him. The Salamanders had shifted, to present a broad side of the safe toward The Shadow. The bullets from The Shadow's .45 were flattened as they clanged the steel surface.

Two cartridges were all that remained in that gun. The Shadow whipped up his second automatic. He did not use it. As he aimed, a huge beam fell between him and the Salamanders. Blazing sparks formed a curtain; smoke poured downward and completely blocked the scene.

The seven Salamanders were gone. The Shadow was caught in a seething oven. Even the stone floor was scorching. Flames from the adjoining cellar told that the Salamanders had departed through another pit of roaring heat.

RISING, The Shadow followed. He stopped short at the opening in the wall. The Salamanders had gone from sight. The next cellar was an inferno. Prompt death faced The Shadow. For a moment, he stood motionless, ready to accept his doom.

A peculiar hissing hissed steadily at The Shadow's feet. Blinking as he peered downward, The Shadow saw the Salamander whom he had shot with a chance bullet. The man's body was half beneath a burning beam. No longer bulky, the grotesque figure looked pitiful.

Grasping the clothy shoulders, The Shadow dragged the Salamander to one clear spot beside the wall. The rogue was dead; the reason for his deflated uniform was explained. It involved that steady hiss.

The Salamander's suit was of asbestos cloth, much oversized. It was rubber-lined; the air hose, also of asbestos, kept it inflated under ordinary conditions. The Shadow's bullet had punctured asbestos and rubber; the suit had emptied like a broken toy balloon.

Nevertheless, air was still issuing through from the hose. It was cool air, that sizzled from the bullet hole. Off in another house, the Salamanders had a portable air-cooling plant, that provided

**A SALAMANDER—
one of the weird group The Shadow
meets in mortal combat.**

them with air, not only fresh, but constantly cool. They were protected against heat as well as suffocation.

The helmet was a metal framework, covered with asbestos cloth. It had not lost its bulk. Fumbling at the neck of the helmet, The Shadow found a tiny lever. He pressed it; the helmet came open. The Shadow saw a sweat-streaked face that glared, even in death.

Tugging the helmet free, The Shadow pulled at the Salamander's uniform and stripped it from the dead man's body. The fire was encroaching upon this last spot of refuge. The heat was stifling; it was with difficulty that The Shadow managed to don the uniform and fix the helmet in place.

His hands were in clumsy gloves. The Shadow found trouble in clasping the spot by the bullet hole. At last he gripped it and twisted asbestos and rubber into one tight mass, which he held firmly with both hands. The fire suit inflated. The air from the hose brought a terrific chill.

Keeping a firm hold on the punctured portion of the suit, The Shadow followed the route of the Salamanders. His eyes could see clearly through the glass. He entered the next cellar and picked his way through a tumbled mass of ceiling that threw up sparks as his asbestos boots encountered it.

The Shadow reached another cellar by following the line of the hose. In this house, the ceiling was still solid; but the cellar itself was filled with oily, burning rubbish.

All seemed secure until The Shadow saw a motion of the hose ahead of him. It was moving forward, rapidly. Doubled coils came snakily from behind The Shadow and passed him with speed.

The Salamanders had reached their base—a cellar free of fire. They were hauling in the loose hose to drag the body of the dead Salamander to them.

THE hose tightened suddenly. As The Shadow groped to another fume-filled cellar, he could feel the steady pull. Suddenly, it stopped. Off ahead, the Salamanders had begun to wonder. The Shadow knew the questions that perplexed them.

Why had the hose pulled so easily, then suddenly offered resistance?

The Salamanders must have guessed the answer. Until this moment, The Shadow had been conscious of a hiss behind his ears, the working of a safety valve that prevented over-pressure from the air that was continuously pumping through. That hiss ceased. The suit dropped loosely from The Shadow's shoulders. The air supply had ended. The Salamanders had kept up pressure in hope that their comrade was still alive. They had known, though, that he could not march through to follow them. That was why they had tugged the hose. The Salamanders at last knew the truth.

The Shadow could not go on to meet them. Entrenched, the Salamanders would be ready with scorching flame, once they had blocked the path. Without the air supply, the asbestos suit would smother its wearer. The Shadow's one chance was to try escape from this house, two doors away from Breel's.

Divesting himself of the Salamander's suit, The Shadow again groped through the smoke. He was looking for a stairway, like the one at Breel's. He found it and gained an unlocked door at the top. His path was lighted by a mass of flames.

Drune's torches had seen to it that there would be fire here. They had made a long route of fire to cover the movements of the Salamanders.

The blaze, though furious, formed a shell about the inner walls. The woodwork had been oiled. The stairs to the second floor were greasy; but the flames had not commenced to lick them. No longer encased in a Salamander's outfit, The Shadow climbed the stairs in agile fashion.

His speedy action was necessary. As he reached the top of the stairs, flames licked the bottom. With a roar, the fire came ripping upward, dashing devastating tongues along The Shadow's trail.

Smoke was everywhere; but The Shadow found a doorway. He pressed into a rear room of the house and saw an outlined window. With sweeping arm and shoulder, The Shadow smashed the glass. Coughing, he crawled through to an outside sill, lowered himself to full length and dropped to a courtyard beneath.

The entire block was burning. Fire engines were parked by a rear-street hydrant when The Shadow reached it. Pausing in one sheltered spot that the ruddy glow of flames did not reach, The Shadow looked along the street. He saw a truck pull from an alleyway where there was no blaze.

The Salamanders had gone. There was no chance to overtake them. Creatures of fire had escaped with their spoils.

AN old roadster came along the street. It stopped abruptly near where The Shadow stood. Firemen shouted angrily at the occupants, who growled in return. The firemen maintained that the roadster had no business coming through this thoroughfare; the men in the car argued that they had no other route. The roadster was ordered to turn about, to avoid running over a fire hose.

As the car backed up on the sidewalk, almost at the spot where The Shadow stood, The Shadow sprang forward to the rear bumper. The car had no rumble seat. Its rear section was a large luggage compartment, with a knob at the bottom.

The Shadow opened the luggage compartment, while the driver still argued with a fireman. Twisting forward, The Shadow wriggled into the ample space. He let the container close above him but stopped it before the catch could lock.

The roadster jolted from the curb. The Shadow lay motionless within, puffing the air that came from a crack at the bottom of his hiding place. Even this poor source of air seemed tinged with ozone. It was reviving compared to the smoke-filled atmosphere which The Shadow had just escaped.

The car rode a few dozen blocks, then jounced upward on a ramp and rolled to a standstill. Growling men were climbing from the front seat. The Shadow could hear their muffled voices; but he made no move.

He had weakened from his ordeal. His only course was to rest. When the men had gone, however, The Shadow wedged the top of the container higher, so that he could gain more air.

This scarcely improved The Shadow's condition. He was in an atmosphere tinged with the odor of gasoline. Bare walls, dimly lighted, proved that the two men had left their car in a large public garage. Nevertheless, as he waited, The Shadow experienced a slow return of strength.

AFTER fifteen minutes, The Shadow resolved upon departure. He crawled from the roadster, steadied himself upon the stone floor. He carefully noted the license number of the car; that done, he picked his way through clustered automobiles and found a side door to a darkened alley. Stopping outdoors, The Shadow took deep breaths that gradually eased the burning of his smoke-racked lungs.

At last, a whispered laugh sounded in the darkness beside the silent garage. The Shadow's tone carried a note of triumph. The Shadow had done more than escape Drune's trap and the power of the Salamanders. He had found a trail for the morrow.

One reason only, could have brought that roadster along the street where fire engines were at work. The two men in the car were henchmen of the master crook. Like others, they had been ordered to cover the departure of the truck that carried the Salamanders and the spoils.

The Shadow had ridden with minions of crime. He had marked their car; he would remember this garage. When crooks came here again to get their roadster, The Shadow would be prepared to follow on their trail.

CHAPTER IX
THE THIRD CAMPAIGN

REPORTS of the fire dominated the next day's headlines. Throughout New York City, eager readers devoured newspapers as hungrily as the flames had consumed the fuel of the night before. The blaze at Lincoln Breel's had been one of the most startling in the history of Manhattan, excepting, perhaps, the burning of the Capitol Hotel.

Only the heroic efforts of competent firefighters had averted a holocaust. Successive alarms had brought out hordes of fire engines. Roaring flames had almost obliterated the block where Breel's house had stood; the firemen had fought valiantly to prevent the conflagration from spreading throughout the entire neighborhood.

It was obvious that the fire had been of incendiary origin. Flames had begun in half a dozen houses almost simultaneously. Breel's home had simply been the focal point.

What had been the purpose of the fire?

That was the baffling point. Insurance men were puzzled. The houses in Breel's neighborhood belonged to half a dozen different owners; none was heavily insured. The fire was classed as arson; but no one had acquired monetary gain of any consequence.

The only theory that gained support was one which involved Lincoln Breel.

It was known that Breel had suffered financial losses in the past; also that he had counted upon regaining his wealth. Probably, Breel had been working on some scheme that might have brought him back to Wall Street.

ASSUMING that Breel's plans had failed, there was sufficient reason to suppose that the financier was disappointed with life. Men sometimes find curious ways to end a thwarted career.

Breel, always a man with dreams of grandeur, could have decided to imitate the Vikings of old; to consign his own body to a self-made funeral pyre.

Fantastic though this theory was, there were facts to substantiate it.

Breel had been away from home. He had returned unexpectedly to New York. No one knew of his activities just previous to his arrival at his house. Breel, himself, could have been the incendiary who started the blaze throughout the block.

The fire had begun immediately after Breel's arrival home, so the servants said. Moreover, Breel had answered a mysterious telephone call. That pointed to paid helpers: "torches," who might have aided Breel in his insane undertaking.

Most significant was the report that concerned the door of Breel's study. The servants testified that Breel seldom closed that door; they added that it had no key. Yet Breel had shouted that the door was locked; and the servants had found it in such a condition. It seemed that Breel had deliberately cut himself off from aid.

There was mention of a muffled explosion that had come soon after the fire. That episode could well have marked Breel's suicide. It silenced the objectors who claimed that no man would have consigned himself alive to flames. The final theory held belief that Breel was dead, a suicide, before the fire reached his study.

Breel had wanted no rescue. That was why the job had been so thorough. Crazed, the financier had seen to it that no human aid could reach him.

Such stories intrigued the public. The morning newspapers began them; the evening journals snatched up the theme and played it up with huge headlines. By mid-afternoon, the later editions had dug up old stories of famous fires in past years. They ran photographs of firebugs who had previously alarmed New York. Breel's picture was included with the others.

Anyone might turn incendiary, so the newspapers claimed. They classed the craze with kleptomania. Any man, thwarted in life, might turn hostile toward the world and use fire to impress his hatred. The burden of the blame belonged to Lincoln Breel.

TWO men were pleased most highly by the rumors that the press had accepted. Fellow conspirators in crime, they were chuckling over a stack of newspapers as they sat in an office high above Manhattan. Those connivers were Gordon Colgarth and Huxley Drune. They had joined in conference at the power magnate's office.

"It worked better than we planned it, Drune," commented Colgarth, in his harsh tone. "Everybody has fallen for this crazy idea that Breel was responsible for the fire."

"Absolutely," agreed Drune, dryly. "We should express our thanks in memory of The Shadow."

"Why thank The Shadow? The idea was yours, Drune."

"To trap The Shadow, yes. But not to have him come there as Breel. That was his own idea."

Drune paused to chuckle. Leaning on the desk, he added: "The Shadow's own idea. A most clever one, to come as Breel. A plan, however, that worked doubly to our advantage. No one will ever look for Breel's body up in the Adirondacks. Nor will concern be expressed when Breel's safe is not discovered in the ruins of his home."

Colgarth arched his furrowed brow in questioning fashion. Drune smiled and spoke an explanation.

"Breel's supposed madness," stated the master crook, "has made everyone—the authorities included—believe that he possessed no wealth. Therefore, his safe will not be regarded as important. We, alone, know the value of Breel's holdings. In fact, we know their precise value, for we have them here with Woldorf's securities."

From a desk drawer, Drune produced two bundles and thwacked them upon the desk. Colgarth displayed an ugly grin as he eyed the double spoils.

"We are ready," declared Drune, "for our third campaign. We need the stocks that are in the Sheffield National Bank, held there for the Cruikshank estate. How soon will all be ready in Sheffield, Colgarth?"

"Everything is ready. We can stage the job tonight."

"You have covered every detail?"

"Right to the dot. Give me pencil and paper, Drune. I'll show you how it stands."

RECEIVING paper and pencil, Colgarth drew four squares in a line, numbering them from one to four. He tapped the first square in the row.

"This is the old garage," he stated. "It is empty, ready to be torn down. The truck went in there this morning. The air-cooling system is hooked up. The passage is finished, underground, straight to the foundations of the bank building."

Colgarth moved his pencil and tapped the second square.

"This is the Sheffield National Bank," he said. "It is strongly barred; but its interior is old. It will burn like tinder, once the fire starts. It is protected by an elaborate sprinkler system that—"

"Which suits us exactly," interposed Drune, "provided that you have made the right arrangements."

"I have," returned Colgarth, promptly. "The water tank on the roof has been filled with gasoline. We did that job a week ago, at night. All that I have to do is plant a potassium bomb, set to go off at the required hour."

"Its flare will be sufficient to start the sprinklers?"

"Yes. The bomb will be packed in combustible material. I tested one like it. The heat will quickly melt the amalgam in the nearest sprinkler. That will mean gasoline, not water. Every sprinkler in the place will open."

Colgarth had settled the matter of the bank building. He tapped the third square in the row.

"This is the old depot," he remarked. "A sore eye to the citizens of Sheffield. They have petitioned often for its removal; but the railroad has kept on using it as a freight station. You should see that depot, Drune. Low and flat, with wooden walls and platforms. A few sparks will ignite it."

Colgarth moved his pencil to the fourth square.

"A block of stores," he explained, "with cheap apartments on the floors above. Well tenanted, as I should know, for I own the block. I couldn't risk fixing the water tank; someone might smell the gasoline after the fire reaches the apartment house. But Broddy and a crew put all the fire hydrants on the fritz throughout that entire block."

"Won't that excite suspicion?"

"Not in Sheffield. My home city boasts one of the worst fire departments in the State. Pipelines are never inspected. The public safety department will take the rap after this fire."

SUMMARIZING his statements, Colgarth lifted his pencil. Ignoring the first square, he tapped those that were marked 2, 3 and 4, naming them in order:

"The bank. The depot. The apartment block. All in twenty minutes. Two hundred tenants in those apartments. Picture the confusion, Drune. The bank building will be forgotten. The whole one-horse fire department will be working to rescue the people trapped in the apartments.

"Meanwhile, we can blast the bank's foundations. Our tunnel will carry us straight into the vault. Leave it to me to grab those Cruikshank securities and put a lot of phony stuff in place of the ones we need.

"I am a director in the bank. I have the necessary keys. The only list of the Cruikshank holdings has been destroyed. No one will suspect a robbery has been accomplished. Best of all, I shall not be seen about town while the fire is underway."

"You will be leading the Salamanders?"

"Yes. We will bring the truck to my country house, five miles north of Sheffield. You can await us there, Drune."

Drune nodded. He studied Colgarth's diagram. A question came to his mind.

"The dynamite," remarked Drune. "Where is it?"

"On a siding near the old depot," replied Colgarth. "It came in this afternoon, in a steel boxcar. It won't be near enough to the fire to make trouble."

"There is sufficient reason for its presence?"

"Yes. It is an advance shipment to a local quarrying company. They do not know that it has arrived. The telegram was intercepted."

"Your men have taken dynamite from the car?"

"Broddy will handle that at dusk. He is in charge of the garage. He will lift whatever amount is needed."

Drune considered further. He asked:

"Where are the Salamanders?"

"At the blast furnace," replied Colgarth, "off in the woods to the west of town."

"On the road that leads past the airport?"

"No, that is south of Sheffield."

Drune nodded, as though recalling the terrain. He picked up the securities stolen from Woldorf and Breel. He packed them in a briefcase.

"I shall go to Sheffield with you," decided Drune, looking steadily at Colgarth. "There is one thing that you have forgotten. I had intended to stay here in New York; but I think it best to accompany you and attend to the detail that you omitted."

"What detail?"

"The matter of the prisoner whom the Salamanders brought from Riverport."

"He means nothing, Drune. He is helpless out at the blast furnace."

"Have you forgotten about The Shadow?"

Colgarth looked puzzled, and then snapped a logical question: "Why bring up The Shadow? We finished him last night. How can he figure in this, Drune?"

"The Shadow has an organization."

"Maybe. Maybe not. He was alone when the Salamanders met him."

"True. That was because he was on a one-man job. But he has followers and we must be prepared to handle them if they try something in the future."

"You think our prisoner was working for The Shadow?"

"Yes. You found him at Riverport."

"I have quizzed him. He claims to know nothing."

"More possible proof that he is an agent of The Shadow."

COLGARTH nodded slowly. The idea had not occurred to him.

"I shall quiz the prisoner."

Drune's cluck was harsh and ominous.

"Go to it," accorded Colgarth. "Suppose we meet at six o'clock and start for Sheffield in my car? We can make the trip in two hours easy."

"When will you plant the box?"

"After we reach Sheffield at eight. The bank stays open until nine. I'll stop off and leave it when I make a deposit. Then we can go to the blast furnace."

"Don't forget the cover-up men."

"The ones still here in New York? Don't worry. I'll call them. If they start before seven, they will arrive in time to join us."

Hands stretched across the desk. Men of crime joined hands in an evil clasp. Plans for the third campaign were completed. Drune and Colgarth foresaw a mutual mastery of wealth.

The pair had forgotten The Shadow. They believed that he occupied the fiery grave that the public had conceded to Lincoln Breel. Because of that belief, Drune and Colgarth had formed their plans too well.

Their last detail, regarding the cover-up men, had paved a route by which The Shadow could again oppose them.

CHAPTER X
THE THIRD CAR

IN their frenzied search for details that concerned the fire at Lincoln Breel's, the New York newspapers had failed to gain a most important item. That was not surprising, for the occurrence in question was one that seemed quite detached from the conflagration of the night before.

A new man had taken a job as a car washer at the West Side Garage, which was located near Eighth Avenue.

Car washers work principally at night, particularly in garages that depend chiefly on overnight storage. The West Side Garage handled cars that belonged to hotel guests.

Hence the new man, applying for a job early in the morning, had been told to wait around until night. The West Side Garage had happened to need an extra car washer. The manager was willing to give the new man a chance.

Old hands at the garage predicted that the new man would not last long. All through the day, he had lounged about the door of the garage, smoking cigarettes that hung downward from his droopy lips. His face was listless; he seemed to lack the slight amount of ambition that even a car washer should possess.

The regular employees circulated the rumor that the manager had been on a "bender" the night before; that he was so bleary-eyed in the morning, he would have hired any "punk" who had asked him for a job. Certainly, the dull appearance of the new car washer bore out the theory that the manager had made a poor choice.

By seven o'clock in the evening, the new man had become too lazy to even light the cigarette that he had thrust between his pasty lips. He was leaning against the wall beside the door, his shoulders slouched, his eyes half closed, when two men entered and walked toward a roadster that was parked in back of a coupé.

THE new hand gazed lazily about, to make sure that no other employees were watching him. Slowly, he came to life; he shambled through the garage and came close to the roadster. One of the two men was at the wheel of the light car. The other was about to enter the coupé, in order to move it from the roadster's path.

"I'll move that car," drawled the new employee. "Lemme handle it, bud."

"All right, punk," growled the man beside the coupé. "Get a move on. We ain't staying here all night. We're in a hurry."

"You paid for the storage?"

"Sure. Over at the hotel. Here's the receipt."

The man flashed a sheet of paper. The car washer eyed it and nodded. Listlessly, he entered the coupé and pushed aside a small satchel that was lying on the driver's seat. He pressed the starter; the motor thrummed, then stalled. His next trial brought another failure.

"Say," growled the man beside the car, "what do you want us to do? Shove that crate out of the way?"

The starter whined again; this time the motor throbbed steadily. Gears clashed; the coupé went jerking forward, to stall again near the garage door. The man on the floor joined his companion in the roadster.

"What a dumb cluck," growled the man at the wheel. "Did you hear the way he jammed them gears, Jing?"

"Yeah," responded the second man, gruffly. "But don't worry about that goof. Keep an eye peeled to see who else is around."

"Nobody that I can see."

"Then get going. I'll take a squint along the street."

The roadster zipped from the garage. The driver gave a guffaw when he saw the car washer still trying to start the coupé so as to reverse it to the place where it had been. The roadster turned toward Eighth Avenue. Jing, watching the lighted street, delivered an approving grunt.

"O.K., Sloopy. Nobody here to spot us."

"Sloopy" grunted in satisfied fashion. He slowed to make the turn into Eighth Avenue.

Back at the garage, the shabby-dressed car washer had changed his tactics with the stalled coupé. The motor thrummed instantly when he pressed the starter. The trim car glided backward, then darted forward without a groan from the changing gears.

Eyes gleamed as a firm hand meshed the gear into high. The coupé swung out into the street. Its driver, no longer listless, spotted the roadster turning left into Eighth Avenue.

There was a whispered laugh within the confines of the coupé; a token of the driver's actual identity. The dull-faced, blundering car washer was The Shadow.

This coupé was The Shadow's own. He had sent it to the garage last night. Today, after talking himself into a job at the garage, he had found an opportunity to move the coupé in front of the roadster. Thereby, The Shadow had been ready at the right time.

He had looked over the two men who had brought him to the garage last night. He had lulled them into thinking that they were unwatched. Finally, The Shadow had taken up the trail of Drune's two minions.

THE trail led northward on Eighth Avenue. The roadster reached Broadway and continued along that thoroughfare. The Shadow recognized that the two crooks were bound for some destination outside of New York.

This was proven finally when the roadster neared One Hundred and Seventy-eighth Street. It headed for the approach of the George Washington Bridge.

Across that massive span, where lights twinkled high above the Hudson. Into New Jersey, then along a main highway. All the while, The Shadow's car continued with the same traffic that carried the roadster. Confident crooks never guessed that the coupé was following them.

As yet, The Shadow had no definite knowledge of the final destination. He believed that the cover-up men were on the way to some new scene of crime. How far their goal might be from New York—how soon they would be needed in new operations—these were matters impossible to guess.

Crime had first begun in Riverport, hundreds of miles south of New York. Crime had then come to the metropolis. It was due to strike somewhere else.

Whether the third crime would be the last was something that did not concern The Shadow. He was banking upon the one possibility that he could find the new scene soon enough to balk the deeds of evil workers.

Twenty miles outside of New York, The Shadow allowed the roadster more leeway. He knew this highway; there were no important side roads within the next ten miles. Traffic had thinned considerably; The Shadow preferred to let the crooks ride on without another car close behind them.

Coming to a small settlement, The Shadow slowed his speed. He observed a gasoline station on the near side of a dirt road. Beyond was a lunch wagon. Its lights showed the roadster parked in front. The crooks had stopped off for a hurried meal.

The Shadow pulled into the filling station. In drawled tone, he ordered the attendant to fill the gas tank. Alighting from the coupé, he strolled into the service station.

IN a manner that befitted his shabby garb, The Shadow shambled to a corner where a pay telephone was located. There was no one else in the service station; The Shadow was free to make an important call. He gave the operator a Manhattan number. Half a minute later, a quiet voice responded over the wire.

"Burbank speaking."

The Shadow had reached his contact man. His conversation with Burbank, however, did not concern the crooks whom The Shadow had followed. In whispered tone, The Shadow gave an order:

"Report on shipment."

"Arrived from Texas twenty minutes ago," returned Burbank, in a methodical tone. "Crofton has shipment at Newark Airport. Instructions awaited."

"Instructions," voiced The Shadow. "Transfer shipment to autogiro. Crofton to remain ready for new call."

"Instructions received."

Leaving the service station, The Shadow paid for the gasoline and started his coupé forward. He passed the lunch wagon slowly; as he guided the car with one hand, he used the other to open the satchel beside him.

From it, The Shadow produced cloak and hat. Halting the car beside the highway, he donned the garments. He then proceeded forward, his rate of speed no more than fifteen miles an hour.

Cars were roaring past the slow-moving coupé. The Shadow watched each automobile's approach in the mirror and checked again when the car had swished past. Soon he saw one coming up behind him with the speed of a rocket. He guessed that it was the roadster.

The Shadow was right. He recognized the license number when the light car whizzed past. Jing and Sloopy were making up for the time that they had lost by stopping at the lunch wagon.

The Shadow had turned on the bright lights of the coupé. He waited until the roadster had swept past a bend; then he clicked his lights to dimmers and jabbed the accelerator. The coupé showed an instant pickup. Seconds later, The Shadow had attained high speed.

He gained sight of the roadster's taillight within the next two miles. The crooks, had they looked back, could hardly have connected the car behind them with the coupé that had been loitering along the highway.

The expedient of brightening and dimming the headlights, while simple, was sufficient to lull the men ahead. The Shadow knew; for he had used the expedient on other occasions.

It was necessary to stay closer to the roadster while connecting highways were near at hand. The crooks kept to the main road; again, The Shadow gave them leeway.

At intervals, he closed up toward them, sometimes with bright lights, on other occasions with dim ones. The pursuit continued. The coupé's speedometer registered the distance of sixty-one miles from the George Washington Bridge.

As The Shadow was closing in on the roadster, he saw its taillight slacken speed. The Shadow slowed; he watched the light bob from view. Moving ahead, he came to an old highway that cut off at an angle to the right. The coupé's headlights showed a sign that indicated the town of Sheffield as being four miles away.

USING a road map by the glow of the dashlight, The Shadow formed an immediate conclusion. The crooks had certainly headed for Sheffield, for they had taken the direct route to that town. There was another turn off, a mile farther on, not quite as short as this one. The Shadow decided to use the second road.

He gave the coupé the gas. The car developed speed that it had not previously showed. All during this chase, The Shadow could have passed the crooks at any time, even though they had been driving the roadster to its limit.

The Shadow covered the mile to the next road

in a space of fifty seconds. Jamming the brakes, he wheeled right; then opened up along a bumpy road.

Few drivers would have dared to travel over forty-five along this battered highway. The Shadow urged the coupé to almost seventy miles an hour.

The lights of Sheffield showed ahead. The Shadow knew the town of more than thirty thousand inhabitants as the focal point of a quarrying district. Though a railroad center, Sheffield was isolated from the main highways.

The Shadow's road joined the one that the roadster had taken. As he slackened speed, The Shadow knew that he had beaten the crooks to the town. The road became the main street; The Shadow took time to study the business district of Sheffield.

On his right, The Shadow saw a decrepit building that looked like an old garage. Past the garage was a narrow street; then a pretentious old-fashioned structure that bore the name "Sheffield National Bank" above its wide doorway. A clock indicated a quarter of nine. The bank was open for late business.

The next building beyond the bank was a squatty stone-fronted structure with a wooden superstructure that showed rows of grimy blackened windows.

Looming above the roof was the beginning of a long train shed, chiefly of wood. A sign said "Freight Depot"; The Shadow recognized that this had formerly been a passenger station.

Through an alleyway next to the freight depot, The Shadow saw a line of railroad tracks that ran parallel to the main street. Those were the yards of the railroad that served the city of Sheffield.

Just after the freight depot, The Shadow came to a business block. This consisted of one large building, at least thirty years old. It was constructed of brick and wood. The ground floor showed storefronts, while the three remaining upper stories served as an apartment house.

As he neared the end of the block, The Shadow saw an important cross street. He decided to wait before he reached it, as the roadster was nearly due. There was a vacant space by a fire plug. No policemen were in sight. The Shadow pulled his coupé to the curb, turned out the lights, then watched from the cover of darkness.

THREE minutes ended The Shadow's vigil. The roadster rolled up and passed the coupé. Its occupants did not even glance toward The Shadow's car. As it neared the crossing, the roadster pulled to the center of the main street. A traffic light showed red; the roadster intended a left turn as soon as the light changed.

The Shadow eased the coupé from the curb. Another car had moved up in back of the roadster. The Shadow joined the line. The light turned green. The Shadow swung left with the cars ahead.

Though he had gained no inkling of the fact, The Shadow had viewed the scene of contemplated crime. He had studied the very buildings that had appeared as squares on Colgarth's numbered diagram. Drune, the master of crime, had given his approval to a campaign of destruction. The Shadow, alone competent to forestall evil, had unwittingly left the very place where trouble was due to break.

Nevertheless, The Shadow still had his trail. The roadster was heading westward from Sheffield. The Shadow had lessened speed; but he was keeping the car ahead in view. Caution was necessary. The roadster was taking to a highway that lacked traffic. The Shadow let the other car ride ahead.

He still had a way to trail the roadster. The road was hilly, with curves. By watching far ahead, The Shadow could see the tiny lights of the crook-manned car. The gleam bobbed in and out from strips of woods. The Shadow checked each reappearance of the lights.

There came a space of blackness. The lights did not reappear. Rounding a bend, The Shadow saw a dirt road to the right. He caught the glimmer of a taillight, a path of brightness beyond it. The roadster had turned off to the right.

Extinguishing his own lights, The Shadow made the turn. The wheels of the coupé joggled roughly on the dirt road.

Guided entirely by the red spot ahead, The Shadow sped the coupé through the darkness. His daring brought him close behind the roadster, just before it took a bend in the road. The Shadow had reached a vantage point.

Close behind the roadster, he was able to drive by the glow of the other car's lights. His coupé, however, had become invisible. Like a ghost car, it was trailing the roadster; the blanketing darkness of the woods concealed the coupé perfectly.

ALL was well for half a mile. The two cars crossed another dirt road; forty feet behind the roadster, The Shadow was sure that the soft purr of the coupe's motor had not been heard by the men ahead. When trouble came, it was from an unexpected source.

The two cars had traveled no more than a hundred feet from the crossing when a glare illuminated the road behind them. Brilliant headlights bathed both the coupé and the roadster. The Shadow's machine was caught in the glowing beam.

A third car had suddenly entered the game, moving in from the crossing that the two machines had passed. The Shadow's darkened coupé was trapped between two automobiles.

The unknown presence of The Shadow was revealed!

CHAPTER XI
DEATH IN THE DARK

IN his dealings with dangerous adversaries, The Shadow preferred quick action. Speedy in battle; accurate in marksmanship, The Shadow had frequently conquered heavy odds when events moved swiftly. His greatest tests came when emergency was slow to arrive. Such a condition gave foemen time to think.

The Shadow had entered a snare that troubled him more than the trap at Breel's. Almost at the end of a trail, his plans had gone wrong. The Shadow had counted upon complete stealth tonight; he had been profiting by the fact that crooks believed him dead. Without any warning, his actions had been exposed to the enemy.

The roadster was going to a rendezvous. The men in that car had been summoned to join their evil chiefs. The masters of crime had taken a precaution. They had posted a follow-up car at the borders of their domain. That third car, deliberately set to make sure the roadster was not followed, had found the dark coupé upon the trail.

Given time for deliberation, the men in the third car would guess that The Shadow was the driver of the coupé. Crooks had believed The Shadow dead on other occasions. They were always prompt to recognize his return.

What action would the enemy take?

One course was immediately possible. The Shadow expected to see the third car leap ahead to overtake him. That would mean battle with the trailers; afterward a fight with the crooks in the roadster, who would come back to join the battle. Such a happening would give The Shadow chance to deal with two groups separately.

The third car; however, failed to close in upon The Shadow. It simply matched the coupé's speed.

The Shadow pressed the accelerator more firmly. He began to gain upon the roadster. Instantly, the car ahead increased its speed. So did the machine that was following The Shadow.

Trying other tactics, The Shadow slowed almost to a standstill. The roadster slackened accordingly; the third car also rumbled at a snail-like gait.

The men in the roadster had noted the coupé by simply looking into their mirror. The lights from the third car had given them a chance to see that they were trailed.

Crooks were playing with The Shadow as a cat would play with a mouse. If he sought to overtake the car ahead, the car behind would close in before he could overwhelm the men in the roadster. If he waited for the car in back, it would not come to him. Nor would the roadster flee and open the road ahead.

CALMLY, The Shadow resumed a normal speed. The other two cars matched him with exactitude.

The dirt road was following an upward slope. The Shadow was content to keep along it. He knew that he was being taken closer to his goal. That was well for the present. Later, however, it could mean a definite trap.

Analyzing the situation, The Shadow knew definitely that there had been no communication between the car ahead and the car in back. Nevertheless, the two machines were acting in accord.

That meant one thing only. This precaution was a usual plan. Crooks had their instructions in advance on how to act should followers appear in this terrain.

The trap lay ahead. Where would it be?

There was a chance that it might lie at the rendezvous—the goal that The Shadow sought. There would be other criminals there, to swell the numbers of the band. At the same time, wise crooks would be wary about bringing an enemy straight into their own camp. It was quite as likely that the trap would be encountered before the end of the trail itself.

One mile had passed. The three cars were high upon the hillside, continuing on beneath the trees. The Shadow could feel a rising urge for action; one that he repressed. He realized well that the average man in his position would be jittery.

He calculated that the crooks had counted upon that fact. Whatever the trap, a clever schemer had devised it. The Shadow was confident that he would recognize the snare when he encountered it.

HIS first inkling that the spot was close by came when the roadster slightly decreased speed. The slope had lessened; the car ahead would logically have gone faster. As The Shadow slowed slightly, he noted in the mirror that the car behind was doing the same.

The roadster's headlights showed a slight turn to the right. As the car passed it; The Shadow observed a road that went left from the curve. Immediately afterward, the roadster jogged more speedily; the car in back, however, slowed a trifle. A soft laugh escaped The Shadow's lips.

The crooks were giving him a chance to duck away. The roadster was going to the right; if The Shadow went to the left, only the third car could follow. That would mean a single group of enemies. The opportunity was the very sort that would appeal to a man in a dilemma. In fact, the opportunity was too good. The Shadow knew that the crooks wanted him to go to the left.

The Shadow had reached the fork. Deep ruts to the left offered inviting tracks along which to guide his car. Lights were unnecessary. The road to the left was bait. Nevertheless, The Shadow took it.

Had The Shadow stopped to take up double battle, crooks would have been prepared. His policy was to draw them off their guard. By entering the trap, he could accomplish that important act. Wisdom merely told The Shadow not to venture too deep into the snare.

The roadster's lights had given The Shadow a forty-foot glimpse of the rutted road. That was the full distance that he drove. He could feel the ruts pulling the front wheels to the left, through absolute darkness. The Shadow estimated the distance before he halted.

SOFTLY opening the door of the coupé, The Shadow listened. He heard the slight throbbing of a motor. The third car had extinguished its lights. It was creeping into the road that he had taken. There was no sound of the coupé; no flicker of light among the trees. The front car, too, had stopped.

The Shadow knew what crooks expected.

They supposed that he was still in the coupé; that sooner or later, he would turn on the lights. If he did that, enemies would surge upon him in the darkness. Perhaps the trailing car would smash down upon his coupé.

If The Shadow lingered in the dark, crooks, too would have the benefit of the gloom. They could attack, en masse, to overpower their lone prey.

There was a third course: to drive ahead in darkness. The Shadow knew that his foemen must certainly recognize that such was possible. Therefore, he decided that to drive ahead would mean a completion of the snare. Waiting in their darkened car, crooks were hoping that The Shadow would push the coupé onward, without benefit of lights.

Standing on the left running board, The Shadow reached across the wheel and pulled the hand throttle on the dashboard. The coupé's motor quickened its rhythm. The Shadow adjusted it to a moderate purr.

Pressing the clutch pedal with his left hand, he used his right to pull the gear shift into low. He shifted his right hand to the clutch pedal. Slowly, precisely, he let the pedal move upward from the floor.

The action brought the car into gear. With a slight jolt, the coupé moved forward. The ground was level; the car reached a speed of five miles an hour. There was no need to handle the steering wheel. The ruts were holding the coupé to the road.

Swinging outward, The Shadow gripped the handle of the door. As the car rode slowly ahead, he clamped the door shut noiselessly. He hung free, ready at any instant to drop to the ground beside him.

He could see nothing; not even the opening of the road ahead, for the sky was clouded, as dark as the overhanging trees. The Shadow had even extinguished the dashlight. The interior of the coupé was a mass of solid blackness.

The road sloped slightly downward. The whining coupé moved faster. The front wheels gave a sudden jounce. Instantly, The Shadow dived sidewise to the ground. He struck sandy soil; his feet slid past an edge. Gripping at rocks, The Shadow checked his rolling. He could feel a swish; he heard a mechanical screech as the rear wheels of the coupé lurched upward into the air.

An instant later, the car was gone. The sound of its motor had vanished. Seconds seemed interminable; at last, from somewhere far below came the thwack of a tremendous splash that brought long echoes from the steep walls of a stony pit. The coupé had plunged a full eighty feet into the deep, stagnant waters of an abandoned quarry.

The Shadow was on the fringe of the cliff. He had acted instantly when he had felt the warning. As he crawled to firmer ground, he could hear the throb of an approaching motor. The men in the third car had heard the splash. They were confident that the coupé's driver had gone with the car into the quarry.

They had moved up behind the coupe, knowing that its fall would tell them when they had reached their limit. They wanted to peer down into the pit; to assure themselves that The Shadow had made no miraculous escape from the submerged coupé.

RISING from hands and knees, The Shadow was drawing an automatic. He expected men to come on foot, with flashlights. He was preparing to give them a surprise. Instead, the driver of the car was the one who unwittingly produced the surprise.

The fellow suddenly switched on the lights, to spot the edge of the quarry. Headlamps and taillight were sufficient to show the outline of the car, forty feet short of the quarry's edge.

The car was still coasting forward; the glare of

The car lurched hard toward The Shadow. Whipping from the path, The Shadow jabbed quick shots from his automatic.

its headlights showed The Shadow. Instantly, the cloaked fighter sprang forward, straight for the radiator of the sedan.

The front of the car afforded The Shadow his only possible cover. Shouts were coming from the moving car; guns were bristling from windows. Revolvers spat wildly in the night. Thuggish marksmen were too late. Five in number, they saw The Shadow dropping in front of the moving car; the sedan's advance was giving him better cover.

The unarmed driver snarled an oath. He saw a chance to beat The Shadow's game. He had thirty feet in which to do it. The Shadow was only a few yards away. Gripping the wheel in readiness for a sharp turn, the sedan's driver jabbed the accelerator. The car lurched hard toward The Shadow.

Whipping from the path, The Shadow jabbed quick shots from his automatic. He aimed for the steering wheel, to cripple the thug behind it. That crook out, the sedan could not continue.

The Shadow could again use the radiator as his entrenchment. In his close-range aim, The Shadow was accurate; but his leap was delayed too long. As his .45 zimmed its third quick shot, the fender of the sedan sideswiped him before he could escape it.

Staggering, The Shadow reeled sidewise. He sprawled and lost his guns. He was clear of the sedan's path; he lay flat on the road, was in darkness off to the side. But bullets were biting the gravel all about him. The moment the car halted, or turned, The Shadow would be a helpless target.

Savage shouts had sounded from the car as crooks stabbed wild shots that were ineffective because of the sedan's motion. As The Shadow rolled to hands and knees, groping to regain a gun, he heard shouts change to shrieks.

The sedan had not stopped; nor had it veered. The driver had slumped without the knowledge of the marksmen who accompanied him. His foot had slipped from the accelerator; but the car was in high gear. On the slight downgrade, it was rolling straight to the quarry's brink.

The thug beside the driver was grabbing for the steering wheel. He gained it; the car swerved left on the edge of the cliff. A door burst open; one frenzied crook made a dive for the ground. He was the wisest of the lot.

Though its left wheels held to solid ground, the sedan's right tires slipped over the stony edge. The car was broadside to The Shadow; he saw its lights topple away from him.

With a slow, outward motion, the sedan took a sidewise plunge. It was gone from the brink, the lights obliterated. Long shrieks became trailing wails that ended in a splash more violent than the thwack of the coupé.

The sedan had carried four crooks as cargo to the fate that they had sought to bestow upon The Shadow. The fifth thug had escaped. He was crawling from the brink.

Bare-handed, The Shadow surged forward to meet him.

PICKING the exact spot where he had seen the crook fall, The Shadow found his foeman in the darkness. The man quavered hoarsely as The Shadow seized him.

Too jittery to offer resistance after his narrow escape from death, the crook subsided to the turf. His thought of fight was gone. He feared the fate that had overwhelmed the others. Whipping the fellow's belt from his waist, The Shadow rolled the prisoner on his face and doubled his legs upward. With the belt, he formed a figure eight that bound the thug's wrists and ankles together.

Carrying the prisoner well away from the quarry, The Shadow placed him against a tree. Producing a flashlight, he looked about for his automatics. He found them, extinguished the light, then returned along the rutty road. The Shadow expected to find others back at the fork.

A motor throbbed its presence. The Shadow recognized the jerky sound. Sloopy and Jing were waiting; they had heard only the sounds of gunfire. Sloopy was peering from beside the wheel, growling because he could not see through the dark. The roadster's dashlight offered a small glow within the car.

"It was The Shadow," decided Sloopy, in a gruff tone. "Couldn't have been nobody else. Thought they croaked him, though, at Breel's—"

A muffled cry from Jing. Sloopy turned. He saw gloved hands from the dark, over the right door of the roadster, yanking Jing from the car. As Jing sprawled outward, Sloopy caught the gleam of fierce eyes. A hoarse shout was Sloopy's challenge:

"The Shadow!"

Yanking a revolver, Sloopy jabbed shots into the darkness—the darkness where sounds of a scuffle told him that Jing was meeting disaster. Echoes followed Sloopy's three shots. All was quiet beside the car. Leaning to the right, Sloopy called out.

"You all right, Jing?" was his query. "Hope I didn't plug you, while I was getting him. It was The Shadow—"

A dying groan answered from the ground beside the roadster. The tone was Jing's. As Sloopy winced, a sinister laugh sounded at his very elbow, on the left side of the car. Coughing an oath, Sloopy swung about. He was too late to aim his gun.

VISELIKE hands gripped Sloopy's throat. Choking, the crook dropped his gun. He subsided, sidewise, to the seat beside him. The Shadow came aboard the roadster. By the dashlight's glow, he bound and gagged Sloopy and huddled him upon the seat at the right.

Jing was dead. The Shadow had twisted him toward the car. Sloopy's shots had finished his pal. By rounding the back of the roadster, The Shadow had completed his victory. Carrying Sloopy as a prisoner, he started the roadster along the road to the right.

Should this road lead nowhere, The Shadow intended to question the man beside him; to make the prisoner talk, a task that The Shadow could easily accomplish.

One mile farther on, The Shadow skirted the side of a hill. He paused to study a distant glow against the clouded sky. A puff of flame rose suddenly, then disappeared. Darkness replaced the short-lived beacon.

This road led to a blast furnace. The Shadow had recognized the flare from the far-off chimney. The furnace was one that worked at night; most observers would not have given it second thought, for such plants were common in this region.

The Shadow, however, delved more deeply.

He was seeking a supercrook who used fire as the means to cover crime—an evil master of death, who controlled the Salamanders as henchmen. A blast furnace would be useful to those rogues as a proving ground for their devices.

The flare puffed anew. It was from somewhere along this old road. The Shadow drove the roadster forward, toward the goal that living flames had revealed.

CHAPTER XII
THE ORDEAL

THE puffs of flame that guided The Shadow were proof that something was afoot at the blast furnace. Master crooks were at their isolated headquarters. Drune and Colgarth had completed their plans for crime; while they awaited a definite hour, they had found time for preliminary diversion.

The two rogues were seated in a small, stone-walled room that looked like a crude office. They occupied battered chairs; near them was a desk, with a telephone. A single incandescent light illuminated the chamber. Beneath the glare, a prisoner lay propped against the wall.

He was bound hand and foot, that captive. Stolidly, he met the glaring gaze of the men who held him helpless. His face showed grimness; his lips remained unopened. He was ready to defeat all efforts that might be used to make him talk.

The prisoner on the floor was Harry Vincent. The Shadow's agent had survived the hotel fire at Riverport. His present plight, however, was as great as when Gordon Colgarth had consigned him to the smoke-filled cellar.

Colgarth, himself, was emphasizing that particular fact. In harsh tones, the hard-faced man was speaking to the prisoner.

"We know your name, Vincent," came Colgarth's rasp. "We know why you were at Riverport, watching Woldorf. You were working for The Shadow."

Colgarth paused to see if he had scored a hit. Harry's expression did not change.

"Why be a fool?" sneered Colgarth.

"The Shadow is dead. Look at these headlines." He picked up a newspaper from the desk and pointed to large-typed words. "They say that Lincoln Breel died in a New York fire. They lie. We rubbed out Breel days ago.

"It was The Shadow who died instead of Breel. He was finished by the same men who carried you from the Riverport hotel. We figured we might make you talk. That's why I shoved you down into the cellar. But The Shadow was different. We took no chances with him."

Harry did not betray the worry that he felt. He had no recollection of how he had been brought from Riverport. His hurtling trip into the hotel cellar had left him senseless. He could recall traveling in a bumpy truck; a final arrival in this stone-walled room. Since then, he had been a prisoner, confined to this one place.

Did Colgarth speak the truth concerning The Shadow?

HARRY feared that the crook's words were correct. Harry knew The Shadow's ability at disguise. He could picture his chief arriving at Breel's, not knowing that the man whom he impersonated had been murdered days before.

"You gain nothing by silence," insisted Colgarth. "We're giving you a chance, Vincent, because we don't want any interference in the future. You worked for The Shadow, so it's a bet that there are others like you. We want to know who they are.

"Maybe you're thinking that we didn't get The Shadow, that we want you to squawk so we can find him. That's not the game. The Shadow is dead, I tell you. He'll stay dead. You can't help him."

Harry remained unimpressed. Colgarth fumed. He was about to rasp new statements when Drune stopped him with a waving hand. It was the gray-haired magnate's time to speak.

Until this moment, Drune had said nothing. He

LINCOLN BREEL—retired financial wizard.

acquisitions. First"—he tapped his left thumb with his right forefinger—"important securities held by Chester Woldorf. We gained those by removing the safe from the Capitol Hotel in Riverport."

HARRY stared. He had guessed why Woldorf had been murdered; but he could not understand how the hotel safe had been lifted. He tried to connect it with his own peculiar delivery from the fire. He wondered how any human being could have braved the flame.

"Second"—Drune was tapping his left forefinger—"we needed securities owned by Lincoln Breel. I, personally, saw to Breel's death at his lonely lodge in the Adirondacks. Later, we set his home ablaze. We removed the safe that was in his New York residence. We now possess Breel's holdings."

In satisfied fashion, Drune tapped his next finger.

"Our third and final acquisition," he stated, "will be securities that belong to the Cruikshank estate. Those stocks are in the Sheffield National Bank. We shall remove them tonight. I might remark that we shall encounter no difficulty whatever."

Leaning back, Drune waved a hand toward his partner.

"This gentleman," he remarked, "is Gordon Colgarth. He is highly esteemed in the town of Sheffield. He owns property in the city. He is a director of the Sheffield National Bank. His residence is a country estate, with a delightful old colonial mansion. It is located several miles north of Sheffield."

Drune's persuasive tone had become almost gentle. Colgarth blinked, then showed a hard smile. Puzzled at first, he realized that Drune was using the best tactics. By telling all, the master crook was making an impression upon Harry.

Drune leaned toward the prisoner. Steadily, each word emphatic, he came to the climax that he wanted.

"We have killed," announced Drune, "whenever necessity compelled us. We have been ruthless, purely through policy. Tonight, one hundred or more persons may perish. Useless persons, who will die only because their plight will divert attention from our place of operations.

"The Shadow was a threat. Therefore, we slew him. Previously we had permitted you to live, because we thought you might prove useful. Colgarth has already expressed that fact. I need not dwell further on the past.

"The future concerns the three of us. Whether you live or die depends entirely upon your own

had simply eyed Harry with a cunning gaze. Drune's shrewd look had made Harry feel positive that the older man was the senior partner of the criminal pair, more important—and, therefore, more dangerous—than Colgarth.

When Drune spoke, his tones were a dry crackle, persuasive because of their careful emphasis.

"Perhaps, Mr. Vincent," stated Drune, "we should clarify this situation. We know your name, thanks to papers that were on your person. You, however, have not heard ours. I am Huxley Drune, president of the Great American Power Company, with offices in New York City.

"Possibly you have never heard of my company? That is not astonishing. Great American Power has not as yet come into the limelight. It was founded upon prospects rather than actual assets. Great American Power will be heard from in the future."

There was an insidious touch to Drune's prediction. The master crook paused to indulge in a dry smile.

"Our prospects," continued Drune, watching Harry steadily as he spoke, "depended upon three choice. Tonight, Colgarth and I shall possess all the holdings that we need. Our wealth, through proper manipulation, will bring us fifty million dollars.

"There will be a stir in Wall Street. One, however, that will excite no suspicion there. The only people who might link our gain with crime are others like yourself. Men who once served The Shadow. We are willing to grant you life because we know that you can offset the efforts of such persons."

Tilting his head in a speculative fashion, Drune spoke pleasantly of the future.

"You will live in comfort, Vincent," he declared. "Let us say in luxury. You will be a prisoner, yes, but good behavior will grant you privileges. You will, of course, provide us with the names of all persons who might make us trouble.

"We shall watch such persons. If they do nothing against us, we shall ignore them. If they trouble us, we shall let you warn them. Unless they persist despite your warnings, we shall not harm them.

"They are your friends, Vincent." Drune lowered his gaze and smiled benignly toward the prisoner. "You can be their benefactor, by keeping them out of trouble. Your work accomplished, you shall have wealth—our gift, in return for your cooperation."

DRUNE stopped. His withered face tilted to one side. His eyes beamed; his lips showed a mild smile. Harry remained stolid. Colgarth showed impatience.

"What about it, Vincent?" queried the junior partner. "You've heard Drune's terms. They're fair—"

Drune extended a restraining hand.

"Come, Colgarth," he suggested. "Let Vincent deliberate alone. We may grant him a few minutes to make his decision."

Colgarth nodded. He followed Drune toward a door at the front of the room. The two stepped through into a passage. Drune closed the door. He chuckled softly as he and Colgarth stood in the darkness of the passage.

"That talk," remarked the master crook in a tone that was complimentary to himself, "can be classed as the proper style of persuasion to be used with a man of intelligence."

"You handled it great," whispered Colgarth. "There's only one question, though."

"What is it?"

"Is Vincent going to be worth all that you promised him?"

Drune's reply was an insidious croak. To Colgarth, it signified more than words. Drune was denoting evil pleasure. Colgarth awaited an explanation.

"So you fell for it?" chuckled Drune. "Well, Colgarth, if you swallowed my story, Vincent probably will."

"You bluffed him?"

"Of course. Of what use is Vincent? Only to tell us the names of others."

"You mentioned that to him—"

"Certainly. All the while, however, I covered the most important fact."

"What was that?"

"The fact that Vincent and those others all come into the class that I mentioned mildly—persons whom we must necessarily eliminate. Once Vincent has told us the names of all who served The Shadow, we shall do away with them, one by one."

"And Vincent?"

"He will be our final victim. Come, Colgarth; we have given him sufficient time to consider my false offer. Let us enter and hear his reply."

Drune opened the door and stepped into the lighted office. He approached Harry and smiled in kindly manner. Pleasantly, he put a question:

"You have considered?"

FOR the first time, Harry showed an expression. Looking up at Drune, he delivered a contemptuous smile. Words were unnecessary on Harry's part. His disdainful look showed that he had seen through Drune's false promise.

Instantly, Drune's manner altered.

His smile changed to a demonish leer. His eyes bulged from their sockets. His teeth showed fanglike, yellow and ugly against the duller hue of his parchment face. Clenching his fists, Drune turned to Colgarth, whose hard face showed harsh anger. Drune's game had failed. He was ready to vent his spite upon the prisoner who had defied him.

"We shall do without Vincent's knowledge," snarled Drune. "His death will mean one more meddler gone. We can meet the others as they come."

"Right," rasped Colgarth. He hauled forth a revolver and jabbed the muzzle toward Harry. "I'll give him what's coming to him."

"Wait!" Drune's firm hand gripped Colgarth's arm. "This prisoner does not deserve so comfortable a fate."

With a leer, he added: "The Salamanders saved him from death by fire. We shall consign him back into the flames."

Bravely, Harry Vincent heard the promised fate. He was ready for his ordeal, although he had no hope of aid. Harry believed The Shadow dead;

his chief, so he thought, had perished in a tomb of fire.

Despite the horror of such death, Harry felt triumph in the thought that he was to end life like The Shadow, fighting against evil.

CHAPTER XIII
THE FIERY PIT

DRUNE snapped a command to Colgarth. The latter yanked open the door and shouted a summons that echoed along the stony corridor. Harry heard the pace of approaching feet. Two brawny, rough-clad men arrived. Colgarth indicated the prisoner.

"Take him to the test room."

The men nodded. Harry was hoisted upon husky shoulders. Helplessly bound, he felt himself being carried through the darkened passage. The men made a turn at a corner. They came to a large door; one carrier kicked it open.

A fierce glow struck Harry's eyes; with it came a crackling roar. A blast of heat swept from the doorway. As the men descended steps, Harry sniffed fumes amid the burning temperature. His captors strode twelve paces forward, then dropped Harry to the floor against a wall. His eyes were straight toward the glow.

Directly in front of Harry was a pit thirty feet wide. It extended fifteen feet to a wall. That pit was a bed of fire, an open furnace that matched all descriptions of hellish depths. Coals were banked high, almost to the level of a concrete curb that fronted the pit.

Looming from the wall at the left was a huge tube that evidently led to a chimney. Harry heard a whirring sound; flames roared as a suction pump drew them crackling toward the tube. Fumes and smoke were sucked upward; with them went a terrific surge of flame.

Harry recognized that this must be a converted blast furnace. He guessed that the sudden suction had carried a sweep of flames up through a tall chimney.

Such was necessary in order to free the room from fumes that no human being could survive.

HARRY'S two captors had gone. Despite the pressure of the heat, Harry glanced to the right. He saw that the right end of the pit ended a few yards short of the wall. Harry saw grimy hands and bare, sweaty shoulders.

Stripped to the waist, three stokers were at work in a shallow pit. They were hauling out ashes from beneath the fire.

Large cans of ashes were stacked at the right wall, on a level with the path where Harry lay. It required tons of coal to feed the fiery pit. Harry was puzzled as to the purpose of so large a bed of flame. He was to learn the reason for it; but before the answer came, he was suddenly impelled to watch a happening at the wall beyond the pit.

A short section of the wall was rising upward, like a curtain. Harry had taken it for stone; he realized that it must be thin steel, fronted with asbestos that matched the dullish color of the solid wall.

The raised curtain revealed a ledge of six-foot width. The ledge was some four feet deep; behind it was a wall topped by a rail. Leaning over the rail was Huxley Drune.

High above the flaming pit, Drune stood like a gloating sentinel. His glare focused upon Harry; the prisoner saw the evil smirk that adorned the master villain's lips.

Wavering fumes from the pit added distortion to Harry's view. He saw Drune as a demon, the controller of the torrid depths where fire held its sway.

Drune's arms were waving in command. Stokers swung huge shovels, to hurl streams of coal across the fire. Flames roared their welcome to the fuel. Hungrily, they turned the coals into an added blaze. The suction outlet whirred.

Again, Harry saw a mass of fire shoot up through the chimney. Fumes cleared and gave a better view of Drune. The fire master was delivering a new signal.

Harry looked to the left. Coming through a door was Gordon Colgarth, flanked by two of the strangest creatures whom Harry had ever seen. They looked like undersea divers, clad in bulky suits with glass-fronted helmets. Each of these underlings was trailing a long hose.

It was Harry's first sight of the Salamanders. He understood, at last, how he had been carried from the toppling, fire-swept structure of the old hotel in Riverport. These asbestos-suited workers were the servitors who made crime possible for Drune and Colgarth. Harry guessed correctly that there must be other Salamanders in the crew.

More than that, he understood the reason for the huge bed of fire that lay before him. That pit was the practice ground wherein the Salamanders tested their ability. The flames of the open furnace made as hot a fire as any that the Salamanders might encounter when they marched forth to crime.

The Salamanders moved onward. Colgarth stopped. Reaching the spot where Harry lay, the monstrous henchmen stooped and picked up the prisoner. Hoisting him high between them, they turned toward the fire. Drune's hand was raised to halt them. The Salamanders waited, holding

Harry, stretched face upward. They had raised him to arm's length.

Harry could see nothing but the high stone ceiling. He could feel the heat of the furnace; he could smell its sulphurous fumes. He heard a whirred puff as the suction pipe operated. For a moment, the heat lessened; the fumes were gone. Turning his head, Harry, saw Drune's arm drop.

The Salamanders stepped squarely into the blazing pit.

THE crackle beneath Harry's back was ominous. Tongued flames were sweltering, though their upward lick did not reach the prisoner, who was borne seven feet above. Step by step, finding solid footing upon the live coals, the Salamanders strode to the inner wall.

Lowering their arms, they placed Harry, face upward, upon a ledge. Six feet above the fire, Harry lay like a victim upon the altar of a Moloch. Drune, glaring down, represented the fiend who was prepared to deliver sacrifice to the fire-god.

Increasing fumes cleared as another blast roared up into the chimney. Turning, the Salamanders marched out through the fire. They joined Colgarth at the door, as he waved for them to hurry.

Harry saw the Salamanders removing their helmets. He guessed that they were leaving with Colgarth upon their expedition of crime.

Stokers hurled new coals upon the fire. Flames licked the wall below the ledge. The fire was ready for its victim. Drune reached to a niche beside him and drew slowly upon a long, stout, wooden lever that was fitted into a steel ring.

There was a grating sound by Harry's shoulder. Looking inward, the prisoner saw the wall inch forward below the rail. It pressed slowly outward. It encountered Harry's shoulder. Harry felt himself move toward the pit, while hidden machinery clattered in response to Drune's slow, steady pull upon the lever.

The fire master was gloating. Stokers showed leers upon their sweaty faces as they watched Harry's slow approach to the flames. They were proper henchmen for a fiend like Drune. The stokers took it that they were to have their reward for long efforts with the fire.

Within the coming minutes, Harry Vincent was destined to lose his balance; to plunge downward toward the white-hot coals. The fire was sufficient to burn any unprotected human to a crisp within the time space of a dozen seconds.

Harry tried to buck the moving wall. The attempt was useless. He was at the edge. One bound elbow was hanging over the fire. Strength left him as he turned his face to the wall.

The fumes were bringing spasmodic gasps from Harry's lips. He managed barely to turn upon his left side facing the wall. The move prevented him from falling; but it meant only a short postponement of the final plunge.

Drune paused a moment with the lever to gloat at Harry's plight. The stokers shouted glee that was drowned out by the fire's roar. Drune's hand tightened on the wooden rod.

Triumphantly, he looked toward the stokers. Two of them were gesticulating their mad joy. The third suddenly became rigid.

With a wild, unheard shout, the third stoker pointed across the fire. His companions stopped their gestures to stare. Drune, his hand stilled upon the lever, looked also.

At the door by which Colgarth and the Salamanders had departed stood a figure of vengeance. The lurid, red-orange light of the fire showed The Shadow. His black-clad form was weird against the reflected crimson that tinged the wall. His eyes were burning with a glow that matched the fire's coals.

Gloved fists held automatics. One weapon was directed toward Drune's balcony; the other covered the stokers at the end of the pit.

DRUNE snarled. The stokers dived away. Automatics spat bullets before a crook could gain a gun. Slugs clanged the wide posts of Drune's protecting rail. Other bullets sizzled the wall where the stokers had been. The three underlings were taking to a doorway below, to get out of range from The Shadow's covering guns.

Drune was alone. Twisting backward into a narrow outlet, he had found luck with him. He had escaped The Shadow's first bullets. He was under cover in his exit, except for his extended right arm, which bent from around a corner and gripped the top of the long, wooden lever.

The Shadow could not aim for Drune's clutching hand. It was protected by the steel rail of the balcony. As his last deed before flight, Drune intended to give the final tug that would thrust the wall six inches farther forward and roll Harry Vincent into the fiery pit.

The Shadow aimed between the rails of the balcony. He took the only target possible, the wooden lever that projected upward in full view. Bullets whistled in a swift barrage. They splintered the wooden rod, just as Drune gave his last pull. The weakened lever failed. It snapped off in Drune's fist.

Promptly, The Shadow sidled to the left. He gained a new position—one that gave him an angle from which he could pump bullets into the exit where Drune had taken cover.

The master crook foresaw the maneuver. Too

Slowly, each step steady, he found his footing in the furnace. The Shadow was using the process of the Oriental fire walkers, who tread bare-footed through beds of flame.

late to pull a gun of his own, he took another course. He made a hasty scramble off through his outlet, just as The Shadow gained the aim he wanted. A .45 spoke half a second too late. Drune had gone to overtake the fleeing stokers; to make a dash for distant safety.

The Shadow looked toward Harry Vincent. He saw his agent prone and motionless, on the very outward portion of the ledge. Though the pressing wall had stopped, Harry was in a forced position.

The slightest waver of his body would cause him to lose his balance. Groggy from the fumes, Harry was holding onto life through sheer instinct. At any moment, he might lose his slender balance.

Rescue was imperative; yet between The Shadow and his agent lay fifteen feet of roaring, fresh-coaled flames!

The Shadow saw the ash containers at the end of the short passage that fronted the fire bed. Swiftly, he dashed toward the containers.

One of those ash-filled cylinders was almost a two-man burden; yet The Shadow hoisted it as easily as if it had been empty. He swung to the center of the low front that ran along the pit. With a lunging motion, he tossed thick ashes upon the fire.

Flames wavered; they lashed the sides of the ashy path and fought to lick up through the surface. The Shadow hurled more ashes; these went farther than the first. They spread halfway across the gap separating The Shadow from Harry Vincent.

Another heave sent chunky ashes to a distance of twelve feet. The Shadow gave a final toss and sprayed the last contents to the far wall.

The chimney roared. Flames swept across the ashy path and formed a flare as they roared through the suction tube. Again, the ashy path lay clear and gray. Fumes had departed. The Shadow sprang across the low barrier and stepped upon the path of ashes.

SLOWLY, each step steady, he found his footing in the furnace. Haste would have spelled his doom. So would delay. The Shadow was using the process of the Oriental fire walkers, who tread barefooted through beds of flame. Their secret was a burnt charcoal surface, with feet toughened by an alum solution.

The Shadow had chosen ordinary ashes, with leather underfoot. His protection was greater; but he was daring flames that no fire walker would have been willing to engage.

Five steady paces. Eyes ahead. The Shadow saw Harry's body waver. Almost pausing, The Shadow made three short strides, timing his steps to the minimum, counting upon Harry's fall. Forward went The Shadow's hands.

As Harry, gasping, toppled from the ledge, strong arms were there to snare him just below the brink. Gauging his approach to perfection, The Shadow had gained advantage through Harry's sudden relax. He had no need to pause.

He had caught his falling agent tightly; turning, The Shadow swung Harry across his shoulders. Stooped forward, he gazed toward the ashes as he retraced his path to safety.

The return was doubly dangerous. Fire had licked up through the ashes. Certain spots were unsafe. The Shadow's strides were zigzagging ones. With the burden of double weight, he needed absolute surety in footing. Anyone of his eight steps could mean doom for himself and the man he rescued.

Steady steps served The Shadow; but his deliberate progress produced another sort of danger. At any moment, the suction tube was due to draw another withering blast of fire across the failing path of ashes. The Salamanders had not feared such puffs of flame; but The Shadow was not equipped to withstand one. Each step made a blast more imminent.

THE SHADOW reached the front edge of the pit. He stamped a scorched shoe upon the low stone barrier. With an upward, forward spring he swung his other foot past the edge, down to the stone path beyond.

Quickly, he leaped entirely clear from the fire's edge and rolled Harry to the solid floor beside the wall. Leaning back, The Shadow drew a lungful of fresh breath. He had been forced to breathe with caution amid the scorching fumes.

A tremendous roar came from the defeated fire. It was the expected suction of the automatic chimney, four seconds too late to ensnare The Shadow. Flames rose and ripped in one wild sheet that lashed across the path of ashes. The chimney howled as it delivered a puff like those that had served The Shadow as his beacon.

That surge of fire obliterated the ashy path; but its destroying force found nothingness. The Shadow had rescued Harry Vincent. He had won his duel with the flaming pit.

CHAPTER XIV
CRIME'S HOUR

NEW vigilance was The Shadow's move immediately after his rescue of Harry Vincent. He had witnessed the full evil of Huxley Drune. He knew that the supercrook might return once he had rallied his scattered squad of henchmen.

Standing above Harry Vincent, The Shadow drew the automatics that he had replaced beneath his cloak. He looked toward the high-railed balcony, then to the stoker's pit.

Satisfied that crooks were not returning, The Shadow put away one gun. While he held the other, he raised Harry from the floor and started a journey through the outer door. The furnace blasted a puffy roar as its conqueror departed.

Cool air seemed frigid in the passage. The contrast was so staggering that The Shadow was forced to ease Harry to the floor. Two minutes passed, while The Shadow watched the brilliant doorway, ready in case enemies should appear. The air became reviving. The Shadow stooped beside Harry.

There was no need to cut Harry's bonds. The Shadow broke them with hard tugs; for the cords had become scorched. Harry's hands showed blisters; so did his neck; but his face had been away from the fire. His clothing, though singed, had protected his body.

Harry's ordeal had been a long one; but he was showing signs of slow recuperation. Producing a handkerchief, The Shadow ripped it in half and used the portions to bandage Harry's hands. Slowly, Harry moved; finding himself free, he tried to rise. The Shadow prevented him. He eased Harry against the wall.

Whispered words reached Harry's ears. Tones of encouragement that came like a voice within a dream. Harry realized that he had been rescued; he recognized the tones as The Shadow's. It was unbelievable; so much so that it stirred Harry to vague mutterings. His words became coherent.

"Drune," spoke Harry. "Huxley Drune—the man above the pit—he runs the game. Gordon Colgarth—he met me in Riverport—he commands the Salamanders—"

Harry mumbled. The Shadow urged him to continue. In response to the commanding whisper, Harry spoke again.

"Woldorf—Breel—both murdered"—Harry paused; his breath came in a choke—"there will be other crime tonight. Sheffield—the bank—a hundred people may die—"

HARRY'S tone subsided. He was sinking back with a tired sigh. The Shadow roused him violently. With a start, Harry tried to connect events.

"I was a prisoner," he recalled. "They kept me in a room like an office. Chairs there—a desk—a telephone. They took me through a passage, to a pit of fire—"

Harry gulped as he leaned forward. He could see the vivid glow from the furnace room. He heard a puffing roar from beyond that door. His nerves began to buckle. Harry sagged backward. The Shadow gripped him. The strength of that

clasp restored Harry's fading confidence. He rallied as The Shadow drew him to his feet.

The Shadow led the way along the passage. He reached the end away from the furnace room. He guided Harry to the right; there was reason for the move.

The Shadow had entered from the other direction, through a doorway that he had found when he reached the building that housed the blast furnace. He knew, therefore, that Harry must have been brought from the opposite end of the passage. The Shadow wanted to locate the office that Harry had mentioned.

Using a flashlight, The Shadow found the door. He opened it, discovered the hanging light and turned it on. He saw the desk; placing Harry in a chair, he picked up the telephone. A few clicks of the receiver hook brought a response from the operator. In careful tones, The Shadow gave a New York number.

Harry had told The Shadow where crime was due. It would strike in Sheffield, with the Sheffield National Bank as its goal. The Shadow knew that crooks would again use fire as their main weapon. Given time, he could offset their stroke.

Burbank's voice came across the wire. The Shadow gave an order.

"Autogiro to leave at once," he instructed. "Make landing at the airport near Sheffield, New Jersey. Await contact."

"Instructions received."

The Shadow had made plans for the mysterious shipment that had come from Texas. Crofton had by this time transferred it to the autogiro at the Newark Airport. He would have the autogiro at the Sheffield Airport within the next hour.

There was a chance that crime would strike before the ship arrived. The Shadow must warn the authorities in Sheffield. He clicked the receiver to recall the Sheffield operator. There was a half-minute delay; then the girl's voice sounded.

"Hello..."

The line was dead. The Shadow clicked the receiver hook twice, then jounced the telephone upon the desk. Drune's work. The master crook had rallied his men somewhere outside. They had cut the telephone wire.

The Shadow turned to Harry for more facts. Revived, the rescued agent gave them.

"Colgarth left with two Salamanders," stated Harry. "The rest are probably in Sheffield. Colgarth has a country house, several miles north of the town."

THE SHADOW nodded. He could picture the country estate as the new headquarters. A stronghold to which Drune had probably headed, leaving crime to Colgarth in Sheffield.

The Shadow had not encountered Colgarth and the Salamanders; but he had heard a car pulling away from one side of the blast furnace while he had been stowing the roadster in the woods beyond the building.

It was time for quick action. First, to make sure that Drune was not still about; after that, to reach Sheffield with the utmost speed. The Shadow had formed an instantaneous picture of the situation. The old garage as headquarters for the Salamanders; the Sheffield National Bank as the building to be burned.

More than that, he recognized what Harry had meant by a hundred lives in danger. The Shadow remembered the old freight depot; the apartment house beyond it. As clearly as if he had Colgarth's diagram in front of him, The Shadow could see the route by which the fire would progress.

The call to Burbank had been important; but it would be useless if the blaze began too soon. The warning to the Sheffield authorities had been The Shadow's alternate move; Drune had tidily balked it. The Shadow's deduction was that crime would not be long delayed.

The Shadow paused long enough to add new cartridges to his half-emptied automatics. Producing an additional weapon, he handed it to Harry. With a sharp order, The Shadow clicked off the light, then used his flashlight to lead the way outside.

When they reached the chilly outdoors, The Shadow extinguished his torch. Clutching Harry's arm, he drew his companion through the darkness. They groped past trees; The Shadow found the roadster. He turned on the dashlight. Harry saw Sloopy bound and gagged inside the car.

Without ceremony, The Shadow hauled the crook to the ground and rolled him close beside a tree. He motioned Harry into the car, then took the wheel. The motor hummed as The Shadow pressed the starter. The car swung toward the road.

"Prepare for Drune."

Harry gripped his automatic as he heard The Shadow's order. The Shadow was driving with one hand, gripping a .45 with the other. He turned on the lights; they showed the road ahead. Harry realized that if they encountered an ambush, The Shadow's plan would be to run it rather than delay the dash to Sheffield.

HARRY'S guess was right. Nevertheless, he had by no means pictured the full extent of The Shadow's deductions. The Shadow was considering facts unknown to Harry.

The Shadow knew that Drune had remained with three henchmen; but they were probably the poorest fighters in his band. Otherwise, they would not have been delegated to their job as stokers. Furthermore, they had scattered when The Shadow opened fire.

Knowing The Shadow's prowess, doubtlessly amazed by the fact that he had reappeared, Drune would be too wary to attempt a hurried ambush with three inferior underlings as his only backers. There were others upon whom Drune would depend.

Drune and his minions, driving away in a car, would keep on until they reached the crossing of the two dirt roads. There, they would expect to find a sedan manned by five sure marksmen. Drune, knowing The Shadow's skill at stealth, would naturally suppose that he had maneuvered past the sedan. The master crook would not jump to the incredible belief that the sedan was at the bottom of the old abandoned quarry.

Not finding the sedan, Drune's only move would be to deploy his three stokers. The ambush would be a forced one, not at all to Drune's liking. Much as he wanted to hold back The Shadow, he would be thinking of the security that Colgarth's stronghold offered.

The roadster roared along the road. Harry gripped the braces of the raised top. He could foresee a quick, sure ride through any early ambush. He did not know that The Shadow was accomplishing another purpose. By his terrific speed, The Shadow was lessening the space of time that Drune would have for preparations at the crossroads.

They whizzed past the rutted road to the quarry. Down the long hill; then The Shadow pressed the clutch pedal and turned off the ignition. He turned the key on again, a few moments later, but the motor did not engage, for The Shadow still held the clutch pedal to the floorboard.

The lights went off; the roadster coasted silently in darkness. The last glimpse along the road had shown The Shadow that they were past the bend, rolling on a straight stretch to the crossing. Only the creak of the car's springs gave token of the approach. Even that sound ceased as the roadster struck a smoother piece of road, close to the crossing.

"Ready," whispered The Shadow. "Aim to the right. Thirty degrees forward. Three shots—"

A pause. The Shadow was aiming similarly to the left. The roadster creaked slowly onward.

The Shadow gave the command:

"Fire!"

Simultaneously, The Shadow and Harry each discharged three rounds. The shots ripped from each side of the roadster, just before it reached the crossroad.

YELLS sounded from the left. A motor roared as its driver jabbed the starter. Lights clicked into view. A taillight formed a target less than fifty feet away. The Shadow gave Harry a quick command:

"Join fire!"

Leaning across the wheel, Harry used his right hand; The Shadow fired with his left. They were at the center of the crossroad, pumping bullets at the car that had revealed itself.

The other machine had been waiting, headed away from the crossing. It shot forward with terrific speed, darting madly toward a bend. There was not a single answering bullet. The occupants of the car had chosen flight instead of battle.

The Shadow did not halt. Instead, he threw in the clutch. The motor throbbed; The Shadow drove the roadster ahead; increasing speed as he made for the road to Sheffield.

The Shadow had cracked Drune's ambush.

The master of crime had lain in wait, his minions ready with their guns. Had they scented the roadster's approach, they would have spread among the trees, to begin a desperate fire.

The Shadow had decided that Drune's car would be headed away, ready for flight if the ambush failed. He had called for fire to both sides, so the enemy's car would surely be a possible target, on whichever road Drune had chosen.

The shots from the night had totally surprised the crooks. Drune had instantly supposed that his location was known. He had jumped to his other plan; a speedy trip to Colgarth's. The absence of the cover-up crew in the sedan had made Drune qualmish. He wanted a bigger band before he dared The Shadow's power again.

The Shadow had let Drune go. Quick shots had not been sufficient to stop the master schemer's departure. Moreover, The Shadow had seen a double purpose in Drune's flight. Drune wanted to draw The Shadow on a futile chase toward the stronghold, so as to keep him away from Sheffield.

Drune knew that The Shadow alone could halt the progress of scheduled crime.

The roadster was at the highway. The Shadow gave full speed along the paved road. Roaring, quivering at every jolt, the light car was riding at its limit. The steering gear was old; the wheel gave a warning shimmy click at every heavy jolt; but The Shadow never slackened speed.

BOUNCING over a final hill, the roadster came in sight of Sheffield. Neither The Shadow nor Harry noted the outspread twinkle of the city's lights. Their eyes were captured by a greater glow.

A mammoth torch glared red against the sky.

The light showed a mass of billowy black smoke. It made a brilliant outline of the building from which the fire issued. The hour of crime had arrived.

The Sheffield National Bank was ablaze. Sprinkled gasoline had done its work. Flames were raging from the roof, licking the water tank that contained gallons more of gasoline. Fanning winds were sweeping the flames toward the freight depot. Even the breeze had favored schemes of crime.

The center of the little city lay full in the fire's path. Destruction had begun despite The Shadow.

CHAPTER XV
THE DYNAMITE BOXCAR

IT was a five-minute ride to Sheffield. Five mad minutes, at The Shadow's furious clip. Not one second could be lost, for The Shadow knew the horror that threatened.

The flames from the bank building had appeared with such suddenness that the origin of the fire could not be held in doubt. Here was a holocaust more terrible than that which had destroyed the hotel in Riverport; a blaze far swifter than the fire in Manhattan.

It was nearly eleven o'clock, a late hour for Sheffield. The fire had begun without a warning; its swift sweep was the sort that would produce chaos. Panic was due in the doomed city. Only quick and efficient work could avert it. The Shadow intended to do his utmost, although he knew that the evil had struck too soon.

His one preparation against this new thrust by fire depended upon his autogiro's arrival. It was less than half an hour since The Shadow had called Burbank. Crofton would not reach Sheffield within the next twenty minutes; he would halt at the airport, a few miles south of town. By the time The Shadow could gain his ship, disaster would be completed in Sheffield.

Hence The Shadow swung straight into town, trusting to the bare hope that he might gain some opportunity to organize whatever firemen he found. Sirens were screeching when he arrived; two fire engines were clanging up beside the burning bank. The Shadow sped to join them.

The only chance was to convince the fire fighters that their task was useless; to send them scurrying to warn the people in the apartment house beyond the depot. Soon the scorching flames would be there. Scores of lives were at stake.

As The Shadow swung to the curb beside the fire engines, a horn squawked from the corner. A red automobile skidded into view and rolled past the roadster. A brawny, beefy-faced man jumped to the curb. He was Sheffield's only fire chief, prompt on the job.

The fire chief turned to view the high-flung fire, which was licking the posts of the squatty water tank atop the bank. He was ready to stride to the fire engines when a uniformed man came dashing toward him, waving and shouting.

The fire chief met the newcomer; The Shadow recognized that the second man must be the chief of police. The two stopped right beside the roadster.

QUICKLY, The Shadow grabbed Harry's arm. He had been about to order his agent from the car. On the point of discarding his cloak and hat, The Shadow, too, intended to join the crowd that was gathering near the uniformed men.

Despite the shabby clothes that he wore beneath his cloak, The Shadow had a persuasive power that would rally men to proper action. This meeting on the sidewalk, however, promised some important consequences. The police chief evidently had a message.

"Will the water tank stop it," he bawled, to the fire chief, "or is it going to spread?"

"Chances are the tank is empty," shouted back the fire chief, above the hideous noise of the flames. The sprinkler system can't be working! That may mean the tank's empty!"

The fire chief had not guessed that the water tank was filled with gasoline. Nevertheless, the man had spoken sense. The Shadow waited, despite the loss of valuable seconds. He was sure that more news was due.

"If it spreads," put in the police chief, "it'll get the depot anyway."

"Sure it will," returned the fire chief. "What're you driving at?"

Neither had thought of consequences after the depot caught fire. They did not realize the fate that was due the business block with its many apartments. Nevertheless, the police chief had brought a real idea.

"We can clear away that depot for you," he shouted. "We'll do it while you're fighting the bank-fire!"

"Go to it!" barked the fire chief. "Only you won't have more than half an hour! How're you going to manage it?"

"Dynamite!" snapped back the police chief. "There's a carload of it back of the depot! Inspected it this afternoon! We can use some of it to blast the depot—"

"Get going! Thirty minutes is all you've got, chief!"

Harry Vincent pointed suddenly. The crowd was shifting; men were darting suddenly across the street. The fire chief was turning toward the engines, which were spraying futile streams of water against the bank building; the police chief had dashed away to summon men. Neither saw the stir that Harry indicated; but The Shadow had spied it.

The identity of the running men was positive. They were crooks who belonged to Drune and Colgarth. Dodging out of sight, they were on their way to block the police chief's plan. They would be the first to reach the dynamite car. Their cunning chief had figured out a possible move like this.

The Shadow urged Harry from the roadster, with quick instructions.

"Cover the garage," he ordered. "Watch for Colgarth and the Salamanders, with their swag. Use caution."

AS Harry leaped out and slammed the car's door, The Shadow swung the roadster round-about. He whizzed across the street, jouncing over a fire hose while firemen shouted angrily.

As The Shadow reached the corner, he heard a clanging of bells; he gave his car the gas; it shot forward, straight across the path of Sheffield's hook and ladder truck. The front fender of the truck skimmed the rear bumper of the roadster.

More shouts, as the hook and ladder swerved to a stop. The Shadow did not pause. He swung his car straight through the alleyway between the bank building and the freight depot.

Above the car roared a mass of flames; chunks of masonry crashed from burning walls. Running the gantlet safely, The Shadow reached the far end of the old train shed, in back of the depot.

As he sprang from the roadster, The Shadow heard a terrific roar above. Glancing up, he saw the water tank topple. It burst into immediate blaze; fire jetted to twice the previous height.

Still partly filled with gasoline, the tank had given the flames a tremendous impetus. As a breeze swept across the burning bank building, the fire became a tidal wave. A broad, crackling sheet, it swept downward to envelop the old depot in its maw.

The flames had begun their spread. The fire chief's half an hour had become a scant five minutes. The police would never have a chance to plant the dynamite in time.

The Shadow had reached the gleaming railroad tracks behind the depot. The fire showed three policemen hurrying from the other side. Gunshots barked suddenly from freight cars on a siding. The police stopped, stupefied, then scattered for cover.

The Shadow saw the dynamite boxcar. It was alone on a siding that led into the old depot; but it was fifty yards away. The Shadow recognized the car by the activity about it. A shifting locomotive had chugged up to the farther end. Men were making a coupling.

They were crooks, who had boarded the shifter, to put it to quick use. Word that the police were seeking dynamite had pushed the criminals to their present task.

Men were leaping back, waving their arms; others were aboard the boxcar, ready with guns should the police approach. The wheels of the shifting locomotive were moving. The engine was ready for a swift trip from the yards, with the dynamite boxcar attached.

Abandoning all cover, The Shadow sprang forward, an automatic in his right fist. The crooks on the freight car did not see him coming; they were looking in the direction of the scattered police squad. The first thug who saw The Shadow was one who stood beside the moving boxcar. He chanced to spy the cloaked figure bearing down upon him.

THE thug whipped out a revolver; he started an outcry. He never used his weapon; nor did his shout materialize. With a mammoth leap, The Shadow was upon him. A cloaked arm drove a downward blow. The Shadow's automatic thudded on the thug's skull.

As the crook fell, another challenger leaped toward The Shadow; this second crook was quicker with his gun. The Shadow beat him by a split-second, again without delivering a telltale shot.

He snapped a backhand sideswing that clipped the crook behind the right ear. The thug slumped, his trigger finger nerveless.

Leaping across ties and rails, The Shadow reached the front of the moving engine. The locomotive was increasing its reverse speed; it jounced, twisted, as it clicked across switches. The Shadow grabbed the pilot rail as it jolted toward him. He boarded the engine with a leap.

Back against the locomotive's boiler, The Shadow clattered along the runway and reached the open cab. Without any attempt at stealth, he sprang into view, to be met by two men who had heard his sudden arrival.

One was the crook at the throttle. He snarled as he saw The Shadow. The thug was holding a revolver ready in case policemen should try to board the train. He aimed quickly at the cloaked invader. This time The Shadow fired. His own aim beat the crook's. The man sprawled to the floor of the cab. The Shadow whirled to meet the other thug, who was acting as fireman.

This brawny rogue was armed with a big shovel that he had used to stoke the firebox of the switching engine. The shovel was descending with a terrific, vicious stroke as The Shadow turned. The Shadow's left fist shot upward, forward.

A shot could not have stopped that swing; but The Shadow's jabbing arm accomplished the deed. Like a trip-hammer, his fist swerved the crook's brawny arm and clamped it to a standstill.

The thug snarled as he grappled for The Shadow's gun. Dropping the automatic against the jouncing floor, The Shadow gave the crook a fast jujitsu hold.

The struggle ended. The thug twisted upward, outward, lost his grasp, then pitched headlong to the track beside the clattering locomotive. As the crook thudded on the ties, The Shadow snatched up the .45 before it could bounce away. He dived into the cab and pulled the air-brake lever.

The engine and the dynamite car came to a sudden halt out in the yards.

From the cab's window, The Shadow could see the flames that had caught the freight depot, on the side nearest the bank. The fire was rising; once it reached the top of the structure all would be over. The wind would sweep the flames into the business block. Brief minutes were all that remained.

Firemen and police had just realized the danger, for The Shadow could see tiny figures dashing toward the apartment building. The warning was belated.

Tenants would not know about the menace before the fire struck. The whole block seemed doomed to immediate destruction, for the fire's intensity had trebled.

The Shadow tugged the throttle. The switching engine started forward.

RABID shouts came from the boxcar. Crooks upon it had supposed that their pals had stopped the locomotive, figuring it far enough out in the yard.

This sudden start, that promised a return to the siding into the freight depot was something they could not understand. Shouts were closer. As the locomotive gathered speed, a crook appeared on the ladder steps of the dynamite car.

He saw The Shadow at the window of the cab. The crook aimed; The Shadow fired first. The thug lost his hold and toppled sidelong from the ladder.

New shouts were raised. Revolvers tongued shots; automatics roared from within the cab. Battle had begun amid this mad return. Shots were almost useless, for the thugs were flattened on the car, and The Shadow's head was bobbing at the locomotive cab. To The Shadow, the fray was mere byplay, to keep the crooks from swarming to the locomotive.

The real result would come when The Shadow completed the bold, swift course that he had undertaken. Every increased gain of the clattering locomotive was to his liking, for it led to the new outcome.

The Shadow was driving the dynamite car ahead of him, squarely into the depths of the blazing depot!

CHAPTER XVI
THE SHADOW'S COURSE

CROOKS controlled the yards outside the old depot. Deployed over a wide area, they had driven back Sheffield's few policemen. A dozen or more—all men like Sloopy and Jing—these thugs were gloating as they watched the flames surge up to the top of the depot. Roof and train shed were both ablaze.

It was the loud rattle of the shifting locomotive that made those outspread thugs turn about. By the lurid glare of the fire, they saw the dynamite car coming toward them, shoved by the fast-moving wheels of the little engine.

The Shadow had yanked the throttle wide. The shifter was driving its one-car train forward at nearly a thirty-miles-an-hour clip.

The fire's vivid light showed the men who fired from atop the boxcar. Other crooks leaped into action. Some vainly tried to throw switches before the dynamite car arrived. Others, guessing that a foeman had captured the locomotive, were prepared to open fire from the tracks.

As the dynamite car ran the last lap into the station, a figure swung outward from the cab. A black shape struck the ground, staggered forward, rolled, then came to a halt. Rising, The Shadow was ready with his guns.

No crooks offered fire. All were ducking to cover. Eyes were riveted by the sight ahead.

THE dynamite car had reached the blazing train shed. The shifting engine was hurling it onward. Crooks were leaping from the car, all except one. He clung in terror, fearful of the drop at such high speed. That thug was doomed to quick destruction.

Locomotive and car covered the length of the train shed in three seconds. Outlined by the fire above, the dynamite car hit a wooden bumper at the end of the track. The bumper was too frail to stop the impetus. The locomotive drove the car straight onward; the bumper was pushed from the track.

The next obstacle was a thick brick wall, the buttressed inner end of the old depot.

A sweep of fire had risen over the top of the depot, all along the roof and train shed. A cataract of flame, it was ready to descend; to clear the roof and swallow the whole depot in its clutches. Once that surge struck, the fire would roar onward, unrestricted. The moment of the fire's triumph had arrived.

Full speed, the dynamite car crashed the thick brick wall. It smashed the buttress; halted; then telescoped as the shifting locomotive drove squarely through it.

All happened in a quarter of a second; yet The Shadow, watching, could sense a distinct instant that formed an ominous lull.

A TERRIFIC explosion made the fire's roar seem puny. The fire that thundered from the doomed boxcar was more vivid than the holocaust above.

Splitting to fragments, the steel car vanished. With it, the shifting engine was shattered, twisted, broken into chunks of hot and jagged metal. The concussion carried instantaneously. The ground trembled as the terrific blast hurled the whole depot into fragments. Walls, roof and train shed went scattering in every direction.

All portions were hoisted outward. The front of the depot hurtled to the street. The rear of the train shed was blown into bits that scattered all over the tracks in the yard. The unburned side of the depot was rocketed against the walls of the business block; chunks of superstructure clattered the roofs of the apartments.

The whole flaming side of the depot was lifted backward, as if swept aside by a giant hand. The tidal wave of fire was carried with it, thrown against the breeze, back upon the flames that rose from the Sheffield National Bank.

The huge roar of the mammoth blast was answered by the echoes of clattering windows and shattering plateglass from the business block. For seconds, there was no other sound.

There was a sight, however, that held eyes amazed. Space had replaced the old freight depot. Low fragments of masonry, a flattened surface of settled debris were all that marked the spot where the structure had been.

Flames writhed, a mammoth, windswept torch above the bank building. Caught anew by the breeze, they took their old direction. Gobbling downward, they reached to the site of the old depot, hungrily seeking fuel which they could no longer find.

The Shadow's blast had isolated the fire. Nothingness lay in its path. The flames could never reach the business block, where startled apartment dwellers had awakened, to show their staring faces at every broken window.

One task accomplished, The Shadow had another. Darkness had blanketed the spot where he stood, for the flames had suddenly exhausted after their last surge. They had almost totally consumed the bank building; its ruins afforded no additional fuel. Darkness served The Shadow.

Skirting wide through the freight yard, he circled hurriedly to reach the old garage beyond the Sheffield National Bank. The Shadow knew that Colgarth and the Salamanders must have timed their underground entry at the very outset of the fire, for they had expected a complete holocaust that would divert attention from them.

Harry was watching. Had he already seen the Salamanders emerge?

PAST the bank building, The Shadow cut straight toward the garage. He had a hundred yards to go. Crooks from the freight yards had taken a shorter course. The Shadow saw the cover-up men scurrying to give the alarm. He had no time to battle with those underlings. His task was to stop the Salamanders first.

Before The Shadow had covered thirty feet, the far door of the battered garage burst open. A truck rocketed into view; it cut toward the main street. The range was too great for The Shadow to halt the big machine; moreover, it was driving off at full speed in the opposite direction.

The Shadow saw a man spring out from beside a building and stab futile shots at the escaping truck. It was Harry Vincent; he had thrown aside all thoughts of caution. He was due for trouble before The Shadow could reach him.

Two thugs jumped into sight. They were cover-up men, the ones who had been nearest to the garage and, therefore, the first to reach it. They grabbed Harry; The Shadow saw them drag him, struggling, off beyond the garage.

The Shadow dashed onward. His cloaked shape was outlined by the waning fire in the bank building. Crooks spotted their deadly foe and opened fire. The Shadow gave them no regard. He intended to save Harry first.

An automobile flashed past an opening between two buildings. Thirty yards distant; it was gone before The Shadow could aim to stop it. Covering crooks were making a speedy getaway. Harry was again a prisoner; there was no chance to overtake the men who held him captive.

The Shadow twisted to a halt. He heard the whines of bullets dispatched by the crooks who

had tried to pepper him at long range. They had failed to find their swift-moving target. They had opportunity for better aim when The Shadow stopped his dash; but they gained no chance to press their new advantage.

Close to the subsiding bank fire, the crouched crooks were visible to a man. The Shadow had whipped out both automatics. He jabbed quick-spurted shots as he turned in turret fashion. Each gun pumped alternately. As one arm drove down, the other recoiled.

Three thugs sprawled in quick succession, while their pals fired wildly toward The Shadow. Weaving, fading, he was an impossible target in that brief fray. Surviving crooks dashed for cover.

The Shadow followed.

He knew that they were heading for a car. The roadster had been crumpled by the explosion. The Shadow needed another machine.

ROUNDING a building beyond the abandoned garage, The Shadow overtook three crooks who were boarding a touring car. Two men dove away and fled past a close corner when they saw The Shadow. The other tried to start the car; at the same time, he peered wildly, gripping a revolver as he looked for his black-clad adversary.

The Shadow came in from the other side of the front seat. Dropping his automatics, he pitched upon the thug. He caught the crook's throat with one hand, the fellow's gun wrist with the other.

The thug choked as his hand lost its hold upon the weapon. Snapping the man up from behind the wheel, The Shadow chucked him headlong over the door beside the driver's seat. The rogue thudded against the paving and lay stunned.

Colgarth and the Salamanders had driven north in their truck; underlings had taken the same direction in their car, with Harry as their prisoner. Instead of following, The Shadow wheeled the captured touring car across the street and swung southward.

Again, The Shadow was beginning a swift ride. He was bound for the airport south of Sheffield. By this time, the autogiro had arrived.

The Shadow preferred his autogiro for new pursuit.

CHAPTER XVII
DRUNE'S DECREE

HARRY VINCENT'S struggles had ceased as soon as he had been placed aboard the crook-manned automobile. The thugs who had trapped him threw him into the back seat, into the arms of another waiting pair.

Threats of slugging guns had quieted Harry. Discretion was preferable to useless fighting. So long as he remained conscious, Harry would have double opportunity; to seek a chance for escape and to learn facts for The Shadow.

The crooks were snarling as they drove along. With harsh epithets, they promised tough times for Harry. The Shadow's agent maintained his composure. He knew that these rogues would not harm him unless he made trouble. They wanted to deliver him intact to Drune.

The car scaled a hill. It rode between brick gate posts and pulled around in back of a sprawly mansion. In the darkness, Harry glimpsed white pillars as they passed the front. He knew that this must be Colgarth's colonial residence.

The crooks jabbed revolvers into Harry's back. They forced their prisoner from the car and marched him to the rear door of the house. One thug rapped with the butt of a revolver. The door opened; an ugly-faced servant admitted the group and conducted them to the front of the house.

HARRY saw Drune and Colgarth rising, startled, from a table in a large living room. The pair had been sorting the securities taken in the bank raid. Colgarth emitted a harsh exclamation to his henchmen:

"What brought you here?"

"Things went sour," growled a thug. "The Shadow blew up the freight station and stopped the fire."

"So that was the explosion that we heard!" ejaculated Colgarth. "We thought it was the gasoline in the water tank!"

"That burned first. Then The Shadow grabbed the dynamite car. After that, he clipped about half of the cover-up crew—"

"So you fools came here! You gave him a sure trail—"

Drune waved an interruption. His eyes gleaming, the master crook had spied Harry in the background. Drune turned to Colgarth.

"They were quite wise to come here," said Drune, dryly. "Look, Colgarth; they have brought us an old friend."

Colgarth craned his neck. He saw Harry. His hard lips showed a vicious grin. He snapped, "You frisked him?"

Nods indicated that the henchmen had deprived Harry of his gun. Colgarth rasped an order:

"Leave him here with us."

Harry's captors departed. Colgarth drew a revolver and motioned Harry to a chair. The Shadow's agent seated himself calmly. Drune and Colgarth buzzed in conference beside the table; all the while, Colgarth kept watch on Harry. Nods proved that the crooked partners were reaching a quick agreement.

The pair arose. Drune gathered up the stacks of securities, while Colgarth waited. Then Colgarth covered Harry and ordered him toward the door. Harry walked out into the hall, where the four thugs were waiting.

Colgarth buzzed orders to the leader of the four-man squad. The men hurried off in different directions. Colgarth marched Harry to a kitchen. He opened a door and pointed to a cellar stairs.

"Go down," ordered Colgarth.

As Harry descended, Drune turned on a light at the head of the stairs. At the bottom, Harry found himself in a square-walled room, empty except for boxes along the wall. While Colgarth kept Harry covered, Drune went ahead and entered another section of the cellar. A light gleamed when Drune found the switch. Colgarth moved Harry forward.

Drune was waiting for them. With a polite bow, he pointed to a lone chair in the corner. It was an invitation for Harry to be seated. Harry accepted, while Drune and Colgarth remained standing.

Drune's actions were more insidious because of the rogue's mock courtesy. Harry remembered the previous fate to which the master crook had consigned him. He expected something equally as undesirable as the fiery pit.

"We congratulate you, Mr. Vincent," crackled Drune, with smiling lips. "Your escape from death was quite miraculous. We assume, of course, that your chief, The Shadow, was responsible for your rescue. I presume that you were with him when he so neatly uncovered my ambush at the crossroads.

"We have learned that The Shadow spoiled our plans for the complete destruction of Sheffield. That, however, does not cause us concern. Our one purpose was to divert attention while Colgarth and the Salamanders completed their foray in the bank. They were quite successful.

"Even the subterranean blast, by which they shattered the foundation, remained unheard during the roar of the fire. It was an expert job. Colgarth completed it in less than the estimated time. We have gained the final spoils that we require. Our need for crime is ended."

DRUNE'S smirk showed satisfaction with the past. His eyes glared suddenly as he began to speak of the future.

"We hold the wealth we want," declared Drune, "but we must protect it. Since The Shadow lives, we shall be forced to evade him. Doubtlessly, you have told him why we delivered death to Woldorf and Breel; also why we raided the Sheffield National Bank to gain the holdings of the Cruikshank estate? The Shadow has us at a stalemate. We cannot cash our wealth until we have settled him.

"To do that, Colgarth and I shall disappear. We possess sufficient funds to wage a relentless campaign against The Shadow. We shall fight from every hiding place. Only The Shadow will know our identities; and no one will believe him if he declares that Huxley Drune and Gordon Colgarth are criminals.

"For the world will class us as unfortunates. As unhappy victims, like Chester Woldorf and Lincoln Breel. Colgarth, as owner of this mansion; I, as his guest, shall presumably perish. For you, Vincent, I decree the fate that you previously escaped: death by fire!"

In a trice, the whole cunning scheme flashed itself through Harry's brain. He knew why Drune and Colgarth had buzzed in conference; why whispered orders had been given to thugs. The underlings had been told to act as torches; to set fire to the mansion.

Other fires had been attributed to incendiaries. The same would be the case here. By this time, the authorities in Sheffield had guessed that the bank fire was intentional. When Colgarth's home broke out in flames, common belief would have it that criminals had done the work.

No one would ever suspect Colgarth of having any connection with crime. Nor would Drune, a chance guest from New York, be considered a party to the deed.

As an answer to Harry's thoughts, a crackling noise came from above. It was the sound of fire, heard from the kitchen stairway. Crooks had started blazes throughout the mansion. By this time they were taking to their car, along with servants who were crooks like themselves.

The situation matched the one in Riverport. It was like the fire at Breel's. Any person held here would be trapped. There was to be one victim in this new conflagration. Harry was to be the man.

A wild impulse seized Harry. He tightened, ready to spring upon Colgarth, on a chance that he could down the rogue and then battle Drune. If Harry died by gunfire, it would be better than the flames. In another second, Harry's attack would have begun.

Then came a sight that stopped him.

DRUNE had shrilled a crackly order. A door swung open in the far wall. Two by two, a squad of men were entering. Six in all, they were garbed in puffy suits of asbestos, with grimy faces glaring through the fronts of their helmets.

They were the Salamanders. They had been given word. They had come from a passage, to take charge of Harry and hold him here while Drune and Colgarth preceded them through a tunnel that led to safety.

Harry saw formidable, gun-like tubes, projecting from clumsy, thick-gloved fists. They were the fire guns that The Shadow had encountered. Though Harry had never seen them in use, he recognized that they were weapons. Rising from his chair, he stood powerless.

Drune and Colgarth withdrew from the space between Harry and the Salamanders. They stood close to the door of the tunnel. A terrific roaring was apparent. By this time, the mansion must be entirely in flames. Soon the flooring would collapse; blazing beams would drop. Then the Salamanders would depart, leaving Harry to his doom.

Drune's chuckle sounded amid the fire's roar. Colgarth held his hard-lipped leer. They were waiting, that pair, to enjoy Harry's plight. They were secure, here in the cellar of the flaming house.

Master rogues believed that they occupied a spot where even The Shadow could not reach them!

CHAPTER XVIII
FROM THE SKY

COLGARTH'S mansion had burst into a complete blaze.

Viewed from the ground below the hillside, the fire produced the same torchlike effect as the flames at the Sheffield National Bank.

Incendiaries had done a thorough job. They had spattered kerosene all about the house. The men had started blazes on every floor.

As the fire roared away, a carload of crooks were looking back with glee. Billows of smoke were reflecting the brilliance of fire tongues that lapped from every section of the roof.

The fleeing men took a side road to avoid persons coming to the hill. They knew that the fire must have been seen in Sheffield. A distant clanging, dimly heard in the night air, told that fire equipment was coming toward the burning mansion. Flames had practically ended at the Sheffield National Bank. Engines were no longer needed there.

Colgarth's house was isolated. No witnesses were present to eye the early stages of the fire at close range. Long wings that ran from the main portion of the house were being rapidly consumed; for they were all of frame construction.

The center of the house still stood; but the fire raged most furiously in that portion. Only the fact that the central walls were brick had kept them from toppling as soon as the wings.

The ground floor was solid, well constructed, directly above the portion of the cellar where Drune and Colgarth held Harry prisoner. The flames had risen upward, consuming the upper stories with rapidity.

The wooden-shingled roof was dropping into the interior of the mansion; but it was too light to complete the devastation. The ground floor would not sag until the walls came inward. They were due to crumble when the upper structure was completely gone.

Once the mansion became a shell, complete disaster would follow rapidly. That time would be soon. The Sheffield fire engines would never reach the hill in time to fight the flames.

Roads to the hill were roundabout. They handicapped all who sought speed on the ground. There was another route, however, that offered direct course to the burning mansion.

That route was the air.

A THRUMMING was audible, off above the town of Sheffield. The drone was becoming louder, significant of rapid approach. It neared the lighted zone above the burning house. Flames, enlarging, hurling their bright light upward, showed the source of the zooming sound.

An autogiro was outlined in the sky above the mansion. It was The Shadow's ship, arriving from the airport, its master at the controls. The autogiro seemed to poise, motionless in the air, except for the whizz of the long-armed blades that rotated atop the ship.

Slowly, the autogiro descended straight downward. It was temporarily obscured by smoke that had risen hundreds of feet above the house.

The Shadow had divined Drune's plan. He knew that both Drune and Colgarth would want the world to think that they had died within their fire. There was a chance that they might still be close at hand.

There was a greater chance that Harry had been left to perish in the flames. That, more than thought of the supercrooks, inspired The Shadow to his dangerous descent.

Witnesses, had there been any to view the scene, would have thought the pilot of the autogiro mad. Seemingly, The Shadow was dropping himself into the midst of destruction.

Smoke, twisted by the wind, uncoiled to show the autogiro hovering directly above the flaming house. Less than a hundred feet intervened between the dropping ship and the high tongues of the devastating flames.

Red light showed a peculiar feature of the autogiro.

Rounded objects were dangling below the ship's wheels. One loosened; like a bomb, it descended toward the flames. At fifty feet, the bomb exploded with a silent puff. A volume of powdery substance rained upon the flames. The effect was instant. Blazing tongues succumbed; when they reappeared, their extent had diminished by half.

The Shadow released a second bomb. Again, the powder burst and scattered, this time at a closer range. Flames withered. Only a few licks of fire lashed in a final effort. From forty feet above the roofless mansion, The Shadow released a third bomb. Its effect was final.

The bomb puffed within the house itself. Powder blanketed every remaining vestige of the fire. Smothered flames were gone. Brick walls stayed upright; The Shadow had arrived in time to prevent their fall.

FROM Texas, The Shadow had ordered these bombs of dust powder—the latest and best devices invented for fighting the merciless oil-well fires. He had foreseen battles with Drune and Colgarth, wherein fire would be used to cover the evil work of the Salamanders.

The shipment had come promptly; but The Shadow had been forced to let it wait in Newark while he located the scene of coming crime. Fire had struck in Sheffield while Crofton was still flying out from Newark.

But the autogiro had reached the airport soon afterward. It had been waiting for The Shadow, its bombs all prepared, when he had arrived to take over the ship.

With smothering dust, The Shadow had conquered the new fire, the last thrust in the schemes of Drune and Colgarth. Attacking from the air, he had found the center of the flames. To insure success, he had dropped the autogiro to the very level of the roofless walls.

There was no chance for the autogiro to soar upward. Dust had banished heated air, to create a vacuum within the house walls. The space sucked fresh air downward, through the open roof. The autogiro was caught in the vortex.

Like the pull of a magnet, the air itself drew the ship to its descent. Blades spun madly, bending as they resisted the pull. Despite them, the autogiro dropped within the flame-scarred walls of the ruined mansion.

The Shadow had expected this descent; he had known that he could not prevent it. He was working only to avert a total crash. He managed that task well. Air had settled like a cushion within the walls.

The space was ample; the way was clear, for the upper stories had completely fallen. The ground floor had not yet weakened; its only fault was its irregularity, for it was heaped with masses of debris.

The autogiro quivered through the last twenty feet of the descent. It struck at an angle; one wheel bounced upon a smoldering beam. For a moment, the ship was toppling; as it rolled forward, it righted. Braking it, The Shadow halted the giro against the farther wall.

WITH a command for Crofton to remain with the ship, The Shadow leaped to the baked house floor. Dust was everywhere; only a few patches of smoking wood remained. There was light from the burning wings of the house. By the fading glare, The Shadow saw the remains of doorways. At one spot, he saw a vacancy in the floor itself.

Hurrying there, The Shadow spied a flight of steps; below, he saw the glimmer of a light. The top steps were burned. The Shadow cleared them with a leap. Stopping short, he saw a square-walled room, that was darkened.

The wiring for that first chamber came from upstairs; and the fire had obliterated it. The Shadow could distinguish the shape of the room only by a light from the opening beyond.

The Shadow heard the buzz of voices. He had reached his goal. Drawing a brace of automatics, he crept forward. Nearing the door in darkness, he saw shapes in the other room. He recognized the baggy figures of the Salamanders. Formed in a semicircle, they were holding their fire guns to cover a corner that The Shadow could not see.

A crackly voice sounded. The ranks of the Salamanders opened. From between the grotesque creatures stepped a gray-haired man whose withered face glared its malicious triumph. He, too, was looking toward the corner.

Edging across to the other side of the door, The Shadow saw Harry Vincent, facing the evil gaze of Huxley Drune.

The master crook had stopped. Easing back, The Shadow covered Drune. He waited, unseen; for the Salamanders were staring in the same direction as their chief.

The time for departure had arrived. Drune had stepped forward to crackle the words that would sound his prisoner's doom. He was ready to fulfill his decree of doom.

While Drune spoke, The Shadow watched.

CHAPTER XIX
THE FINAL FRAY

"THE fire has lessened," snarled Drune to Harry. "The walls have not fallen as we had hoped. That last crash was not sufficient."

Drune was referring to the thump of the autogiro. He had heard it on the floor above. He had mistaken it for an inward fall of bricks and masonry.

"Nevertheless," sneered Drune, "fire shall be your mode of death. My decree stands. Blackened to a crisp, your body will be found. You will be identified as Colgarth or myself."

Backing, Drune motioned to the Salamanders. The asbestos-clad henchmen raised their fire guns. They opened ranks, that Drune might pass. Once he was behind them, they would be ready for the order to blast withering flame upon Harry Vincent.

The Shadow started forward. He wanted the Salamanders to see him when he attacked. They would remember that fight at Breel's. His presence would confuse them, better than shots from the dark. An instant more would have brought The Shadow's surprise attack.

A harsh cry intervened.

The shout came from Colgarth. Standing beyond the Salamanders, Colgarth was holding a well-padded briefcase beneath his arm. It was the precious bag that contained the stolen securities.

Colgarth, looking through the space between the Salamanders, had chanced to glance toward the outer door. He saw The Shadow springing forward.

The Salamanders turned. They swung their heavy fire guns. Six in number, they sought to use their ungainly weapons before The Shadow could down them with his automatics. The Shadow opened fire as the Salamanders aimed.

THE SHADOW'S shots were speedy. The nearest Salamanders fell, like toppling puppet figures. Slugs scarcely staggered them, because of their heavy garb; but each one tumbled as his punctured suit lost its air. Every hit was marked by the same phenomenon.

A suit withered, shriveled. Air hissed from the interior. Overloaded by a heavy helmet, each stricken Salamander wavered back and forth, to fall with a crash.

The Shadow bagged three Salamanders in a row. Two made clumsy leaps for the farther doorway. One of the six, however, held his ground. His thumb was on the trigger of the fire gun. He had his chance to drive a blast of fire before the next shot came.

It was Harry Vincent who stopped the Salamander's stroke. Unbound, Harry had seized his chair from the corner. He was driving forward as the Salamander thumbed the lever. Harry swung the chair downward, with terrific force, upon the Salamander's helmeted head.

It was the force of the blow, not the result, that staggered the Salamander. His helmet was sufficient protection to save his skull. Harry's stroke, however, was terrific. It shattered the chair and sent the Salamander reeling.

The fire gun puffed; a blast of flame seared forth. The Salamander's aim was altered. The scorching fire lashed the wall, instead of The Shadow's doorway.

As the Salamander rallied, The Shadow fired again. The Salamander's baggy suit deflated. His clumsy thumb slipped from the lever. The weapon clattered from his fists and struck the floor.

Drune was diving through the far door, barking to Colgarth to follow. Colgarth obeyed; the last two Salamanders joined the flight. They knew that the range was long for their fire guns. With their leaders in rout, the Salamanders did not care to stay.

The Shadow delivered one quick, stabbing shot, directly between the Salamanders. He had aimed for the darting form of Colgarth, who was a few steps nearer than Drune. A cry told that The Shadow had clipped the man with the briefcase; but Colgarth staggered onward.

Harry was leaping forward. The Shadow thrust forth an arm to hold him back. One chance blast from a fire gun would have spelled Harry's finish. The Salamanders must be met at long range.

By his action, The Shadow had saved his agent from a false move; but the Salamanders profited. They were gone, following Drune and Colgarth, when The Shadow turned in their direction.

"The tunnel!" cried Harry. "They're making a getaway—"

The Shadow sprang forward, knowing well that crooks had fled for safety. At the door, he halted, to rip quick shots along a gloomy passage. Those shots would spur the flight of the Salamanders. The Shadow paused for a short interval, then leaped through the doorway.

THE SHADOW saw a low, lighted tunnel, leading down through the slope. It was a route that offered outlet somewhere down the hillside. The passage turned, a hundred feet away. Drune was at the bend. He stood beneath a ceiling light; The Shadow saw his hand upon a massive switch.

Drune was ready to inject a current that would dynamite the tunnel. It was a piece of evidence, that passage, that crooks did not want the law to find. Drune was waiting for the Salamanders. In clumsy flight, they were halfway down the passage.

Colgarth had stumbled when the Salamanders passed him. He was closest to The Shadow; less than thirty feet into the tunnel. He had lost the briefcase in his fall; he was groping for it as he rose. The Shadow dashed toward Colgarth. The crook saw him coming.

Colgarth's right arm was dangling. He did not have a gun. Instead of offering fight, he turned and scurried after the Salamanders, who had formed a two-man file, still dashing clumsily, handicapped in their asbestos suits.

Drune saw The Shadow gain the briefcase from the floor where Colgarth had dropped it. With a savage snarl the crime master tightened his hold upon the switch.

In this moment, Drune cared nothing for Colgarth and the Salamanders. Nor did he care about the rescue of his wealth. He had one incentive only: to destroy The Shadow.

Within the dangerous sector of the tunnel, The Shadow chose the quickest course. He had emptied one automatic; he had three shots remaining in the other. Aiming the .45, he pumped three rounds above the shoulders of the Salamanders. Every bullet found its lodgement in the stooped form of Huxley Drune.

Reeling, clawing blindly at the wall, the chief of crime still sought to pull the switch. Though mortally wounded, he held to life, seeking by one evil effort to doom The Shadow with him. There was no time to linger; no way to deal further with Drune.

Gripping the briefcase, The Shadow made long strides back along the passage. As he reached the cellar, he flung the briefcase ahead of him; with a dive, The Shadow rolled out into the room where Harry stood. Twisting to his hands and knees, he stared through the tunnel.

The Salamanders, like The Shadow, had thirty feet to go, in order to reach the other end. They had covered less than twenty. Colgarth, faltering, had failed to overtake them. Drune, clawing blindly, collapsed against the wall.

As he sagged in a death throe, Drune found the switch and pulled it with him. His gasped cackle sounded along the tunnel. Drune thought that he was completing The Shadow's doom.

WITH a muffled roar, the walls and ceiling of the tunnel broke inward. Mined for its entire length, the passage collapsed with a single blast. The Shadow caught one fleeting glimpse of Drune, sprawling headlong. He saw Colgarth and the Salamanders, still within the tunnel.

There were shrieks as the stony walls obliterated the view of the men. Lights were gone; not only in the tunnel, but in the cellar room as well. Pungent fumes stenched from the tunnel. Groping away, The Shadow clicked a flashlight and opened the path for himself and Harry to reach the stairs.

Huxley Drune, master of crime, had failed in his final effort. Clutched by death, he had done his best to finish The Shadow. All that he had accomplished was the doom of his partner, Gordon Colgarth.

Both supercrooks had perished. With them had died the last of the Salamanders.

The Shadow had triumphed over fiends who fought by fire. He had conquered murderers and their well-trained henchmen who could dare the wrath of devastating flames. Through smothering their own element, fire, The Shadow had shattered crime's last bulwark.

The Shadow had forced the final battle. The menace of the Salamanders was ended.

CHAPTER XX
THE DEPARTURE

WHEN The Shadow and Harry Vincent reached the floor above, they saw the autogiro against a dimly flickering background. The burning wings of the house were almost entirely consumed. Spurts of flame were only occasional, places which the dust had hit lightly.

Harry saw Miles Crofton by the autogiro. He heard his fellow agent report. Crofton had cleared a path across the ground floor. It was a rough one; but the distance was great. It offered the ship a fifty-foot path to the farther wall.

The Shadow and his agents boarded the autogiro. Crofton had rolled the ship a dozen feet back from the nearer wall. The Shadow started the motor; he waited while the propeller and blades gained top speed.

Outside, shouts told that people had arrived from Sheffield. A loud clanging marked the progress of fire engines up the hill. Soon the burned mansion would be entered. The Shadow did not care to remain.

BRAKING one wheel, he started the autogiro forward. It spun about because of the unequal pressure. It gathered speed by the turn, swung clear about, the ship rolling toward the wall at the other end of the house. It rolled freely, its wheels jouncing hard, then left the roughened floor.

Ordinarily, the autogiro would have risen rapidly. Surrounding walls impeded its lift. For a moment, Harry feared that the ship would crash the wall ahead. The air within the pitlike building was too restricted for the last few feet of rise.

Suddenly, the autogiro jolted upward. Its horizontal blades had cleared the level of the roofless walls. The blades had clutched the outer air. They hoisted the ship's wheels over the blackened surface of the threatening end wall. The autogiro circled upward, to avoid tall, surrounding trees.

Astonished burghers from Sheffield stood gazing at the sight. Brief flames from the wings of Colgarth's house gave them a view of the mysterious ship. They were totally amazed, unready to believe their senses.

To them, the autogiro might have been a phoenix—that fabulous bird that ancients claimed could rise from its own ashes, to soar away to a new existence. They gaped as the ship vanished suddenly into the night.

Staring vainly, they heard its motor hum off into the distance. The clanging fire engines arrived, to rouse the few witnesses from their stupor. They began their tale, to listeners who scoffed their disbelief.

Firemen entered to search the ruins. They found the open path to the cellar. Descending, they made a discovery that proved as amazing as the story of the autogiro. They found the bodies of the four dead Salamanders, still clad in their asbestos suits.

The fallen tunnel did not gain the attention of searchers. Its wreckage had been complete. The tunnel's mouth looked like a side room of the cellar, where debris had fallen. The foundations had failed to withstand the pressure of the floor above.

The autogiro was forgotten in the surprise at the discovery of the Salamanders. There would be no new facts uncovered regarding the ship's presence in the vicinity of Sheffield. Crofton had landed at a deserted airport which had long been no better than an emergency landing field. No witnesses had seen the autogiro prior to its take-off from the ruins of the mansion.

Only The Shadow and his trusted agents knew the full story of the conquest. Flying the darkened autogiro back toward Newark, The Shadow was silent at the controls. On the floor beside him lay the briefcase that he had risked his life to gain.

Later, he would examine its contents. The heirs of Woldorf and Breel; the administrators of the Cruikshank estate—all would gain their rightful property.

The Shadow's agents heard a grim laugh from their chief. The tone was the summary of the episodes that The Shadow had undergone. He had striven for final conflict with the Salamanders. He had gained. Monstrous men who marched through fire had perished with their evil leaders.

The Shadow's laugh was an aftermath of talk that had once passed between Huxley Drune and Gordon Colgarth.

The supercrooks had talked of three elements—earth, water and fire. They had agreed that The Shadow could have survived the first two on the list. They had applied the third. Fire had failed to doom The Shadow.

Yet the crooks had still believed that fire could protect them. They had forgotten another element: air.

From the air had The Shadow come to gain his victory. To the air had he returned.

THE END

VOICES FROM THE SHADOWS

It started with a bone-chilling laugh, and an eerie mocking voice that chilled early radio listeners: "This is—The Shadow!" The haunting tones first materialized over the CBS airwaves on July 31, 1930, narrating tales from the pioneering mystery fiction magazine. "The Shadow knows," intoned the sinister host, "and you too shall know if you listen as *Street & Smith's Detective Story Magazine* relates the story called—The Serpent Stings!"

The popularity of network radio's first sinister host led Street & Smith to revive the long-dormant single-character publication. The groundbreaking success of *The Shadow Magazine*, which jumped from quarterly to twice-monthly publication in less than 18 months, led to a profusion of imitative "hero pulps," and the arrival of Gibson's pulp Shadow on the MBS airwaves in 1937 (with the young Orson Welles in his first prominent radio lead).

The revamped *Shadow* series quickly earned a reputation for the wildest plots on the airwaves as Lamont Cranston and the lovely Margot Lane* each week confronted a bizarre array of evildoers. Many of the Welles episodes seem more believable today than in 1938: a shell-shocked former soldier trained as a sniper opens fire on crowds below in "The Silent Avenger," teens are lured into a religious cult in "The Bride of Death," and a U.S. senator is accused of accepting a $50,000 bribe in "The Phantom Voice." In "The Tomb of Terror," deaths blamed on an Egyptian mummy's curse turn out to be caused by a radiological device that destroys the human immune system.

In the early Welles shows The Shadow, following in the footsteps of the omniscient narrator of the early seasons, often telepathically manipulated events that led to the well-deserved deaths of his sinister adversaries. As the series evolved, Lamont Cranston became less shadowy and more of a dilettante as the scripts grew formularized and his occult mental powers went unexplored. During Bill Johnstone's 1938-43 tenure, The Shadow developed a warmer, less mysterious demeanor. The villain might still die horribly, Johnstone explained to the *New York Times,* "but The Shadow himself never kills anybody."

With the departure of script editor Edith Meiser, "the lovely Margot Lane" was reduced from a capable partner to a cliched damsel-in-distress who seemingly existed only to be captured by a different villain each week. If a maniac was conducting a

secret experiment in a forsaken haunted house, Lamont and Margot were certain to blunder onto the hideout when their car broke down on the lonely road outside. Inevitably, Margot would be captured by the fiend, and strapped to an operating table or imprisoned in an ancient torture chamber.

When advertising executives claimed his pulp stories contained too much "blood and thunder," Walter Gibson countered that their radio shows focused on "thud and blunder." The limitations of a half-hour time slot required that Cranston be quickly dropped into the action. In a real world, both Lamont and Margot should have learned to be leery of invitations from former friends. Margot would have quickly realized that Cranston's old college crowd and professors were a bizarre lot, just as Lamont should have been equally wary of invitations from Margot's friends.

The radio Cranston made an unusual foray onto the printed page in the December 1946 issue of *Best,* when Gibson Scott Fox's script for the March 3, 1946 broadcast was adapted to text form. "Island of Ancient Death" was the first of Fox's half-dozen *Shadow* radio scripts, and was followed by "Vampires Prowl by Night" (September 8, 1946), "Die, Lover—Die!" (September 22, 1946), "The Corpse Without a Skin" (November 10, 1946) and "The Bones of the Dragon" (January 11, 1948). Fox was one of several pulp writers who sold scripts to the radio series, along with Shadow pulpscribe Theodore Tinsley and science fiction writers Alfred Bester and Max Ehrlich.

Despite his success with macabre thrillers, Fox appears to have had a personal preference for cowboy stories, pounding out pulp Westerns and scripts for the *Lone Ranger* and *Hopalong Cassidy* radio series, and later serving as George W. Trendle's personal representative on the set of the *Lone Ranger* television series.

The 1946 pulp adaptation of "Island of Ancient Death" remains an enigma, since it appeared in a pulp released by a publisher other than Street & Smith. Could Fox have adapted his script on his own, without authorization? If the adaptation was sanctioned by the Mutual Broadcasting System or the Ruthrauff & Ryan advertising agency, why did *Best* incorrectly credit *The Shadow* to the Columbia Broadcasting System (which hadn't aired the series since 1935) instead of Mutual?

"Island of Ancient Death" was severely condensed in its original pulp publication, so key scenes and dialogue from Gibson Scott Fox's radio script have been restored.

Though its origins are lost in the shadows of time, this unique pulp adaptation features a rare appearance of radio's Lamont Cranston on the printed page.

—Anthony Tollin

---

*Though Walter Gibson spelled "Margo" phonetically in his pulp novels, the radio scripts (and this adaptation) retain the spelling from the name of Margot Stevenson, the Broadway ingenue who inspired The Shadow's "friend and companion" and played the role opposite Welles during the 1938 Goodrich summer season.

Bret Morrison as The Shadow

ISLAND OF ANCIENT DEATH
by Gibson Scott Fox

Adapted from *The Shadow* over the Mutual Broadcasting System

Yet we are the movers and shakers of the world, forever, it seems. Let your child dream his dreams! —Arthur O'Shaughnessey

"HESTER. What's the matter? Why don't you unlock the door?" Diane Madeira looked at Hester with cold, black eyes.

"Madam—have you thought what you're doing?"

Diane was impatient. "Of course I have."

"You're a stranger here, Madam," said Hester. "The island of San Angelo is small, but it's belonged to your husband's family for many generations. It has certain traditions. No one, for instance, ever enters this pavilion. And Madam—isn't it true that Dr. Madeira has forbidden you to enter it? Isn't it true, Madam?"

"Never mind my husband, please, Hester—just open the door."

"If I do, he'll—" Hester's mouth relaxed and she said: "Very well, if you insist, Madam." Slowly she placed the key in the lock and turned it. The door moaned and slowly turned on its hinges.

"There. Will Madam … enter?" Slowly, unsurely, Diane stepped inside the dark musty room. The bright sun had blinded her for a moment so she could not see in the darkness.

"Hester. It—it's so dark. I can't see."

"I shall have to open the shutters, Madam. Madam, listen to me. Go back while there's time. There's an evil here that no one should see. An evil that—"

"Open the shutters, Hester. Open them."

"Yes, Madam." Hester felt her way to the window and the shutters flew open with a startled bang. "Then look," she cried. For a moment Diane glanced about the room and then her eyes focused on the wall. She gave a step back, put her hands to her head, and choked back a short scream. Then she sank to the floor and burst into low, moanful sobs.

"Dr. Madeira!" Hester drew back as if incredulous that someone else was in the room. From behind a large desk a short, dark man with straight black hair and a long mustache stood up and advanced slowly toward Diane. For a moment he placed his hand on her shoulder, and then pulled it back. "You disobeyed me, my dear," he said. His voice was cold and emotionless. "Are you so determined to die, Diane?"

Lesley Woods and Bret Morrison starred in the March 3rd, 1946 MBS broadcast of *Island of Ancient Death*.

That night, in her room, Diane sat at her desk and finished a near-completed letter. When she had put her pen away, she walked to the sofa and read it before placing it in an envelope and sealing it. She read part of the letter half-aloud:

"… and if this letter convinces you I'm losing my mind, I'll not blame you—but oh, Margot darling, you're one of my best friends. There's no one else I can turn to—and if you could come—better still, if you could persuade Mr. Cranston to make the trip as well … then I'd be so much more grateful than words can say …"

A WEEK later Lamont Cranston and Margot Lane sat beside Diane Madeira in a buggy drawn by two black horses. Diane was pale, and she held fast to the reins in her left hand.

"Oh, I'm so grateful, Margot … more than words can say. I never dreamed that you and Mr. Cranston would really come … but I'm so frightened, Margot. If something doesn't happen soon …"

Margot looked apprehensively at Diane and then turned to Lamont.

"Now stop it, Diane. Lamont, you'd better take the reins. She's in no condition to drive."

Lamont obligingly took the reins from Diane and offered each of the two ladies a cigarette. After they politely refused, he lit one and threw the dead match between the two horses. Then he asked:

"Is that the pavilion up ahead?"

"Yes. This … this cliff we're climbing is Devil Rock. The pavilion is at the top of the cliff."

"Then we'll soon be there. Miss Madeira, isn't it time you told us exactly what's happened?"

"You said that you're not allowed to leave the island, didn't you, Diane?" asked Margot.

"That's true, Margot, I'm not. And I don't even know why we came here. Pablo was doing research in New York and I thought he meant to stay. Then all of a sudden he made me leave without the least warning."

"What's he doing in that laboratory you mentioned?"

"I don't know. He won't tell me anything. All I do know is that he's changed completely and the natives are terrified of him. I'd wanted to write Margot for a long time, and when I saw that picture in the pavilion, I knew that I had to."

"What sort of a picture is it, Diane?"

"It's horrible. It's a painting of a man killing a woman. He's got some kind of queer, three-bladed knife and he's torturing her and she's trying to scream." Diane almost broke down and Lamont placed his hand on hers.

"Easy now—easy."

"I—I'm all right. But that isn't what frightened me so. It's an old picture—a mural—a hundred years old, at least. But, Mr. Cranston …"

"Yes?"

"Someone's painted the woman's face to look like mine."

Margot got up and gasped, "Diane."

"Someone just recently—you'll see it, Margot. Mr. Cranston, is it a warning? Does it mean that I'm to die? That—"

"I'm afraid I can't answer any of your questions, yet, Mrs. Madeira. You'll have to give me a chance to look around first." The buggy pulled up in front of the pavilion and Lamont and Margot jumped out.

"Aren't you coming in with us, Mrs. Madeira?" asked Lamont.

"Oh, no, I couldn't. I never want to see that picture again. I'll wait for you here."

"All right. Coming, Margot?"

"Of course, Lamont."

Diane called from the carriage, "The door's unlocked. You can go right in."

"Thanks, Diane," said Margot. "We won't be long." Lamont and Margot entered the pavilion and stood for a moment at the door.

"Just a minute, Margot. I'll open the shutters."

The light cast clear beams on the portrait. Margot gave a slight "Oh," and grabbed Lamont's arm.

"She didn't exaggerate, did she?" Lamont's voice was queer, too.

"Oh, Lamont, this is horrible."

"It isn't pretty."

"And someone *has* painted that face to look like Diane's."

"Yes!"

"I don't blame her for being frightened, Lamont. Look at this knife … and these scratches and the blood—"

"What the devil? No artist painted this blood, Margot!" Cranston started tapping the edges of the panel with his knuckles.

"What are you doing?" asked Margo.

"Don't you see?" he replied. "It's seeped through from behind, so there must be a way this panel can open!" He stopped tapping.

"Wait! I think I've got it! I felt something give!" He grabbed the picture by the edges and slowly it swung outward.

"Stand back! It's swinging open!" Lamont shouted.

"What on earth—" Margot's eyes grew large.

"Feel that draft? That means a tunnel or passage of some sort. Wait—"

The panel continued swinging open. Then it abruptly stopped. Margot gave a stifled scream.

"Great Scott—"

"Lamont! Something's standing there! It's holding something in its hand! It—it's grinning at us! What is it, Lamont?"

"A body, Margot."

"But it's grinning!"

"A trick played by rigor mortis."

"Are you sure?"

"Yes. Just a second. What is this he's holding? Oh, a book, eh? Hold onto this, Margot. We'll look at it later. I'd like to know why a murdered man should be left with a book in his hand."

"Lamont—"

"Yes?"

"That—that man was a native—"

"I know he was. What about it?"

"But don't you remember what Diane said about her husband ... that the natives are terrified of him? And look there ... look at the scratches on his arms and shoulders. Couldn't those have been made by a three-bladed knife?"

"Listen, darling ..."

"No, Lamont! *No!*" Margot cried out in growing terror. "We've got to get out of here! I don't know what's happening on this island, but we've got to get out! And if we don't ..."

"Margot!" Lamont spoke sharply.

"I—I'm sorry, Lamont. I—I lost my head."

"Margot, we're getting Mrs. Madeira back to the house."

"All right, Lamont."

"Then you and I are coming back and exploring this tunnel!"

LATER that day, after Mrs. Madeira had been taken home, Lamont and Margot did return to the tunnel. The narrow passageway extended for almost a half mile before they came upon a door. They broke it in to find a room filled with cells and human bones. Lamont explained that in the old days, San Angelo used to be a slave station, and that the room probably was used for barracks.

From the distance they had come, Lamont conjectured that they probably were under Dr. Madeira's laboratory in the main house. Suddenly they heard a bloodcurdling scream. They stopped and it was repeated. "That's coming from Madeira's laboratory," Cranston called out "Margot, get upstairs while I see what it is!"

The two rushed upstairs, and after a long wait, Dr. Madeira opened the door. He was haughty. He did not even attempt to explain circumstances. He simply stated that Lamont and Margot were unwelcome guests, and demanded that they depart on a boat sailing from the island the next day.

While Lamont and the doctor were talking, Margot called her friend from upstairs. She had taken the book found in the dead man's hand at the pavilion and upon discovering it was a diary, showed it to Lamont. It read ...

March 3rd, 1835: How strange it is to know that this is the last time I shall ever sit at this desk—and make an entry in this diary. How much more strange to realize that if I had never posed for that horrible picture in the pavilion, I might not have had to die. And, strangest of all, to realize at last that my husband's experiments were meant to have their climax in my death! Even now, as I write, I hear my husband's footsteps in the hall. Now, he stops. He is at the door. Now, I hear nothing—he must be raising his hand to knock. Oh, yes, and now—and now—

When Lamont had finished reading the passage, Diane slumped into a chair. As Margot rose to rush to her, there was a knock at the door. When Lamont opened the door, a body, slashed from head to foot, fell into the room. Diane screamed, "Lord, another one," and then passed out.

THAT night, a stiff wind began to blow.

"There's going to be a storm," said Lamont.

Margot looked at him. "Oh, I hope not."

"There's not much doubt about it. The weather's been getting ready for one for the last couple of days and these semitropical storms are practically hurricanes."

Margot was assured that everything would be all right. And then Lamont, sure that the coast was clear, took her with him to Dr. Madeira's laboratory. They opened the door and there Cranston made a bizarre discovery in the trash. "Look, Margot, it's human flesh, as it might look if it was cut from someone's body's with a three-sided knife like this one on the lab table."

"Have you told Diane about the body at the pavilion?" questioned Lamont.

"No. Of course not," replied Margot.

"Then don't mention this either. There is no use worrying her more."

While Margot stayed with Diane, Cranston set out for the pavilion to find the doctor.

AT the pavilion, Doctor Madeira was talking to Hester.

"Stop it, Hester."

"You love her, don't you?"

"Yes, I love her."

"Then how can you hesitate? Isn't the man in that painting in the pavilion killing the woman he

Lamont Cranston and the lovely Margot Lane (as portrayed by Bret Morrison and Lesley Woods)

loves? And doesn't he get a wild pleasure from it? Listen to that—the storm. It's here! Kill her now and throw her body into the sea. Let the storm hide her before these fools, who think they've come to help, can discover what our real purpose is."

Madeira sat silently.

BACK at the house Margot was following Diane, who insisted on finding where her husband was. "Pablo wasn't in his laboratory," Diane explained. "He must have come down here. I have to know what he's doing. I'll go crazy if I have to stay in my room."

"I know the feeling. I can see faces staring at us from every shadow," Margot observed.

There was a sudden noise in the dark passageway.

"What was that?" Diane exclaimed. "I think it came from behind this door." Fumbling with the knob, she cried out, "Margot, something's in here!"

Before Lane could object, Diane rushed ahead into the darkened room, and the door suddenly slammed shut in Margot's face and was being locked tight from the other side!

Helpless, Margot heard Diane screaming and the sounds of a struggle within. When Margot cried out for help, Lamont suddenly showed up with a flashlight. "Wait here," he told her. "I think I know where Diane is!"

"What have you found out, Lamont?"

"I haven't time for questions now, darling. Just do what I say. Go to your room and lock yourself

in. I think I know what's happening here and if I'm right, it's worse than I imagined. I think Madeira has gone to the pavilion, and if I'm not mistaken—so has *she!*"

AS Lamont approached the pavilion, the storm was beginning to rage furiously. He glanced inside the window and saw Diane and Madeira talking. Disguising himself as The Shadow, he furtively entered and listened to their conversation. Madeira was the first to speak.

"Diane."

"Yes, Pablo."

"You—you knew about the panel—and the tunnel."

"Yes. Yes, I knew."

"What are you doing with that gun? Diane—don't—"

"I'm going to kill you, Pablo."

"No, Diane."

"I'm going to kill you as you meant to kill me."

"But I didn't. Listen, Diane. Go back to the house. Do you hear that wind? It's a hurricane. The pavilion isn't safe here. Get back before—"

"Are you trying to trick me again, Pablo? Are you trying to trick me now—as you've been trying to trick me into madness?"

"Diane, I swear I'm not! Can't you hear? Go back. *Go back!*"

"What are you trying to hide, Pablo? What's that on the floor behind you? Isn't that a body? Isn't that Hester's body?"

"Diane!"

"It *is* Hester. She's dead. You've murdered her. Look at the mark of the knife, Pablo. You've murdered her."

"You are mad!"

"No, but—"

"You killed her."

"Who will believe that?"

"The Shadow will believe it, Diane." The sibilant tones filtered from the dark recesses of the pavilion.

"The Shadow?" echoed Madeira.

Diane was frightened.

"Who are you? Where are you? I'll kill you if I find you. I'll kill you!" She fired three times but only mocking laughter echoed through the room.

"How can you hope to kill a shadow, Diane? Drop that gun. Drop it, I say!" The pistol thudded to the floor and Diane struggled for a moment.

She cried, "Something has hold of me. Something I cannot see. Pablo, help me!"

"Do you call to your husband for help, Diane? Have you forgotten that you meant to kill him also?"

"Only because I had to! He meant to kill me!

**Disguising himself as The Shadow, he ... listened to the conversation going on.
(Bret Morrison poses as The Shadow in a WOR/MBS photo by Lou Nemeth.)**

He was driving me mad!"

"No, Diane, you were <u>already</u> mad!"

"That's not true!"

"But it is! That's why your husband brought you here. That's why he refused to let you leave the island. Isn't that right, Dr. Madeira?"

"Yes! Yes, it is!" replied Madeira.

"And isn't that why you carried on those experiments in your laboratory? Because you hoped to find a way to cure her?"

"Yes!"

"He couldn't tell you that you were losing your mind, Diane, and that's why you failed to understand. Perhaps if you had understood, you wouldn't have murdered those two natives!"

"I didn't! Why should I?"

"Because you had already planned to kill your husband in order to regain your freedom. And you planned to justify yourself by making him appear a murderer! And you sent for Miss Lane so that she and Cranston could vouch for your story!"

THE next day, as Margot and Lamont boarded a ship for home, Cranston explained everything to her.

"Lamont," Margot asked, "was Diane really insane?"

"Yes, Margot, Dr. Madeira brought her to the island on that account. However, he made one very serious mistake. He confided in Hester that his wife was insane. Hester was in love with the doctor, so naturally she did all she could to make her more insane. I felt the diary was faked. It was too much of a coincidence. Diane had planted those pieces of flesh in the laboratory just for us to find.

"But the clue that tipped me off was when Diane shouted 'another one' when we discovered the second body. No one had told her of the first one, so she would have had to have killed the first man to know—"

"But what about those cries we heard in the laboratory?"

"Diane was in there. We heard her murdering the native. Madeira and Hester covered up for her when we came into the laboratory, so we wouldn't learn the truth."

"But darling, Diane got locked in that passageway, and then she disappeared—"

"Oh, that's very easy to explain. When the storm put the lights out, she slammed the door, faked that business of being seized and took advantage of the darkness to skip out again and lock the door behind her. She'd made up her mind to kill Hester, so she had to go through all that in order to get rid of you."

"The poor girl—"

"Look, Margot, the sky's clearing up."

"Yes, darling, the sun has come out. The storm must be over."

"Yes, the storm is over," Cranston intoned, "for the island and for the people on it."

Margot snuggled close to Lamont and the two watched as their ship slowly pulled away from the mainland.

THE END

The weed of crime bears bitter fruit. Crime does not pay. The Shadow knows!

Illustration by Stephen Fabian

Walter B. Gibson (1897-1985) worked as a newspaperman, carnival conjuror, insurance policy writer, crossword puzzle creator, prolific novelist, comic book scripter, and advance man for touring magic shows. Thanks to the powerful voice of The Shadow, this amazing jack of all trades owed his greatest fame to radio. But Walter Gibson was a radio pioneer in other ways.

As early as 1923—seven years before The Shadow was born—Gibson began working in the young medium. Twice a week over Philadelphia's WIP, he did magic tricks and recounted puzzles for early radio listeners. His family took turns at the earphone of a primitive crystal radio set to hear his performances on *After Dinner Tricks*. It was an offshoot of his popular *Philadelphia Ledger* column of the same name.

In the summer of 1930, Gibson helped magician Howard Thurston develop a variety radio show devoted to the magical and mysterious. Gibson often recalled the day he and Thurston sat listening to the radio in search of ideas when The Shadow's mocking laugh first caught his ear: "We were discussing radio so naturally we turned on the radio from time to time to hear what was on it …but I was more interested in reading what was going on in the magazine on Friday because I was wanted to write magazine stories." He had no inkling he was destined to transform that sinister sound into a new American phenomenon, and because of that would be unavailable to work on the Thurston program when it finally aired.

Over the next dozen years, The Shadow kept Walter Gibson far too busy to bother much with any radio work. He did script a *Shadow* pilot episode that aired over WMCA in New York in 1934, and when *The Shadow* was revived in 1937, consulted on the show's development.

In 1943, with *The Shadow* approaching the height of its radio popularity, Gibson was lured back into the broadcasting world by Street & Smith. His forte was not scripting, but plotting shows in the Shadow mold that others could flesh out and dialogue. Gibson helped launch *The Return of Nick Carter,* which he coscripted with Edward Gruskin. They teamed again on a spinoff serial called *Chick Carter, Boy Detective.* After that, Gibson brought several classic Street & Smith heroes to the airwaves. *The Avenger* was inspired by the S & S pulp hero Gibson helped develop, but was reinvented for radio audiences. Biochemist Jim Brandon, through use of an ultra-violet "diffusion capsule," turned as invisible as The Shadow himself. A telepathic device enabled him to mimic The Shadow's mental powers. His radio tagline was "The road of crime is a trap that justice sets!" Gibson laid out the storylines, leaving it to the husband-and-wife team of Gil and Ruth Braun to break them down into script form.

Gibson and the Brauns teamed up again for *The Adventures of Frank Merriwell* in 1946. *Blackstone, the Magic Detective* was based on Gibson's comic book interpretation of his close friend, master illusionist Harry Blackstone. Nancy Webb was his collaborator on that 1948-50 dramatic series.

Gibson's involvement with *The Shadow* radio program was limited, but that was fine with him. With two Shadow pulp deadlines a month to make, and the monthly *Shadow Comics* to script, he was lucky to find time to listen to his own character on radio!

As he once explained, "Generally the writer had to be in New York with the director. Oh, they would massacre these scripts when they'd get them. The director wouldn't like one thing. The sponsors of course were even in on it. The scripts only paid 75 bucks. I would get ten dollars a page for the Shadow comics. Hell, I could sit down and knock out an eight-page comic much faster than I could do a radio script, with no criticism."

In the post-Shadow era, his abiding interest in ESP and related phenomena inspired Gibson to create and narrate the ABC radio program *Strange.* It ran for over 100 episodes in 1955.

When The Shadow returned to the airwaves in 1963, Walter Gibson was a prime mover in the nostalgic revival of his most famous creation. With this rich background, Gibson was much in demand for radio talk shows. He could be heard on everything from Mary Margaret McBride to Long John Nebel, expounding on his life in radio and outside it. And of course imitating The Shadow's marrow-chilling laugh, which he loved to do.

"I don't know how The Shadow managed to capture the imagination of hundreds of thousands of readers and millions of radio listeners," Gibson once mused. "But he did. And for that I am grateful."

The man who owed everything to the medium, and who ended up contributing so much to it, was also most comfortable speaking into a radio microphone.
                                                    —Will Murray